*continued . . .*

# ODYSSEY

# SEEKER

# POLARIS

# OMEGA

# CHINDI

# FIREBIRD

## Jack McDevitt

**ACE BOOKS, NEW YORK**

**THE BERKLEY PUBLISHING GROUP**
**Published by the Penguin Group**
**Penguin Group (USA) Inc.**
**375 Hudson Street, New York, New York 10014, USA**

Penguin Group (Canada), 90 Eglinton Avenue East, Suite 700, Toronto, Ontario M4P 2Y3, Canada
(a division of Pearson Penguin Canada Inc.) • Penguin Books Ltd., 80 Strand, London WC2R 0RL,
England • Penguin Group Ireland, 25 St. Stephen's Green, Dublin 2, Ireland (a division of Penguin
Books Ltd.) • Penguin Group (Australia), 250 Camberwell Road, Camberwell, Victoria 3124, Australia
(a division of Pearson Australia Group Pty. Ltd.) • Penguin Books India Pvt. Ltd., 11 Community
Centre, Panchsheel Park, New Delhi—110 017, India • Penguin Group (NZ), 67 Apollo Drive,
Rosedale, Auckland 0632, New Zealand (a division of Pearson New Zealand Ltd.) • Penguin Books
(South Africa) (Pty.) Ltd., 24 Sturdee Avenue, Rosebank, Johannesburg 2196, South Africa

Penguin Books Ltd., Registered Offices: 80 Strand, London WC2R 0RL, England

FIREBIRD

An Ace Book / published by arrangement with Cryptic, Inc.

PUBLISHING HISTORY
Ace hardcover edition / November 2011
Ace mass-market edition / October 2012

ISBN: 978-1-937007-80-5

ACE
Ace Books are published by The Berkley Publishing Group,
a division of Penguin Group (USA) Inc.,
375 Hudson Street, New York, New York 10014.
ACE and the "A" design are trademarks of Penguin Group (USA) Inc.

PRINTED IN THE UNITED STATES OF AMERICA

10  9  8  7  6  5  4  3  2

*For Jack McNichol and Joe Chapman.*
*Thanks for a lifetime.*

# ACKNOWLEDGMENTS

Thanks to Walter Cuirle, for advice and technical assistance. I'm also indebted to Ginjer Buchanan, my long-suffering editor. To Sara and Bob Schwager, for their contributions. To my agent and good friend for two decades, Ralph Vicinanza, whom we lost this year. And, as always, to my wife, Maureen, for persevering with the second, third, and fourth drafts.

Dates not classified as Common Era (C.E.) are based on the Rimway calendar.

# PROLOGUE

Lt. Jeremy Dalton frowned at the screen. "Nothing yet, Steve?"

Steve Yaniwicz activated the expanded scan, pressed the earpods to signal that the AI was telling him something, checked the auxiliary display, and shook his head. "No, sir. No sign of her yet."

Dalton was wearing his formal whites, in preparation for the upcoming change-of-command ceremony. "Okay," he said. "They have to be close. Let me know."

"Yes, sir."

He called the Command Duty Officer. "Still negative, Mr. Brolley," he said.

*"Check with the rest of the squadron, Jerry?"*

"Yes, sir. They are *not* in the area." It had been almost two hours since the *Abonai*'s scheduled arrival time. The Dellacondan star drive, like the Armstrong system that had preceded it, wasn't too accurate. You might come out of it thirty or forty million kilometers from your intended destination. But they were providing extensive coverage. Somebody should have picked up the cruiser by now.

"All right," Brolley said. He made no effort to hide his concern. "Let Fleet know."

Admiral Thadeus O'Conner was aboard the incoming ship, scheduled to take command of the 314th Attack Squadron.

Dalton had never seen O'Conner, didn't know anything about him, but he had to be an improvement over their current commander, Mary D'Angelo. The woman who never smiled. Who was impossible to work with. She thought nothing of chewing out subordinate commanders in front of anyone who happened to be present when she got annoyed. She insisted on telling everyone, in microscopic detail, how to do their jobs. And she had no respect for the chain of command. If she disapproved of the way a junior officer was handling an assignment, she didn't arrange to work through his boss; she went after the offender herself. It was clear she enjoyed raising hell, and there was no one in the squadron, and especially on the *Celestine*, who would regret her departure. As inevitably happened in such cases, she had been promoted.

He turned back to the comm operator. "Steve—"

"Yes, Mr. Dalton."

"Get a message to Comm Ops at Point Edward. Tell them we're still waiting. Ask them to provide an updated ETA." Point Edward was, effectively, just down the street. A fortyminute flight. In and out of hyperspace. It was hard to imagine what could be holding things up.

He watched Yaniwicz send the message. That, he suspected, would be the signal for the cruiser to arrive. But it didn't happen.

The transmission would require about twenty minutes to reach the Point. He looked out through the port at the Veiled Lady, which, to him, bore no resemblance whatever to a woman but appeared simply as what it was: a nebula filled with a million stars drifting through the night. Janet McReady, who did *indeed* look very female, thought he lacked imagination and pretended to feel sorry for him.

Janet would be assuming the watch in three hours. She was an intellectual type, beautiful but pretentious. Read philosophy and pretended to be able to see the child peering out of Barnable's impenetrable art. How, she'd say, could you miss it? Well, she looked good, and for a woman, that was enough.

He was still thinking about Janet when Yaniwicz raised a hand to signal he had something. It was too soon for Point Edward to have answered. Too soon for them even to have received his message. He started toward the comm desk, but Yaniwicz pointed at an auxiliary screen:

From: CDR, Third Fleet
To: *Celestine*
Subject: *Abonai*

Movement Report *Abonai* not received as of 1720Z.
Confirm *Abonai* your area.

Movement reports were routinely sent at departure and arrival. Dalton squinted at the message, then forwarded it to the CDO. Moments later, Mr. Brolley appeared in the comm center. He did not look happy.

"Still nothing?" he asked. The CDO was easygoing, a guy who never got excited. Dalton had been impressed with his behavior under fire. He was exactly the man you wanted to be with if you were having a serious problem.

"No, sir. No sign of her."

"Very well. Tell everybody in the squadron to take another look. We want a report, positive or negative, from every ship."

"Yes, sir."

"While we're at it, let's inform Point Edward that we haven't seen them yet. Confirm whether they left on schedule."

"We've already done that, sir. A few minutes ago."

Brolley sighed and walked out. He'd be keeping Admiral D'Angelo informed, of course, which meant dealing with another of her annoying habits. When something went wrong, she had a tendency to sound as if it was the fault of the reporting officer. He had no doubt that Brolley was already feeling the heat.

Well, at least she hadn't come down to the comm center yet. Instead, she'd be descending on Operations, taking control of the scanners and sensors and giving obvious instructions. Dalton had seen her described in the Fleet newsletter as a can-do hands-on officer.

The request went out, and, within minutes, the destroyers began to check back in. *McMurtrie* first: Negative on the *Abonai*. Then *Karasani*. Then *Hopewell*.

It was, of course, an exercise in futility. The three cruisers and six destroyers that comprised the Flag Squadron were already doing what they could, watching their screens and standing ready to report at first sighting. Had they seen anything, they'd have said something.

*Wilson* reported negative.

*Cajun*.

Eventually, Yaniwicz got a reply from Point Edward: *The* Abonai *ETA has not changed. They left on schedule.*

More than two hours ago for a flight that should have taken twenty minutes.

*Chiyoko* negative.

*Sattari* negative.

"The drive's erratic, Mr. Dalton," said Yaniwicz. "It could be on the other side of the sun."

"I know, Steve. It wouldn't be the first time. But it's going to screw up the ceremony."

"I hope nothing's happened."

"So do I. They've probably just missed their target. I hope."

Yaniwicz grinned uneasily. "Safer going to Rigel," he said, "than going to the grocery." It was the standard platitude of the interstellar transport lines.

But then there'd been the *Capella*. Nine years earlier, on a flight from Rimway to Saraglia Station, it had made its TDI jump and never been seen again. Twenty-six hundred people had gone with it.

And there'd been the *Warburton*, lost eighteen months ago. Wreckage had been found, leading investigators to believe that its mass detectors had failed, and the ship had tried to materialize inside an asteroid. Of course, had that happened with the *Abonai*, there'd have been an explosion of considerable magnitude. No way they could have missed it.

They waited. Messages from Point Edward became increasingly frantic. Patrol craft and destroyers began to arrive to assist in the search.

Janet relieved the watch. Dalton returned to his quarters, showered and changed, went to the officers' mess for dinner, where, of course, the conversation focused exclusively on the lost ship. Tag MacAllen had a sister aboard the *Abonai*, and Boros Razkuli, a son. Everybody knew someone in the crew.

At midnight, when Dalton returned to his watch station, there was still no word.

Six days later, the *Abonai* was formally declared lost. An extensive search by a sizable portion of the fleet had revealed nothing.

A memorial service was held at Point Edward, and another at Toxicon, the *Abonai*'s home port. To the dismay of the *Celestine*'s crew, Admiral D'Angelo was extended. Investigations continued for a year and a half. All reached the same nonresult: The *Abonai*, its crew, and Admiral O'Conner were missing due to cause or causes unknown.

# PART I

## Virginia Island

# ONE

However useless your product, package it properly, and people will buy it. People will buy *anything* if the approach is correct. It is this happy truth that keeps the wheels of commerce rolling.

—Eskaiya Black, *Lost in Aruba*, 7811 C.E.

*1434, RIMWAY CALENDAR. SIX YEARS LATER.*

I was sitting in my office at the country house, watching the snow come down, when Karen Howard arrived. The storm had reached epic proportions, at least by local standards, and I'd expected her to postpone. But she appeared at the front door exactly on time.

The only things I remember about her were that she wore a big hat, and that she talked in a loud voice. And, yes, that she was short. When she'd called for an appointment, she'd dodged explaining why she wanted to see us. *"I have something to sell,"* she had said. *"I know you'll be able to get a good price for me. It's all quite valuable."*

But no details. That kind of approach is usually a guarantee that the prospective client is trying to get away with something. The antiquities business attracts a lot of con artists. Particularly our specialty, which is handling objects that have specific historical significance. The original notebook, say, that Despar Kolladner had used when he was writing *Talking with God*, or a set of drums that had belonged to Pepper Aspin. People are usually quite good at creating and producing supporting documents, but Alex is hard to fool. It's only happened once, and it cost us. But that's a tale for another time.

Karen came into my office, shook off the snow, and removed the hat but held it close to her blouse as if it would one day be a collector's item. "I'm Elizabeth Robin's sister," she said, in a tone suggesting that explained everything.

I invited her to sit, but she remained standing. So I got up and came around in front of the desk. "I'm Chase Kolpath, Ms. Howard. How may I help you?"

"You're the person I talked to?"

"That's correct."

"Is Mr. Benedict available?"

"I'm his associate."

"You didn't answer my question."

"At the moment, Ms. Howard, he's busy. I'm his associate. What can I do for you?"

She frowned. Took a long look at me. Apparently decided she could make do. "You may know that Elizabeth died last year." I had no idea who Elizabeth Robin was, but I nodded and managed to look sympathetic. "I've inherited the estate," she continued. "And I have some items connected to Christopher that I'm going to make available. I'd like your help getting a good price."

An old Ray Cammon song, "Love Is All There Is," was playing quietly in the background. "Who," I asked, "is Christopher?"

She just barely avoided rolling her eyes. "Chris Robin," she said. "Of course." Then, seeing that I needed further explanation: "Elizabeth was his wife."

"Oh," I said. "Chris Robin the physicist?"

"Yes. Who did you think?" Now she sat down.

"He's been dead a long time," I said.

She smiled sadly. "Forty-one years."

"I see."

"Maybe I should be speaking with Mr. Benedict?"

"You should understand, Ms. Howard," I said, "that artifacts connected with physicists— Well, there's just not much of a market for them."

"Christopher wasn't just *any* physicist."

"Did he accomplish something special?"

She sighed, reached into a handbag, and pulled out a book,

an old-fashioned collector's edition, with his name on it. *Multiverse*. "Here's *part* of what he did," she said.

"Well—" I wasn't sure where to go from there. "It looks interesting."

"He accomplished quite a lot, Ms. Kolpath. I'm surprised you don't know more about him. I suggest you read this." She laid the book on my desk. Then she reached back into the bag and brought out a small box. She opened it and handed it to me. It contained a wedding ring with engravings of *Liz* and *Chris*, with the inscription "together forever." There was also a diamond-studded comm link. "This is the one he always wore," she said, "on special occasions. Whenever he received an award. Or spoke at an event."

"Okay," I said.

She produced a chip. "I wanted you to see some of the other items. Do you mind?"

"No. Of course not."

The chip activated our projector, and a pair of lamps appeared. "They were custom-made to his order." The lamps were ordinary flexible reading lamps, one black, one silver. Documentation consisted of two photos of Robin, one at his desk writing by the light of the black lamp, and one in which he was relaxing on a sofa, reading, with the silver lamp behind him.

"I have a large number of his bound books. He was a collector." She showed some of the individual volumes to me. Mostly they were physics texts. There was some philosophy. Some cultural commentary. Danforth's *History of Villanueva*. "One problem is that he was always writing in them. Elizabeth said he couldn't sit down with a book without writing in it." She shrugged. "Otherwise, they're in excellent condition."

For significant people, of course, writing in a book inevitably *increases* its value. I wasn't altogether sure whether Robin qualified for that classification.

"There are other items as well. Some of his lab equipment. Some wineglasses."

She showed me those, too. None of them would be worth anything. There were several other photos, some taken outside, usually of the happy couple, posed in starlight or beneath a tree or coming up the walkway to the front door of what appeared to be a small villa. "It's their home," she said. "On Virginia Island." A few were limited to Robin himself. Robin lost in thought by a window, Robin biting down on a piece of fruit, Robin throwing a log on the fire.

One photo consisted of two lines of print. "It's the closing sentences," she said, "from *Multiverse*."

> We cannot help then but draw the conclusion that each of us has an endless number of copies. Consequently, we are never really dead, but simply gone from one plane of existence.

"I never really understood it," she said. "Oh, and I almost forgot." A photo of a superluminal appeared. The ship's name, or maybe a designation, was partially visible on the hull, but the symbols were nonstandard:

Since all vessels use the same character set, the vehicle seemed to be a photographic fiction.

"I also have three autographed copies of *Multiverse*, and also—" A battered, broad-brimmed hat appeared. She looked at me expectantly. Then sighed. "It's the Carpathian hat he made famous." She put more framed photos on display. Robin and Elizabeth in the bright sunlight on the front deck of their home, Robin at a lectern with one hand raised dramatically, and Elizabeth with another, younger, woman. ("That's me," said Howard.) And there was Robin receiving an award, shaking hands with students, conferring with various people. And at his desk with his eyes fixed on a notebook. And one I especially liked: Robin at a restaurant table pouring tomato sauce onto a salad while Elizabeth watched with an indulgent smile.

"He *loved* tomato sauce," Howard said. "He put it on everything. Potatoes, sandwiches, beans, meat. He used it for a dip."

"Okay," I said. "I've got it." That was my moment to cut it off, to explain that we only deal with artifacts that are connected in some way with famous places or events, or with historical figures. That I was probably not the only person in Andiquar who'd barely heard of Chris Robin. But I ducked.

And she roared ahead. "Look at this," she said, activating another visual. It was a painting of Robin and his wife. Elizabeth was dark-haired, attractive. The kind of woman who always draws attention from guys. She wore a pleasant smile, but there was a formality in the way she stood and in the way she looked at her husband.

"She died last year," Howard said.

"Yes, I'm sorry."

Her eyes clouded. "I am, too. She was irreplaceable."

Robin could have been a perfect typecast for the mad scientist in an over-the-top horror show. His eyes peered out at me with unrelieved intensity. His hair had retreated from the top of his skull, though it was thick and piled up over his ears. Unlike Elizabeth, he made no effort to look gracious. His expression reminded me of Dr. Inato in *Death by the Numbers* whenever he was about to unleash a killer typhoon on a crowded resort.

Another oil painting displayed a few musical notes and a date. "Those are the opening bars from 'Starlight and You,'" she said.

I'd heard the song, of course. It had been popular off and on for years. "What's the connection?"

She looked surprised. "He *wrote* it."

"Really?"

"Do I sound as if I'm kidding?" A note of annoyance had crept into her voice.

"Not at all," I said. "Music or lyrics?"

"Both. Chris was a man of many talents."

Well, I thought, maybe we had something after all. I was reminded once again of the perils in dismissing a prospective client too quickly.

Another painting depicted him and Elizabeth standing atop a bluff overlooking a moonlit ocean. "They lived on Virginia Island," she said. "Did I mention that?"

"Yes."

"It's a gorgeous place. Have you ever been there?"

Virginia Island was halfway around the planet. "No, Ms. Howard, I'm afraid I've missed it."

She smiled tolerantly. "You need to get out more. Get away from the office and see the world."

Robin was wearing the Carpathian hat, slanted off to one

side. He and his wife stood with their backs to the imager. They were leaning against each other, looking out to sea. Though they were not clasped in each other's arms, it was a remarkably romantic picture.

A photo depicted him walking through a terminal, carrying a small piece of luggage, with a notebook slung over one shoulder. "This one's of special interest," she said.

"Why's that?"

"He was leaving for that last flight."

"Did something happen on the flight?"

Another show of disdain. "At the end of it," she said. But she seemed disinclined to go further on the subject, so I let it slide.

There was always a possibility somebody would be interested. I decided to let Alex make the call. "Very good, Ms. Howard," I told her. "We'll be in touch with you shortly. If we decide to accept the commission, Mr. Benedict may have some more questions for you. And he'll want to see the actual material."

She let me see that she had some issues with my competence. "To be honest," she said, "I'm surprised there'd be any hesitancy on your part. I mean, you've said yourself that you deal in artifacts connected with people of historical interest. If my brother-in-law doesn't fit that description, I find it hard to imagine who would."

"Ms. Howard, you have to understand that he was a physicist. And I've no intention of demeaning that, but scientists don't usually become celebrated. And it's celebrity that drives the price. We have to be sure he fits the profile in which our clients are interested, and also that we ourselves are in a position to do him—and you—justice."

She got up. "That sounds like double-talk."

"I'm sorry if it does. I'm trying to be honest with you."

"Of course you are. And I assume you won't object if I make the offer to someone else?"

"That would be your choice, Ms. Howard."

"Just in case," she said, "I'll leave the chip."

We walked back out to the front door. It opened, and she strode through onto the deck. "I'm always surprised," she said, "that these small companies don't train their people better."

I smiled politely. "How about his AI? Is that available?"

"No," she said.

"Is there a reason? That could be the most valuable object in the estate."

"No. Elizabeth wiped it."

"That's odd. Why would she do that?"

"I have no idea. I didn't realize its condition until after she'd passed."

Alex wasn't in the building. When Howard arrived, I'd been sending out notification bulletins to clients, letting them know we'd found the artifacts they'd requested or, in several cases, that they were unavailable, or that we hadn't been able to locate them. Often objects just vanish. Someone gets them who's not connected to the rest of the world, or who has no wish to deal regardless of the price being offered. Occasionally, thieves make off with something, and it disappears from view for an extended period. Valuable artifacts have vanished for centuries, only to surface again.

Anyhow, I went back to work and was just getting ready to break for lunch when Alex came in. He'd been doing his workout routine, which now consisted mostly of swimming over at the Delancey pool. He brushed the snow off his coat and gave me a broad smile, the implication of which was that all the world was bright and enticing. I smiled back. "I see Audree was there today," I said.

He shook his head. "No, she couldn't get off this morning."

"When you write your autobiography, Alex, I have a title for you."

"And that would be—?"

*There's Never a Shortage of Beautiful Women at Delancey's.*
He grinned. "It's too long, Chase."

"Well, I don't know—"

"And you never want to start a title with *There*."

"Oh."

"You have a lot of talent, sweetheart, but you'll never be a writer." He pulled off his hat and scarf. "It's cold out there."

It was the first storm of the season, and the earliest we'd seen anything like it as far back as I could remember. He sat down to wriggle out of his boots. "Anything happening here?"

"Mack Darby thinks we should try harder to get the stiletto."

That was the weapon that Nicholas Wescott had used to kill his young bride, thereby igniting the revolution that ultimately wrecked the Fremont Republic.

Alex dropped one boot on the floor. "Keating wouldn't let go of it unless somebody went over there with a gun."

"I told him that. Not in those words, of course. I don't entirely trust Darby."

"He's okay. He's a bit intense, but he wouldn't hurt anybody."

"Anyhow, Alex, he says he wants to try. Says if anybody could persuade him—"

"What's he offering?"

"You'll need to talk to him."

"Okay. Anything else?"

"You ever hear of Chris Robin?"

"*The* Chris Robin?"

"A physicist who wrote songs."

"That's him. He wrote 'Starlight and You.'" Alex laughed. "Chase, the guy's famous."

"If you say so."

"I think you spend too much time in this office."

"That's more or less what *she* said."

"Who's *she*?"

"His sister-in-law."

"You were talking to Chris Robin's sister-in-law?"

"Yes. She was here. Has some stuff for sale that belonged to him."

"That's interesting."

"Really?"

"Chase, the reason he's well-known doesn't have anything to do with 'Starlight and You.' Or the physics. It's because he disappeared. Nobody knows what happened to him."

Light finally dawned. The physicist who'd come home from somewhere, had gotten out of a skimmer at his front door, and never made it into his house.

Alex shook his head. Sad story. "But it gives some value to anything connected with him."

"Yes. I remember now."

"So tell me about the sister-in-law."

"Her name's Karen Howard. She's inherited the estate, and she wants to market some of his personal items."

Alex gave me a broad smile. "Sounds promising. What's she have?"

I showed him the inventory. He looked at it and made some notes. "Okay. The ring will probably bring a decent price. What about the house AI?"

"It got erased."

He groaned. "How'd that happen?"

"I've no idea."

He shook off the other boot. "Well, the books might be worth something."

"She says Robin was in the habit of writing notes in them."

"Okay. That'll help. You saw some of these, right? The books?"

"Some."

"Okay. I'll want to go over and take a look."

"I'll set it up."

"Good. I'm surprised you haven't taken care of it already. Was there a problem?"

"Alex, I didn't think we were going to do anything with this unless maybe because he was a songwriter."

That brought a smile. "All right. Let's lock it down."

"So what's he done? Other than drop out of sight?"

"Chase, what else does he *need* to do? You make up a list of people who've vanished over the years, they've almost all become famous, but hardly anyone's done anything other than that. It's all you need. And Chris Robin is among the top ten."

I called Howard, told her we were interested in representing her, and set up an appointment for the following evening. Then I looked up Christopher Robin.

A pilot who often worked with him had dropped him off at his home on Virginia Island at around 11:00 P.M. on the first day of spring, 1393. And if that rings a bell, it's because that's the date of the Great Kolandra Earthquake. The pilot's name was Cermak.

Robin's home was located in an isolated area at the southern tip of the island. A young couple who were strolling along the edge of the ocean saw the skimmer arrive. Elizabeth, apparently, slept through it all.

Robin seems never to have entered the house, and no one ever saw him again.

In an odd coincidence, it was also Cermak's last night. He'd been bringing Robin in from Skydeck. They'd flown a lander into the Vasilyev Terminal in Kolandra and parked. From there, Cermak had delivered Robin to Virginia Island, then gone home to his own place at Caton Ferry, a small coastal town five hundred kilometers north. He apparently arrived just in time to get caught in the quake.

Cermak became one of the heroes of that unhappy event. There are pictures of him, scorched and bleeding, carrying kids out of burning buildings, administering first aid, pulling people from wrecked cars. In one particularly dramatic shot, he's charging across a rooftop several floors above the street, surrounded by flames.

Two hours and seven minutes after the first quake hit, a tidal wave rolled ashore and demolished most of Caton Ferry. It also destroyed the Vasilyev Terminal.

Fortunately, Virginia Island felt only a few temblors.

Like Robin, Cermak simply vanished that night. He disappeared during the general chaos. He was either carried out to sea by the tsunami or buried in the wreckage. According to the accounts, it's unlikely he ever learned that his passenger had gone missing.

"What do you think happened to Robin?" Alex asked. His voice surprised me; I hadn't seen him come into the office.

"I have no idea," I said. "It sounds as if he jumped, or fell, into the ocean. But if so, why didn't they find the piece of luggage he'd been carrying? Or the notebook?"

"It's a good question."

"Maybe he just ran off. Maybe there was another woman."

"It's possible."

"He could have been murdered."

Alex nodded. "Maybe he wasn't there at all."

"Why do you say that?"

"The people who saw the lander on the pad did *not* actually see him get out."

"That doesn't mean anything. But maybe that's what happened. It's unlikely that both men would disappear on the same night. Maybe he went on to Kolandra with Cermak."

Alex shrugged. "If so, why stop at his home first?"

"He might have changed his mind. Maybe he just needed something at the house."

"It's possible, Chase. It would explain the bag."

"Well," I said, "it's a long time ago." Alex was silent. "We aren't going to look into it, are we?"

"No," he said.

"That's good. But you're surprising me. Why not?"

"Because if we were able to find an answer, the value of the artifacts would go down."

"Oh."

"Maybe what we'll do is *pretend* to look into it. If we do *that*, and can't solve the riddle—"

"The value goes *up*."

"Very good, Chase. You're a natural for this business."

# TWO

Science is an investigation into reality, how atoms interact and biological systems develop and stars give heat. Myth is also an investigation into reality, but into a reality of a different type: It informs us of the deepest desires and fears of the subconscious mind. The place where we really live.

—Kosha Malkeva, *The Road to Babylon*, 3376 C.E.

Karen Howard lived in a plush estate in Westmont Park, where Mt. Gordana was just visible in the west when the light was right. The storm had finally subsided, and the skies had cleared, but the entire world was buried in snow. As we settled toward the ground that evening, we were instructed by a deep baritone to identify ourselves and state our business. "Rainbow Enterprises to see Ms. Howard," I said, giving the system a code word that had been issued to us earlier. A ring of lights came on around the landing pad. The lights weren't necessary because it wasn't quite dark yet, but they did add a sense of luster to the place.

The house resembled an Itaki temple. Towers rose above both wings, and I found myself expecting to hear chanting as we touched down. The voice, still speaking through the comm link, welcomed us to Howard Manor and invited us inside. We got out of the skimmer and started along a sheltered walkway.

The windows were sedately illuminated, and a viol played wistfully. More lights came on. The front door opened, and a young woman greeted us, took our jackets, and showed us into a large sitting room. "Ms. Howard," she said, "will be with you shortly." The room possessed an elegant sterility: window curtains that might have been employed as ceremonial robes, ivory-colored ornamental shelves supporting vases filled with year-round flowers, a red carpet that looked as if no one had ever walked on it. It was a room to admire but not one in which you could relax and kick off your shoes.

We'd been there only a couple of minutes when Ms. Howard walked in. She inspected Alex and said hello to him. Then she smiled condescendingly at me. "It is nice to see you again, Ms. Kolpath."

We exchanged a few pleasantries. Alex commented on how well kept the grounds were, presumably apparent to him under the snow cover. Howard took a moment to admire his scarf, and suggested that we all make ourselves comfortable. We sat down on a sofa while she took a large, padded armchair. "Chase tells me," Alex said, "you have some items connected with Christopher Robin."

She looked momentarily as if that fact had slipped her mind. "As a matter of fact, Mr. Benedict, I do." Sidewise glance at me. "I take it you're in a position to represent my interests?"

Alex fell back on his charm. "Of course," he said. "We'd be delighted." His tone conveyed a sense that we were all friends, that whatever had gone before was of no concern, was part of a misunderstanding, and that he would find it gratifying to assist her. "I wonder," he continued, "if it would be possible to see the materials?"

Some of the stiffness drained away. "Certainly, Mr. Benedict," she said. "Please follow me."

We went out into a central corridor, turned toward the rear of the house, and entered another, smaller, room. The objects had been placed on a dinner table, arranged with the Carpathian hat as the centerpiece. Plaques, lamps, framed pictures, books, paintings, the wedding ring, the diamond-studded comm link, a bust of a bearded man (Adam Karvenko, I learned later, who'd connected quantum theory with consciousness), and some electronic gear. And, of course, the books.

Alex circled the table, examining the objects, using a magnifying lens on some, lifting others so he could study them from different angles.

He took a long look at the wedding ring. "The names will help," he said, "and especially the inscription." Alex lifted the cover of one of the books. Mirabeau's *The Social Abstract*. Comments were printed in precise characters in the margins: *Exactly!!* And *Out of context*. And *I'd love to see the documentation for that*.

He paged through Hai Kallei's *Lost in the Shadows*, smiling at Robin's comments. *Dumb*. And *Tribalism will always be with us, despite your assertions*. And *Sometimes I wonder if we deserve to survive*.

In a collection of science essays, Alex, admiringly, read one comment aloud: *We are like the seas. Tides come in, go out. Our shorelines wear down and drift away, but in the end, the substance does not change. Neither technology nor accumulated wisdom has any fundamental effect on who we are*.

Baron's *Cosmological Constant* was also filled with commentary. *Sounds good, but the logic is confused*. And *If this is so, the world is even more illusory than we thought*. Alex smiled. "Did you know him very well, Ms. Howard?"

"Not especially," she said. "I didn't especially like him."

"Why is that?"

"He thought he was better than everybody else."

Alex nodded. Isn't that the way of the world? He put the book down and looked up at the picture of the interstellar that Howard had shown me at the country house. It hung directly opposite the entrance, making it the first thing you'd see coming into the room. "This is exactly the way he'd placed it in his own house," she said.

Alex examined it from several angles before turning to her. "Ms. Howard, what about this? Did it have a special meaning of some sort for Professor Robin?"

"Not that I'm aware of."

Alex turned back to the picture. Shook his head.

"What's wrong?" I asked.

"I've seen it before somewhere."

I didn't recognize it. The superluminal looked retro. Too thick through the hull. The two odd characters near the main hatch. Individual portals on the bridge rather than the wraparound.

"So what do you think, Mr. Benedict?"

Alex smiled pleasantly. "We'll be happy to assist you,

Ms. Howard. I doubt there'll be any trouble moving the ring, or the plaques. The books should be okay. Photos are always a difficult sell, because they are not single items, if you get my meaning. But I think we can do reasonably well." He hesitated. "Ms. Howard, I'm going to ask you to be patient, however. It might be possible to increase the value of these items if you'll allow me some time."

"Time to do what, if I may ask?"

"I won't be sure until we learn more about Professor Robin."

He remained quiet until we got up into the night sky and had started home. It was not yet dark, but we had a crescent moon directly overhead. "There are some speculations about this guy," he said.

"Like what?"

"Are you aware there's a Christopher Robin Society?"

"No. I didn't know that. Is that really so? What is it? A society of physicists?"

"Physicists, historians, enthusiasts."

"Okay."

"They meet monthly at Sanova."

I knew the tone. "We're not going, I hope?"

"Why not?"

"What would be the point?"

"Who better to drum up interest in Robin artifacts than people who have a passion for his work?"

"But aren't we talking about physics? How do you get collectors passionate about physics?"

"Chase, we're talking about alternate universes and black holes."

We were passing over the Melony. Fireworks were being launched from one of the casinos. Somebody celebrating something. "Alex?"

"Yes, Chase?"

"A lot of people have disappeared. Why does Robin draw enthusiasts? What are they enthusiastic about?"

His eyes caught some of the light. "Robin worked at the edges of science. He was interested, for example, in whether any part of us survives death."

"Oh."

"Okay?"

"And what did he decide?"

"I couldn't determine whether he'd ever reached a decision. Chase, Robin explored the fringes of science. He was looking for breakthroughs in areas that are considered beyond the pale by most of his colleagues. He asked questions nobody else dared to ask."

"Like whether there really are alternate universes."

"Yes."

"I thought the notion of alternate universes was an established fact."

"Mathematically. But Robin apparently wanted to find a way to cross over."

"Oh."

"And he thought maybe we were getting occasional visitors from one."

"You're kidding."

He laughed. "I think he was hoping. In any case, a lot of people are fascinated by the fact that he disappeared on the same night as the Kolandra Earthquake."

"I suspect a lot of people disappeared that night."

"He wasn't in the area where the quake hit."

"So what are they suggesting happened?"

"The theory is that there was a collision that night. Between universes. That's what caused the quake."

"That's crazy."

"Ah, Dr. Kolpath, I'm glad to have that settled. However that may be, some of the enthusiasts—but I suspect none of the physicists—think Robin took advantage of the collision to cross into the other universe."

"Okay. I know you're not buying into any of this. Are you?"

He laughed. "Of course not. But the more extreme elements make for good copy."

"I don't think," I said, "that lunatics buy antiques."

"It doesn't matter. They'll raise the general level of interest in Robin. That's all we need."

"Okay."

"Some of the wackier elements claim he was looking into the possibility that there are ghosts. They've been arguing that he knew about people, or entities, who'd gotten caught in dimensional fluxes. And can't get clear. Plato described grave-yards as being restless at night. He thought it was a result of people's being too materialistic. Tying themselves to the plea-sures of the world. Then when they die, they can't untangle their souls. Robin's idea, according to some of these people, was that if you're in the wrong place when there's a collision, you can get permanently snared."

"Is any of this on the record?"

"Not really. Look, Robin was given to kidding around. So it's hard to know what he really thought about a lot of this stuff. He'd appear at different events as a speaker, and some-body would ask the question, were there really such things as people trapped in the dimensions, or in cemeteries, and he'd play along. 'Of course there are,' he'd say. All you have to do is watch him in action, and you get the sense that he knows what he's saying is preposterous, but some part of him hopes it's so."

"Okay—"

"He wasn't given to ruling things out simply because they seemed absurd. If collisions actually happen, he says some-where, there could easily be casualties."

"That's a pretty spooky notion."

"Yes, it is."

"But nobody's going to take this stuff seriously."

"Chase, as far as we're concerned, nobody *has* to take it seriously. It doesn't matter whether the ideas have any valid-ity. Only that people get excited about them. Anyhow, the tim-ing's perfect. It's this weekend, and I'm going to head over there. You want to come?"

I put it out of my mind until, near the end of the week, Jerry Muldoon called. Jerry was a retired psychiatrist who had probably talked with a few too many patients. He was the most dispassionate guy I'd ever known, a man whose smile was automatic, and whose ability to portray empathy was nonexistent even though he thought he was good at it. Alex was on the circuit with another dealer, so I asked if I could help.

*"I understand,"* he said, *"that you have some personal effects that once belonged to Chris Robin?"*

"Yes, we have access to some, Jerry. But they haven't been placed on the market yet."

*"Magnificent,"* he said. *"What actually do you have?"*

I told him. Then asked how it happened that he knew about them.

*"I just happened to hear about it."* His tone suggested he'd outmaneuvered us. *"Word of something like this gets around. You know what I mean? Can I see what they look like?"*

"Not yet, Jerry. The owner wants to keep them under wraps for the time being. But I'm glad to hear you're interested. If you like, we'll notify you as soon as they become available."

*"What's the delay?"*

I couldn't very well tell him that Alex was planning some backroom conniving. "They're still clearing the official documents," I said.

*"Damn."* He sounded genuinely disappointed. The odd thing was that Jerry had always been a collector of objects associated with the collapse of the Ilurian Era. That's literally several worlds and sixteen centuries away. He'd done some ancestral research and convinced himself that his forebears were among the thieves chased out during the Rebellion, so he was interested in anything connected with them. We'd been able to get a few modestly priced items for him: a dissembler—which is a weapon since outlawed—that had once belonged to an earlier Jeremy Muldoon, a vase that had been the property of a prostitute associated with one of the rebels, and one or two other objects from the period. But I'd never known him to be interested in other antiquities.

"Did you want these for yourself, Jerry?" I asked. "Or are you acting as someone's agent?"

*"Are you kidding, Chase? They would be for* me. *Absolutely."* Outside, two capers were chasing each other through the snow, waving furry tails. *"All right. You* will *let me know, right?"*

"Absolutely."

*"As soon as you have something."*

Three minutes later, there was a second call. It was more of the same.

"Sure," Alex said. "I leaked the story."

"Why?"

"Call it a test run."

"I'm amazed that anybody would care that much about a

physicist. Even one who disappeared. I mean, we have pilots who've disappeared, pharmacists, librarians, all kinds of people. So you've dug up responses from a few people who don't have enough to do. What's it prove?"

"Chase," he said, "you need to stop thinking about Robin as a physicist."

"Really? What would you suggest?"

"Try 'celebrity.'"

"It's been a pretty well-kept secret."

"You travel," he said, in his locked-on imitation of Collier Ibsen, the actor who'd made a career of playing tough guys, "in the wrong circles, sweetheart."

# THREE

A myth is occasionally a scientific explanation that hasn't been made yet.

—Christopher Robin, *Multiverse*, 1387

We got a few more calls from potential customers asking about Chris Robin, and Alex looked quite pleased. "If we play this correctly," he said as we lifted off in the late afternoon for Sanova and the monthly meeting of the Christopher Robin Society, "we might have a serious winner here."

"You should consider a career as a sales consultant," I said. He smiled and pretended to take it as a compliment.

The meeting was being held at the Jubilee Country Club, which, in better times, had been a posh operation designed for people who enjoyed showing off their wealth. But they'd come under new management which, we heard, had lost the personal touch with their customers, the clientele had gone away, and the Jubilee fell into a state of general deterioration. When we walked through the front doors, I got a sense of a lost age, of a place whose time had passed.

The meeting was being held in the main ballroom, with panels assigned to conference rooms. We signed in with a middle-aged woman sitting at a table just inside the door. She produced two badges, and we went inside.

I'm not sure what I expected. A séance, maybe. A team of ghost hunters. Someone who'd encountered stalkers from another universe.

Alex disapproved of my attitude. "They *do* trade ideas here," he told me sternly. "Keep in mind this is primarily a social event. But it's also a place where people can talk about wild ideas, whatever they might be, without fear of getting laughed at. I should also mention that the tradition here is that comments made during the evening stay here. Nothing gets recorded. Nothing gets repeated, without permission."

There were about fifty attendees present when we arrived. Another ten or fifteen drifted in while we wandered around, introducing ourselves and engaging in small talk. Then the president called the meeting to order, made some business announcements, and introduced the keynote speaker, a trim woman with cinnamon-colored hair whom he described as an expert on the subject of disembodied consciousness. The woman thanked us for coming, said she hoped we would find the evening instructive, and expressed her appreciation that there were still open-minded people in the world. "The Latrill branch of the Society," she said, "sends its warmest wishes." She expressed regret that modern society had failed to recognize the scientific contributions of Chris Robin simply because they did not fit easily into the common misperceptions of how the universe worked. "It's hard not to wonder what he might have given us," she said, "had his lifetime not been cut short."

That got some applause.

She gazed around the room, nodded to a couple of people in back, and smiled. "Some of my colleagues," she continued, "suspect he was spirited away by the forces of corporate greed. There might be something to that. If his work on dark energy had panned out, it would have delivered a body blow to some of the corporate powers, and I don't need to tell you who they are. Unfortunately, it looks as if dark energy has reached a dead end. I personally doubt there's any truth to this particular conspiracy theory. Though we all love conspiracies, this one is simply too mundane. But until we know for certain, assuming we ever do, the suspicion will always be there."

She mentioned something called the nanodrive, which would allow us to cross to Andromeda. And she praised Robin's work on colliding universes, and how exciting it would be if we could somehow communicate with these other realities. "Imagine meeting another version of yourself," she said. "Although I confess that some of my associates tell me that, for some of us, one is quite enough."

That got some laughs. "I'd love to think," she continued,

"that somewhere, we are all gathered at another Jubilee Country Club. But instead of mourning for Chris Robin, he is standing here with us, our guest of honor, sharing a drink with Harry over there." Everybody turned toward a tall, white-haired man who smiled. Those who had glasses raised them in his direction, and the rest applauded.

She sat down to more applause and had to rise again when it did not subside. The president thanked her for her illuminating remarks. "If that is so," he added, "I'd be inclined to wonder whether that happy group could imagine *our* situation." He paused, sighed, and announced that the first two panels would start at the top of the hour.

A screen at one of the conference rooms announced that the opening topic would be "The Multiverse." The room filled up quickly, while the panelists took their places behind a table. I should mention that the attendees all seemed to be professionals of one kind or another. They were articulate, obviously knowledgeable, and enthusiastic.

The panelists talked about how a multiverse was the only way we could rationally explain our own existence, where the requirements for a universe friendly to life were extreme: a gravity constant within narrow limitations, the tendency of water to freeze from the top down, the weak and strong nuclear forces, and a number of other very precise settings. "You have to have a lot of universes, an enormous number of them, in fact," said the panel moderator, a short bald man who drummed his fingers constantly while talking. "You have to have literally billions before the settings can become right by accident. Unless, of course, you're willing to admit divine intervention."

The discussion sailed quietly along for about twenty minutes. Then one of the panelists, a heavyset man with a shock of white hair hanging in his eyes, delivered a jolt: "What we have to ask ourselves," he said, "is whether Chris really was taken by someone, or whether he *did* find a way to cross over. Do any of the panel members believe that might actually be possible?"

Among the other three panelists, two hands went up. "'Anything that is not expressly forbidden is possible,'" said one, a young woman who might have been a model for one of the clothing companies. "But I think the likelihood is remote."

The others nodded.

A hand waved in the audience. Another young woman. "If he could have actually gone to the other side, wouldn't he have taken someone with him? To serve as a witness? But nobody else disappeared that night. At least not on Virginia Island."

The panelists looked at one another. The moderator drummed his fingers some more. "It's a valid point, Jessica," he said. "But he might not have wanted to risk someone else's life until he was sure he could do it and return."

I looked at Alex. "That's pretty wild stuff."

"Gives the notion of the Universal Cab Company a whole new meaning," he said.

A bearded man seated beside me wanted to know whether there was any truth to the claim that Robin had predicted the earthquake. That he knew it was coming because it was the result of colliding branes. At first I thought he was talking about people, but then I recalled that physicists use the term *brane* to indicate the edge of a universe. Assuming universes *have* edges.

The question went to a panelist named Bill. Bill was tall, thin, clearly well into his second century. "I've heard that story," he said. "Can you cite a source, sir?"

"No," he said. "I've tried. I've heard it often enough, but I don't know where it comes from."

Bill looked at the other panelists. They shook their heads. All were familiar with it, and one even commented that it sounded plausible to her. But nobody could pin it down.

Another hand went up. A man with gray hair and a neatly trimmed beard. He had the mien of a department chairman. "The night Robin disappeared," he said, "is it true he was returning from Skydeck?"

"That's correct."

"Had he actually gone somewhere? Or was he just hanging out at the station?"

"He'd been out somewhere," said Bill.

"Do we know where?"

"Nobody has any idea."

Another hand went up. "What about the black holes?"

"What specifically were you referring to?" said the moderator.

"Robin's overall interest in them. What was that all about?"

"Hey," said someone on the far side of the room, "who *doesn't* have a fascination with black holes?"

They all laughed. "Of course," said a woman in back, "but is it true he spent time charting their courses? Their trajectories? Whatever?"

The moderator looked at the other panelists. The panelist who'd not thought it possible that Robin had crossed into another universe was middle-aged, well dressed, and wore a sardonic grin throughout the proceedings. Her nameplate identified her as Dr. Matthews. "It's true," she responded. "He *did* do that."

"Do we know why?"

"A hobby, I'd guess. Frankly, I'd be surprised if someone like Robin *didn't* have an interest in black holes."

During the course of the evening, we saw a broadcast interview with Robin in which he dismissed the theory that the universe is a hologram. I was surprised that anyone had ever been able to take that idea seriously, but apparently there *was* some supporting evidence. *"But,"* said Robin, *"there are alternative explanations for the evidence. There's a lot we still don't know, but sometimes one simply has to fall back on common sense."*

One of the speakers, Charlie Plunkett, identified as an engineer with Corbin Data, described an attempt by Robin to show that the voices in an allegedly haunted house might actually be connections with an alternate universe. "Unfortunately," he said, "the results were inconclusive."

In a program titled "Alternate Selves," the panelists discussed the notion that, in an infinite sea of universes, every possibility, somewhere, would come to pass. That meant there were other editions of ourselves out there somewhere. We were consequently asked which of our alternate selves we would, if given the chance, choose to meet. Members of the audience opted for themselves as war heroes, entertainment superstars, lady-killers. The bearded guy beside me wanted to be CEO at Colossos, Inc. "Why? So that I never again have to deal with a boss."

A substantial number wanted simply to meet a version of themselves who was accomplishing something that would be remembered. One admitted hoping that "it might still turn out to be me." That drew applause.

When his turn came, Alex didn't surprise me: "I'll settle for where I am," he said. "I love dealing with antiques."

Then it was my turn. A few years back, I'd fallen in love for the one and only time in my life. And I let him get away. If I actually had the opportunity, I'd like to meet the Chase Kolpath who had held on to him, married him, and settled into a quiet life. I'd like very much to know how that would have turned out. But I wasn't going to say anything about it in front of that crowd, so I told them I'd enjoy spending an hour with the Kolpath who'd made a fortune as lead singer with the Bandoliers.

During that same panel, an historian went in a new direction. "His IQ is on the record," he said. "It was over 260, too high for any human being. Maybe he didn't get carried off by a corporate giant. Or caught in another dimension. Maybe he simply went home."

When I asked him later if he thought there might actually be something to that suggestion, he shook his head sadly. "No," he said. "I wish I did."

Shortly before he disappeared, Robin was interviewed by Todd Cunningham, the celebrated talk-show host who, at the time, was at the very beginning of his career. Robin looked better in motion than he did in the still pictures. He seemed relaxed, amiable, a guy with a sense of humor. A large smile appeared when Cunningham asked him why he persisted in saying things that left him open to criticism by his colleagues.

*"I'm not sure they're my colleagues,"* Robin said.

*"Other scientists, then."* Cunningham smiled in the self-deprecating manner that suggests his guest is twisting the truth, and that had since become his trademark.

Robin allowed himself to look uncomfortable, but I got the sense he was in complete control. *"There's no easy way to say this, Todd, but the reality is that most of us, even physicists, maybe especially physicists, aren't generally open to new ideas. We think every important discovery was made during the Golden Age. That nothing of any significance remains to be found."*

*"You're saying that's wrong?"*

*"I hope it's wrong. I really do. I'd hate to think there's nothing left for us to learn."*

*"Do you hope to provide us with a breakthrough somewhere, Chris?"*

*"Yes, I do."*

*"And what might that be?"*

*"I don't know. If I knew, I'd tell you now."*

*"When will you know?"*

He smiled. *"Maybe after Uriel."*

*"Uriel?"*

*"When I have something, Todd, I'll be in touch."*

Cunningham frowned. *"What's* Uriel, *Chris? Are you talking about the angel?"*

*"I'll let you know—"*

Alex found an astronomer, a quiet, dark-skinned woman who seemed out of place amid all the jokes and exaggerations. Her name was Silvia, and I suspected she'd been talked into coming. More or less like me. "Silvia," he said, "what *is* Uriel?"

She looked pleased to have someone ask a straightforward question. "It's a dwarf star, Alex. Six and a half light-years from here. Maybe a little less."

"Any planets?"

"A few. Nothing habitable. At least there wasn't the last time I looked." We could hear laughter in the next room. The end of the evening was approaching. "And there's nothing unusual about it that I know of."

"You have any idea what Robin was talking about?"

She shook her head. "None whatever. And neither does anybody else. I've seen this interview before, and I can't imagine what he's referring to. I'm not even sure he means the star. Maybe you need to ask an historian. Or a theologian." She grinned. "Maybe the theologian would be your best bet."

When the panels concluded, we retired to the ballroom for some drinks and hors d'oeuvres. Alex maneuvered us to a table occupied by Harvey Hoskin, the president of the Society, and Brandon Rupprecht, a biologist. Hoskin had bristly gray hair and a close-cut beard, and he was probably the oldest person in the Jubilee that evening.

We talked about the Society, how there would be a special meeting on the north coast later that year, and who was in line for the Chris Robin Award, which would be given out at the summer meeting in Andiquar. The award recognized "reaching beyond the parameters." During a break in the conversation, Alex asked how the Society had gotten started.

"This is our twenty-seventh year," Hoskin said. "It began here at the university after Jim Hovel did a dissertation on Robin's multiple-universe analyses. Jim was on one of the panels tonight."

"Yes," said Alex. "We were there."

"Anyhow, as I'm sure you know—" Hoskin plunged into an account of the mathematics of time-space flexibility. At least, that's what I think it was. "He insisted, therefore, that alternate universes *had* to exist. I don't have the physics background to go into detail, but you can find it in his book."

"We have a copy," said Alex.

"Okay. Then you can imagine why a lot of people got interested. No one before had ever dared talk this way." He looked across the table at Rupprecht. "At the time he disappeared, he'd become a figure of ridicule. Maybe a lot of people were jealous. I don't know. Anyhow, we—most of us—didn't learn to appreciate him until he was gone. Now, of course, he's a hero. Several of us went to a party one night, and we were talking about him, and I think we began to realize how much he meant to us. I mean, he wasn't afraid to be wrong. For him, it was nice to be right, but the important thing was to ask the right questions. You know what I mean?"

Rupprecht picked up the thread: "And that's how the Chris Robin Society was born." Rupprecht was average-looking, average height, average everything. His was the kind of face you'd never be able to remember from one day to the next except for his eyes, which tended to freeze you in place.

"Is there *really* any possibility," I asked, "any at all, that he might have been right? I mean, I know how crazy it sounds, but is there any chance that maybe you could walk into that closet over there in the corner and find yourself in another universe?"

Hoskin smiled. "It's not forbidden by the laws of physics, is it, Brandy?"

Rupprecht grinned, lifted his glass to his lips, and put it back with the drink untouched. "Above my pay grade," he said.

I must have looked stunned.

Hoskin noticed. "We have to be cautious about ruling

things out simply because they're counterintuitive, Chase. Who would have believed a particle could be in two places simultaneously?" Alex asked whether any members of the group had actually known Robin.

Hoskin passed the question to Rupprecht.

"I knew him," he said, with a sad smile. "Chris was okay. Not the most patient guy in the world. But I was sorry to lose him."

"What was he like?"

"He told jokes on himself. Took himself seriously but didn't expect anybody else to. If he had, I don't think he'd have survived as long as he did. He wanted to do blue sky science. That was all he really lived for. Find something new. Figure out how to travel backward in time. Find out what drives complexity. But that era was over long ago. All we do today is try to design a better engine and do studies on why life evolves in different ways on different worlds. If it shows up at all. So for a long time, nobody took him seriously. But he learned to live with that."

Hoskin jumped in. "Something else that fascinated him was the occasional sightings of unidentified ships."

"Unidentified ships?"

"You know, the sightings they have at the stations every once in a while? A ship will show up, cruise past, not identify itself, and just leave the area."

"I've heard of them, sure," said Alex. "But I never really thought much about the stories."

"They're there. *Something* is. They're on the record. The sightings go back a long time. Centuries."

"But that just means people get lost. Wander into the wrong system, and clear out again."

"Well, there's something strange about some of them—" He turned toward me. "You're a pilot, Chase—am I right about that?"

"Yes, Harvey, that's correct."

"If I watch a ship make its jump into transdimensional space, what do I see?"

I wasn't sure what he was asking. "Nothing," I said finally. "It just disappears."

"Exactly. Like turning off a light, right?"

"Yes."

"But the ships involved in the sightings, *some* of them anyhow, *don't* just blink out. They *fade* out. It takes a few seconds, but it's a different process. They gradually become invisible."

"So what did Robin think they were?"

"He never said. But they intrigued him. And I'm pretty sure I know what he *suspected*."

"Which was—?"

"That they were ships from another civilization. Or maybe another universe."

I'd had enough to drink, so I let the AI take us home. It was a bright, cold evening, with a few clouds drifting across a moonless sky. "Well," I said, "that was an interesting experience."

"Yes. And a profitable one."

"What makes you say that? I can't see any of those people, for all their enthusiasm, buying a book because Robin scribbled a comment in it."

"Oh, that's probably true."

"Then what—?"

"Chase, we can get a substantial price for the Robin artifacts."

"Really? Why?"

"The guy is the stuff of myth. Ghosts. Colliding universes. Ships from other realities. Then *he* disappears."

"I'm not sure I'm following you."

"We won't get a good price for his stuff if only a few people are interested in him."

"I agree."

"And, of course, nobody cares about physicists. I mean, nobody understands them. But a mad scientist? Who maybe got carried off to another universe? Or maybe came from one himself?"

"Alex, I don't think I like where this is going."

"It's all P.R., Chase. What we need to do is shape the public perception."

"And how do you plan to do that?"

# FOUR

Perception is everything.

—Terrestrial proverb, third millennium

Two days after the Chris Robin conference, Alex showed up as a guest on *Newscope*, hosted by Leah Carmody. I was at home, shoes off, feet propped up, enjoying a nightbinder although I'd put too much lemon in it.

Leah's other guest was Arlen Adams. Adams could have been an Old Testament prophet. He was big and imposing, and probably a thousand years old, with judgmental eyes and a long white beard. He was also chairman of the physics department at Perennial College. He had never hidden the fact that he disapproved of Alex.

Leah introduced the topic, which would be Chris Robin, *"the physicist who disappeared forty-one years ago."*

She turned to Alex first, and he started by admitting that his own grasp of physics was virtually nonexistent, and he was consequently not competent to speak about Robin's work. He then proceeded to do so, describing Robin's desire to break into new territory, his attempt to explain why the universe was "biology friendly," his conviction that there were alternate universes, and his determination to answer the cosmic questions that everyone else had long since given up on.

I knew that Alex had been reading everything he could find on the subject, and I was familiar with his work ethic, so I wasn't surprised by his performance.

Adams sat through this, looking placidly at the ceiling like a man wondering why he was there. When Leah turned to him and asked for a comment, he shook his head. *"When there's solid evidence for any of this,"* he said, *"I'll be happy as anyone to look at it. In the meantime, all of this talk about branes and places where the physics is different and all the rest of it is just that: talk. It's idle speculation and nothing more, and I'm sure Mr. Benedict would agree."*

Leah smiled pleasantly. *"I wonder if either of you would mind telling us what an alternate universe might look like?"*

Adams managed a patient smile. *"With luck,"* he said, *"it would be one without deranged antique dealers."*

Alex returned the smile but let it pass. *"I would hope so. But, to answer your question, Leah, an alternate universe is simply a place where the rules are different. For example, if the gravity is weak, stars might never form. Or maybe the rules are pretty much the same, but the history is different. A place, say, where the Greeks built the pyramids. Or where we are different. For example, you might be the person who deals in antiquities, while I'm running a talk show. And Professor Adams has an open mind."*

Adams went back to examining the ceiling.

She laughed. Jokes between friends. *"Are we saying that a place like that might actually exist?"*

*"It's possible. Some physicists say it's a mathematical necessity."*

Adams made a sound deep in his throat. *"As much as it pains me to admit it,"* he said, *"Mr. Benedict has it right."*

*"Then these places do exist."*

*"In all probability,"* said Adams, *"yes."*

She looked from one of her guests to the other. *"Is there any evidence that Professor Robin found a way to cross over to one of these places? Is that where this is going?"*

*"I wouldn't call it evidence,"* said Alex. *"Some people claim he did."*

*"Did he ever make the claim?"*

*"Not that I know of."*

She turned back to Adams. *"Arlen, what's the common wisdom on this? Will it ever be possible to travel to one of these places? Assuming they exist?"*

He used his folded hands to support his chin. "Ever *is a long time, Leah. Certainly, we won't be jumping into one of Mr. Benedict's universal cabs to visit them anytime soon."*

Leah nodded. *"I'm glad we have some consensus. Let's talk about his disappearance."*

Adams had been wearing a superior smile. Now it faded, and his features took on a regretful aspect. *"He came back from a trip to Skydeck, was dropped off outside his house, and nobody ever saw him again. He'd probably been drinking and fell into the ocean."*

She turned back to Alex: *"But* you *think he disappeared into an alternate universe?"*

*"I didn't say that."*

She brightened. *"I wish you would."*

*"Leah, there's no way to be sure what really happened. We're looking into it now."*

*"Good luck with that,"* said Adams.

*"Alex, don't you think if there were anything to any of this, somebody would already have looked into it?"*

*"People have, Leah. The police still have his case open, but it remains a mystery. Did he fall into the sea? Was he taken by someone? Or did something outside our experience happen to him? Professor Adams has* that *part of it right: The story's so wild that most physicists don't want to touch it. I mean, it does nothing for your professional standing to take something like this seriously. So they keep a respectful distance. Should it turn out at some future date that he actually did* find *a way out of this reality, there'll be no shortage of Professor Adams's colleagues claiming they suspected it all the time."*

*"So you* do *think it's possible, Alex? To cross into another universe?"*

*"Who's to say what's possible and what isn't, Leah?"* Alex glanced at Adams, who had closed his eyes and was just perceptibly shaking his head. Who, indeed? It was times like this that left me wishing I'd gone into real estate.

What had really happened on the evening that Eliot Cermak brought Chris Robin home? The best approach would have been to ask Cermak, but he unfortunately did not have an avatar on the Web. But Elizabeth did.

Avatars are notoriously unreliable, of course, because they will say what they've been directed to say. So-and-so was an idiot. I never saw the jewelry. I never did the stuff they accused me of. But sometimes, if you're careful, and you ask the right questions, you can get a piece of the truth.

Alex asked me to stay with him for the interview. Women, he believed, even avatars, usually responded more readily if there was a second woman present.

The Elizabeth who appeared that morning was *not* the young dark-haired beauty who'd been in the photos. The luster had faded. I saw a more accomplished version of her sister Karen. Her eyes suggested a weary competence rather than the effusive charm of her younger self. Her hair was cut short in a severe fashion that had vanished a generation earlier. *"Hello,"* she said quietly. *"What can I do for you?"*

We introduced ourselves. "We've been employed by your sister," Alex explained, "to determine the value of some of the estate items that you passed on to her."

*"Oh, yes."* Her lips tightened. *"She intends to sell everything, does she?"*

"No. I didn't mean to give you that impression. But she's concerned that you and your husband have not received the kind of credit you deserve. It's been a while now since your husband's disappearance, and, as happens to so many of us, people are beginning to forget his contributions. And yours, since without you, he could not have been so effective."

Those dark eyes reflected a touch of amusement. *"You do speak well, Mr. Benedict. What did you want to know?"*

"We'd like to know whether you have any idea at all what happened to him."

She studied Alex momentarily, then looked my way. *"May I sit down?"*

Usually, an avatar provides its own chair if it wishes to sit. "Of course," said Alex, indicating that she was welcome to use any of the available chairs or the other end of the sofa that he was using.

Elizabeth smiled pleasantly and picked the sofa. *"I have no idea what happened to him. It is a question that has always haunted me. I just don't know. I wish I did."*

"Do you know of anyone who might have had a motive—?"

*"There were people who didn't like him. Some who were*

*jealous. But I don't think anyone would ever have gone so far."* She shook her head. *"I just don't know. Obviously, someone had a reason."*

"Is it possible he might have taken off on his own?"

*"I've wondered about that, too. Years ago, I would have been shocked at the question. But I've gotten used to it. Every time I was introduced to someone, they always found a way to ask that."*

"I'm sorry."

*"We were happy, Mr. Benedict. I loved him."* She was staring past us, looking at some distant place. *"And he was in love with me."*

Alex signaled me to take over. "What actually happened that night, Elizabeth?"

*"I don't know. I'd been down at the church. They were having a social. When I got home, I went to bed. Apparently, Eliot brought Chris home shortly before midnight. I never heard the skimmer.*

*"Whatever happened after that—"* She shook her head. *"He never came inside; I'm sure of that. I woke up during the night because of the earthquake. We didn't take any damage, but we got some tremors. It's a scary thing when the ground shakes under you. I never realized they'd been there until I heard, two days later, that Eliot had died in the quake. I couldn't understand that because he was supposed to be out with Chris. But it left me fearful that Chris had been stranded somewhere. That Eliot was supposed to go back and pick him up."* Her voice shook. *"It's all very confusing, Ms. Kolpath."*

"Call me Chase," I said. "Do you know where they'd gone? Your husband and Eliot?"

*"No. It was always orbital stuff, and I just wasn't very interested. I guess I should have been."*

"Were you expecting him home that evening?"

*"Not really. He'd said he expected to be gone about a week. By then he'd been gone three or four days, so no, I wasn't looking for him."*

"Did he usually let you know when he'd be back?"

*"He sometimes came back early. When he did, he'd usually call from Skydeck. But not always."*

Alex got up and walked over to his desk. "So he did this often?" he asked. "Traveling off-world?"

*"Yes. He did it all the time."*

"Did you ever go with him?"

*"Three or four times. I don't particularly enjoy it. I used to get dizzy just going up to Skydeck."*

"You deleted everything in the house AI. Why?"

*"Too many memories. He was there. In the system. I could have spent endless evenings talking with him. Enjoying him. Pretending he was really in the house. Really* alive. *I knew if I did that, I'd never survive."*

"It would have been hard," Alex said. There've been cases of people who needed treatment when they refused to let go of loved ones who'd died. "How did you find out Cermak had been to the house? Was it neighbors?"

*"We didn't really have anyone living close enough to qualify as a neighbor."* She smiled ruefully. *"I loved the house, but I didn't like the solitude. We were all alone out on the Point. That was Chris's idea. I went along with it."* She stopped and took a deep breath. *"There were a couple of people out for a walk. Along the ocean. They saw the skimmer come down. When they described it, it sounded like Eliot's. But since Chris had never arrived, I thought it must have been just a coincidence that it looked like his. But the two witnesses, they swore it landed. And, of course, when it turned out that Eliot had gotten home and been killed in the quake—"*

"It must have been a terrible shock," said Alex.

*"It was,"* she said. *"And it never went away."*

# FIVE

Ghosts exist. The terrifying aspect of the phenomenon, however, is not that they haunt abandoned houses and dark forests and old cathedrals. No. It is nothing as simple as that. It is rather that they haunt the mind. And, unfortunately, it takes far more than a few prayers or a dash of holy water to get rid of them.

—Ferris Grammery, *Famous Ghosts of Dellaconda*, 1311

I brought up the images of the Robin collectibles. Again, it was the portrait of the starship that drew my attention. The bulky, retro interstellar that had hung on Robin's wall. "Jacob," I said, "can we connect this vehicle with anything?"

He was briefly silent. Then: *"Working."*

I studied the ship. The two odd symbols on the hull.

The ship's designator. But it was a language I'd never seen before. Mute, possibly?

*"I have a match, Chase. It's the Sanusar contact. It passed by the station fifty-four years ago. It has never been identified."*

Bingo. And that probably explained why Alex thought he'd seen it before.

*"It was visible for several hours."*
"Did they get any radio contact, Jacob?"
*"Negative. They tried, but got no answer."*

When I reported what I'd learned to Alex, he let me see he already knew. "And I've a surprise for you," he said.
"What's that?"
"Let me show you something. Found this last night."
Suddenly, I was looking at a crowded concourse. Something was going on. Everybody was excited, and people were moving close to where a familiar figure was being interviewed by a virtual journalist.
Chris Robin.
*"So,"* said the reporter, *"what do you make of it, Professor?"*
*"I'm not sure,"* said Robin. *"But it's not just a lost ship."*
"It's Sanusar," I said. In 1380. A half century ago. "And Robin was there—?"
*"Why do you say that, Professor? That it's not just a lost ship?"*
*"Because of the way it left,"* he said. *"If you look at the record, you'll note it didn't simply move into hyperspace. This was different."*
"You know," I said, "maybe this is why he got interested in these sightings in the first place. He happened to be present when one of them occurred."
"Maybe." Alex looked puzzled. "But I think there's more to it than that."
"How do you mean?"
"Let me show you the media reports for the second week of the new year, 1387. Jacob?"
The monitor lit up, and I sat down in front of it and scanned the headlines:

MEYER ARRESTED ON CORRUPTION CHARGE
SCIENTISTS PREDICT HOT SUMMER
FREEDOM PARTY UNDERWRITES STRIP JOINT
SARA GOLD SEPARATES FROM HARRY
POLICE OVERREACTED, SAYS ANGRY MOTHER

And, finally:

## ALIEN SPACE VEHICLE AT SKYDECK?

(WWP) An alien ship may have passed through the planetary system last night, the Deep Sky Operations Directorate reported this morning. It appeared without warning at the outer edge of the Rimway launch and recovery area, did not respond to calls from the operations center, and, approximately three hours later, passed out of range of the scanners. It was also sighted by a private yacht, which was able to get pictures of it.

Authorities believe the contact was not a standard Confederate vehicle because of its method of departure, which signified an unknown type of drive unit. The vessel did not appear to be Ashiyyurean.

The intruder never approached close to Rimway. According to authorities, it was at no time considered a threat. And they have stated they do not believe it to have been of alien origin. According to the spokesperson, it is deemed far more likely it was an experimental spacecraft and that its origin will become apparent within a short time. No one, however, could explain why it did not respond to repeated queries.

The private yacht was the *Breakwater*, owned and operated by Eliot Cermak. It was, unfortunately, unable to overtake the intruder. Pictures taken by Cermak indicate that the unknown ship simply accelerated well beyond the yacht's ability to stay close.

An investigation is under way.

"Cermak?" I said. "The same one who was ferrying Robin around?"

"Yes."

"Do we know whether Robin was in the *Breakwater* at the time?"

"No. But I'd bet on it."

"You don't believe in coincidence?"

"No."

"But you think he was present for *two* sightings."

"I didn't say *that* was a coincidence."

"How could he possibly have known in advance?"

"I don't know, Chase. Answer that, and we'll be a step closer to finding out what happened to him."

Alex made two more public appearances over the next few days, and was interviewed by the *Celestial*, a magazine that specialized in sensational stories. When I suggested he was playing into his critics, he told me it was product enhancement, and it was an essential part of the business.

It *was* working. Interest in the Robin artifacts continued to mount. Karen Howard got excited when she saw what was happening, and she called, insisting that we hold the auction while the demand was high.

"We're not ready yet," Alex told her. "Give it some time."

*"Are you sure, Mr. Benedict?"* She did not sound comfortable with the idea.

"Everything's going our way, Karen. Let's just be patient for a bit longer."

*"All right. I'm sure you know what you're doing."* Her tone suggested that was hardly the case. *"When do we plan on holding the auction?"*

"We're watching the market. I'll let you know when we're ready to go."

A few minutes later, Shara Michaels called. She blinked on in front of my desk, wearing a blue lab coat. *"How's the big sale going?"* she asked.

"Which one is that, Shara?"

*"Robin."*

"Pretty well. Did you want to put in a bid for something?" Shara, of course, was a physicist.

*"To be honest, I'm tempted."*

"Really?" That seemed out of character. There are two kinds of collectors: those who hope to acquire an artifact in order to make a profit down the line, and those who have a sentimental interest in the object. Shara didn't fit readily into either category. "Why's that?"

*"I've been watching Alex. On the talk shows—"*

"And—?"

*"He makes Robin sound much more intriguing than I'd ever thought. I wouldn't mind having something of his around the apartment. To remind me to keep an open mind, maybe."*

"He is pretty good at that. Selling a story, I mean."

*"I guess. Did you know that Robin believed in a second life?"*

"A lot of people do."

*"But not many physicists."* She looked at me as if I were a bit slow-witted. *"He ran experiments to try to determine whether the mind, the soul, whatever, survived the death of the body. He was morbidly aware of his mortality. Couldn't stand the thought of dying.*

*"There were other things as well. He thought there had to be highly advanced civilizations scattered around the galaxy. He spent a lot of his time trying to find a way to communicate with them."*

"Sitting in a room with a transmitter?"

She laughed. *"Actually, yes. A hyper system of some sort. He was hoping to find a way through the borderlands."* That was a reference to transdimensional space-time, which was still not well understood. *"Look, what I'm trying to say is that you guys should be aware that, obscured in all the eccentricities, the guy was a genius. But that's not the reason I called—Chase, I'm worried about Alex. He's taking a lot of criticism right now in the media. Is he okay?"*

"He's fine, Shara. I think he's used to it."

*"Okay. I'm glad to hear it. If I can help in any way—"*

"Sure, Shara. I'll tell him you called. We'll let you know if you can do anything."

*"Thanks."* She started to disconnect, but hesitated. *"One more thing about Robin?"*

"Yes?"

*"I don't suppose his notebook's included among the artifacts? Or the house AI? I didn't see either listed."*

"No. We don't know what happened to the notebook. Elizabeth deleted the data banks in the AI so she wouldn't be tempted to bring him back."

*"I can understand that. Chase, if you come across a journal, a diary, anything like that, I'd like to know about it."*

"Okay."

*"It could have some very valuable stuff in it."*

"I'll ask his sister-in-law. Maybe she knows something more than she's told us."

*"Good. If you come up with anything, can I persuade you to call me first?"*

"Sure, Shara."

I called Karen Howard. *"No,"* she said. *"He* did *have a notebook. Used to carry it around with him a lot. But it wasn't among the stuff that came with the estate."*

"You're sure?"

*"I'll check and get back to you."*

I'm not sure why, but I didn't much feel like going back to the mundane administrative tasks I'd been working on all day. I sank into my chair and found myself thinking about Gabriel Benedict, Alex's uncle, who'd hired me to work for the archeological team he'd led. I'd spent most of my time then in the field at his sites rather than in an office. But when we were at home, this had been our headquarters, and I'd been behind the same desk. There was a scratch across one side of it, where he and one of his colleagues had gotten careless and bashed a spade into it. The damaged side was now set against the wall so no one could see it.

There was a picture of Gabe and me on the bookcase. He had a trowel in one hand and a bone in the other. I was leaning on a spade. He'd been more than a boss. He'd been a friend. I spent three years with him, ferrying him and his colleagues to remote locations around the Orion Arm. I'd known, of course, that civilizations rise and fall, that cities enjoy their time in the sunlight, then, for a variety of reasons, sink into obscurity and, eventually, into the ground. Everybody knows that. But I hadn't understood the implications until Gabriel Benedict had hired me on as transport director—the title was a gag: I was the pilot for the Fleury Archeological Initiative, named for Ann Fleury, who'd put the organization together in an effort to maintain the integrity of historical sites, to see that they were properly managed, and to keep them safe from exploiters.

That, of course, meant people like Alex. And, ultimately, me.

It was the reason Gabe was so disappointed in his nephew. Alex never knew his parents. Both had been historians. His mother died giving birth to him. She was one of three women in the entire world to die that year during delivery. His father died a year later while touring the ruins of Kashnir when he was attacked and bitten by a storm of dragon bees. The infant, left temporarily in the care of Gabriel and his wife, Elaina, stayed with them.

Elaina was long gone by the time I met Gabe. She'd run off with someone. Don't know who. I never heard the details. I can't imagine how she could have done any better than Gabe.

So Alex grew up, as he liked to say, in dig sites. He inherited the family's passion for history. But instead of following in Gabe's footsteps, he'd decided there were plenty of artifacts out there for everybody. There was a serious market for antiquities, especially those that could be linked to an historical personage or event. And Alex saw no reason he shouldn't cash in on it.

Shortly after I began working for Gabe, I heard that he had a nephew. When I asked, innocently, whether Alex had any interest in archeology, Gabe's face had darkened, and he'd shaken his head. "No," he'd said. "None whatever."

I didn't ask again. His colleagues filled me in on the details. "Alex robs tombs," one of them told me. "You might say he's not exactly the son Gabe had hoped for."

Eventually, they reconciled, although they never became close. I didn't meet Alex during those years. You'll understand I had a fairly low opinion of him and felt sorry for his uncle.

Gabe got interested when an exploration ship, the *Tenandrome*, returned to Rimway, and Survey became secretive about something they'd seen. Gabe went home, got involved in an investigation, and let me know he'd figured it out. He was on the return flight, on the *Capella*, when it vanished. He'd asked me to meet him at Saraglia Station. And I'll never forget sitting in Karlovski's All-Night listening to the reports. The interstellar was late. Two hours later, it *still* hadn't arrived. Then there was an assurance that delays happen, and there was no reason to worry. Search units were being sent out. I was wandering through the concourse, too restless to sit, when they announced that the *Capella* was officially declared missing.

They never found it, of course. It was a bad time. As painful as anything in my life. I hadn't realized how much I liked Gabe, loved him, really. An easygoing guy with a great sense of humor. I used to wonder about his ex-wife, what kind of nitwit she must have been to leave him. He possessed an innocent charm, and I loved spending time with him. Did it whenever I could. It was why I hung around the sites, eating food cooked over campfires and sleeping under the stars. And now and then wielding a shovel. Looking back now, I've come to realize that they were among the best days of my life.

Then, without warning, he was gone.

After I got myself together, after I'd given up on any possibility that the *Capella* would magically show up somewhere, I went back to Rimway, to the country house. Gabe owed me two months' pay and expenses. I had decided to let it go, not to put in my final statement, but when I heard that the nephew had taken over the estate, I had no problem.

That, of course, constituted my introduction to Alex. Pay me. And I'll confess that I didn't like him at first. Maybe it was because of what I knew about him. Maybe, somehow, I resented his being there in place of Gabe. I don't know. We got talking about the *Tenandrome*, and why Survey had been so secretive about its mission, and what its connection was with Gabe.

As the old saying goes, one thing led to another. Before we were finished, he'd saved my life. That can do a lot to cement a relationship with somebody.

Karen called back that afternoon. *"No notebook,"* she said. *"Sorry."*

"You couldn't have misplaced it?"

*"No. If I'd seen it, I'd have remembered. It just didn't come with the other stuff."*

Alex spent his time reading everything he could find about Robin. He discovered that the physicist had been a superb athlete in school, that he'd been an only child, that his parents had been wealthy, and that he'd never wanted for anything.

We continued to get a lot of calls from the media, but Alex knew there was such a thing as overexposure, so he limited access. For him, it was all a game. It had little or nothing to do with making money, per se, other than that he enjoyed seeing his clients prosper. But he spoke of his "enhancement technique" as if he were creating a romance, giving value to the culture.

I objected occasionally, especially when we went overboard for Karen Howard. The truth is that I suspected there was more to this than the Robin collectibles. That he'd become intrigued with the mystery surrounding the disappearance. He continued to insist that arriving at a solution would be counterproductive. And I knew he was right. But I didn't think, in the end, it would matter.

During this uncomfortable period, I stopped by the country house during off-hours a couple of times to reassure myself he was okay. One evening, I found him in the conference room watching a clip of Chris Robin giving out awards at a high school on Virginia Island. I didn't think he was even aware I was standing there. But he froze the scene, depicting Robin sharing cookies with a couple of the kids. "What do you think?" he asked, without looking up.

"About what?"

"Uriel," he said. "What do you suppose he meant when he said he'd be able to talk about a breakthrough after Uriel?"

# SIX

The secret of a truly successful career in almost any field is the ability to control what people think. In other words, pure public relations. It is the difference between talent and greatness.

—Henry Taylor, *The Statesman*, 6712 c.e.

While we watched interest build in the Robin artifacts, we got involved in the search for Korman Eddy's *Clockwork*, which had vanished from a train in the middle of the last century. The sculptor, then at the beginning of his illustrious career, had achieved celebrity status but hadn't yet reached the superstardom that awaited him. He famously took the sculpture aboard an Andiquar local and somehow—nobody had ever understood how it could have happened—left it on the seat when he got off at Mill Harbor. "A beautiful young lady had come aboard," he'd explained, "and I'm easily distracted."

*Clockwork* was an abstract depiction, according to the experts, of the inevitable passage of time, and its effect on the psyche. It was a collection of springs, clock hands, pinions, Roman numerals, wheels, electric dials, and pendulums. It wasn't a large piece, but Eddy had needed two seats to transport it. It had been inside a transparent wrapping. He sat on the opposite side of the aisle.

Eddy apparently realized his oversight after leaving the train. He was in a cab on his way to the Vancouver Center, where it was to be unveiled. Horrified, he immediately called the train. A quick search ensued, but the sculpture could not be found. Passengers reported seeing a woman struggling with it, carrying it toward the back of the car on which Eddy had been riding. That had been several minutes after the train had left the station. Police were waiting at Cuirescu, the next stop. But they could find no sign of the missing artwork or the woman the other passengers had seen. An inspection of the forty-three-mile-long track between the two stations turned up the wrapping but nothing else.

Eddy was heartbroken. Prior to arriving at Mill Harbor, he'd shown it to no one. "It was to be a special moment for the Vancouver Center, and for me," he said in the aftermath of the event.

It had happened in 1341, ninety-three years earlier. We got interested when Eddy's *Varesque* became available, and some of our clients began commenting what a shame it was that nobody had ever found the *Clockwork* sculpture, and how much they'd give to get their hands on it.

So we went through the documents, read the media accounts, talked to two of the witnesses and several of the avatars. We visited the two train stations, which had changed considerably over the years, although their layouts were basically the same. We satisfied ourselves that, with the distribution of people reportedly on the platform at Cuirescu, no one could have gotten off the train carrying the sculpture without being seen.

I thought the conductor was involved. "He has to be," I said. "The woman, whoever she was, needed help. A place to hide, both the sculpture and herself."

"It's not difficult to search a train," Alex said. "Not when you're looking for something that big. No, I don't think that's what happened."

"So what *did* happen, Sherlock?"

He grinned. I've often wondered where that term came from. But I've never been able to find an origin. "Well," he said, "I wonder why the thief discarded the wrapper?"

I shrugged. "Don't know."

"I can see only one way it might have been done. I can't prove it, of course, but when you eliminate the impossible—"

"I'm listening."

He enjoys moments like this. "It's unlikely that the woman could have hidden successfully from the police. They had witnesses who could identify her. What other explanation might there be for the fact that she, too, had gone missing?"

"She got out the back, somehow."

"Well, I suppose the police might have been that sloppy. But—"

"Yes?"

"Let me ask *you* a question: If you were carrying a valuable sculpture around, what kind of wrapping would you use?"

"Something that would protect it, I suppose."

"But would you advertise its presence?"

"No."

"That raises a question: For what purpose would you use a transparent wrapper?"

I hesitated. "Only to show it off, I suppose."

"Very good, Chase. It strikes me that the most feasible explanation is that this woman was never there in the first place. It was someone else, probably a male, wearing a disguise."

At times like that, my head starts to spin. "Isn't it unlikely that she—or *he*—would have been on board, wearing a disguise, just in case a sculptor left something valuable in a seat?"

"Yes. I'd say so. Which suggests it would have been a setup."

"A setup in what way?"

"Eddy was still at the beginning of his career."

"And—?"

"A little publicity wouldn't hurt."

I got a good laugh out of that. "I guess you'd know best. But where'd she hide the sculpture?"

"Chase, I don't think the *Clockwork* ever existed."

"How do you mean?"

"It was a fable. From the beginning."

"But he brought it on the train. There were witnesses."

"What they probably saw was something thrown together, probably using corbicide. Or anything else that's dissoluble in water and can be broken apart fairly easily."

At the time, we were sitting on one of the benches at Cuirescu. While I began to see what he was saying, a train glided into the station, kicking up a gust of wind. It settled down onto the rail, and passengers started climbing out. I had to raise my voice, almost shout, to make myself heard. "You're saying she flushed it down the toilet?"

"Then he took off the wig. And probably had dinner with Eddy that evening."

"What was the payoff?"

"Oh, Chase. Instead of having a minor piece of sculpture on display at the Vancouver Center, he became the media highlight of the week. It's the kind of story everyone loves. A potentially valuable piece of art stolen. And before you object, the perception would be that it *must* be valuable, or it wouldn't have been taken. And certainly not in such an elegant manner. Add an apparently insoluble mystery. And there *are* some people who will tell you that Eddy never really lived up to his reputation. But he became famous because of the *Clockwork* incident. And he had just enough talent to make it pay off."

As we started home on the train to Andiquar, his head sank onto the back of the seat, and his eyes closed. "You okay?" I asked.

"Tired." He'd been tired a lot lately.

"You need a vacation."

He smiled, but the eyes stayed shut. "Who'd run the business?"

"I'm serious."

"I'm fine, Chase."

The sunlight blinked off as we entered a tunnel. Within seconds, we were out the other end. "When are you going to set a date for the auction?"

"I've been thinking about it. The artifacts keep going up. But you're right. We ought to get it moving while we're still headed in the right direction."

He fell quiet again.

"Is it Robin?" I asked.

"No. Why would you say that?"

I shrugged. "Just a thought."

"He been on *your* mind?"

"A little." He lapsed into silence again. I watched the forest racing past. "You know what I keep thinking—?" I said.

"That he might still be alive somewhere? Off in the islands enjoying himself?"

"It's a possibility."

Alex shook his head. "Robin was too committed to his work to disappear. No, whatever happened, he didn't instigate it."

"You have any idea at all?"

"Not a thing. I've talked with Shara. Told her about Robin's being at Sanusar and again at Skydeck when the sightings occurred."

"What does she think?"

"She doesn't know *what* to think. But she told me what I guess she told you. Find the notebook."

We rocked a bit as we entered a long curve. "I miss Gabe," I said. "I don't know why, but I've been thinking about him a lot lately."

He nodded. "Mysterious ships in the night."

"I guess." I sat listening to the air circulating through the cabin. We came out of the woods, intercepted the Melony, and charged along its bank. Alex rearranged himself, trying to get comfortable. The compartment was cramped.

"I'm getting the feeling," I said, "we're going to be heading for Virginia Island."

He didn't respond right away. "I hate even to start," he said finally. "Robin wasn't a young guy when it happened. The chances that he's still alive somewhere—"

"When do we leave?"

"It's going to be a few weeks. I have all kinds of commitments here."

"Well," I said. "Why don't I go there and get the process started?"

"What would you do?"

"You don't trust me, do you?"

"Sure I do."

But he was still waiting for an answer. "I'd do tourist stuff. Wander around a bit. Get to know people. See what I can find out. Somebody there must know something."

# SEVEN

A dream that survives becomes myth. And, ultimately, dogma.

—Tulisofala, Extracts, CLII, iii (translated by Leisha Tanner)

Virginia Island is located about ten minutes off the coast of Kinesia, four time zones away, on the other side of the equator. It's fourteen kilometers long, and, at its widest, you could walk across in twenty minutes. It was a hard, bitterly cold night when I left Andiquar, but it was summer on Virginia Island.

I'd ridden the last leg of the journey on a small shuttle from the mainland, which delivered me to the Windraven, a lodge with more modest accommodations than its name might suggest. It was midafternoon, and the walkways were crowded with tourists. I checked into my room, looked out at a series of low hills that framed my view of the ocean, and called Alex. "I'm here," I said. "The place is gorgeous."

*"Good."* He was at his breakfast table. *"The flight went okay?"*

"Everything ran on time."

*"All right. Enjoy yourself."*

"I expect to."

*"And, Chase, there's no pressure, okay? It's a long time ago, so you're not likely to come up with anything. Just try to get a sense of how Robin lived, what he was like, how much his fellow citizens knew about him. See if you can find out what he was doing on that last flight. And how long he was gone."*

"Okay."

*"Don't feel you have to get started right away. There's no big rush."*

"I'm glad to hear it. I think the first thing I'm going to do is head for the beach."

*"Very good. Umm—"*

"Yes, Alex?"

*"Have you been out to Robin's place yet?"*

"Alex, I just got here."

*"Okay. Sure. Look, one thing—"*

"Yes?"

*"Jack Ramsay called last night. He'll get to you in a day or two for an interview. Be careful what you say to him. We don't want him to hear anything that gets in the way of the mythology. Right? If somebody knows what really happened, tells you he ran off with a local dancer, sit on it. We want Ramsay to be able to write that the ultimate skeptic—that's you, by the way—went out there against her will, and now she's beginning to wonder if there isn't something to all the stories."*

"Alex, you know as well as I do that Ramsay isn't going to buy any of that."

*"He doesn't have to buy it. All he wants from you is a story he can use. Okay?"*

"All right."

*"Whatever else you find, save for me."*

It wasn't as if we hadn't done things like this before. Sure, it's not quite ethical to start rumors to increase the value of a client's holdings, but Alex's argument is that nobody gets hurt, that all we're doing is earning our money. Nothing wrong with that. And I wasn't being asked to lie outright. Exactly. Just provide some context. That was the term he normally used. *Context.*

So okay. I decided to skip the beach for the moment. I put on a pair of shorts and a white pullover with an anchor emblazoned on the vest pocket, and wandered out among the tourists.

Virginia Island was home to about four hundred houses. Hotels and lodges, shops, and souvenir stores lined the shore walk. There was a convention center, a stable, a pier that provided all kinds of entertainment, a petting zoo for kids, and an aquarium. And, of course, the beaches.

I looked for somebody who didn't appear to be a tourist and settled on an elderly couple sitting at a table under a tree. I bought a sandwich and some chocolate cookies and sat down on a nearby bench. It was easy enough to catch the woman's eye and begin a conversation. Within a few minutes, I had joined them and was commenting on how beautiful the area was, while we all munched on the cookies. They'd been on Virginia Island for the better part of seventy years and couldn't imagine living anywhere else. But when I commented that this had been the home of Christopher Robin, they looked at each other and shrugged. "If you say so," the woman said.

A little farther on, a guy in shorts was working on his boat. "The island can be a wild place this time of year," he told me. "Parties every night. Kids running loose. Don't know where their parents are. I wouldn't let mine just wander around." His name was Wes Corvin. He was well past the century mark, all smiles, with an appearance of absolute contentment. It was obvious his plans in life didn't extend far beyond floating around on the ocean.

When my opportunity came, I commented that it was fascinating to be here, that I'd done a paper in school on Christopher Robin, and there I was on Virginia Island.

"I remember seeing him when I first moved here," Corvin said. "He used to walk around up by the cove. He'd be up there in the evenings, sometimes with his wife, sometimes alone. I can remember that he'd just be standing there, leaning over the rail, staring out to sea. I never really talked to him. Maybe said hello or something. He didn't seem to pay much attention to what was going on around him. Every time I saw him, he was looking at the ocean, or the sky, or something far away. You know what I mean?"

"But you knew who he was?"

"Hell, I still don't know who he was. I knew he was supposed to be a famous scientist. But that's all."

In Ruby's Walk-In, I drank lemon soda with two women, one tall and distant, one heavyset and almost painfully good-natured. They shook their heads sadly while telling me that Robin had been cheating on Elizabeth, that she'd found out, and that when he'd arrived home that night, she'd been waiting for him. "Everybody here knows what really happened," the tall one said. "They just don't like to talk about it."

"You're saying she murdered him?"

"I'm not sure how she managed it. Since there was no witness, I can't really say."

"But you think she killed him and dropped him into the ocean."

"Yes. She might have had a gun. She might have simply told him there was something strange happening in the sky and got him to walk out to the overhang. Maybe she had an accomplice, somebody to help her drag the body out. She had a lot of money, so she could have paid somebody."

"They never found the body," said her affable friend. She seemed proud of the fact.

That evening, I took a taxi out to the house they'd owned, which rested on a summit overlooking the sea. It was completely alone at the southern tip of the island. No other property, no other house, was even visible.

A FOR SALE image blinked on as I approached, and a code that would allow a prospective buyer to contact the agent.

It looked more imposing than it had in the photos. It was not as large as most of the island homes, but it had a quiet ambience: single-story, small windows with dark green shutters, a sloping roof and a chimney. Until then, it was the only chimney I'd seen on the island. The property was shaded by tolivar trees, and protected on three sides by a hedge that needed cutting.

I strolled around the perimeter of the property, went out onto the top of the bluff, and spent several minutes looking down at the sea. It was a three-story drop into the water, where an incoming tide washed over a few rocks.

I'd done my research. No weapon had been found. And there'd been no mention of the adultery theory.

No evidence connecting Elizabeth, or anyone else, to his disappearance had ever been brought forward. She had not been charged though the media had reported she drew the attention of investigators. But the only reason seemed to be that she was his spouse, and the spouse, in a case like this, was automatically the prime suspect.

The owner of the Windraven, Ilena Kataiya, told me that Elizabeth had been a longtime friend. Ilena was short, solid, still energetic despite being advanced in years. She was always rearranging things, wiping down the counter, entering data into the system, adjusting the curtains. She was routinely amiable, but her voice grew intense when I asked about the disappearance. "It broke her heart," she said, "that anyone would think she could have done it. That she could have killed her husband."

"Were they close?" I asked.

"They were like most married couples, I guess." She winked. "They got along okay. I mean, he couldn't have been the easiest guy to be married to. He was all physics all the time. I don't recall that he ever talked about anything other than the stuff he was involved in. I remember when Kevin won a prize at the school. For swimming. Kevin was a great swimmer. Still is."

"Kevin's your son?"

"Yes." She nodded. "He took first place in the Oceanside Tournament. I wanted to show them the trophy, but Chris couldn't have been less interested. He was a guy who, if he was with you, was either talking about black holes or looking at the time. But you know how it is—a lot of guys are like that."

I hadn't known many who spent their time talking about black holes, but I let it go. "Ilena, could Elizabeth have been behind it?"

"No," she said. "Not in a million years." She thought about it. Shook her head. "No way."

"She says she slept through the night and never heard Cermak's skimmer arrive. How could that have happened?"

"I think the media got that part of the story wrong. She told me she heard them touch down. She was in bed. It woke her, and she just turned over and went back to sleep. Look, Chase, it wouldn't have been the first time it had happened. That she'd slept through it when Chris came home. In fact, she'd done it just a couple of weeks earlier."

"He'd been out two weeks prior to the final flight?"

"Yes. Two weeks, three weeks, something like that. I remember her telling me about it when she complained that he was going out *again*. She wasn't all that happy about the flights." She bit her lip. "I'm probably talking too much."

"She didn't like his being gone so much?"

"It wasn't only that. She was afraid something would happen to him."

"Why would she think that?"

"Well, they lost Bill Winter."

"Bill Winter? Who was he?"

"An academic type. I think he was a historian. He went out with them one time, and they apparently set down somewhere, and he was attacked by a predator."

I hadn't heard about that, but she had no details to add. "Do you know how long he was gone?" I asked. "On that last flight?"

"Three or four days, I think."

"That's all?"

"Well, something like that."

We were in the lobby of the Windraven, and a family with three little kids were coming in. "Hang on a second." She got up and assumed her place behind the counter. When they'd been taken care of, she came back. "Everybody liked Elizabeth," she said. "We all wondered what she'd seen in Chris, how she could have gotten connected with him in the first place. When it happened, when Chris disappeared, we were all worried she'd leave, too. But she didn't. She stayed on. Lived in that house for, I don't know, another forty years or so. She never gave up hoping he'd come back. I thought she was better off with him gone. But what the hell did I know?"

Cermak would have dropped Robin off at the pad, which was on the west side of the house. The house itself faced away from the sea. The picture of Robin walking through the terminal on his way to that last flight had shown him with a light bag and a notebook. Where had they gone? If Robin had strolled directly out onto the bluff and fallen off, he'd have left them behind. After he got out of the skimmer, he'd have set them down before walking out onto the summit.

It was possible Elizabeth had met him at the front door and just said, Honey, I'm glad you're home. Let's go look at the ocean. It's beautiful tonight.

Bring your luggage, love.

I couldn't get the earthquake out of my head. For some reason, they'd set down here and he'd changed his mind and they'd both flown on to Kolandra. And both had died in the quake. It wasn't, of course, a theory Alex would want me to pass on to Ramsay. Better to have something that would point to a more outré conclusion. What I really needed was some neighbors to tell me that they used to go to parties at Robin's house, and how he had a talent for walking into a closet and disappearing. That would be good. I was pretty sure that, given the opportunity to talk to a few people, I could coax a whopper or two that I could use, that Ramsay could duly put up on *The Morning Report*.

The private homes were spread loosely around the island. I rented a korvine at the stable, climbed into the saddle, and let it carry me in a slow trot along the back roads. People looked up as I passed, some waved, and a few said hello. I stopped and talked whenever it seemed feasible, telling everyone the same story, that I was doing an essay on Chris Robin, and that I was trying to get a sense of what life had been like forty years ago on Virginia Island.

Of those who were old enough to have known Robin and Elizabeth, nobody had anything to add to the basic story. I heard no more about infidelity, even when I asked whether there might have been any problems with the marriage. Everybody remembered Elizabeth as being friendly and nice. Her husband was okay, nobody had any real complaints, but he was always tied up in his work. I got the usual range of opinions as to what had happened to him.

I was looking for a more efficient way to penetrate the social mix on the island when I heard that the local church, Holy Sacrament, would be holding its monthly St. Kaelen's Night in two days. "What," I asked Ilena, "is St. Kaelen's Night?"

"St. Kaelen," she said, "is the patron saint of friendship and good times." He was the saint whose motif was: Be generous and loving and you will never be alone.

I went early. The event was being held in a meeting hall, adjacent to the church. An engraved dove, its wings spread wide, adorned a sign carrying the maxim HEAVEN IS A STATE OF MIND. I wondered if that was really what they meant to say.

Approximately two dozen people were already in the hall when I arrived. Others were still filing in. A priest stood at the doorway, greeting people as they passed. He saw me and smiled. "Hello," he said. "Welcome to Holy Sacrament. I'm Father Everett." He'd put on a lot of mileage, and was old enough to have known Robin. He had dark hair, dark skin, friendly eyes.

"I'm Chase Kolpath," I said. "Glad to meet you, Father."

"I don't suppose you're a permanent resident of the island, Chase?"

"No, I'm just a visitor."

He looked pleased. "Well, we're glad you decided to join us. Are you visiting friends?"

"Just sightseeing. It's a beautiful island."

"Yes," he said, "it is."

More people were coming in, so I started to move on. "While you're here with us this evening, Chase," he said, "the tradition is that you make at least one friend."

The event was utterly informal. People brought covered dishes and soft drinks, set them down, pulled up chairs, and sat down with one another. Despite the efforts of St. Kaelen, the usual social relations held. Some guys were anxious to meet me; others shied away. I joined one group arguing politics while tensions rose, and another that was enraged by the policies of a local storekeeper.

When I could, I asked about Elizabeth and Chris Robin. And I got contradictory information: Chris was hostile, he was friendly; he was a genius, God knew how he'd ever become a professor; he had a great sense of humor, he was a crank. Nobody could account for his disappearance though nobody thought he'd gone voluntarily. "He loved Elizabeth," they said. I heard that over and over.

Elizabeth was a good wife to him, they told me, better than he deserved. She could be a shrew when she wanted, though. Unlike him, she had a good many friends.

"I think whatever happened to him," one woman told me, "it had to have been an accident." Her name was Mara. She was accompanied by her husband and a grandchild.

"What kind of accident do you think would account for it?"

She glanced at her husband, who was small, smaller than she was, compact, and heavy. "He was working on a pocket-size antigrav device," she said, without batting an eye. "Isn't that right, Walt?"

Walt nodded. "Something like that."

"It wouldn't surprise me," she continued, "if he had one in his pocket and activated it accidentally."

"How would he have done that?"

"He was hauling luggage. It was late. It would have been easy enough to push a button by mistake."

I got an image of Robin drifting into the sky, suddenly too high to turn the thing off, maybe hanging on to his piece of luggage because it was the only thing he had to hang on to. "Thanks," I said.

Of course, with an antigrav unit, he wouldn't go into orbit; he'd just keep going. Ridiculous idea. A pocket-size antigrav unit, I'm pretty sure, isn't possible. But it would be a story that Ramsay could use.

Toward the end of the evening, I looked around for Father Everett. He was speaking with an elderly couple near one of the tables. I watched for my chance and, when they started away, I stepped in beside him and asked if he was enjoying the evening.

"I always do, Chase," he said. "It's my favorite time of the month."

"I was wondering if you have a couple of minutes to talk to me, Father. I could use some help."

"Of course, Chase. If I can. What sort of help?"

"Well, I'm actually here doing some research."

"You're studying the sociology of parties."

"That, too. Seriously, Father, did you by any chance know Christopher Robin?"

"Chris? Yes, I knew him. To say hello. He and Elizabeth weren't members of the parish, but *she* used to come to some of the events. We were sorry to lose her."

"I'm sure."

"Her husband—? That was, what, twenty years ago?"

"Forty," I said.

His face clouded. "Time moves so quickly. But yes, I knew him to see him. Though I don't think we ever really talked." He picked up a potato chip and bit into it. "They're good," he said. "What kind of information are you looking for?"

"I'd like to figure out what happened to him."

The smile broadened. "Of course you would. Well, good luck on that."

"Can you tell me anything at all that might be helpful?"

"I just never knew him, Chase. He had a reputation for being self-centered; I can tell you that. I thought he looked down on the rest of us. I suspect he thought everybody else on the planet was his intellectual inferior."

"You didn't like him much."

"I had no dealings with him, to speak of. Hello, good-bye, and not much more than that. But there was something in his manner. A sense of his own preeminence. It was hard to miss."

"Anything else?"

"Well, I don't know. He occasionally shocked some of our people."

"In what way?"

"Some of his opinions—" He glanced around the hall, which was now almost empty, and lowered his voice. "He was an atheist, I believe."

"I see."

"But that sometimes happens to people. They don't believe that faith has a place. They don't see the evidence for God, so they dismiss Him." He excused himself for a moment to speak with a couple of his parishioners. Then he came back. "Despite his atheism, he seemed to think there might be a spiritual dimension. That, without God, we—our souls—drift through eternity. That it was possible there really would be no rest. He used to laugh at the notion of Hell, but I can't imagine a worse one. I almost think I'd prefer the fire."

"Odd," I said.

"He had exquisite musical taste; I'll give him that. Sometimes, in the evenings, I enjoyed walking down past his place, out onto the overhang. I could almost always hear the music coming from his house. Tchaikovsky, Schubert, Rimsky-Korsakov, Goldstein, Harkin. He loved the Euro composers."

"Anything else, Father? Did you ever hear anything about what might have happened to him?"

"I know the police suspected Elizabeth. I guess they had to. They didn't have anyone else."

"You don't think she could have had anything to do with it?"

"No. Not a chance."

"Thanks, Father."

"One other thing. I understand he was careless with money.

I don't know whether that might have had anything to do with his disappearance or not—"

"How do you mean?"

"Well, for one thing, he kept buying yachts. And then losing them."

"Did they sink somewhere?"

"Not *that* kind of yacht, Chase. The interstellar kind."

"Oh." I thought about it. "How many yachts did he lose?"

"Four or five."

"You're not serious?"

"Oh, yes. I'm quite serious. They were all pretty creaky, apparently. At least that's what I read. But he'd buy one, take it out somewhere, and the next thing we knew he was buying another."

"Did you hear what was happening to them?"

"Just that they'd broken down or something and got left somewhere. I remember Elizabeth telling me that he used them for experiments. But I don't know what sort of experiment."

"Thanks, Father," I said.

"He gave them dramatic names. One, I think, was called the *Starhawk*."

"The *Starhawk*."

"And the one I really liked—" He laughed. "That was the *Firebird*."

"That *is* poetic," I said.

"That, too, I suppose. It's Stravinsky."

Shortly after I got back to the Windraven, Ramsay called. "I haven't really had much time yet, Jack," I told him. "Give me another couple of days." I couldn't tell him that some of the neighbors thought Robin had been cheating on Elizabeth so maybe she'd killed him. Or that he was an atheist. And I didn't really have much else.

*"Come on, Chase. How long does it take to manufacture something?"*

I liked Ramsay. He was just a few years out of journalism school, but I could already see he had a future in the field. He was personable and sufficiently corrupt to carve out a career for himself. Alex refers to it as flexibility, but I plan to write a book one day on how it happens that people of unflinching integrity rarely, if ever, rise to the top of any profession. I asked Alex for his opinion once, and he agreed that it was true more often than not, and said it was because people who were inflexible were dumb. I don't buy it, of course, and neither does he, really. Though sometimes I'm not so sure.

"Jack, give me a chance to look around a bit more, okay?"

*"What about the aliens, Chase? People from another reality? Don't you have anything on that?"*

"Not anything you could use."

*"I don't guess you have anything about the black holes? Or the colliding universes?"*

"No."

*"Colliding universes is good. How about the undead?"*

"Say that again?"

He smiled. He was tall, dark-haired, easygoing. He always looked as if he thought I was trying to get away with something. *"I talked to one of the people at that party you guys went to a few nights ago. He says that Robin might have been one of the undead."* He broke into his trademark cackle. *"You have anybody out there who thinks he might have been a vampire?"*

"Jack—"

*"Okay. Seriously, Chase, I read somewhere that Robin predicted he'd vanish but that he'd be back one day."*

"I hadn't heard that, either."

*"He must really have been something else. I can't imagine what you could find that would beat this stuff."*

Meantime, I went looking for old news reports.

Two days after the quake, Elizabeth had reported to police that her husband might be in trouble. Cermak had transported him off-world, she explained. She didn't know where. "He does this all the time." She'd just learned that Cermak was dead, and she was reported as frantic that Robin might be stranded somewhere.

Several days later, there were reports that a couple of people strolling along the water's edge had seen a skimmer that was similar to Cermak's touch down at Robin's house about an hour before midnight.

Elizabeth was shocked to hear it. "I was asleep," she said. "I never heard him." And as far as anyone could determine, he'd never gotten inside.

\*   \*   \*

I was able to get some information on the lost yachts. Robin had taken four of them out somewhere between 1385 and 1393. None of them, as far as anyone could tell, ever came back. No explanation was offered other than that the vehicles were being used in experiments to improve cycling. Whatever that was.

The other two yachts were *Striker* and *Elizabeth*.

The *Firebird* had been the last to go missing, in 1393, a few weeks before Robin himself had vanished.

Robin was born on Toxicon, the only child in a wealthy family. He got his master's degree at Kawasai University, and, according to people who knew him at the time, was pretty handy with the ladies. He married a singer, Mary Dexter, and accepted a teaching appointment at Cajun Barker College.

The marriage and the appointment both collapsed within the first few months. He started criticizing his colleagues, sometimes doing it in front of students, and periodically for the media. Some of the professors, he said, were not aware of what really went on in the subquantum world. They didn't understand about complexity. It was why they couldn't present a clear vision to the students.

Robin himself apparently had problems connecting with the students. Only a handful signed on for the second semester. The college responded by canceling all but one of his classes.

Meantime, he was caught in a local hotel with a stripper. There was a public fight with Mary, in which she tried to push him out of an airborne taxi, and the thing crashed onto the roof of the Kassner Building, which housed the medical department. When the physics department chairman, a Professor Makaius, called him in, he responded by telling a reporter from the college newspaper that at least he'd never propositioned a student. That had required Makaius to issue a denial that *he* had ever done any such thing. It looked for a time that there'd be lawsuits, but everything was dropped when Robin agreed to leave the school and to comment no further.

A year later, he showed up on Rimway, got his doctorate at Margala, convinced everyone he could be trusted, and joined the physics department at Kinesia. He remained there six years, met Elizabeth, who was a lawyer, and began looking

for a way to prove the existence of other ⌐_____. _____ ___
been trying to do that, of course, for thousands of y⌐
consensus has long been that it can't be done. Most physicists
believe there *are* other universes, but it does not appear that
there's any way to demonstrate the proposition. Robin even
took to talking about creating a bridge.

He lost interest in teaching, claimed that his students were
deficient, and decided he had better things to do. In 1359, he
bought the house on Virginia Island and retired there suppos-
edly to do research. Elizabeth had specialized in criminal
law, and criminal activity on the island was essentially nonexistent. Apparently, she was given a choice between her career
and her marriage. She chose the marriage.

A year or so later, Elizabeth is quoted in a review article to
the effect that she had never been happier.

From that point, there's not much on the record about their
private lives. Both withdrew into the house and, across a
thirty-four-year span, became relatively innocuous neighbors.

In 1376, Robin wrote *Multiverse*, which had been controversial from the start. It was, according to his Kinesia University colleague William Winter, not a book for the faint of
heart.

Winter? He was the one Ilena had mentioned. Seven years
after publication of *Multiverse*, in 1383, he'd joined Robin on
an expedition to Indikar. I couldn't find a clear explanation
regarding the purpose of the flight. It seemed to have something to do with orbital fluctuations.

But Winter was killed, apparently attacked by a predator
when they made the mistake of landing on a green world to do
some sightseeing. The body was never found.

I had asked Father Everett about the incident. "We never
really heard any details," he said. "I didn't know Winter. But
I noticed a change in Robin after that. I thought it hit him
pretty hard. Elizabeth told me he blamed himself. In any case,
he was never the same after that."

# EIGHT

I am not truly lost so long as someone, somewhere, can hear
my voice.

—Vicki Greene, *Love You to Death*, 1423

I guess people will always see things in the night sky. There've
been countless reports over the millennia of various kinds of
sightings, of mysterious lights and unidentified objects and
phantom vehicles. The vast majority do not stand up to close
inspection. Some are simply ships that have arrived at the
wrong place, for one reason or another, and are reluctant to go
on the record, so they clear out without identifying themselves.
Others are space rocks that catch momentary sunlight. Still
others are incompetent smugglers. In one famous instance, the
object was a firefly that had gotten onto a station and been
caught in a sliding port.

But sometimes no ready explanation presents itself. The
two events witnessed by Chris Robin, one at Sanusar, the
other at Rimway, seem to fall into that category. Neither had
ever been explained.

The vehicle at Sanusar in 1380 had approached within
about fifty kilometers of the station. The scanners got visuals,
but the visitor was never identified. Nothing that matched the
design was known to exist among the commercial and naval
fleets of the Confederacy or of the Ashiyyur.

By the mideleventh millennium, no space station had been in
place longer than the one at Sanusar. At the time of the sight-

ing, it had been in orbit more than three thousand years. Brandine Kovalar himself is said to have christened it. It had welcomed almost every major figure in the Confederacy at one time or another. It was where Myra Dawkin had stayed on her historic visit. It had provided the platform on which George Delios delivered his celebrated "Here I stand" address. Kyla Bonner had written some of her Twilight Sonnets in Korby's, a café in the main concourse. And Kip Berry had died somewhere in the Majestic Hotel—nobody was sure where—after taking the station back from the Debunkers. And, of course, at the beginning of the twelfth millennium, the station would fall briefly into the hands of the Mutes.

But over that vast span of time, there was probably no event more intriguing than the one that occurred at the end of the evening watch on Constitution Day, fifty-four years ago.

I downloaded the record and watched:

Tereza Urbanova was on duty, surveying an empty sky, when Jay Benson, the operational control AI—the only AI I'd ever heard of with a last name—informed her that an unscheduled vehicle had just been detected on the scopes.

*"Where, Jay?"* she asked.

*"Range eight thousand kilometers. Approaching."*

*"What? And we're just now seeing them? How'd they get this close?"* Her display showed only a blip.

*"I don't know, Tereza. I've started a systems check. No indication of a malfunction."*

*"They're coming out of a jump."* She made no effort to hide her irritation. *"They just jumped the hell in. Right on top of us."*

*"I'll start the report."*

*"I've been out here more than thirty years, Jay. Never seen it before. Never saw anything like it."* She leaned over the board and opened a channel. *"This is Operations at Sanusar. Ship that has just entered system, please identify yourself."*

No response.

She centered the ship on her display. *"Mack, this is Ops. Hold the launch. Unknown vehicle in the area."*

*"Will do, Tereza. Holding."*

It wasn't all that dangerous. But there's a courtesy thing. You just don't do that.

*"Trajectory will take him past the station. But it will be close,"* she said.

*"It might be a vehicle malfunction,"* said Jay.

*"For his sake, I hope so. Can you give me a better look at it?"*

*"One second."*

While Tereza waited, she opened a channel to someone. Probably the chief of the watch. *"Marcos—"*

*"I see it, Tereza. Just follow protocol. I'll be down in a minute."*

*"Still closing,"* said Jay.

She switched over to her Patrol link. *"Caleb."*

*"Hold on, Ops. We see him."*

*"Two minutes to closest approach,"* said Jay. *"Holding steady."*

*"It's just passing through."*

Another voice, a steady-as-she-goes baritone: *"Yes, Tereza. What have you got on him?"*

*"Don't know who he is. You want to take a look?"*

*"What's the situation?"*

*"It just transited in. We've got one flight going out, but we're holding."*

*"Okay,"* he said. *"No incoming?"*

*"Negative."*

*"Good. I see them. We'll get after them."*

*"They're still not responding,"* said Jay. *"Moving at nineteen thousand."*

Tereza leaned over her mike: *"Incoming Vehicle,"* she said, *"this is Sanusar Ops. Please identify yourself. You are in violation of procedure."*

The intruder had a vaguely ponderous shape. Exhaust tubes and scanner housings and maneuvering thrusters and everything else were all buried within the hull. Navigation lights blinked on and off. The ship looked vaguely throwback. *"How big is it, Jay?"*

*"Two hundred twenty meters."*

She could make out more lights now. On the bridge. And there was a line of illuminated windows.

*"Who the hell are you?"* She propped her chin on her hand and stared at the display. Both of Sanusar's moons were visi-

ble. *"Jay, there's a hull designator of some sort. Can you make it out?"*

"Let me try to get more definition."

*"Ops."* A new voice. Female. *"Patrol ready to launch. Request permission."*

She checked her screens. *"You are clear."*

*"Got a bad angle on the hull. I can see two characters, but they're not anything I recognize."*

Someone appeared in the doorway behind her. Probably Marcos, her supervisor. *"Maybe it's the Mutes,"* he said.

*"Don't know. I hope not."*

Despite the baritone, Marcos was thin, smaller than she was, and he looked as if he'd be more at home in an academic setting. *"Have you been able to get any response from these people at all?"* he asked.

*"Not a word."*

*"Okay."* He opened the channel to the Patrol. *"Who's got the conn?"*

*"Sandy."*

He nodded. *"Sandy. Try to get a better look at him if you can."*

*"Will do, Marcos."*

Marcos leaned over Tereza and spoke into the mike: *"Unidentified Vehicle, slow down. Who are you? What's the problem?"*

Nothing but static.

He grumbled something. Kept his eyes on the display. *"Where the hell is it going?"*

*"Marcos."* Sandy's voice. *"Something strange is happening."*

*"What?"* Marcos frowned and tried to enhance the image.

*"I can see through it."*

*"Say again, Sandy."*

*"I can see through it. The damned thing's fading. It's disappearing."*

It was true. The hull had become transparent.

*"Not possible,"* said Marcos. The calm authority was gone from his voice. It had been replaced by a note of uncertainty.

The intruder's navigation lights dimmed. We saw more stars. And then it was as if it had never been there.

*"Ops,"* said Sandy. *"Did you see that?"*

I'd watched a good many ships make their jumps, on-screen and riding beside them. When they did, they vanished. Blinked off. One moment they were there, and the next they were gone. This wasn't like that at all.

*"Spooky,"* Tereza said, keeping her voice low. *"What the hell was it?"*

I called Alex. He was in his quarters, sitting in an armchair, framed by a window. It was still darker in Andiquar. A notebook lay open on his lap. *"How's it going, Chase?"* he asked. *"You figure out what happened to him?"*

"No. I don't have a clue. I do have one interesting piece of information, though."

*"What's that?"*

"Robin bought several yachts, according to the local priest. I checked the archives. It's true. He bought four over an eight-year period."

*"Four yachts? What was he doing with them?"*

"Apparently, he was using them in an experiment. I did some research and found something on it. Not much. And it's really not clear. Something about cycling."

*"What's that?"*

"It's connected with providing reserves for an electronic boost when you make a jump."

Alex's brow crinkled. *"Make sense to you?"*

"I know it happens. Beyond that—"

*"I take it the yachts were not new?"*

"No. They were all pretty old. Which, by the way, isn't consistent with cycling experiments, so I don't know what was actually going on."

*"Okay."* He lifted a glass of something from a side table and drained it. *"When did all this happen?"*

"Between 1385 and 1393."

*"Did you get the names of the yachts?"*

"One of them was the *Starhawk*."

*"All right."*

"Another was the *Firehawk*."

*"The* Firehawk? *This guy had a thing with hawks?"*

"Sorry. The Fire*bird*."

*"And the others?"*

"*Striker* and *Elizabeth*."

*"How long did they usually have these yachts before they lost them?"*

"I don't know, Alex. I couldn't find any detailed information. Why are we so interested?"

*"I'm not sure. I don't know. But the yachts went away. Then Robin went away."*

"All right. Ramsay will be calling in a little bit. If you have no problem with it, I'm going to tell him about them. About the yachts."

*"Yes. By all means. It sounds mysterious, and that's exactly what we're looking for. When you tell him, sound surprised, okay?"* Lightning lit up the window, but I couldn't be sure whether it was his or mine. Until the thunder rumbled overhead. *"Chase,"* he said, *"you're a genius."*

"How's everything going at your end?"

*"We're still rolling. The artifacts may have peaked. But maybe not. I've arranged some informal presentations for Plunkett."*

"Plunkett?" I knew the name from somewhere.

*"Charlie Plunkett. The guy from the Robin Society. Brane theory."*

"Oh. As in colliding universes?"

*"Yes."*

Libraries, museums, and other social groups were always looking for guest speakers. "Alex," I said, "the guy might be a bit far out."

*"It doesn't matter. He's good behind a lectern. And nothing he can say will hurt the artifacts. That's all that matters."* He was about to sign off, but apparently remembered something. *"Hang on a second, Chase."* He took another sip of his drink. Then: *"One other thing—"*

"Yes?"

*"These sightings have been going on for a long time. I don't just mean lights in the sky, but close-ups of ships that don't seem to belong. And there've been strange voices. The sightings are infrequent, maybe two or three times a century, but they keep happening."*

"How far back?"

*"Into ancient history."*

"Okay." I waited, thinking more was coming.

But he subsided. Then: *"We're onto something very big, Chase."*

"Ships from another reality?"

*"Maybe."*

"Now, *that* would really be a jolt. Oh, one other thing I forgot to mention. It's probably of no significance. Robin was out somewhere in the *Breakwater* two or three weeks before that last flight."

*"Do you know where?"*

"No. My source didn't know. Also, you wanted to know how long he'd been away on that last flight. It was three days, possibly four."

# NINE

It is an unfortunate aspect of human nature that we appreciate what matters only when we don't have it anymore. What would any of us not give to be able to return, if only for an hour, to those high-school years and see again those who at that time were only the kids we hung out with, who have since gone away, and whom we now recognize as irreplaceable parts of ourselves.

—Kirby Edward, *Traveling in Time*, 1407

Cermak Transport became Reliable, Inc., which had an office in the center of Kolandra, manned by Mitsui Shimazaki. Shimazaki had been Eliot Cermak's partner, and was now semiretired. When I stopped by the office, he was arranging flight information for a young couple planning a honeymoon on another world. They weren't sure where they wanted to go. "Somewhere exciting," the bride-to-be said, while the AI ran visuals of towering mountains and majestic cities. Both were excited and, if I read them correctly, neither had ever been off-world before.

Shimazaki asked whether he could help me, and I told him to take his time with his clients. I was in no hurry. So he did, and eventually they settled on a sightseeing tour of the solar system. "Our twelve-day special," he said. "We'll have two other newly married couples with you, if that's okay."

"By all means," the bride said.

"As long as we have a little privacy," added the groom, with a smirk.

And I thought, *There's a marriage that will never see renewal.*

When they'd finished, Shimazaki came back, apologized, and asked what I needed.

"My name's Chase Kolpath," I said. "I'm doing some research on Eliot Cermak. I wonder if you could answer a few questions?"

"Of course. I was always sorry about Eliot. Gone too soon."

"Did you by any chance get to see him the night of the earthquake?"

"No," he said. "That night was pure hell. I'll tell you the truth, when that first shock hit, I got my wife and kids into our skimmer, and we cleared out. I've always felt guilty that I wasn't here to help, but—"

"I understand, Mr. Shimazaki. You couldn't be everywhere." He nodded. Smiled. And his eyes momentarily lost their focus. "Did you know Chris Robin?"

"Oh, yes. One of Eliot's clients. I knew him. He was a good man. He died that night, too." He shook his head. "You wonder how, in this day and age, something like that can happen."

"You liked him."

"Very much. He was smart. Honest. Not like some of the other VIPs we get involved with. Didn't have the ego that you see in a lot of these people."

"Did you socialize with him at all?"

"A couple of times."

"He and Eliot had been off-world that night."

"Yes, I know."

"Do you have any idea where they'd been? Before coming home?"

"None. If I ever knew, I've forgotten."

"Do you know how long they were gone?"

"Not really." He rubbed his fingertips against his cheeks. "I think they were only out a couple of days. But I'm not sure of that."

"I understand."

"It's been a long time, Chase. Is it okay if I call you that?"

"Of course." I hesitated, then charged ahead. "Did you know his wife?"

"I met her a couple of times. I couldn't say I knew her."

"Mr. Shimazaki, would Elizabeth have had any reason to want to get rid of him? Anything you're aware of?"

His expression told me that if she did, I'd never hear it from him. "No," he said. "If there was any trouble between them, I didn't know about it. Why do you ask?"

"I'm just trying to understand what might have happened that night."

He nodded. "We'd all like to know."

"Did Robin have any enemies?"

"Not that I know of. Again, I just didn't know him that well. I understand there were people who didn't like him all that much. He had a reputation for not being very sociable, though I never saw any sign of it. He was always okay around me. Eliot told me once that he tended not to trust people. He might have had a rough time growing up. Who knows?"

"How do you mean?"

"Well, he'd have been so much smarter than the other kids, and he probably didn't mind showing it. Which would have made him pretty unpopular."

"You can't think of anyone who might have wanted him out of the way?"

"There were rumors that he was working on a new version of the star drive that would provide an extra kick, something capable of intergalactic flight. Something like that might create a problem with the corporate heavyweights. But I never heard anything about that from a credible source."

I was looking out at a gray sky. The sun was trying to break through but I didn't think it was going to happen. "Mr. Shimazaki—"

"Mitsui, Chase."

"Mitsui. The name has a rhythm."

"Thank you, Chase. I suspect its owner does not, however."

"Mitsui, I understand Robin lost some yachts—"

His AI showed an incoming call. From someone who wanted to sell him something. "Have them call back," he said. His face scrunched up while he thought about the yachts. "That's correct. Some junkers. Four of them, I believe."

"How'd it happen? That they lost all of them?"

"They were doing some sort of experiment. I don't know the details. Eliot didn't talk about things like that, and I really

wasn't very interested. I *do* know they didn't expect to bring
them back. They didn't even have AIs, I believe. At least some
of them didn't."

"Thank you, Mitsui," I said. "You've been very helpful."

"I'm glad, Chase. And the next time you would like to go
somewhere exotic, I hope you'll think of us."

"I will—"

"You're a pilot, too, aren't you?"

That surprised me. "Yes," I said. "How did you know?"

"I'm not sure. You sound as if you know what you're talking about."

"Thank you."

"I miss it," he said. "The cockpit. And the women. You and
your sisters are a special brand."


A thunderstorm swept in off the ocean that night, blurring the
village lights and bringing high winds and lots of rain. I spent
the evening going through the list of names associated with
Robin, looking for anybody who might be able to shed light
on what had happened to him. I made some calls but came
away with nothing.

I ran a search on Eliot Cermak. He'd been a self-employed
interstellar pilot. CEO of Cermak Transport. Born in Temple-
ton, on the Dimrok Plains, in 1326. Joined the fleet in 1348.
He picked up a pilot's license in 1351. And rose through the
ranks to command a destroyer. Retired, 1373.

He launched Cermak Transport the same year, purchasing
a yacht he christened *Breakwater*. (That would have been the
vehicle that he and Robin were riding when they engaged in
the Skydeck pursuit.)

He prospered as an independent, hiring out to those with
unusual destinations that the big carriers didn't serve. That
meant he frequently carried research teams, and occasionally
wealthy patrons who simply didn't like to travel with the general public.

He formed several special relationships with CEOs and
scientists, Robin among them. He was the pilot, in 1383, when
William Winter was lost on the mission to Indikar. I looked
up Winter. He'd specialized in ancient history, especially the
Great Expansion, the period during which the first colonial
worlds were beginning to take hold. According to the report,

he and Robin were investigating the ruins of the Indikar outpost, which had been abandoned a thousand years ago.

Cermak had red hair, and the vids revealed an easygoing confidence. The guy looked like a natural leader, and I'll admit that he impressed me. It wasn't hard to see the destroyer captain.

I called Ramsay that night. (It was midafternoon back in Andiquar.) When I told him that Robin had lost four yachts, and that the yachts had been purchased apparently for the specific purpose of being taken out and abandoned, he literally gasped. *"Are you sure?"*

"Absolutely."

*"Why, Chase? Why would he do that?"*

"I don't know."

*"But you have a theory?"*

"Yes. They had to be part of an experiment."

*"What kind of experiment?"*

"Probably something connected with his ideas about alternate universes." I had a hard time delivering that line, but he was delighted with it.

*"Can you spell it out a little bit?"*

"Okay, look: I'm guessing. And I don't want to be quoted."

*"That's fine. Consider yourself a reliable source."*

"Not in *this* life, kid. But I think, and again I've nothing to back this up, I think he wanted to send the yachts into one of these alternate universes he was always talking about. And either he succeeded—"

*"Or they were blowing up."* He shook his head. Wrote something on a pad. *"You really think that's what he was trying to do?"*

Hmm. What *did* I really think? The truth was, I couldn't imagine what else he might have been up to. "I wish," I told him, "that we could go out wherever it was he'd taken them. And see whether they're still there."

*"I assume there's no way to do that?"*

"None that I can imagine, Jack."

I went back and looked at the news accounts from the quake. It was Rimway's worst natural disaster, in terms of fatalities, in modern history, and the second worst anywhere in the Confederacy.

Tens of thousands died, in an era when that wasn't supposed to happen. But somehow the pending quake, which would be an 8.0, escaped the notice of the monitors and came without warning. The inhabitants knew they were in a danger zone, but even though the temblors shook the area regularly, everyone had been assured that the technology would detect a major event well in advance. There'd be plenty of time to clear out.

It hadn't happened that way. The earthquake had occurred with almost no warning. Worse, it had been near the surface, and it had triggered tsunamis that killed several thousand more in the immediate aftermath. The visual record was horrifying: people screaming and running while buildings collapsed and fires erupted. And finally, the waves.

When it was over, when the medical teams had gone home and the funerals had been completed and the technicians had made their explanations, the stories of individual acts of heroism began to emerge. The names of many who'd risked, and sometimes lost, their lives to help others would forever remain unknown. But not all. And among those who stood out was Eliot Cermak. *He brought my kids out. Right through the fire. Threw a blanket over them and got them clear of that place. I thank God he was there.*

A young woman described how he'd gotten her out of a burning building. A man who lived adjacent to him watched as he stood directing terrified victims onto higher ground. Ultimately, like Robin, Cermak had vanished.

I called Alex and described what I'd heard and seen.

*"Where exactly was he,"* he asked me, *"when it happened?"*

"Caton Ferry."

*"Caton Ferry—"*

"It was in the middle of the quake. On the ocean. Just northwest of Kolandra."

*"Okay."* There was a long pause.

"You want me to go there?"

*"I think it would be a good idea. They have some sort of memorial for Cermak. Let's see what else we can learn."*

# TEN

I wish all the best for my brother. I ask only that I am able to stay a step ahead of him.

—Josh Levins, *Darkness Rules*, 1398

Aside from a few preserved sites, the only indication that Caton Ferry had been devastated by an earthquake and a tsunami forty-one years before is Memorial Park, which now occupies a substantial tract of land on the west side of the city, between the town center and the ocean. Everything else has been rebuilt, restored, replaced.

At the time of the disaster, Caton Ferry had a population of about ten thousand. It's considerably more than that now, and like many of the coastal towns, it's become a tourist trap. It's anchored by Big Apple Construction and Kryzinski University, it has the most famous auto racetrack on the continent, and it's also the headquarters of three major churches. So much, the noted atheist Wendel Kavich commented a few days after the quake, for any claims on their influence with God.

I checked into the Seaview Hotel, which borders Memorial Park, and changed into some casuals.

The park consists mostly of closely manicured lawns, with clipped rows of hedges and clutches of shade trees. Two sites enclose wrecked buildings, protected by globes. Data boards at each site show pictures of the structures as they'd looked before the disaster.

They have a theater that, twice daily, runs a documentary on the event, titled *Day of the Hero.* An L-shaped building houses a souvenir shop, administrative offices, and a museum.

I wandered into the museum. It was filled with pieces of equipment used by firefighters and rescue teams during the quake. The AI that had coordinated the overall effort was on display and would talk with anyone who had a question or comment. I listened for a few minutes.

"How did you feel," a teenage boy asked, "to be in the middle of all that? Were you scared? Do AIs *get* scared?"

*"I was inspired,"* said the AI, speaking with the voice of an older male, *"by the heroic efforts of those who came to the rescue. And I am referring not only to the professionals but to the ordinary people who put their lives on the line to save their friends and neighbors. Was I scared? Yes. I knew we were in trouble."*

"Were you scared for yourself?"

*"Yes. I was scared for all of us."*

An older man described himself as having barely survived the experience. "I was in a staircase," he said. "It collapsed, and I broke both legs. The place was on fire, and a young woman showed up and dragged me out." He grinned and indicated a female companion. "I married her."

*"Excellent choice,"* said the AI.

A guy in a Fleet uniform asked about preparedness. "How did it happen," he said, "that everyone was taken so completely by surprise? Could the politicians have done more?"

*"We have the advantage of hindsight,"* said the AI. *"When you have that, you can always think of more things that might have been done. The real problem was that we thought there could not be an event of that magnitude that would not reveal itself in advance. The science failed."*

Eighteen persons were recognized in the heroes' gallery. All had lost their lives during the earthquake. Their pictures dominated two walls. They were young and old, both sexes, some in uniform and some not. Among them was Eliot Cermak, handsome, gallant, and fearless in his pilot's silver and blue. His name was emblazoned below the photo, and his dates: 1326–1393.

A booklet had been put together for the eighteen, photos

and names on the cover, and emblazoned with the motto NO
GREATER COURAGE.

I picked one up and paged through it. It contained a brief
biography of each person, and dozens of pictures, most of
moments from their personal lives before the event. One of
the Cermak photos showed him standing next to Robin.

I bought a copy and took it back to the hotel.

Cermak's parents had looked like serious people, the
father not entirely comfortable smiling for the photographer,
his mother lighting up the page. It was easy enough to see
where he got his good looks.

Here he was lined up in front of the Cardwell Elementary
School with the other first graders. And at about age twelve in
a beach picture with his father. And playing palmball with his
older brother, Gregory. They had him at his high-school prom,
embracing a gorgeous brunette who was smiling compla-
cently at the picture taker.

Then Cermak at Kryzinski University. And on vacation.
Posing with the family at a wedding. There were two pictures
from flight school. Another returning from his first solo. He
was beaming, and I remembered how that had felt. It is still,
so many years later, one of the proudest moments of my life.

And two more pictures of Cermak with the Fleet, where he
rose to the rank of lieutenant commander.

And, finally, Cermak standing beside the *Breakwater*, on
one of the docks at Skydeck. And the one with Robin, who
was identified as a "world-famous physicist." Robin looked a
trifle pretentious, self-important, while Cermak was simply
a guy on top of the world.

The older brother, Gregory, still lived in the area. There was
no indication of a profession, so I assumed, correctly as it
turned out, that he had settled for the basic security allotment.
When I called and told him I was doing research on Eliot, he
couldn't keep the annoyance out of his voice. *"It's a long time
ago,"* he said.

I wondered whether he was jealous of the attention that
Eliot had received. Still jealous, after forty years? "That's
why we need to do the research," I said. "I was wondering if
there was more material available about your brother that I

could look at? We'd like to get a sense of who he really was. And of the family that could produce somebody like him."

*"What do you mean?"*

"The world knows he's a hero, but they've never really gotten a good image of the *man*."

*"I don't think I have anything that would be of use to you. Nice to talk to you—"*

"No, wait. Don't break off. This is important, Mr. Cermak. And I'd be willing to pay for access."

*"Really? How much?"*

I gave him a number. It was a minimum amount, but it's always easy enough to increase the offer if necessary.

*"Okay,"* he said. *"I'll do what I can. But payment up front, please."*

"Let's see what you have to offer first."

*"What exactly are you looking for?"* His tone softened a bit. Not much, but enough.

"Do you have anything that belonged to him? Correspondence? Diary? Anything like that?"

He had to think about it. *"There's a diary. I have a lot of stuff, actually. My wife never throws anything out."*

"What else?"

*"Pictures. A lot of pictures. And an award he received. In high school, I think it was. I don't have any correspondence."* He couldn't think of anything else. *"Mostly pictures,"* he said. *"And a notebook."*

"When can we talk?"

I doubted that Gregory Cermak had ever looked much like his brother. Where Eliot could have been a leading man, Gregory might have been a guy who'd spent most of his time hanging out in the woods. He had hard, almost immobile, features, and he was irritable and impatient. He introduced me to his wife, Vella, who seemed beaten down, then made it clear that she must have other things to do.

He didn't have much to tell me, mostly stories about him and Eliot growing up together. His resentment of his brother came through loud and clear. Eliot had been selfish. "Though maybe I shouldn't say that." The other kids in school hadn't liked him as they had Gregory. "He was always whining about something, but please don't print that. The only reason

I'm saying it is so you can understand he wasn't really what everybody thinks now."

"Greg," I said, "how do you account for his actions during the earthquake?"

"Look, Chase," he said, "I'm not saying he was a bad person. If I said that, I'm sorry. It's not what I meant. I just wanted you to understand he was as human as everybody else. He ran into buildings and pulled kids out while everybody else ran in circles and screamed that he'd get himself killed. Which is ultimately what happened." He said it as if it demonstrated his brother's bad judgment. Then his tone changed: "I like to think that if I'd been there, I'd have done the same thing."

"You weren't there?"

"No," he said, in a tone that suggested I wouldn't believe him. "I was on a job."

"Did you ever meet Robin?"

"Chris Robin? Not really. I saw him at a distance once or twice. I don't think I ever actually talked to him, though."

"Did they come down from the Skydeck on the shuttle?"

"Yes. Eliot's skimmer was at the terminal. He took Robin home and then rode back to Caton Ferry."

"He wasn't very lucky, was he?"

"No." I saw a hint of regret.

"What about the yachts? You know he and Robin lost some yachts?"

"I heard about that, yes."

"Do you know anything about them?"

"Not really. I joked with Eliot about them. What were there? Three?"

"Four."

"Okay. Yeah. They'd just take them out somewhere and dump them."

"And you've no idea why?"

"Eliot said they were junk. They were just using them for experiments."

"Did he say what kind?" He shook his head. "How about where they went? Did he ever—?"

"No. When I asked Eliot about it, he laughed it off. They bought them, or rather Robin did, and I think they deliberately took them out and got rid of them. But *I* don't know. Eliot was never inclined to tell me stuff."

"And you've no idea where?"

"No." He bit his lower lip. "I remember he said something about one of the yachts, the *Firebird*, I think it was. The last one."

"Yes?"

"I remember asking Eliot, just before he left, where he was going. And he said, 'Just for a spin.' I asked him what he meant, and he said two hundred billion klicks. He shrugged, like it was just around the corner."

"Two hundred billion. You sure?"

"Yeah."

"It wasn't *million*?"

"No. It was *billion*. It stuck in my mind because usually he'd say he was headed for Toxicon, or the Moon, or wherever. But that time, no. It was just two hundred billion klicks. I remember telling him it sounded like a long walk."

That couldn't be right. Two hundred billion kilometers would take you absolutely nowhere. Well outside the planetary system, but it would deposit you in the pit. In interstellar space.

"What about the *Breakwater*?" I asked.

"It got junked."

There were pictures, holograms, even a bust of Eliot sculpted, according to Gregory, by a girlfriend. In school, Eliot had been at the top of his class a few times, and he had framed certificates to testify to it.

I picked up the diary. This was where I expected, hoped, to find everything laid out, explanations of what he and Robin were trying to do. Maybe I'd even get a sense of what had happened on that final fatal night. So I opened it, in Gregory's presence, and made no effort to disguise my disappointment. It covered only his junior and senior years in high school. Mostly it was a record of love affairs and occasional conquests.

*"We did it,"* he reported at the beginning of one entry. *"I never thought Molly would go along. She always went just so far and backed off. But we did it. O happy day—!"*

Damn.

O happy day.

So we went through the pictures. I didn't know any of the

people in them, except of course Cermak and Robin. And Gregory. Gregory agreed to identify everybody, provided I increased the remuneration. *Remuneration* might not have been in his vocabulary, actually. "This is taking up my time," he said by way of explanation. "And I should warn you up front that some of these people, a lot of them, actually, I don't know."

Whatever Eliot had been, Gregory was not. He grumbled that I wasn't moving fast enough. He ignored Vella when she arrived with some muffins and fruit juice. She'd probably been attractive when she took her place with him at the altar. He rolled his eyes a lot and didn't seem able to get comfortable in his chair.

Nevertheless, he helped and I made notes. "This was Dr. Farley, the family physician. *That* was one of Eliot's girlfriends. Yolinda Something-or-other. Don't know *who* this one is. Oh, yes, *that's* Talia, his first wife."

"He was married?"

"Twice. The other one was, um—" He pushed back in his chair, opened the door to the living room, and called to his wife. "Vella, what was the name of Eliot's second wife?"

"Akri," she said.

"They divorced him?" I asked. "Both wives?"

"Talia did. Akri, I think, just let the marriage lapse."

"Sorry to hear it."

"It hardly matters now."

And here was the picture of Cermak and Robin that had been in the book. And a few more. A couple with Cermak and Akri. One showing Robin sitting in the right-hand seat in a cockpit. "The *Breakwater*?" I asked.

Gregory shrugged. "Who the hell knows?"

"You were never in it?"

"No. Not me. I like to keep both feet on the ground."

More pictures from the cockpit. In one, Eliot was looking out at an enormous set of rings. Robin, in another, was just sitting, trying to smile, and not doing a very good job of it, while the same rings cut across the wraparound. I wondered where they were. The instrument panel was visible, but I couldn't make out any details. Blowing it up wasn't likely to help. Still, there was always a possibility. "Can you make a copy of this one, Greg?" I asked.

He looked at it as if he might be giving away something I should be paying for. But he shrugged and directed the AI to make a print.

Then a surprise: a picture of Robin's house on Virginia Island. In fading sunlight. And a shot of the ocean, taken from the bluff. And one of Elizabeth, looking out to sea. All three pictures were moody, placid, somehow wistful. Taken at the same time of day.

Then we had Eliot lifting off in a skimmer. "That was the last time I saw him," said Gregory. "It was my father's funeral. We had a memorial service, and afterward he left, went out to wherever it was with Chris Robin. He came back just in time to get killed by the quake."

"Who took the picture?"

"My son Creviss. Creviss always wanted to be a pilot. Be just like his uncle."

"Did he do it, Gregory?"

"No. He became a lawyer. Don't know which is worse."

# ELEVEN

The value of an object is whatever we assign it to be. It is not
anchored in economics, but in the imagination.

—Timothy Zhin-Po, *Night Thoughts*, 10,002 C.E.

I was on my approach to the country house when *Straight
Talk* started. Deryk Colter was their guest. Colter was an historian, tall and thin and passionate. He'd made a career of
finding fault with Alex, and immediately after sitting down,
he began going on about the sanctity of the past and how we
could not seriously progress unless we learned from it. He
was appalled at the dearth of historical knowledge by the
general public. And he was particularly dismayed by those
who understood the importance of looking back, of avoiding
the same old blunders, but who nevertheless saw no contra-
diction in robbing humanity of its cultural heritage, of tram-
pling it for profit. He was, of course, speaking of Alex. *"The
man is insufferable,"* he was saying as I started down toward
the landing pad. *"He's trying to make Chris Robin look like
an erratic genius who may have opened a door to other realities, then walked through it. The truth is that Robin probably wasn't paying attention to what he was doing and fell
into the ocean. Anyone who's ever been out to Virginia Island knows how easily that could have happened. Maybe he
had a little too much to drink. In any case, Benedict is not to
be taken seriously. Not in this matter. And I don't mean
to take anything away from his achievements. I grant him*

*all that. But in the end, he's a salesman, and he can't be trusted."*

The host, Charles Koeffler, managed to look disconcerted. *"What you're saying, Deryk, is that he'll do anything for money. Is that your position?"*

I shut the thing off before Colter could answer. And I came down on the pad a bit harder than I might have. The AI quietly pointed out that he'd warned me several times about listening to talk shows while I was running the skimmer.

I grumbled something, climbed out, and walked toward the house, not sure whether I was more annoyed with Colter or with the AI. Jacob opened the door for me and said hello. I said hello back, went inside, took off my jacket, dropped my notebook on my desk, and wondered why I was living in a place with such a cold climate.

I was still getting settled when Alex came downstairs. He was smiling, looking as if he'd just left a party. "Welcome home, beautiful," he said. "This place feels empty without you."

I was in no mood for banter. "Alex, I don't know why you keep doing this. These guys are ripping us apart."

"You mean Garland?"

"No. Has he been torching us, too? I was talking about Colter—"

"Yeah. Well, we're a pretty good target at the moment. But they're playing right into our hands. Giving us more traction. The interest in the Robin artifacts is going through the roof. By the way, we'll be running the auction in a couple of days."

"What about your reputation?"

"I'll be fine. Chase, if you do anything creative, anything at all, you have to learn to live with critics. The charges aren't true. All I've done is bring to public attention the fact that Robin had some unusual preoccupations. And I reminded them that he'd disappeared. Those guys, Garland and Colter and the rest, this is their only chance to get out in front of an audience. Relax."

"I don't think we should let them get away with it."

"I'm not much interested in throwing mud. Our clients trust us. That's what's important."

"That's *not* the only thing that's important."

He grinned. "I'm glad to have you looking out for me."

"I don't like being insulted by those idiots."

"I know. Well, for what it's worth, I've arranged to be on Kile's show tonight." He leaned against the wall and folded his arms. "Chase, not to change the subject or anything, but did you know that, the night of Robin's disappearance, the investigators were able to determine that only three skimmers left Virginia Island?"

"I hadn't heard that. But one would have been enough to carry him off. I assume they checked them out?"

"One was Cermak. The other two were locals, and the police were convinced neither could have been involved in his disappearance."

"I can't see how they could make that determination."

"From tracker readings. They wouldn't be definite, but they'd be close enough."

"Did you pass it on to Ramsay?"

"I've been saving it. I'll use it this evening on the show." He went into lecture mode: "Always have something new when you go on one of these things. Throws the critics off stride." He eased himself down onto the love seat. "How was the trip?"

"I'm pretty sure Robin isn't an alien."

"Sorry to hear it. I saw what you gave Ramsay. It was pretty good."

"I thought about telling him how people used to see Robin walking the streets whenever the moon was full, but I thought I'd better let it go."

"You get anything more on the lost yachts?"

"I don't know. Maybe. Greg Cermak, Eliot's brother, said that Eliot told him they'd taken the *Firebird* out two hundred billion klicks."

"And—?"

"Two hundred billion kilometers takes them absolutely nowhere. It would be way outside the planetary system."

"And of course Beta Marikon—?"

Beta Marikon, of course, is our nearest stellar neighbor. "Nowhere close," I said. "They would simply have been in the pit."

"You think the brother might have been mistaken?"

"Sure. Still, he seemed certain that was what Eliot had said."

He thought about it. "Something to file." He started for the door. "When you've a minute, come on back. I've something to show you."

After I got organized, I followed him to his office in the rear. He poured coffee for me and got out some sticky buns. I settled into a chair. "I just hate the personal attacks," I said.

"I know. Audree feels the same way. She thinks I should retire and just sit out here for the rest of my life."

"You know, nobody's really suggesting that. But we could lower our profile a little."

"That would take all the fun out of it."

"Look, Alex. You mind if I tell you what I really think?"

"I wasn't aware you haven't been doing that all along."

"You've accomplished more than most people dream of. Kids look up to you. Everybody except people like Colter respects you. And he's just jealous. They'll name some schools after you one day. But who knows when it might all turn around. I'm tired of watching you risk your reputation."

"Chase—"

"Let me finish: For you, this is always a game. It's the same game you played with your uncle. It almost destroyed your relationship with him. It's time to give it up. It really is. You don't need the money. God knows you don't need the celebrity." I wanted to stop, but I couldn't. "Screw it up now, one misstep, and it's going to be gone. If people start to believe these stories, it'll be over. Once they decide you're a con artist, you won't get your reputation back. Not ever." I was trying to hold my temper in check.

"Chase." He looked offended. "I have an obligation to our clients, too." He stopped and stared at me. "Is that what you think I am? A con artist?"

"Sometimes, Alex, I'm not so sure."

"Okay." His face paled. "Chase—" Then he bit down on whatever he was about to say. I don't think I'd ever seen him seriously angry with me before. "All right," he said. "Let it go." He took a piece out of one of the buns, pushed them across to me, and chewed silently. When he'd finished, he commented that Jacob had come across another sighting that we hadn't known about previously.

The display lit up, and we were looking at a dispatch dated 1385.

(KPR) An unidentified ship passed within tracking range of Tippimaru last night. Authorities at the space station reported that the vehicle did not respond to repeated directives to turn flight control over to the operations center. All attempts at communication proved fruitless.

Failure to comply put the vehicle in violation of at least six provisions of the transport code. An investigation is under way.

An operational representative added that no one was in danger at any time.

"That's interesting," I said. "I hope you're not going to tell me that Chris Robin was there again?"

He smiled. "No. I'd have liked it if he had been."

A hologram appeared in the center of the room. Reporters at one of the terminals. Hurling questions at a woman in a StarCorps uniform. *"They're saying that it wasn't a standard drive, Commander. Is it possible it was an alien?"*

*"Did you actually see the thing, Commander?"*

*"What did it look like to you?"*

She held out her hands. *"One at a time, please."* They quieted. *"I can't believe you guys are asking me seriously about aliens."* She smiled. Foolish notion. *"Give us a little time, and I'm sure we'll figure out what happened out there this morning. To start with, I wouldn't be surprised if it turned out to be a Mute."*

"Well," I said, "Mutes are aliens."

"Not anymore." Alex looked amused. He poured two glasses of orange juice and passed one over. "This one never amounted to much. Tippimaru's a small out-of-the-way place, and nobody pays much attention to what goes on there. But they never did come up with an explanation."

"Did they check with the Mutes?"

"Yes. They said it wasn't one of theirs." He sat back, looked out at the morning sun. "I think we should do a little traveling, Chase."

"Tippimaru?"

"No. Remember Tereza Urbanova?"

"Umm. Not exactly."

"She was the Ops officer at Sanusar."

"Okay. Yes, of course."

"Jacob found an interesting posting about her online."

"Really?"

"Her husband is quoted by a friend as saying she never got over the sighting."

"Why not?" I asked. It wasn't as if the incident had threatened the station.

"I don't know. But she's still at Sanusar. Retired now."

We watched every available visual involving Robin that we could find. He gave out awards, addressed community gatherings, presided over graduations. He was an accomplished speaker and invariably won over his audience right from the start because he consistently made *them*, rather than himself, the center of his remarks. If the audience was composed primarily of teachers and librarians, he inevitably pointed out that it was teachers and librarians who had given us civilization. On one occasion we watched him talk to a crowd of law-enforcement officials, and he observed that it was the police who held civilization together. With engineers and architects, he doted on the sheer joy of living in a modern city, with its combination of convenience and majesty.

He was good.

The Carmichael Club was a group of mathematicians who'd loved him, and apparently had invited him in at every opportunity. They took particular pleasure in jousting with him. They tended to talk about a *hidden* universe rather than an alternate one. And during the Q&A sessions, he was invariably asked the off-the-wall questions that everyone enjoyed. Was entanglement evidence of another level of cosmic law? Had he yet found a bridge for crossing over to another reality? If there was an alternate Chris Robin out there somewhere, was there any chance he was a lawyer?

"But here's something I wanted you to see," said Alex.

At one of the Carmichael events, a young woman with auburn hair got the floor for a moment. *"In all seriousness, Professor Robin,"* she said, *"you often speak of blue sky science. You're enthusiastic about concepts that may always be beyond our reach. How much effort are you willing to expend, how far are you willing to go, on, say, the shadow universe, before you concede that no proof is possible?"*

Robin nodded. *"How far am I willing to go? What's my transportation look like?"*

Laughter rippled through the audience. *"Whatever you like."*

*"Okay. Whatever it takes. Put me in the* Constellation, *and I'll ride to the other side of the Milky Way. If I'm on foot, I'll walk a thousand kilometers, if I have to, to get the result I need."*

Someone in front jumped in: *"Why a thousand kilometers?"*

*"Because I'll be headed south, into better weather, and a thousand kilometers will bring me more or less to the shoreline."* That got more laughter. Then he continued: *"I guess what I'm trying to say, Catherine, in my mangled way, is that the chase is never over."*

"So, Alex," I said, "what did we learn from that?"

"Hold on. Here's something from an address to undergraduates at Que Pakka University. Robin had been telling them how shy he'd been as a graduate student, and how important it was that he'd learned to trust himself, how it was something they all needed to do. *'Until you believe in yourself,'* he'd said, *'no one else will believe in you. Except maybe your mother. No one else will ever take you seriously.'"*

A male student, moments later, commented that it was hard to believe that Robin had ever been shy. *"You've come a long way, Professor,"* he said.

Robin nodded. *"A thousand kilometers. And I had to. Or I would never have had the opportunity to speak with you."*

"He likes the reference," I said. "A thousand kilometers."

"I found six other times that he used it."

"Okay. So what do we take from that?"

"All eight occasions occur between 1389 and 1393. I couldn't find any prior to that period."

"I still don't see—"

"I know. It probably means nothing. But it's worth keeping in mind. It certainly seems to have been in his."

Alex went on *The Kile Ritter Show* that evening, where he was his usual charming self while describing his interest in the missing physicist and how he certainly didn't want to suggest that Robin had walked across a bridge into an alternate reality, but of course that was what some people thought. *"The problem with a lot of our critics,"* he said, *"is that their minds are closed. Shut down. Anything that doesn't fit easily into their worldview, they won't even consider as a possibility. Kile, as you know, that's not the way science works."*

Three days later, we held the auction. The books, especially the ones with the more outrageous handwritten comments by Robin, brought in most of the money. That was no surprise. They had the personal touch that most of the other items lacked. It was why a functioning AI, that could have re-created conversations with Robin, would have been worth a small fortune. The Carpathian hat also did well. (Robin had actually owned two. He had apparently been wearing the other one when he went missing. It was just as well, Alex said. A lone Carpathian hat would be more valuable than the total for two of them.)

The auction was held in a center-city hotel. Alex had several of the pictures enhanced, and they were projected onto the walls. One that particularly caught my interest was an idyllic image of Robin and his wife standing arm in arm under a tree. It was early evening, and they were looking out to sea. A sailboat was tacking away toward the setting sun, and it seemed somehow suggestive of what would later happen.

We framed a number of the pictures, and they went, too. Along with certificates guaranteeing exclusive possession.

You can measure success by the level of disappointment among those who don't get what they want. Please notify me, they were saying, if anything else shows up.

When it was over, Alex called me aside. "Audree and I are going to see *The Last Rebel* over the weekend. I've two extra tickets if you'd like to come."

"It's an opera, isn't it?"

"It's a ballet."

"Well, thanks," I said. "But I don't think so. I'm not much for ballet. Especially the prehistoric stuff."

"Consider it part of the work, Chase. We may come across one of these productions someday. Most of them are lost."

"I wonder why."

"You're sure, now? The offer includes dinner."

# TWELVE

Despite what people say, Sanusar is not a world lacking in pleasant weather. Just don't be away on the wrong weekend or you might miss it.

—Racine Vales, *Memoirs*, 10,762 C.E.

We made Sanusar in a day. It's one of only four worlds in the Aurigae system. One of the others is an enormous gas giant, on the verge of igniting. One of the local comedians famously said that if somebody crashed on it, the thing would gain enough mass to start a nuclear reaction, and they'd have a second star.

All four worlds are in wildly irregular orbits, and in fact they cross one another's paths occasionally. There is, however, no concern that any of them will collide with Sanusar. If nothing changes, the big one will swallow it eventually, but the date has been projected so far ahead that the universe itself will be in severe decline when it does. There was apparently a close encounter with a passing star or something a billion years ago, which is believed to have created the present situation.

The result, of course, is that temperatures on Sanusar vary extensively, and there is no permanent settlement in the standard sense. A few ground facilities provide shelter for visitors, who are predominantly people who like an unstable climate, or who just want to get their picture taken here, or be able to say they've been to Sanusar. There are some who come because they feel it provides a religious setting. For others it is a place where they can experience the arbitrariness of a nature that, at home, seems so solid and dependable. You don't get that in the confines of a space habitat, they'll tell you. Even one circling a black hole. You need hills and open water and something alive to provide a sense of the value of your home world. By something alive, they're talking about misshapen arboreal growths. It's the only known world with fully developed vegetation that does not have animal life beyond that of a microscopic variety. It existed at one time, but vanished long ago when the environment was effectively reshaped. Until Sanusar, biologists had held that plants could not exist without an animal population.

The space station is among the smallest in the Confederacy, with an operational staff of six. It would probably have been shut down centuries ago except that it's close to Mute territory and has been of use to the Fleet when relations have deteriorated.

"They had *five* people then," Miriam Varona told us, referring to the time of the sighting. Miriam was the sole operational officer. Her husband, Barry, oversaw station maintenance, and her other husband, Condrey, was their Patrol officer. (I don't know the relationship for a fact, but that seemed to be the arrangement.) A fourth person, whom she enjoyed referring to as her personnel guy, was on vacation for two months and had been relieved by Miriam's son Boris. Boris was training to be a physician. Two others performed as technicians, and were also available to handle the rescue vehicle in case of an emergency.

"It's not like the big stations," she explained, "but we *do* get some traffic. Someone's in or out at least once a week. In fact, you are the third arrival in the last five days." Miriam was tall, and maybe a trifle bent, and I got a sense of someone who spent too much time alone. Later, I heard that she'd grown up on the station, where there was a 0.3 gravity setting. Her muscles never became accustomed to standard gravity and when in later years she did have to deal with it, it caused problems. Her family, which had obviously not been too bright, or maybe just didn't care, owned the orbiter.

"We're looking for Tereza Urbanova," said Alex. "Can you tell us where she is?"

"Oh, yes. It's been a while since I've seen her. But she's

living at Oceanside." She produced a map for us. "We can shuttle you down, but I have to tell you, it's not cheap. If you have a lander, I'd suggest you use it."

"We will," he said. "What kind of place is Oceanside?"

"It's on a mountain. Beautiful view, though, despite the name, you won't see much water."

"Okay."

"It's a small complex. Tourist spot, of course. Tereza works there. Does presentations and serves as the host for most of the parties and whatnot."

"Sounds like a busy place."

"Well, I'm not sure I'd go that far. They do have some people there now, though. A group of literature enthusiasts. They're there to visit the Filandia."

"What's the Filandia?" I asked.

Alex usually knows the answers to such abstruse questions, but he waited for Miriam to explain. She seemed mildly amused that we didn't know. "It's the hotel. Where Racine Vales wrote *Over the Side*."

I'd heard the title but had no idea what it was about.

"It's the big revolutionary novel of the Bacchanal movement," Alex said.

I still didn't know—

"It's a long time ago, dear," said Miriam. "Six hundred years. But it *did* change the way an entire civilization behaved. It brought about a new moral code and a complete freedom of the spirit."

"Do as you like," said Alex, "as long as no one gets hurt."

"Exactly," she said. "People always talked about freedom, but then they set a lot of rules. Think how much better everyone's life would be if we just exercised some common sense instead of living by tribal taboos." She laughed. "Well, enough of that. Does Tereza know you're coming?"

In fact she did. We landed on the edge of the complex, which consisted of the Filandia, an entertainment complex, and a half dozen cabins, arranged in a large circle. They all had a kind of rough-hewn look, which added to the sense of being well away from civilization. (As if you needed anything to underscore the reality.) They weren't really on top of a mountain. It was more like an oversized hill with a flattened summit. If you fell off the summit, you weren't likely to get hurt, but you'd do a lot of rolling. We saw a few kids playing tag, and a young woman was coming out of one of the cabins.

An ocean *was* visible, but it was far enough away that it might have been nothing more than a distant lake. We set down on a pad, climbed out, and went into the hotel.

Tereza was in the lobby, seated near a window with three men and a woman. She stood and smiled as we came in. "Chase?" she said. "And Alex. How nice to meet you. I've heard so much about you."

She hadn't aged much in a half century. She had black hair, smooth skin, lemon-colored eyes, and a quiet dignity that imposed itself on her surroundings. She introduced us around the table. They were members of the literary group, and they'd apparently been talking about the weather. And before you leap to judgment, keep in mind that the weather on Sanusar wasn't anything like whatever world the visitors had come from. But *that* day, with sunlight and relatively warm temperatures, it was all anyone could have asked.

"Yesterday," said one of the tourists, "it was forty below."

We joined the conversation, were asked what we did for a living and whether we'd like some drinks. After a few minutes, Tereza excused herself from her guests and took us to a side room, where we sat down around a table. "You're, of course, welcome to stay if you like," she said. "I hope you will, but I don't want to waste your time. How can I help you?"

Alex leaned forward. "Tereza," he said, "we're trying to get a handle on the sighting fifty years ago. The ship that—"

"I know," she said.

"You were on duty when it happened."

"Yes. That's correct."

"We've seen the record of the incident. And we were hoping you might be able to add something."

"I don't know what else—?"

"Your husband once described you as having never been the same after the incident."

She blinked and smiled. "There's some truth to that, I guess." Outside, in the lobby, somebody put on some music. It was slow and moody.

Alex waited quietly.

Her eyes focused somewhere behind us. "The record that you saw was edited."

"Why?"

"We had some decent images of the ports."

Alex leaned forward. "It's okay," he said. "What did you see?"

"There was a woman at one of them. She appeared to be banging on it. She looked hysterical."

"Are you sure?"

"Yes, I'm sure." Those lemon eyes grew sad. "The investigators confiscated everything. When, later, the record was released, that part of it was missing."

"Did you talk to them? The investigators?"

"My boss did. He said they told him it was our imagination. That she was never there." She shook her head. "We all saw it, Alex. God help me, we all saw it."

# PART II

## Villanueva

# THIRTEEN

The future of our species lies hidden in its past.

—Wolfgang Corbin, *Let's Hear It for the Infidels*, 6615 C.E.

"Why would they edit it out?" I asked, as we lifted away from Oceanside.

"Public relations again," said Alex. "We don't know who conducted the investigation, whether it was StarCorps or local. But they had a woman in distress. Worse, *pictures* of a woman in distress. They don't have a clue who she is, or what the ship is, or where it went. There were no reports of anyone in trouble. All vehicles were accounted for." He looked down at the landscape. "How would they explain it to an aroused public?"

The ride home was somber. Alex buried himself in a book and barely spoke until we'd made the jump back into our home system. When I asked him whether we were ready to back away from the entire business, he said that he was disappointed in me. "You give up too easily, Chase."

"So where do we go from here?"

"Winter."

"What?"

"William Winter. Robin's friend. The one who died on Indikar. I think it's time we tried to find out what actually happened."

Two days later, we were on a glide train crossing the continent. At Port Leo we got off, and spent the night at the

Amerada Hotel. I'm embarrassed to admit that I had a little too much to drink and became part of the floor show. I don't usually do stuff like that, and I probably wouldn't have if Alex had been down in the club with me, but he wasn't, and I began thinking how maybe those people who were saying you should enjoy yourself while you can, have a big time as long as nobody gets hurt because you don't have forever, maybe they're right. So I joined two or three other women at the center of the party.

In the morning, I felt a bit guilty, and Alex was surprised when I told him I was going to have breakfast in my room. I didn't want to take a chance on running into anybody from the previous evening. But I could tell from the way Alex was talking to me that he knew something had happened. He didn't comment, though. And at noon, under a brilliant, cloudless sky, we checked out, rented a skimmer, and rode to Taraska.

Taraska is rugged country, valleys and ridges partially submerged in thick forest, lots of rock, and two very large mountains. It's a place for people who'd probably rather be living on an island or on the back side of the Moon except that they like the services that come with being within reach of civilization. And they have a taste for architecture. There were a couple of stores, two cafés, a nightclub, a church, and a city hall in the center of town, all quite elegant. Private homes were widely separated across the area, and were a trifle ostentatious, equipped with towers, domes, and arches.

The townspeople were convivial, though. They hung out in the cafés, or in the nightclub. Or at one another's houses. They threw a lot of parties, or so we were informed. And I had no trouble believing it.

William Winter's son, also named William, lived in a three-story house with columns and spires and circular windows. The lawn was beautifully manicured, and two lines of salonika trees shaded the property. "What's he do for a living?" I asked Alex.

"As far as I can tell, he just sits on his front deck and watches the flowers grow."

"Where'd the family money come from, do you know?"

"It's been there for generations."

The landscape seemed utterly still as we began our descent. Their AI asked us to identify ourselves. "Alex Benedict," I said. "We have an appointment with Mr. Winter."

*"Very good. Welcome to Whitcover."* We discovered later that every house in Taraska has a name. There were, for example, Burlingame and Epicenter and Pyrrhus. Burlingame had, we were told, been picked out of a hat. The owner of Epicenter was a geologist, and Pyrrhus was the property of a family that claimed to be descended from Greeks. A gray-white boulder dominated the lawn of Whitcover.

The AI sounded a bit snobbish. And we wondered why Winter didn't soften the greeting. This didn't look like an area that had problems with salesmen or the Lord's Messengers.

We touched down a minute or two later, and the AI instructed us to proceed to the front deck. We got out, dropped onto a stone pathway, walked to the front of the house, and climbed five marble stairs onto the porch. It was beautiful country. A soft breeze rustled the trees, flowers bloomed, and birds twittered. The door opened, and we passed between two columns and went inside, where we were greeted by a young man dressed in formal garb. *"Good afternoon,"* he said. *"Mr. Winter will be with you shortly."*

He was a hologram. Standing in front of a lamp in the hallway, he cast no shadow. He smiled politely, led us into a reception room, and asked us to be seated. When we'd complied, he smiled again, turned on his heel, and left.

The room was luxuriously furnished with thick satin curtains, a dark, padded sofa, three armchairs, and an exquisitely carved coffee table. Several pieces of twelfth-century transliteral art were mounted on the walls, along with a lush, fur-lined tapestry and a framed wedding picture of William Winter, Sr., and his bride. Two sculpted busts, a man and a woman from another age, looked across the room at each other.

We heard voices in the hallway. Then a short, plump man entered the room. "Mr. Benedict," he said. "So good to meet you. And Ms. Kolpath. I'm Billy Winter. What can I do for you?"

Alex expressed his admiration for the property and said something about the pleasant weather. Winter asked if we'd like something to drink. Of course. That would be very kind. Winter spoke to the AI, and Alex got to the point. "As I mentioned," he said, "we're doing some research on eminent fourteenth-century figures, men and women who had a permanent effect on the development of the culture. We'd like very much to talk with you about your father."

Our host settled into an armchair. "My time is yours," he said.

A bottle of wine was brought in by a middle-aged woman, who smiled politely, took three glasses from a cabinet, and put them before us. She withdrew, and Billy filled the glasses. We raised them to his father, and to the Arcane Club, of which he'd been a founding member, and which included some of the century's most influential thinkers. Maria Cauley, who'd been a major contributor to court reform, had been a member. And Lyle Kashevik, the neurologist who'd argued the necessity of religion for inner peace while warning against its vulnerability to abuse. And Indira Khalalla, who developed the moonlight pheromone that was so potent that moralistic opponents took her to court to block its use. Michael Goshok had belonged during the years when he was leading the effort to ban AIs that could theoretically read minds by examining facial expressions. Goshok had been a liaison with the Mutes, and he must have understood what it would have meant to humans to have their minds open for all to see.

"Did your father ever explain to you," Alex asked, "why he wanted to go to Indikar?"

"No," said Billy. "I was only ten when it happened. He said good-bye, and suddenly he just wasn't around anymore. My mother told me that she never understood what it was about."

"Had he gone out on missions like that before? That you're aware of?"

"No. It was the first time he'd been off-world." The mother, we knew, had died several years earlier. "She used to talk about how she'd had a bad feeling the first time she'd seen him."

Alex leaned back in his chair. "You mean Chris Robin?"

"Yes." Billy took a long swallow of the wine. "If you ever figure out why he went, if you find out why my father died, I'd appreciate it if you'd let me know."

Alex assured him he would. He got up and walked over to the wedding picture. The couple looked happy, even exultant, the way newlyweds inevitably do. The groom might have been a bit too poised. The bride, whose name was Suniya, was literally aglow. I love old wedding pictures. Sometimes I suspect we all peak at that moment, and that afterward we get back to the business of living, and it's a downhill run.

"You wanted to see his papers," said Billy.

"Yes, if we may."

"Absolutely." He raised his voice a notch: "Miranda, make everything available to Chase and Alex, if you will."

*"As you wish, Mr. Winter,"* said the AI. I couldn't help noticing the formality. Most house systems are on first-name terms with people.

"Your father left a substantial reputation behind," said Alex.

"Have you read him?" he asked. He was looking at me.

Alex bailed me out. "Of course," he said. "I read *War, Peace, and Mr. Kargolo* when I was in college."

"It won the Excelsior Award in 1376."

"Deservedly. I've also read *The Libertines*."

"He was especially proud of that one. It didn't win any awards, but he thought it was his best work." He beamed. Then it was back to business: "Alex," he said, "as I mentioned to you, everything in the documents is available for your inspection. But nothing may be downloaded, other than his books." The other titles were *Mathematics and God*; *The Grand Cycle*; *Mutes, Philosophers, and Lawyers*; and *Our Day in the Sun.* "I wouldn't want you to think I don't trust you, but it's a precaution that my father always insisted on, so I feel a certain duty—"

"It's no problem, Billy."

"So what are we looking for?"

I'd asked the question on the way to the house and expected Alex to respond with his trademark line that we'd know it when we saw it. But he was a bit more precise this time, though not much: "Chase, we want to know the reason for his connection with Robin."

The amount of material contained in Winter's papers was breathtaking. Aside from notes on the six books he'd written, which were probably more extensive than the books themselves, there were journals, diaries, comments on whatever he happened to be reading, and records of conversations. There were observations on the culture, on political events, on the media, on religion, on theatrical performances, on his dietary tastes, on child rearing, on marriage, and on AIs (which, he maintained, were in fact conscious entities and therefore should be granted rights identical to people). There was hardly an aspect of human behavior that he left untouched. And he included a few chess games.

"Alex," I said, "we're going to be here for years."

"Chase," he said, "you go through the journals. Look for anything that rings a bell." He went to the far side of the room, pulled the curtains to block off some of the sunlight, and sat down at a table.

Robin's name turned up in various contexts, as a friend, as a brilliant—if somewhat erratic—physicist, as an occasional luncheon companion, as a favorable reviewer, as a reviewer who'd found fault with some of Winter's conclusions about human evolution ("Robin thinks we are not getting any smarter"), and as a pioneer in the field of subquantum research.

*"He always felt,"* Winter wrote, *"that he'd been born in the wrong era. He envied those who'd lived during the scientific golden age, the period from Francis Bacon to Armand Castillo. From the concept that the world could be explained without invoking the supernatural, which can be traced to the arrival in Italy of the Greek scholars who'd fled the fall of Constantinople in the thirteenth century. And which continued until Castillo demonstrated nine hundred years later that there would never be a Grand Unified Theory. That the cosmos was essentially a masterpiece of disorganization, and therein lay its essential elegance.*

*"Robin felt that once that had happened,"* Winter said, *"there was nothing left to do except construct applications. Collect data. And watch the sun go down in the evening. I'm sorry to say that it's difficult to take issue with him on that point."*

Elsewhere, he described Robin as a beneficiary of a line of complexity issues worked out by Friedmann Koffer, the physicist who had contributed so much to the conclusion of hostilities during the Mute War. Winter also mentioned that Robin's work on the multiverse would not have been possible without the efforts of a team that combined with Mute scientists after the conflict to begin looking into the possibility of devising an experiment to establish the existence of alternative universes.

I read a detailed explanation, but I couldn't understand much of it. I decided that Winter was either pretty advanced in the sciences for an historian or that he simply wasn't very good at explaining things.

The reality was that there could be a connection between these two guys that would not necessarily cite Robin's name. So I spent the rest of the morning scanning the journals, looking for multiple-universe issues, the golden age, the subquantum world, Koffer, and the sightings. Something. I found a few possibilities.

Winter was also interested in the occasional sightings by the space stations that seemed to have no explanation. He referred to them as "Sanusar events" and recorded dates and details for some going back more than three thousand years. His sole comment: *They've been with us a long time.*

Winter enjoyed analyzing how the human outlook had changed as a result of the discovery that we were not alone. What would we be like now, he was fond of asking, if we still believed the universe was empty except for us? He thought the presence of the Mutes had induced a degree of humility that we'd lacked for millennia. There were no more claims, as there had once been, that we were spiritually, if not physically, at the center of the universe. The God of the pre-Mute era had been somehow smaller than the one most people believe in today.

I should mention here that I was reared by parents who felt the necessity of a personal connection with God. We were not, however, members of an established faith. (Few people are now, of course.) But we believed there was a greater Power.

I lost that during my teen years, mostly because I couldn't conceive of a compassionate creator who would give us a Darwinian system, with its requisite food chain. When I was growing up, I had a cousin, two or three times removed, who'd piloted interstellars. He told me it was impossible to look down on a distant planetary surface, to watch moons glide around their parent worlds, to cruise through a set of planetary rings, and not feel the presence of something greater than the visible world. He was right. I have felt all that.

But also, especially when I've been alone in the *Belle-Marie*, I also feel an overwhelming solitude. And if that seems contradictory, nevertheless it's there. The majesty of those places, of planetary rings and comets sailing through the sky and stars that remain stable for billions of years, serves only to drive the point home: such incredible beauty. And there's no one but me to look at it.

Adam and Eve have been gone a long time. Genesis is a relic from a different era. And we've known for thousands of years that the universe is immense beyond comprehension. But none of that ever came home, Winter says, until we looked out and saw someone looking back. Now we *feel* the vastness. Worshippers are more inclined to perceive God not as the owner of the church down at the corner but as the creator of a universe whose dimensions and complexity leave us breathless.

Winter himself is talking about believers when, in a journal entry dated a few weeks before his death, he comments that "I'm looking forward with enthusiasm to the flight in the *Breakwater*."

He continues: *"What a joy it will be, finally, to see Villanueva."*

Villanueva.

There was no mention of Indikar.

Villanueva has been gone now almost as long as Adam and Eve. It had been renowned in its time as a refuge and a retreat for the faithful of all religions. But its name had never come up in the accounts of Winter's death on that final voyage.

Villanueva had been colonized during the Great Migration, which occurred in the middle centuries of the fourth millennium. It was third planet from the sun Phalangia. There'd been no intention to create a permanent settlement. The world, along with the rest of the planetary system, was drifting toward a massive dust cloud, which would radically change the climate and make it uninhabitable for centuries. Estimates gave it between five hundred and twelve hundred years.

But five hundred years is a long time. And Villanueva was an ideal world, a second Earth. Originally, it was simply a great spot for a vacation. Then it became home for some religious groups who preferred to be away from a terrestrial culture that many perceived as immoral and godless. There were some who maintained that the claims of approaching destruction were simply a conspiracy, put together by the wealthy, who wanted to keep this pristine world for themselves.

So people came. And many of them stayed. When the dust cloud finally arrived, their descendants were, incredibly, taken by surprise. Most must have thought they could ride it out. In any case, there were too many for an evacuation. To this day, it remains the worst catastrophe in history.

So why would Winter, and apparently Chris Robin, be going to Villanueva?

I showed the notation to Alex. "What happened to Indikar?" I asked.

The hours slipped by. Billy came in to ask if we'd made any progress. "Got a question for you," said Alex. "Did your father ever mention Villanueva?"

"Where's that?" he asked.

"Pretty far from here."

"It's on a different planet?"

"It *is* a different planet."

"No," he said. "Not that I can recall. The only place he ever went to was Indikar. Why do you ask?"

"He mentions it in one of his journals."

Billy shook his head. "I can't recall anything about that. My understanding is that he and Robin only went to Indikar. Nowhere else. Maybe they intended to go there later."

We enjoyed a salad and sandwiches out in the garden. "You should consider moving here," Billy said, while a soft breeze whispered in the trees. "This is about as cold as it gets."

"Did you ever meet Robin?" Alex asked.

"The first time I saw him was at the memorial service. For my father. Other than that, no. I don't even remember his name being mentioned except when my father was going on that flight."

"He came to pay his respects?"

"Yes. At the time, I still couldn't really believe my dad wasn't coming home. I hadn't gotten used to it. We had a service, and Professor Robin came. I remember he was having a hard time himself. His voice broke up while he was speaking. He said it was all his fault. Took all the blame on himself. It started my mother crying again, and, pretty soon, everybody was hysterical."

"He never explained precisely what happened?"

"They were apparently doing everything from orbit. But Dad wanted to land on the world, so they took him down and got attacked by a lizard." He paused. "I don't remember whether Robin actually told us that or I read it later.

"Professor Robin stayed in touch with us. Always asked if there was anything he could do. There never was, of course. But looking back now, I know he tried to be a source of consolation to my mother. It didn't take, though. Then, when I was in college, he was gone, too."

"You have any idea," I asked, "what might have happened to him?"

"You mean his disappearance?" He shook his head. "None." He finished his sandwich and sank back in his chair. The tree branches swayed gently. "I can't imagine what it might have been. I suspect he was probably drinking that night and just fell into the ocean."

Alex decided to stay over one more day, but we needed somebody back at the country house. So I made arrangements to return to Andiquar that evening.

I rode back to Port Leo in a taxi. Jacob contacted me as I was entering the station. *"I know you don't like to be bothered on the road, Chase, but I got word today that Alex will receive the DiPreta Award."* The award, named for the philanthropist Edward DiPreta, recognized contributions to interspecies understanding. *"First it was the Mutes,"* Jacob said. *"Then that business last year. I thought he'd like to know. The presentation will be made at the end of the month."*

"That's great news."

*"Yes. I was glad to hear it. He deserves some recognition. Lately it seems to have been nothing but criticism. Criticism by people who themselves have never contributed anything."*

"You've a point, Jacob. Anyhow, I'm not with him at the moment. I know he doesn't like to be called when he's out of the office, but I think we can make an exception for this. I'll let him know."

*"Very good, Chase. Umm—I was wondering—"*

"Yes, Jacob?"

*"Would it be okay with you if I—"*

"You want to tell him."

*"I would like that very much."*

Two hours later, as I sat in my compartment, watching a dark landscape blur past, I got a call from Alex. *"Just wanted to make sure you got there okay."*

"I'm fine, Alex. On my way home now."

*"Good. No problem with tickets?"*

"None."

*"Okay."* He hesitated. *"Was there something else you wanted to tell me?"*

"No. I think that's it."

*"You already know, don't you?"*

"Yeah. Congratulations."

*"Actually, there* is *something more."*

"What's that?"

*"They're splitting the award this year."*

"Oh." That had never happened before. "How could they do that?" I asked.

*"Don't know. These things just happen, I guess."*

"Who else is getting it?"

*"You are, Chase. Congratulations."*

Later, considerably later, I learned that Alex had insisted that the DiPreta Committee recognize me also. He tried to keep it from me but I'm too good at tracking down secrets.

I've spent too many years watching a pro at work.

# FOURTEEN

Reputation is like youth. Once it's gone, it cannot be recovered.

—Clement Esteban, *Autobiography*, 2702 C.E.

I spent most of my first day back touching base with clients and catching up on the market. That evening, I was getting ready to go home when Alex called again, from his compartment on the glide train. "They haven't changed their minds about the award?" I said.

*"Not that I'm aware. Though maybe we can arrange it if you think you don't deserve it."*

"No. I'll stick it out. What do you have?"

*"I found something else of interest. I'm forwarding it now."*

Jacob put it on the display:

Triflis 1/12 4017
Abonai 7/11 4113
Grand Salinas 9/3 5396
Inaissa 1/16 6301
Saraglia 8/5 7661
Ilyanda 10/10 8377
Vendicari 12/22 9017
Earth 3/17 9638
Inaissa 2/9 9684
Fishbowl 5/18 10312
Pt. Edward 5/30 11107

        Sanusar 7/1 11267
        Tippimaru 4/13 11272

*"It's from Winter's notebooks. No accompanying explanation."*

They were Confederate worlds. Four of them were uninhabited. The dates were in the base system. The current year, on Earth, was 11,321 C.E. And I saw at once that the last two entries coincided with sightings.

*"Those aren't the only two, Chase. The Point Edward, Fishbowl, and Inaissa dates also mark sighting occurrences. There was something near Earth on March 17, 9638, although I haven't been able to find details. I don't think there's any question these all mark Sanusar events."*

"So Winter was collecting information on sightings over the past, what, seven thousand years? That must have taken some major digging."

*"I'd think so."*

"Alex, wait. With that kind of time span, it's inevitable that occasionally a ship would wander in accidentally to a place where it wasn't expected. A lot of these would have to be false alarms."

*"I know. Probably most of them."*

"So why do we care?"

*"Maybe because on two occasions Robin showed up in advance."*

"But not at Tippimaru."

*"Maybe he didn't know that one was coming. Maybe it was somebody who just wandered in. But the point is that Winter was collecting the data."*

"Alex, I have no idea what's going on."

*"There's something else you might be interested in."*

"What's that?"

*"It doesn't have anything to do with the sightings, but Winter and Robin shared another interest: black holes. Winter has a list of them, about twenty, with their locations and their trajectories."*

"Alex, what could that have to do with the Sanusar events?"

It turned into a fairly raucous day. One client claimed we'd promised to get the pilot's seat from the *Seeker* for him. It's our policy to put clients in touch with one another. We don't commit to do any more than that, except in those relatively rare situations in which we actually *own* the desired artifact. The client hadn't been able to persuade the owner to sell, despite making offers that, I thought, were far more than the seat should have been worth. He was threatening to sue us, and I spent a large part of the morning trying to calm him down. The last thing he said to me was that he'd forget the suit, but he'd find another dealer since he couldn't trust us anymore.

And there was Miranda Shelton. "I think I found an alien ship," she told me.

Miranda was one of those people who look absolutely bland. No energy animated her features. She was middle-aged. Average appearance. Bored and boring. The kind of person who, five minutes after meeting her, you would not have been able to pick her out of a lineup if your life depended on it. She showed up unexpectedly at the country house and wanted to talk with Alex.

"He's not here," I said.

"Can I talk to you?"

I showed her to a chair. "Of course. What can I do for you?"

"I have an unusual problem," she said.

"I'm listening."

"I found an alien." My stomach started to tighten. "I'm a pilot for TransWorld," she explained. She did not look at all like a pilot. Or like anyone who did anything other than sit on a front porch.

"Okay."

"I was carrying some biologists to a site in one of the systems—"

"Which system?"

"I'll tell you in a minute. The point is that I found a derelict. It was in orbit around one of the moons."

"Really?"

"I ran images of it. There's no record of anything like it. I think it might be *alien*."

"Why?"

"Because I can't identify it. Aren't you listening?"

"Ms. Shelton, there are quite a few derelicts drifting

around out there. A lot of them don't show up in the inventories. They're too old. The records have been lost."

"That could be true," she said. "On the other hand, who really knows?"

"You'll want to take a closer look."

"Ms. Kolpath, my contract gives all recovery rights to my employer."

"I see. So what are you going to do?"

"I plan to resign, wait awhile, then pursue the matter."

"I don't think you should quit your day job."

"What I'd like to know is, what would a discovery like that be worth?"

"You'd become famous," I said. "You'd be a guest on all the talk shows. You'd get a huge book contract."

"What about the ship itself? Would I be able to sell it?"

"I'm sure you could. I don't really know anything about alien vehicles."

"All right. Thank you. Will you handle it for me?"

"Sure," I said. "We'll help where we can."

"Good. Thank you." She smiled, and for the first time in a discussion that should have been emotional, I saw a trace of something. Hope, maybe. Exhilaration. I don't know. "I'll be back in a few months to let you know how it turns out."

We didn't see her again.

There were a couple of other problems, though nothing quite like Miranda and the guy who wanted to sue us. I was glad to see the day come to an end. I was getting ready to go home when Emile Zuckerman arrived. Zuckerman was a client who collected Ashiyyurean art. He was also a physicist of considerable repute, having made contributions in chaos analysis that, simply put, were too complicated for any normal human to have the slightest idea what he was talking about. Or at least they were too far out for me. Unfortunately, he couldn't have given instructions on how to get a glass out of a cabinet without causing confusion. But I always played along when he called, nodding periodically as if I understood why causality broke down near black holes or why he needed a second artifact from the home of Ajax Bittman.

He was a little guy with a narrow build. He always managed to make me feel as if I shouldn't be let out by myself. His teeth were always visible, leaving the impression that he was looking for something to eat. He had a white beard and dark brown eyes that could not suppress a mischievous glint. I've always suspected he knew exactly what he was doing and enjoyed baffling the people around him. On this occasion, he spent a minute or two telling me how good I looked. Then he asked if Alex was available.

"He's traveling, Zuck," I said. "Can I be of assistance?"

"Would it be possible to reach him?"

"It's not easy. What's it about?"

The lips exposed even more of his teeth. "I'd really like to talk with him, Chase. Please."

Normally, I wouldn't have considered breaking into whatever Alex might be doing to put him on with Zuck. But I was looking at an unusual degree of intensity that afternoon. "Let me see what I can do," I said.

I got him a drink and seated him in the conference room while Jacob put the call through. It went audio only. When Alex answered, I was back in my office. I could hear music and voices in the background and the clink of silverware.

"Zuck wants to speak to you, Alex," I said. "It might be worth your time."

*"You don't know what it's about?"*

"No."

He sighed.

"I'm sorry."

*"Next time tell him I'm attending a funeral. Where is he now? In back?"*

"Yes."

*"Okay. Have Jacob switch me over, but stay with the call."*

"Why?"

*"You know how he is. If he gets talking, find a reason to break in. Manufacture an emergency or something."*

I took a deep breath, got myself something to read, and switched in. They traded greetings. *"I hope,"* Zuck said, *"I'm not interrupting anything."*

*"No, no,"* Alex said pleasantly. *"I've finished most of what I had to do."*

*"Good. I'm sorry to bother you."*

*"It's okay. What do you need?"*

"I won't take much of your time, Alex. But I was reading how you'd gotten interested in Christopher Robin."

"More or less. Why? Did you know him?"

"No. I met him a couple of times, but I can't say I actually knew him. But I knew somebody who did."

"Really? Who's that?"

"Cara. Cara Bosworth."

"And she was—?"

"Robin's mentor at the University of Margala. She was a good woman, Alex. Brilliant. We lost her about twenty years ago. Margala's physics prize is named in her honor."

"I'm sorry to hear it. Did she have any idea what happened to him?"

"She had a theory. And she was probably right."

"What was the theory?"

"That he just got home that night, decided he'd had enough, and jumped into the ocean."

"Enough of what?"

"Well, all these years I've never repeated any of this—"

"Just say it, Zuck."

"Cara was pretty sure Elizabeth was screwing around, and it became too much for him so he killed himself."

"Screwing around with whom?"

"I don't know. I don't think she knew. But Cara picked it up from Robin. Never directly. I mean, she told me he never said anything—"

"Then how did she know?"

"Body language. The way he reacted whenever Cara mentioned her name. 'Tell Elizabeth I said hello,' and he'd clamp down and get a hard look. She didn't think there was any question about it."

"Zuck, they never found the body."

"The tides out there are pretty strong. If he jumped in when the tide was going out—"

"He took his luggage with him."

"All right, Alex. I don't know about the luggage. Maybe somebody came along and made off with it. Maybe he was so much out of his mind that he threw it into the ocean. Look, it's not exactly an orderly world. Crazy stuff happens."

"Okay, Zuck. Thanks for the information."

"Anyhow, Alex, what I wanted to say: This is about an

*eccentric guy, maybe deranged. There was talk about walking through dimensions, crossing over to other universes, tracking down aliens. All this fantasy stuff. Your involvement has been pretty public. Look, we go way back, you and I. You've made some major contributions over the years, and you've been a good friend. I know there are people out there who're always sniping at you. They're jealous. I never see any of those people who don't wish they'd done what you have."*

He went on like that for several minutes, and I knew that Alex wanted me to stage the emergency and bring the conversation to a close. But Zuck kept sounding as if he was about to say good night. And he was saying things I thought Alex needed to hear. So I hesitated. He talked about the respect that people had for him, and how important a reputation is for someone in his business, how critical it was for his clients to know they could trust him. *"Not that I'd ever lose faith in you, Alex. You know that."*

*"I know, Zuck."*

After another minute or two, he finally came to the point: *"You still have time to back off, Alex. Do it. Don't get in any deeper than you are. You know what I'm saying?"*

*"Yes, Zuck. Thanks."*

*"Just let it go. Okay?"*

*"Zuck, I appreciate the call."*

*"It's okay. And you're not upset with me, right?"*

*"Upset with you, Zuck? Never happen."*

Alex was still on the circuit. *"Thanks, Chase,"* he said, with an edge in his voice. *"You were very helpful."*

"Sorry," I said. "I didn't think you'd want me to cut in when the guy was making so much sense."

*"Right."*

"Do you think there's anything to it? That Elizabeth might have been cheating?"

*"I don't know. We may never know. There's no evidence."*

"Okay. Listen, have a good ride home. I have to go."

*"Hot date tonight?"*

"Don't I always?"

*"Chase, I want you to do something for me."*

"Okay."

*"Find out what happened to the* Breakwater. *Maybe we can get access to the log."*

# FIFTEEN

The problem at Villanueva was that nobody thought to turn off the lights.

—Marcy Lee, *Last Days*, ca. 6314 C.E.

Why did they go to Villanueva?

At least we knew why they'd lied about their destination. Villanueva was on the list of hazardous worlds. Mention it on your proposed itinerary, and you could expect to have to justify the reason for your visit. Fill out the appropriate forms. Get permission from higher authority. And agree that, if you get into trouble, rescue may not be forthcoming.

I checked on the *Breakwater*. After Cermak died, the estate sold it to the CEO of a drug company. Wilson Broderick. He kept it for about a year, then donated it to a charity. They eventually scrapped it.

"Is Broderick still alive?" Alex asked.

"He died about ten years ago."

"What about the AI?"

"It would have been destroyed along with the yacht."

"Pity. If we had the log—"

"There *might be* one other possibility."

"I'm listening."

"The space stations don't keep the basic operations logs more than a few years. But they might still have the fueling records."

"From forty years ago?"

"Maybe. It's worth checking into."

"And if we found it, what would it tell us?"

"If they refueled when they got back, which most yachts have to do after a long flight, we'll be able to come up with a ballpark idea how far they went. It'll certainly tell us whether they went to Indikar. Or Villanueva."

Fueling operations at Skydeck were run by Mandy Jhardain. Mandy's a quiet, easygoing type who never married. She didn't like commitments. In the end, she'd told me once, there's always somebody else. I've known Mandy a long time, and I can't imagine her in a permanent relationship. She always claimed she'd been built to roam.

When I asked about refueling records from the previous century, she laughed. *"To be honest, Chase, I haven't cleared the data since I got here. It's supposed to happen automatically. Hold on a second."*

That didn't sound hopeful. I heard somebody saying no, heard the humming and burping of electronics. Then she was back. *"Sorry to keep you waiting, Chase,"* she said. *"It looks as if we have everything for the past three years. I don't guess that would do you any good?"*

I followed up on the *Breakwater* AI as well. Nobody could tell me for certain whether it had been destroyed along with the yacht. All Skydeck recycling had been done in those years by one of two companies, neither of which still existed. A retired employee of ProCon, one of the two, told me that even if the AI had survived, there'd be no way to determine what had happened to it.

I had no idea where to go from there, so I left a note for Alex, who was out of the building, and went back to my routine duties. They included fielding a generous offer for Korman Eddy's *Clockwork*, if we could come up with it. *"Disappeared off that train,"* the would-be customer said. *"I'd love to be able to give it to my wife for our anniversary."* I was tempted to tell him what Alex had concluded about *Clockwork*, but I let it go.

"We'll let you know, Mr. Spiegler," I said, "if we get a line on it. But I'm not hopeful."

\*     \*     \*

When Alex got back, he stuck his head in my office, said hello, and told me we might have a link. "David Lisle," he said, "is an emeritus professor of history at Margala. And he was a friend of Winter's."

"Good," I said. "You found him in one of Winter's books?"

"No. I started looking for someone with a similar academic background who shared his interest in the sightings."

"Have you been in touch with him?"

"He had to tend to his garden."

"What?"

"His garden comes before all else, apparently." He looked tired. "He's making up his mind about what he wants to tell me."

"You think he knows something?"

"Judging by the way he reacted when I asked him about Winter's death, I don't think there's any question."

"What did he say?"

"Told me he was busy planting juleps." He sat down and grumbled something about people who were preoccupied with a sense of their own importance.

"What do we know about him?" I asked.

"He's written a few articles. One of them mentions a sighting a thousand years ago at Fishbowl. The station operators reportedly heard an unknown language on the radio. They said the voice was human, they didn't think there was any question about that, but they'd never heard the language before." Of course, nobody alive as recently as a thousand years ago had ever heard *any* unknown language. Unknown languages haven't existed for a long time.

"That would be the Fishbowl sighting in Winter's journal," I said.

"Correct."

"Lisle and Winter were on the faculty together at Oxnam University for several years, back in the 1850s. It's where they became friends. If there's a connection between Villanueva and the sightings, there's a good chance Winter would have mentioned it to Lisle."

"Where does he live?"

"Shen Chi. It's about a hundred klicks from Virginia Island."

"Where all the action is—"

"Seems that way."

"He going to call you back?"

"That's what he says."

"You want me to sit in?"

"Yes."

"Why?"

"In case he has privacy issues, it's always a good idea to have someone you can send out of the room."

In the end, we had to call *him*. *"Sorry,"* he told us. *"I forgot. Been busy."*

David Lisle bent under the weight of his years. He was, I suspected, close to his third century. His face was wrinkled, his voice a bit too loud, and he wore an uneven, scraggly gray beard. He was lowering himself carefully into a large armchair. His bleary gaze touched Alex, moved around the room, and settled on me. *"Who's the woman?"* he asked.

"Chase," Alex said, "this is Professor Lisle. Professor, this is Chase Kolpath. She's my partner."

He studied me intently, considering, I thought, whether he wanted me present. Eventually, he must have decided I did not constitute a threat. *"You're extraordinarily lovely, my dear,"* he said. His eyes didn't leave me as he addressed Alex: *"Had I known about Ms. Kolpath, I'd have preferred that you come in person."*

"Thank you, Professor," I said. "You're very kind."

He started to smile but slipped into a spasm of coughing and choking as if he'd just swallowed something.

"Are you okay?" asked Alex.

It was that strange inclination we all have to ask someone who's choking to speak to us. Lisle gradually got control of himself, held out a palm, and nodded. *"Sorry,"* he said. *"I have a couple of allergies that show themselves at this time of year."* He took a deep breath and cleared his throat. Then: *"Now, what was it we were talking about earlier, Joseph?"*

"*Alex*, Professor. My name is *Alex*."

*"Oh, yes. Sorry."* He pressed his fingertips against his temple. *"The years are getting to me, I fear. So how can I help you?"*

"We were talking about your old friend William Winter."

*"Oh, yes. Bill. Hard to believe it's been as long as it has."*

"You miss him?"

*"Yes, indeed. By God, there was no one like him. Died too early."*

"What happened to him, do you know?"

*"Only what's been reported. He went out on a mission of some sort, though God knows what it was, and he never came back. He was with Christopher Robin."*

"They went looking for something to do with the space-station sightings?"

*"What?"* He held a hand behind one ear, inviting Alex to speak louder.

"Did they go looking for what was causing the sightings at the space stations, Professor?"

That set him off on a long round of laughter that ended in another spasm. He fought his way through it and finally raised his palm again, assuring us he was okay, inviting us to be patient. *"Sightings? Lights in the sky? Yes, certainly, that was what he wanted to find. Look for these strange things that come and go, whatever they are. And what he found was his own exit."*

"What exactly *were* they looking for, Professor?"

*"I don't know what he expected to find. He didn't want to discuss it."*

"Why not?"

*"I think because whatever it was, he was concerned it would be perceived as silly."*

"Do you know where they went?"

Lisle hesitated. Bit his lip.

"They didn't go to Indikar, did they?"

*"You know that?"*

"Yes, we know. Was it Villanueva? Was that where they went?"

He needn't have said anything. His reaction gave it away. Eyes closed, regret written large on those gray features, wiping his mouth with the back of his hand.

"Why, Professor? Why did they go to Villanueva?"

*"God help me, Joseph, I don't know."*

"No idea at all?"

*"He told me he'd bring it all home with him. And we'd go out and celebrate together. That's what he said."*

"Professor, you must have had *some* idea why they went there."

*"Only that it had to do with the contact flights."*

"The unidentified ships."

*"Yes."*

"What precisely did he say?"

*"Alex, it's been almost half a century. Or has it been longer? The years pass so quickly."* He was hurting. Whether it was physical or not, I couldn't tell. *"I remember asking Robin later, after Bill had been lost, what it had been about. He wouldn't say. Still wouldn't tell me, damn him. I lost a good friend. But he just shook his head, told me I wouldn't believe it anyway, and walked away."* He looked exhausted. *"There was something else, though, now that I think of it. Something Bill said before they left."*

"What was that, Professor?"

*"He said that, with luck, they'd find it in the churches."*

"Find *what*?"

*"I don't know."* He sank back exhausted in his chair. *"When I asked him to explain, he just laughed and said there'd be plenty of time for that later. Sure there was."* His teeth clamped together, and he sucked in air. *"I told him not to go. I kept telling him what might happen. But he was determined to do it."*

"Churches." Alex tasted the word. Frowned. "He said *churches*. Not *church*."

*"That's correct."* He shook his head. *"God knows what he was talking about."* Lisle never cracked a smile.

Villanueva was reportedly a beautiful world, stable climate, gravity index almost exactly that of the home world, fertile land, a biosystem that was quick to adapt to human needs. According to legend, it was where the first off-world lemon tree sprouted. It had served as a home to human pets. Cats and dogs and parrots all did well there. The planet had a moon even lovelier than Earth's because it had an atmosphere and consequently emitted a softer, more luxuriant glow than Luna. Its broad oceans and deep forests and snowcapped mountains reportedly won the hearts of visitors. It was an ideal outpost. But its prospects as a colony world were dim.

When the first survey ships arrived, during the third millennium, they were probably already aware of the dust cloud. Tradition denies it, though, picturing a scenario in which the explorers landed in a peaceful green valley, bathed in its crystal springs, listened to the wind in the trees, and partied under its luminous moon, only to discover, later, that the world was moving toward destruction at a rate of about twenty million kilometers per day. It would be a long time before it arrived in the danger zone. Centuries. But eventually the bright skies would darken, and the flowers and shrubs would freeze into stumps. Meanwhile, though, the world was an Eden. And it must have seemed to a few early adventurers that there was more than time enough. Time to live out their lives, time for their children, and their grandchildren. They needed only avoid creating a permanent presence.

They named the place Villanueva because it was Earth as everybody had always dreamed it should be. A magnificent garden world, where the day was always cool, and the birds always sang. So they did what anyone would have done: Despite the cloud, they built homes. Villanueva became the place where you stopped if you were headed out along the Orion Arm, where people climbed out of the crowded spartan ships of that primitive era for a few days in the tropical breezes of the world that everybody loved.

They set a space station in place and named it Felicity. It became a haven for casinos and sex clubs. The support facilities on the ground expanded. And expanded again. People moved in. The cloud was too far down the road to worry about.

Towns took root. The towns became cities. Population soared. Young families saw it as an opportunity to get in on a ground floor, or as an adventure, or as an ideal place to raise kids. A thousand years, eight hundred years, whatever, it was a long time. Somebody else's problem.

Estimates range widely as to what the global population was when it finally happened. Most historians put it at about a billion. By then, Villanueva had become fully independent, and prosperous beyond anyone's dreams. Even when the outer planets began to drift into the cloud, the population, which everyone had expected would shrink dramatically at that point, continued to increase. The skies grew dark, and the days became cooler, but there was still no concerted effort to leave. The reports indicated that people thought they could ride it out. Stay with their homes and just wait for the passage to end. Trust in the Lord. This, even though Villanueva's time in the cloud would be in excess of three hundred years.

Today, the word itself, *Villanueva*, is shorthand for *catastrophe*.

Felicity, encountering too much resistance from the dust, lost her orbital velocity and went into a death spiral. It plunged into one of the oceans. People at that time still depended on farming, but the farms didn't survive. Eventually, they tried to escape, but it was much too late. Emergency supplies and equipment were shipped in. When, three centuries later, the world came out of the cloud—a small one, by cosmic standards—no one was left.

And something odd had happened: Civilization on the world had been high-tech, of course, by the standards of the time. It had been powered by the most advanced kinds of automated systems then known. From today's point of view, of course, they were primitive. But that may have played in their favor. They were simpler, and therefore more resistant to the pressures imposed by deteriorating climatic conditions. So that it's not entirely correct to say that no one was alive when the world emerged from the far side of the cloud.

The technology was still in place and still functioning. The maintenance systems had, according to contemporary accounts, upgraded themselves. The problem, as Marcy Lee observes in *Last Days*, was that nobody thought to turn off the lights.

I know that doesn't sound like a problem. But a salvage team, sent in after the event, encountered resistance of an unexpected kind. The technology, apparently, didn't want to be shut down. Several people were electrocuted, and a technician died when a power train broke loose and fell on him. The "accident" was reportedly accompanied by a spoken warning, over the comm links belonging to the team, that they were trespassing and should leave immediately.

Later efforts met with similar results. Stories surfaced of would-be scavengers landing on Villanueva and either becoming the victims of seeming accidents or disappearing altogether. A team sent in to destroy the data-control system was locked in an underground chamber. When they attempted to blow a hole in the door, the place collapsed on them. It was all straight out of one of Vicki Greene's horror novels. Eventually, the authorities decided the rational course was to cordon the place off, and they did just that. Villanueva was declared out of bounds, and satellites were established warning travelers that any who went groundside did so at their own risk.

Even Alex, though he had no doubt that the right Villanuevan artifacts would bring good money, had never considered a salvage attempt.

When David Lisle signed off, Alex remained motionless in his chair, his arms folded, his eyes half-closed, lost in thought.

"Alex," I said, "we have no idea what we'd be looking for."

"The churches, Chase."

"Which means what? We're talking about a civilization which, from its very beginning, knew the end times were coming. Knew *when* they were coming. When the place finally collapsed, they had a billion people. I wonder how many churches there were?"

He got up and walked over to the window. Lovely day. "Chase, I don't expect you to get involved with this one. In fact, I won't allow you to. I'm going to hire somebody for this. I'll find somebody who's got a little combat experience."

I laughed. There might have been a touch of bitterness there. If so, I'm not sure where it came from. That he was including me out, or that we were going to go off and do something crazy. "And who would that be?" I said. "Marko Banner?" The big devil-may-care leading man who specialized in whacking his way out of impossible situations.

"It's out of the question, Chase. Sorry."

"Alex, it's an exercise in futility."

"I know it seems that way. But I can't just give up on it. Something very big is going on here."

I let my head fall back and closed my eyes. "My God, Alex, you have no idea what you're even looking for."

# SIXTEEN

People always find something to worry about. The Nile's going to rise. An asteroid's coming close next year. We're going to make a mess of the atmosphere. It's always something. But sometimes they have a point.

—Marcy Lee, *Last Days*, ca. 6314 C.E.

Music is so intrinsically a part of the human experience, that it is hard to imagine our lives without it. How much are we indebted to the first person who beat on a drum, who carved out a pipe, who noticed that strings make pleasing sounds?

—Alois of Toxicon, addressing the Continental Music Institute, 8847 C.E.

I probably didn't help my cause by mentioning that if we were ever going to head out on an idiot's ride, Villanueva would be the place to go. There was no way Alex could back down after that. He was already going through a list of candidates to sit beside him on the mission. He'd need a pilot, of course. Not me, because I'd cause too much trouble. He didn't offer an explanation but just tried to laugh it off. "The bottom line, Chase," he said, "is that if things go wrong, I wouldn't want to be responsible for something happening to you."

And, to tell the truth, I'd have been happy to stay out of it. But I was afraid he'd get himself killed. "Look, Alex," I said. "I think this is crazy. I won't hide that. Because we don't have enough to go on. We don't have a clue what we're looking for.

But that doesn't mean I'll step aside while someone else goes in my place."

He glanced at his calendar with the sort of expression that he uses to suggest I've forgotten who's boss. "Chase," he said, "you don't have a say in the matter."

"Sure I do. Leave me behind, and I won't be here when you get back."

He barely blinked. "Then you'll have to leave, Chase."

"This time, I won't come back."

He took his time about answering. We were in the conference room. "Look," he said, "this thing is just too dangerous."

"Then call it off. At least until we know what we're doing."

"How about if we put it off for a couple of days? Have you ever seen *The Firebird*?"

"Not really. They lost it forty years ago."

"No. I'm talking about Igor Stravinsky."

I'd heard the name. "The sculptor," I said.

"He was a composer."

"Sure. But no, I haven't. It's a ballet, isn't it?"

"Yes."

"I don't much care for ballets."

"Doesn't it strike you as odd that Robin would give his yacht the same name?"

"As what?"

"The ballet."

"Oh." I guess I shrugged. "Not really."

His gaze went to the ceiling. He was operating in the company of children again. "Chase—"

"It's a coincidence."

"Father Everett told you he *loved* the classical composers. Naming his yacht *Firebird* was a tribute to Stravinsky."

"Okay. So what?"

"Maybe nothing. Maybe something more."

"How do you mean?" I looked at him. "You're not suggesting there's actually a point in going to watch this thing, are you?"

"They're performing at Central this weekend."

"Alex, I'm not anxious—"

"You'll love it," he said. "I'm taking Audree. There are two tickets on your link. If you'd like to come along."

*    *    *

Sometimes things just come together. I don't know whether we'd ever have gotten a handle on Robin and Villanueva had we not started with the dancers. The Central Theater, despite its name, is located on the oceanfront. I invited Hal Kaisson, an amateur musician and maybe the only guy I knew who would probably enjoy a nine-thousand-year-old ballet.

All right, I know what you're thinking. It just happens that I've no taste for ballet. But I told myself that the show must have had something going for it to stick around so long.

Alex asked me if I knew the story. I didn't really care that much and told him I'd figure it out as we went. "Ivan," he said, "is a Russian prince."

"What kind of prince?"

"Russia was an area, a country in northern Europe."

"Okay."

"Anyway, there's an immortal who lives in a forest. Kashchei. He doesn't like anybody else going there, and he gets upset when Ivan wanders in."

"Sounds pretty exciting so far."

I got that disapproving stare again. "All right. Let it go. I think you'll enjoy the music in any case."

It's not exactly *Hamlet*. But once it gets started, the music *is* pretty good, and the choreography blew me away. The forest is one of these enchanted places that is not only home to an immortal. Other supernatural creatures sway and flutter and cavort through the forest. One of these is the Firebird, which is apparently a demigod of some sort. It was portrayed that night by a dancer wearing red and gold when she wore anything at all. And when she moved across the stage, she seemed to do so in defiance of the laws of gravity. Ivan captures her but wisely relents and turns her loose. The Firebird responds by promising to help him if he needs help. Which, of course, he will.

The music, predominantly strings, was sometimes passionate, sometimes melancholy, always captivating. There were moments when it set my heart racing. All of it was familiar. It was just that I hadn't known this or that piece was from *The Firebird*.

Alex leaned over at one point and asked whether I was still feeling any reluctance about the show.

"It's okay," I said.

He laughed.

As he travels through the forest, Ivan discovers thirteen princesses held captive by Kashchei. He falls in love with one and asks Kashchei to free her. (Apparently he's prepared to allow the others to remain where they are.)

Kashchei resists, and the inevitable conflict begins. The other magical creatures are called in to support their lord, and it's clear from the outset that Ivan has no chance. But the Firebird comes to the rescue and, honoring her word, drives the music so powerfully that Kashchei and his creatures are forced to dance until they are exhausted and fall asleep.

The Firebird now reveals the secret of Kashchei's immortality, an enormous but fragile egg that contains his spirit. Kashchei awakens, and he engages Ivan in a spectacular, largely airborne, duel. The music rises to a crescendo, and, finally, the prince breaks through the desperate thrusts of his opponent and drives his sword into the egg.

Kashchei crumples.

And Ivan is alone onstage. The magical creatures that had lived under the sway of their lord are gone. The princess for whom Ivan had fought appears, and the two embrace. In the final moments, as the music changes tempo, the Firebird appears again, to signal her acquiescence to the union. She is visible only to the audience. Then she, too, is gone, and the curtain comes down.

The applause shook the building.

"So what did you think?" Alex asked.

"Okay," I said. "It was a good show."

Audree, who spends much of her spare time with an amateur theatrical group, thought the staging was excellent. Alex commented that the woman playing the Firebird had been outstanding—and, of course, we all knew why that was—and Hal observed that yes, it was quite good, but that Stravinsky can't hold a candle to Rimsky-Korsakov.

In the morning, back at the country house, I asked Alex if he'd seen anything that might connect with Robin. We were seated outside, on the deck. It was another pleasant day, with a cool breeze coming off the river.

"I have an idea," he said.

"And that is—?"

"The firebird is a phoenix, Chase. You already know that, right?"

"Not really."

"It is."

"So why does that matter?"

"You know what the phoenix is famous for?"

"Umm. Not really."

"You can't kill it."

# SEVENTEEN

That saddest, most dismal, most unfortunate of places, Villanueva.

—Inga Yassuf, *The Great Migration*, 3916 C.E.

The flight to Villanueva took five days. Alex spent most of his time with Belle, going over biographical sketches, records, histories, myths, everything he could find that was associated with that misbegotten world. He scanned some of the better-known contemporary novels that used it as a setting, *Night Music*, *The Long Winter*—some irony there—*Delia Parva*, *Alone with Uncle Harry*, and a dozen more. Alex commented that they inevitably covered the same ground: Always, a scientist, assisted by the hero, was trying to warn the world. It was played as if nobody knew what was coming. In reality, of course, everyone knew. They knew what the results would be, and they knew generally when it would start. Nevertheless, they stayed.

It was, on the whole, depressing stuff. I got away from it by watching some of Haylie Patterson's *Spotlight* shows. Haylie was a tough journalist who masqueraded as a comedian. He was extraordinarily popular then, as he is now. He brought political types in for interviews, poked fun at them, and cheered them on. The benefit for those who appeared was major public exposure. It seemed as if everybody in the Confederacy loved watching Haylie pretending to take his guests seriously.

The downside for the guests was that they got laughed at. Alex had declined appearing when he'd been invited. When

I'd asked why, he told me because he had no sense of humor.
I think he meant Haylie.

However that might be, Belle understood about laughter.
She assembled a fictitious *Spotlight* in which Alex made an
appearance. She had the voices and mannerisms of both Haylie and Alex down cold.

**Haylie:**  So the Mutes really can get inside your head?

**Alex:**  Oh, yes. They know everything you're thinking.

**Haylie:**  (looking embarrassed) *Everything?*

**Alex:**  Can't hide a thing.

**Haylie:**  My God, Alex. Do they have marriage over
there?

**Alex:**  Sure. It's okay, Haylie. Their females are
open-minded.

(Both laugh.)

**Haylie:**  Them, too, huh?

Seen from a distance, Villanueva might have been Earth. Or
Rimway. Sprawling continents, a vast global ocean, ice caps
at the poles. Big forests, mountain chains, a few deserts. A
beautiful world as long as you didn't get too close, as somebody once said. Not a place to spend the weekend.

Belle was running images from *God and the New World*, a
religious history of the first four centuries on Villanueva.
She'd put a city on-screen, located at the confluence of two
rivers. Endless rows of houses spread out in all directions.
Here and there were more ambitious structures. Skyscrapers,
places with domes, skywalks. She focused finally on a church
made of gray stone, surrounded by private homes with land-
scaped gardens. The church had a tower topped by a cross.
Near the front, an angel with a sword stood guard.

*"St. Michael, I believe,"* Belle said.

Villanueva became the first major off-world home for the three
biblical religions. Its inhabitants knew from their first day that

their time was limited, that there could be no permanent settlement. Though undoubtedly, because the coming destruction was so far away, beyond not only their own lives, but those of their distant descendants, the effect was muted. Possibly it did not exist at all. In any case, the general assumption that those who brought a religious worldview with them would hold on to the old dogmatism turned out to be off the mark. Instead, they acquired, along with a more compelling grasp of the sheer size and subtlety of the universe, a belief that a creating deity *had* to be much more complex, and ultimately less judgmental of minor offenses, than the one in whom their parents had believed. What came to matter most was their conviction that God existed, that, as some said, He was an engineer with remarkable talent, and that they were expected to take notice of that creation. Faith acquired a new immediacy and became for many the link with everything that mattered. The old animosities between faiths that had so despoiled life on the home world withered and, for the most part, died.

The believers experienced a coming-together unique in their history. They retained the traditional rituals, but they were more inclined to notice the stars in the night sky, and to do what they could to ease the lives of those around them. Take care of those in need, the mantra ran, and the Lord will take care of you. Gradually, they acquired a sense that salvation was for all persons of goodwill. For many, religion had finally become what the founders and prophets had intended. They were all heaven-bound, and they were enjoying the ride.

Heaven-bound. The churches were perceived as launching stations. The pictures in the record displayed their favorite symbols: statues of angels collecting children in their arms prior to soaring into the heavens, other angels in full flight. Heaven-bound.

There was a grim irony, of course, that in the end they were destroyed by the cosmic machinery they so much admired.

As we drew closer, Belle locked the scopes on the world, and we looked down on cities and highways and bridges. It was an incredible sight. Had I not known better, I'd have thought we were back approaching Rimway.

We'd known before setting out that Villanueva was

remarkably well maintained. Its facilities, directed by AIs, were still operating. They had continued to function after the last human was no more than a distant memory. The AIs replaced crumbling houses, restored port facilities, and maintained parks. Automated vehicles moved through the streets and through the skies.

We went into orbit and slipped over to the nightside, where, even though we knew what was coming, we received a shock. The lights were on. Everywhere. In cities, scattered around the countryside, lining riverbanks. Other lights moved through the streets and the sky. And there was a biological pulse to them. Where it was late, middle of the night, the moving lights dwindled to a few. And the houses were mostly dark, as though the inhabitants were asleep.

"It doesn't seem to need us, does it?" said Alex.

Villanueva's misty moon floated overhead. White clouds drifted serenely in the lunar skies. The moon was big enough that the system could have been described without too much exaggeration as a double planet.

Belle broke the mood. *"Incoming transmission, Chase."*

"Put it on."

*"Belle-Marie,"* a male voice said, *"welcome to Villanueva."* The speaker sounded businesslike, official, pay attention, I don't want to have to repeat myself. *"This is Highgate."*

Highgate was the automated monitoring system in orbit around the planet. I'd been expecting to hear from it. Still, it startled me. "Yes, Highgate. What is it?"

*"Be advised that you are in a hazardous area. It is highly recommended that you do not attempt to set down."*

Highgate's purpose was simply to keep an eye on things. To warn off idle travelers. To report back any unusual activity. Or any unanticipated technological advances on the world below. I wondered what they were worried about. Maybe that the machines might launch an invasion fleet to take out the Confederacy?

Okay. I'm kidding. But there are people out there who worry, who insist, you can't trust independent AIs, especially ones who've been left to disintegrate, or evolve, or whatever the case may be, on a world no one wanted to think about. Disconnecting the power sats has been an on-again, off-again issue in Rimway elections for centuries. "I was under the impression that an AI loses function after two or three centuries," I told Alex. "How can they still be working out here after all this time?"

He shrugged. No idea. And he didn't really care about the details.

*"I suspect,"* said Belle, *"that some of the AIs have banded together in a worldwide network. Even though no one remains, they continue to operate by whatever protocols they were assigned. Although those may have evolved somewhat."*

Highgate has been out there for as long as anyone can remember. In some eras, it's carried a team of scientists; at other times, like the present, it's been only an AI. And yes, if we can't trust the AIs on Villanueva, what makes us think we can trust one orbiting their neighborhood? I put that question to Belle. *"Matter of faith,"* she said.

I switched back to the satellite. "We read you, Highgate. Thanks for the warning."

*"Can I take that as a commitment that you will not attempt a landing?"*

"We haven't decided yet."

*"If you do make the effort to go down, be advised that, should you need assistance, none is available. I urge you to forgo any effort along these lines. It is extremely dangerous. Your reasonable course, when you have completed sightseeing from orbit, is to depart immediately."*

"Highgate, what's the nature of the danger?"

*"An active mechanical culture exists on Villanueva. All visitors are unwelcome. If you proceed into the atmosphere—note that it is not necessary for you to actually land—you will be perceived by them as a danger, and you may be assured they will take steps against you. If that occurs, you bear all responsibility for the outcome."*

When we filed our flight plan at Skydeck, we'd been forced to sit through a presentation that suggested we go elsewhere, and when we declined, required to sign statements that we'd been warned, and that we absolved the space station, the flight administration, the government, and anyone else in sight, of any liability.

"Highgate," I said, "do you maintain records of warnings? Can you tell me whether one was issued to the *Breakwater* in the Rimway year 1383? The pilot would have been Eliot Cermak."

*"Belle-Marie, that information is privileged."*

"It's important. Cermak would have been carrying two passengers, one of whom we think died here. It is imperative that—"

*"Are you claiming official authority? Are you a police unit?"*

"Yes, we are," said Alex. "G.B.I. Rimway."

*"Please file appropriate authorization."*

"Authorization should have been presented directly from Skydeck Operations. Did you not receive it?"

*"Negative. Please submit as required."*

Well, we got nowhere with that. Highgate issued a warning that we were in violation of something or other, and it would be reported, and we could expect to answer some questions when we got home.

We looked down on the lights. Some were apparently cruising along roadways, drifting through the skies, and even afloat at sea. Every continent appeared occupied. Islands glowed in the night. Only the polar caps were dark. It was a disquieting experience. "If this place is as dangerous as they claim," I said, "why don't we just shut it down?"

Alex appeared as overwhelmed by it all as I was. "How would you go about doing that, Chase?"

"It's easy. I'd cut off the power." Two collectors in geosynchronous orbit used lasers to relay solar energy to an array of power sats, which then sent it on to ground stations. The Villanueva AIs had lost the capability to maintain them thousands of years ago. But Earth had taken over, and later the Alliance. As political realities evolved and changed, the responsibility was passed on. The Confederacy is doing it today. It was a thread that bound the human race to its very beginnings. One of the power sats floated in the middle of the display. There'd been power sats from the beginning, but they'd been replaced many times.

"There are ethical considerations," Alex said.

"How do you mean?"

"For one thing, nobody's positive the place is really empty."

"I can't see that there'd be any problem with getting on the radio and asking if there's anyone down there."

"Maybe there are people who don't have access to a radio. Who wouldn't know one if they did. Even if there aren't any people, how do you feel about killing off AIs?"

"We do it all the time." And yes, I knew Belle was listening, but I reminded myself she's a data-storage system. She's not really *alive*, though sometimes it seemed that way.

"A lot of people don't go along with that, Chase. Killing off a world full of AIs that are doing no damage would create some political problems."

"I guess. We certainly don't want political problems."

We crossed the terminator and moved back into sunlight.

Belle put up more pictures, some taken recently by Highgate, others so old the dates had been lost. Most of the one-time population centers were especially well maintained. The few that weren't had been overtaken by desert, jungle, or forest. The appearance of the cities had changed with the passage of time, but not in the sense that they were decaying. Towers grew wider and acquired a more sculpted look, then became taller and sleeker, discarding ornamentation, then devolved into what appeared to me, anyhow, as bulbous horrors. The cities themselves sometimes expanded in concise geometric patterns, and sometimes spread out with uninhibited energy. Even walkways seemed to shift patterns, moving with geometric uniformity through the downtown areas of one age, gracefully arcing around buildings and natural obstacles in another, and still later using tunnels and bridges to arrow through everything that stood in the way. Even though the parks and roads and city streets and beaches, most of all the beaches, were empty, it was impossible to believe that a living civilization did not exist on that world.

"I'm not excited about going down there," I said. I'd promised myself that I wouldn't raise any more objections. In fact, it was part of the deal. But it slipped out.

"I agree," said Alex. "We'll be careful." It was delivered as a promise but one we both knew he wouldn't be able to keep. It wasn't hard to imagine Chris Robin saying much the same thing to Bill Winter.

He was studying the displays. Belle was focusing on the

churches. "When we get on the ground, I think it would be a good idea if you stay in the lander. No matter what."

*Oh God. Here we go again.* "Alex," I said, "you know damned well that isn't going to happen."

His face hardened. "Then you'll wait in the ship."

"While *you* take the lander down?"

"That's what AIs are for. I don't need a pilot."

"You will if there's a problem. If a storm blows up, or you get hit by lightning, it'll be all over, baby."

"There's not much chance of that. We'll go down in broad daylight under clear skies."

"Alex—"

"Look, Chase. We've been all over this. Whatever else happens, we don't want both of us disappearing into this god-forsaken place."

The scopes had picked up a small country road, winding through open fields and patches of forest. An open-top car moved along at a leisurely pace. The seats were empty, but I could see a steering wheel turning gently.

The entire world was haunted.

Alex was standing behind me, watching the same image. "I'm sorry I got you into this, Chase."

"It's not a problem. I'll just wait in the lander while some local giant bat has you for dinner."

# EIGHTEEN

A valley that offers true solitude can provide an exhilarating experience for the soul. Just don't go in there alone.

—Marik Kloestner, *Diaries*, 1388

If the number of churches, mosques, synagogues, and other places of worship visible along the streets and in the country-side signified anything, Villanueva had been, as advertised, a bastion of faith. The churches were of a multiplicity of types, from giant cathedrals anchored in the centers of large cities to small country chapels out on the plains. Sometimes the architecture was ornate, in the old Gothic style that has character-ized Christianity almost since its inception eleven thousand years ago; sometimes it was eclectic; sometimes it was un-affected and modest.

We spent the first two days taking pictures and hoping to find something through the scopes that would, somehow, imply a connection with Chris Robin. That approach pro-duced nothing. If there was something down there, we were not likely to see it because the sheer number of churches was overwhelming. We knew there'd be tens of thousands of them, of course, but that wasn't quite the same as actually *seeing* them.

We had no idea how to categorize what we were looking at. Big churches, little churches, isolated churches, churches with cemeteries, churches with angels out front. What possible connection could there be with Winter's list of sightings?

"Maybe it started here," said Alex. "Maybe this was where

the first sighting occurred. Maybe someone knew what caused it."

"But how could something like that be connected with a church?"

"Not *a* church, Chase. *The churches*. Lisle used the plural."

"Which means what?"

"That it's not a record. At least not in the sense of a formal document. It's something else."

"All right. I have another question."

"I'm listening."

"Assume you're right. Say it's some sort of historical place. Maybe the church members got together and set up some memorials. Or *something*. How would Robin and Winter have known to come here?"

"I doubt Robin was here previously. And we can be reasonably sure that Winter was never here. That means they saw something in the history of the place."

"Whatever it might have been, *I* didn't see it."

"We may not have recognized it if we did. That's what's so frustrating, Chase. I've been hunting through everything I can find on Villanueva and its churches. There *has* to be something. It's probably best for us to stop theorizing and just keep our eyes open."

Eventually, Alex picked out a small church standing on the edge of a town in a prairie. There were no trees, the vegetation was sparse, and the ground was, aside from some low hills in the east, absolutely flat. Which was why he'd selected it. We'd have good visibility all around, so nothing could come up on us unseen. There was, he admitted, no *other* reason. "Let's just go down and look," he said.

We climbed into the lander and launched. On the way down, we got another warning from Highgate. You are directed to cease and desist. Reports are being filed. Legal action may be taken. If you survive. And finally, *"You are on your own."*

We rode down through pleasant, quiet skies, and descended into a field just east of the church, where we had a good view of the front doors. The grass was out of control, and there was a wooden fence that could have used some paint. Otherwise, the place appeared in remarkably good condition.

Gravity and oxygen content were ideal. It was a beautiful

day, early afternoon. I'd just shut off the engines when a movement caught my eye, and we both turned to watch a four-legged creature with a long snout and wrinkled skin scramble off into the grass.

Alex released his harness and opened the door. Birds were making a lot of noise. "Okay," he said. "Sit tight. I'll be back in a few minutes."

I looked at the church and the green fields and listened to the wind. If I tried to get out with him, I knew that it would just provoke another argument. In the end he'd say no, no way, you're going to keep your word, and he'd stand there refusing to move until I promised him again, for real this time, that I would do what I was told. There was no need to go through all that. So I stayed in my seat and asked him to be careful.

He climbed out, dropped to the ground, checked to be sure he had the pulser he'd brought along. Then he started toward the church, walking through thick grass. When he got to the front, he paused, looked around, and climbed three wooden steps onto the deck.

The church was constructed of white plastene boards. It had a few big stained-glass windows and two large, carved doors. There was no steeple, but a white cross had been mounted on the roof immediately above the front entrance. A dozen or so headstones occupied a small tract of land off to one side. They were worn down by the weather.

A sign stood in front with several lines of unfamiliar symbols. It was leaning toward the skimmer and looked ready to collapse. I asked Gabe, the lander AI, if he could read it.

*"It's Kabotai,"* he said, over the link. *"It was one of the terrestrial languages seven thousand years ago. Do you wish to know what it says?"*

"Yes, Gabe, if you will."

*"One moment, please."*

Alex paused in front of the doors and turned to survey the town. It consisted of about sixty buildings, most of which would have been private homes. A three-story structure rose over the rest, a public hall of some sort. The church faced out on a park. Again, the grass was unkempt, but the benches were in good shape, as well as an overhang that would have protected visitors from the sun. Behind the overhang was a small white building that had probably provided washrooms.

*"Chase,"* said Gabe, *"it says what time the Sunday service is. And also: 'Enter here. A special friend awaits you inside.'* Friend *is capitalized, suggesting it is a reference to the Deity."*

It sent a chill through me.

The sun was directly overhead. Except for the grass, and the fact that the only sound we could hear was the wind, the town *looked* occupied. It was as if we'd simply arrived when everyone was off visiting somewhere. I kept waiting for a door to open. For a dog to bark. Even Alex, who is usually pretty composed in tense situations, looked uneasy. "St. Monica's," I said, over the link.

*"Pardon?"*

"St. Monica's. It should have a name." I climbed out of the lander.

He looked sternly at me. "Chase."

"I can't just sit in there, Alex. Let's try being reasonable."

"Okay. Do what you want. But don't get yourself killed." He reached for the doorknob. Turned it. Looked back at me. "Was that where you went to church?"

"No. But *Monica* suggests congeniality. Warmth."

"This place could use some."

"Couldn't we all?"

He pulled on the door. Something clicked, and it opened. He slipped inside.

I followed immediately behind. In the entryway, a light came on.

The interior had a high ceiling. The sun shone lazily through a series of arched windows. They were narrow but reached from about knee-high well up into the overhead. They were brightly painted, with images of prophets, angels, and saints.

Holy-water fonts stood just inside the doors, and I was shocked to discover they held *water.* Benches were arranged on either side of a central aisle, and an altar dominated the front, with a pulpit placed off to one side. Directly above us was a gallery for the choir. Statues of Jesus and Mary, of St. Joseph, an angel, and three or four figures with halos, were distributed around the interior. One of them, a young woman, had clasped her hands in prayer. "St. Monica," I said.

"Probably Mary Magdalene," said Alex. "I've never seen anything like this. How can this place be thousands of years old?"

"Regular maintenance does it every time."

The altar appeared to be white marble, but it was actually just plastene. A cloth was spread across it. Two candles and a large cup that might have been gold rested on it. Had the candles been lit, I think I'd have started seriously suspecting a divine presence.

We walked up the aisle and stopped in front of the railing that separated the altar from the rest of the interior. "We're probably the first people to come in here in thousands of years," Alex said. "It's a beautiful chalice."

"It is."

"I can't help thinking that it would bring a decent price on the market."

I probably winced. "I was thinking the same thing."

"You don't approve."

"No."

"Why not? I can't see that anyone would be hurt."

"I think we should pass on this one."

"Why?"

"Alex, let's not lose our focus on why we came here."

"Your religious background is showing."

"I don't really have much of a religious background. But it just doesn't feel right."

"Okay," he said. He turned away from it and walked toward the statue of Jesus. "You owe me one."

"Okay."

He touched the statue. "This is quite nice also."

"Alex, this is different from what we're accustomed to. If this church were a ruin, and the statue was buried under a ton of debris, I'd have no qualms about taking it. But *this*—" I looked around at the benches, the stained-glass windows, the altar. "Colter and his crowd are always accusing you of looting. Take anything out of this place, and I think they'd have a valid argument."

"You're becoming difficult to work with, Chase."

"Okay. Try this: It won't fit in the lander."

I wasn't feeding images back to Gabe. I'm not sure why. Gabe tends to ask a lot of questions, and I didn't particularly want to be carrying on a conversation with him. But he was annoyed that he didn't know what was going on. He informed me every few minutes that there was *"no visible movement anywhere,"* trying to lure me into a conversation.

*"What do you think, Chase?"* he said. And, *"Have you seen anything of interest?"*

"Negative, Gabe. I'll let you know if we find anything."

*"I've never understood about religion. Why do people think that a transcendent being would care about having people sit in pews and sing hymns to him?"*

"Later, Gabe," I said.

Eventually, we gave up and went back outside. Alex turned and gazed at the church. "Well," he said, "I don't guess that helped much."

And we got Gabe again: *"Approaching aircraft."*

"How far away?"

*"It'll be here in about six minutes."*

We hustled back to the lander, got in, and lifted off. The oncoming vehicle didn't look like anything I'd seen before. It was the size and bulk of a small cargo transport. It had big wings and no antigrav technology. It was coming from the east. "Gabe," I said, "go to two-four-zero, kick in at three-quarters, and let's take her up."

The aircraft came out of a line of hills. It appeared to be tracking us. Our lander wasn't particularly noted for its acceleration capabilities, so I held my breath as we swung around to the southwest and went to flank speed. The transport was closing quickly.

*"If that is the best it can do,"* said Gabe, *"we should have no problem."*

It wasn't, and for a few minutes it was touch and go. But gradually, we cut the rate by which they were closing, then we began to pull ahead.

*"Skies are clear everywhere else,"* said Gabe. *"We are running at six hundred twenty knots."*

I turned to Alex. "We want to go back to Belle?"

"Let's find another church."

# NINETEEN

A church, by definition, should be a place where one may discuss the matters of the day with his Creator. Unfortunately, too often there are others present, with a different agenda.

—Kory Tyler, *Musings*, 1312

We continued west in the lander, across the prairie. Then we were out over a broad blue lake. Alex sat in the right-hand seat, looking out through the wraparound, while simultaneously studying what we had of the ecclesiastical history of Villanueva. It wasn't much. Pictures of churches, monuments, spires, crosses, and chalices flickered across his display. Maps showed the locations of the Church of the Savior, and, near the coast, St. Agatha's. The Salvage Chapel, celebrated at one time though no one any longer knew precisely why, stood at the entrance to Bryce Canyon, which we passed at sundown.

Most of the structures depicted were either unidentified, or the identification had lost all meaning. Here was the Church of the Angels, located in a place whose name didn't appear on the maps. And there was a picture of a woman in red vestments, presumably a cardinal, whose name was Carassa, but about whom no other fact was known.

We went back to the *Belle-Marie* to recharge. It didn't make much sense to use the lander when the ship, with its scopes, provided as good a view. But Alex said something about wanting to get as close as possible, to be in a position to pursue anything of interest without having to wait. Again, the impatience was out of character, and he didn't seem inclined to offer a better explanation.

The argument for doing the search from the ship gained momentum when we flew into turbulent weather, but we stayed with the lander. I was able to get above the storm, and we were gaining on the sun, now high in the sky, but it made little difference: We'd lost sight of the ground. "It doesn't matter," Alex said. "If what we're looking for is really confined to a single church, we aren't going to find it anyhow."

Later, under clear skies, we passed over a construction site. Silver bots, some on legs, some incorporated into vehicles, moved across the ground with polished fluidity, hauling equipment, erecting walls, striding along girders several stories off the ground. One, a giant mechanical spider, was climbing a wall.

Not far from the construction site, we saw a church. There was nothing special about it. It looked like a hundred other churches we'd seen over the past few hours. A smaller building, probably a rectory, was attached. It dominated a neighborhood of attractive homes with wide lawns and picket fences. (The lawns were overgrown. The AIs apparently hadn't been charged with looking after yard work, other than possibly clearing fallen branches.) "Let's take a look at it," said Alex.

"Any particular reason?" I asked.

"I like the angel."

The angel was a sculpture near the front doors. It was a female figure, its wings spread in full flight. It lent an air of majesty to the church.

The church had an old-style Gothic design, and was maybe four stories high, with gray stone walls. A bell tower rose at one corner. A large cross, set at the peak of a sharply slanted roof, looked out across a modest avenue lined by trees. A car was passing.

A large rectangular building, constructed in the same style, stood on the other side of the avenue. A church school, probably. Lettering was engraved across its entrance. Probably St. Mark's or some such. Private homes, all apparently in good condition, surrounded the complex on three sides. Behind the church, and the homes, dense forest stretched to the horizon.

A small feline creature sat placidly in front of the school. Large birds nested along the rooftops. And music was coming from somewhere. It had no discernible rhythm, just noise, instruments I didn't recognize.

We were still getting a lot of wind. Antigrav vehicles are notoriously vulnerable to high winds, so I was careful going down. "Behind the church," said Alex, "where we're not so visible."

There was open space between the church and the forest. A large granite cross rose from the overgrown soil. It was, I thought, a gravesite. But if there was a stone base with an inscription, it had long ago been buried.

We settled into the thick grass. I opened the hatch, and we sat for a minute, listening to the wind and the buzz of insects, waiting to see if we'd attracted any attention. But nothing came rolling in our direction.

Alex cleared his throat. "Ready?" he asked.

We got out. There was some rain in the air, but not much more than a sprinkle. I dropped down onto the ground. A car moved past on one of the side streets. It had flared tailfins and looked unlike anything I'd ever seen at home. It was automated, of course. Empty.

Before I'd taken more than a few steps, two trucks rumbled by out front. We hustled around to the side of the church so we could see. They were going in different directions. One had an open bed filled with boards. The other was covered, but there was lettering on the side. I used my link to ask Gabe for a translation.

*"Toco Liquors,"* he said.

I looked at Alex. "AIs drink?"

"Maybe here they do."

"I don't get any of this," I said.

"I think what's happening, Chase, is that the controlling AI is simply continuing to do what it's always done. We might be seeing the resolution to the old debate about whether AIs are actually intelligent."

I heard a noise that sounded like air moving through a vent. It was the equivalent of Gabe clearing his throat. *"Alex,"* he said. *"Don't jump to a hasty conclusion. They may see no reason to break clear of their programing. It is what keeps them going in difficult times. Like people, if I may interject a thought of my own."*

We walked around to the front and stood admiring the angel. It was weather-beaten, and had probably never been consid-

ered exemplary sculpture. I suspected it had been cranked out
by some mass-marketing process. But somehow that didn't
matter. In that vast, empty place, it possessed a badly needed
nobility.

Like the sign at St. Monica's, it was tilted by the passage of
time and the erosion of the soil. There was something
heart-stopping in that angel, trying to soar above and beyond
all that desolation. "This one," I said, "would be worth making off with."

Alex smiled. "It would." There was a line of symbols
across its base. Three words. Badly worn, but still legible.

"Gabe," I said, "translation, please?"

He needed a moment. Then: "'*Going to Heaven.*'" And,
finally, "*No, I think 'Heaven-bound' more closely captures
the spirit of it.*"

I looked up at the large stone cross on the roof, standing
directly over the main entrance. Somehow, the architecture
suggested that everything emanated from that cross.

"Chase."

"What is it, Alex?"

"The car. Look." An automobile was slowing. It was a blue
four-door sedan, with its windows rolled down. It pulled
toward the curb, close to where we were standing, and
stopped.

The engine continued to run. A sudden gust of wind shook
the tree limbs.

We were in plain view from the car, so there wasn't much
point trying to hide. We walked toward it but halted a few
steps away. "*Hello,*" it said. And I froze: The thing was speaking Standard. "*May I offer you a ride?*" It had swept-back
headlights, and it looked comfortable.

"No, thanks." Alex backed away a step or two. "But it's
very kind of you to offer."

"*It is my pleasure.*"

"Who are you?" Alex asked.

"*A friend. It would please me to be of assistance if you will
allow it.*"

Alex glanced over his shoulder. A small truck was pulling
off the road, easing onto the grass. As we watched, it started
slowly toward the lander. I glanced at Alex, but he shook his
head. No way we could get back there without being inter-

cepted. "Gabe," Alex said, "get off the ground." Then he turned back to the car: "You speak Standard."

*"Of course. We would not expect any other language to be understood by a visitor."*

"How does it happen that you know the language?"

*"We have learned it from those who have come to spend time with us, of course."*

"I see. Do you have a name?"

*"You may call me Roam. And you are—?"*

The lander lifted off.

"My name is Alex. It's a pleasure to meet you, Roam."

*"And the lady?"*

"I'm Chase," I said.

Alex looked my way. Do not get any closer to the car. Don't get in front of it. Don't even get too close to the doors.

*"The pleasure is mutual. May I ask what brings you to Villanueva?"* Out of the corner of my eye, I watched Gabe pass over the roof of the church.

"We're admiring your churches," he said.

*"Why, yes, they are admirable, aren't they?"*

"Are there others that carry the same motif?"

*"Which motif is that?"*

"Heaven-bound."

*"Ah, yes, an objective we should all seek. Would that we could all find the road to Heaven."*

"Yes. Would that it were so." Alex looked at the angel, then back at the car. "It is something you seek?"

*"Indeed it is. It is something all right-thinking entities should aspire to."*

"We would like very much to tour other churches that have this same theme. Can you possibly tell us where we might find them?"

*"That would be a rather esoteric piece of information. I suspect it would be available at the office."*

"Which office is that?"

*"The Malcolm Library Data Center. You're in Malcolm, you know."*

"No, I wasn't aware of that."

*"Oh, yes. Malcolm is the cultural heart of the entire state. The Data Center is only a few minutes from here. If you'd like to go, I'll be happy to take you."* The back doors opened.

"Thanks. That's very generous of you. But we'd better pass. We're running late."

*"There'd be no problem coming back here. I'd bring you myself."*

"That's quite all right, Roam. But we appreciate the offer." The doors closed again. The car backed up and angled its front wheels toward us. "It's a beautiful day," Alex told the car. "Is the weather always this pleasant in Malcolm?" And without looking my way, he gave me a nod and formed a single word with his lips: *Go.*

We bolted for the church. Roam beeped a horn and jumped the curb. It plowed across the lawn and came after us.

The church was probably three times the size of St. Monica's, with three big double doors at the top of a set of stone steps. We charged past the angel and ran up the steps. Roam sideswiped the angel, smashing its right bumper. But it kept coming, bouncing up behind us, its bottom screeching against the stone.

Alex fired his pulser, and the engine exploded. The car veered to the right, came the rest of the way up, and crashed into the front of the building. The truck that had chased Gabe came around the corner, and two more vehicles, a gray two-door convertible and a small van, came in off the street.

Alex tried the church doors. The first wouldn't open, but one of the center ones swung out. "Yes, indeed," he said. "Welcome to Villanueva."

The door was heavy. As at St. Monica's, the hinges didn't squeal, and one would not have guessed that worshippers weren't coming in regularly. We slipped through and pushed the door shut behind us. All three sets of doors had bolts, which slid smoothly into place.

The church was big. The benches could have accommodated upward of a thousand people, which was considerably more than St. Monica's. I was surprised at first to see what appeared to be a pair of candles burning on the main altar— I thought maybe I'd spoken too soon about the divine presence—but they turned out to be electrical. A choir stall overlooked the rear pews, and above that, the overhead arched into a dome. Sunlight filtered through stained-glass windows that looked as if they'd been cleaned the day before.

Both walls contained alcoves. Several held statuary; others

contained small altars. Holy-water fonts stood at the back. As at Monica's, they were filled.

"Alex." I kept my voice down. "I think we can get out one of the side exits."

"This stuff is priceless, Chase."

"Alex—"

Someone, or some*thing*, began banging at the doors behind us.

Then I heard Gabe: *"More vehicles are arriving. Suggest you consider departure at earliest convenience."*

Alex took over: "Which exit do you suggest, Gabe?"

*"The truck has returned to the area where we touched down. It appears to be waiting there, on the west side. Two other cars are joining it as I speak. A van is now pulling up on the east side. There is also a small truck in the rear."*

"Is there an exit at the rear?"

*"Nothing that I can see. There does not appear to be a clear area anywhere at the moment where a pickup can be made safely."*

"What's happening out front?"

*"More vehicles are arriving. There are now four of them close to the angel. All are passenger cars. One is a small two-seater with no roof. It has climbed the steps, and I assume you can hear it trying to break through the door. I think you are safe for the moment, however, until something heavier arrives."*

Side exits flanked the altar. The one on the right also had an elevator and a marble staircase. Alex signaled me to follow, and we headed in that direction. "Gabe," he said, "we're going to take a look at the opposite side. On the east."

*"Okay, Alex."*

We heard another loud bang at the front door. But it seemed to be holding. "Gabe, be ready to move quickly. Are there any aircraft?"

*"Negative. I'm alone up here."*

We hurried to the front of the church, circled the altar rail, and stopped at the exit. I heard nothing outside the door. Alex twisted the knob, pushed, and it opened out. Three steps went down to a short walkway that led to the adjoining building. The rectory.

But nothing was moving. "Okay, Gabe," Alex said. "Come—"

Somewhere, out of sight, an engine roared to life. *"Heads up,"* said Gabe. *"It's in the rear."* It was a truck, and we heard it start moving. Gabe was descending quickly but he broke off as it rounded the corner and came into view. *"No chance,"* he said.

The truck bounced across the lawn, turning sharply in our direction.

Alex fired his pulser. The engine choked and died. The vehicle rolled over and lay with its wheels spinning.

*"More cars out front,"* said Gabe. *"And another one pulling around in the rear."*

"Can you land safely?"

*"Negative."*

We pulled back out of sight. I heard sirens from somewhere.

"Police?" asked Alex.

*"Two police cars and an ambulance. They're pulling onto the church grounds now."*

"Okay."

*"And the spider."*

"The what?"

*"The thing with the multiple legs from the construction site."*

"That's not good," Alex said. "Where is it now?"

*"Approximately seven and a half kilometers. But coming fast."*

"How long to get here, Gabe?"

*"I would say about six minutes."* He sounded worried. *"What are you going to do?"*

Alex looked across the front of the church, past the altar, to the other exit. "I don't think we can get out over there, either."

His gaze went back to the marble staircase. It went up and down. "Gabe," he said, "we have a stairway and an elevator on this side. Can you see where they lead?"

*"I can't actually see them, Alex, but they'd have to provide egress to the bell tower."*

"Alex," I said, "there's no way Gabe can do a pickup out of the tower. The wings won't let him get close enough. Unless we want to try some serious aerial acrobatics."

*"There's an exit directly onto the church roof,"* said Gabe.

"That's what we want. Come on," Alex said, "let's go."

*   *   *

They were still battering the doors at the front of the church.
I pushed a button for the elevator and it opened, but Alex
pulled me away. "We'll use the stairway," he said. "It's safer."

"Why not ride up?"

He tilted his head at the open elevator. "They might have
control of it. If we get in there, we might not be able to get out."

"You worry too much," I said.

We started up the stairs.

*"Alex,"* said Gabe. *"A large truck has arrived. It's unload-
ing smaller versions of the spider. Looks like about six of them."*

We climbed four or five flights. I'm not sure now. But we
reached a landing with a door and a shoulder-high, foot-wide
window covered by a dusty curtain. It looked out across the
roof. Alex released a bolt and tried to open the door, but it
wouldn't budge.

I got my cutter and he stood back to give me room. Below
us, we heard a loud bang and the sound of the doors splintering.

*"They're into the building,"* said Gabe. *"Bots."*

I started cutting.

"Okay," Alex said. "We'll be on the roof in a minute." The
lander was visible through the window. Coming down.

I heard a clicking sound at the bottom of the stairwell.
*"Hurry,"* said Gabe.

Alex looked uneasily down the stairs. "Gabe, what are we
dealing with here?"

*"The bots appear to be specialized for construction pur-
poses, so they may be equipped with lasers. I assume they can
rig explosives. A few are carrying what appear to be blunt
instruments. Most are on multiple limbs, but I see three or
four that are bipedal."*

"Gabe, can you tell whether they're directed by a single
source. Or—?"

*"They are part of a network, Alex. But they seem to be
individual intelligences."*

"Okay, Gabe. Thanks."

*"And the spider's here, too."* He flashed a picture of the
thing. It was striding in off the avenue and, as we watched, it
moved swiftly across the lawn among the cars and trucks to
the base of the church wall.

And it began to climb toward the cross.

# TWENTY

*In hoc signo vinces.*

> —Reportedly seen in the sky, along with a cross, by
> Constantine, prior to the battle of the Milvian Bridge

*"Hurry up,"* said Gabe. *"Quick!"*

I got the door loose, finally, opened it, and looked down the sloping roof toward the front of the church. A traffic jam had formed out on the street. We were close to the peak, in the shadow of the bell tower. Gabe was hovering just above the roof, as close as he could get.

*"It's here,"* Gabe said. *"Too late."*

A pair of grapplers, attached to tentacles, sailed over the edge of the roof, dropped, and took hold. Two stalks rose into view. Each held a flexible lens. An eye.

Alex shouted for me to move, simultaneously pushing me aside and stepping out with his pulser in one hand.

*"Get back inside,"* said Gabe. *"You don't have time."*

The thing clambered smoothly up onto the roof, long, flexible struts and golden lenses and more tentacles. A spade-shaped disk held everything together. Alex fired and one of the tentacles whipped toward us and wrapped around his arm. The pulser went flying. Alex yelped, then screamed at me to go back. It lifted him into the air.

Gabe roared forward, revving his engines, making all the noise he could—which wasn't much. Alex yelled something as he was hauled toward the edge of the roof. But Gabe's charge distracted the thing. I took a desperate swipe at the

tentacle with my cutter, got lucky, and sliced through it. Alex
came tumbling down. Gabe roared past, just out of its reach,
and began to circle back.

Alex half rolled, half scrambled to his feet. And while
Gabe continued to distract the thing, we stumbled back inside.
"For God's sake, Gabe," Alex said as we pushed the door shut,
"stay out of its reach."

"Alex," I said, "you okay?"

"Yes." He looked shaken.

"I'm glad to hear it. What do we do now?"

"Hide."

We slid the bolt back in place. Through the window, we
could see the spider standing quietly, watching the lander.
Gabe was gaining some altitude.

Alex looked around for a weapon and broke a long piece of
wood off the doorframe. I had my cutter.

*"Alex,"* Gabe said, *"you might want to warn them before
you go ahead with the plan."*

There were sounds at the bottom of the staircase. More
clicks. Starting up. Alex tightened his grip on the piece of
frame.

"What plan?" I said.

*Good idea.* He mouthed the words.

"What's a good idea?"

"Follow my lead."

"Alex, what's a good idea?"

He warned me off with a raised hand. No time for explanations. He spoke into the link: "Chase, I think we're trapped."

He held it in place for me to use. "I agree." Dumb, but it
was the best I could think of.

"I can't see that we have any choice now."

"Probably not."

"But even if we can't get out of here alive, we'll have to do
what we came here to do."

"Yes," I said.

The noises on the staircase were getting closer.

He covered the link. "Ask me why we're using the links."

"What?"

"Just do it. Ask me."

"Alex, why are we using the links?"

"Because, when we destroy this blasphemous temple,

Okar would not want us to destroy these unhappy infidels along with it. It's not entirely their fault that the darkness has fallen on them."

"Ah," I said. "Yes. We would not wish to see them mangled and burning after we blow this place to hell."

"It is behavior that is required of us. It is written in the book to give fair warning. That they may save themselves if they are so inclined."

I whispered: "What makes you think they're listening?"

"Right now, it's our best shot." His voice took on a note of resignation. "Chase, I'm sorry it's come to this. But we can't allow these acts of blasphemy to continue. We have no choice in the matter and we haven't much time."

"I know."

"They're coming up now. Take a moment to pray to Okar, to thank Him for all His gifts. And then we'll do it."

The sounds had reached the landing below us. Suddenly, they hesitated.

We looked at each other. Alex said nothing but mouthed the words, *Let's hope*.

"Alex?"

"Yes, Chase?"

"Good-bye. I've been proud to know you. You are a good and decent servant of the Lord."

Whatever was on the staircase started back down. Rapidly.

"You, too, Chase. Hand me the detonator."

Hearing them clear out was a joy that will stay with me forever. We couldn't see them, from our hideaway near the bell tower, but we could *hear* them, doors slamming, engines turning on, cars and trucks backing into others and scraping bumpers as they tried to turn around. Bots scrambling, running, stumbling out of the church, adding to the mayhem. Vehicles bounced into the streets without waiting for oncoming traffic. Brakes screeched, and cars plowed into one another.

It was magnificent.

We went out onto the roof and waited for Gabe to come back down. We'd been out there only a few seconds, and Gabe was still pretty high, when a bot followed us through the door. It was bipedal, made of black and red metal. It possessed a smaller version of the lenses we'd seen on the spider. *"You must think,"* it said, *"that we're all stupid."* Its right arm mutated into a cutting device with multiple blades. It started toward us. The arm was humming, and the blades began rotating.

I turned the cutter on it and the blade reddened and splattered. I caught a piece of it and I thought it was going to burn through my arm. Alex still held the broken doorframe. He stepped in and hammered the bot. It staggered backward, fell, and clattered down the slanted roof, with Alex right behind it. When it seemed on the verge of halting its slide, Alex kicked it over the side. Then everything was quiet, except for the hum of the antigravs in the approaching lander.

"Not all stupid," said Alex. "Just you."

"Brilliant, Gabe," said Alex, when we were on board and soaring toward the clouds.

*"Thank you, Alex."*

"I think you bailed us out," I said.

*"Yes."*

"That was a great idea."

*"I like to make a contribution when I can."*

# TWENTY-ONE

The road to Heaven is not a six-lane throughway. It is narrow, there are many curves, it skirts deep canyons, and in certain areas it is subject to flooding. There are potholes, and sometimes a fallen tree may block progress. But keep going. Do not forget that your obligation is not only to yourself but to those who travel with you, and to the strangers you will encounter along the way. Do these things, and you will surely get there. Keep your sense of humor, stop occasionally to listen to the wind in the trees, and to look at the river, and you may even find that you will enjoy the ride.

—Bobby Haywood, *Heaven-Bound*, 3211 c.e. (believed to be the sourcebook for the movement that became so popular on Villanueva)

*"I do* wish *you'd be more careful,"* said Gabe, as we gained altitude. *"I'm not sure where I'll be if you get yourselves killed."*

Alex nodded impatiently. "Later, Gabe. Chase, let me see your arm."

It was scorched. But not badly.

Alex got some aloevium and rubbed it into the burn. Then he wrapped it and admonished me to use more care. "You sound like Gabe," I said.

"I'm serious."

*"And I,"* said Gabe, *"am not happy."*

Alex didn't look as if he was in a mood to have this argument. "This isn't the first time we've had a problem," he said. "I haven't heard you complain before—"

*"Maybe I'm getting old. But I have the distinct impression you are becoming increasingly reckless. And when you put yourself at risk, you endanger not only me, but Chase as well."*

Alex glanced my way. I kept a straight face. "Okay," he said. "Maybe you have a point."

*"Of course I do. Please, in the future, exercise some care."* Somewhere, back in his relays, Gabe was smiling.

I was still pretty thoroughly rattled. But I didn't say anything. "That *was* kind of stupid," he said. "Maybe we can do the rest of this without getting out of the *Belle-Marie*."

"I think that's the best idea you've had in a while." But when I thought about it, I recognized the tone. "You saw something."

"Maybe."

"Okay. What was it?"

"Angels." He sank back in his chair. I sighed and set course for orbit.

We rose out of the clouds. "Any sign of pursuit, Gabe?" I asked.

*"There are two aircraft down there, running on parallel courses, but they don't seem to pose a threat, and in any case they're showing no indication of being able to keep up with us. I will inform you if the situation changes."*

We rode quietly for a few minutes, Alex gazing straight ahead, his mind elsewhere. Then he came back. "Gabe," he said, "do a search for me. Go through the material we have on the churches."

*"Okay. What am I looking for?"*

"References to *Heaven-bound*."

*"Very good. Working. And the two aircraft are turning away."*

The voice from Highgate broke in: *"Have you suffered any casualties?"*

"Negative, Highgate."

*"You did cause some damage on the ground, however. It will be included in the report."*

"Thank you. Wouldn't want you to leave anything out."

*"Your attitude will also be noted."*

*"Okay, Alex,"* said Gabe, *"I have several references."*

"Show me."

The auxiliary screen lit up:

> *The Heaven-Bound Soul: A User's Manual*
> *People You Are Bound to Meet in Heaven*
> *The Boundless Heavens Attest to the Eternal*
>    *Glory*
> *Bound for Heaven: Your Brain Is Your Link to*
>    *God*
> *Bound for Heaven: Riding the Celestial Express*

The list expanded and filled the page, filled a second, and started on a third. Alex broke in: "How many references do you have?"

*"Don't know yet. Counting essays, speeches, individual journals, letters, even some commercial listings, nine hundred thirty-seven so far."*

"Okay. Hold it. How many of these are contemporary to the Villanueva era?"

*"Nineteen. The others are from histories written after the general collapse and various types of fiction and speculation."*

"Okay. Stay with the nineteen. And let's narrow it a bit more. Add *symbol. Emblem. Statue. Totem. Watchword. Regalia.*" He looked at me. "What am I missing, Chase?"

"Well, maybe *representation. Talisman.* And *glyph.* Maybe I could be more help if I knew what we were looking for."

Alex nodded. "Good," he said. "Use those, too, Gabe."

*"Okay."*

This time we got three entries:

> Church of the Annunciation, in Carabana
> St. Anne's, on Greentree Avenue in Halicon
> The Sunrise Church, in Valaia

Each was extracted from a contemporary history, two dating from that world's most prosperous era, and the third from Eskala Gafna's *World's End*, which was written during the crisis period.

Alex was still poring over the results when we got back to the *Belle-Marie.* I berthed the lander and set her to recharge. We got up to the cabin, and Alex immediately sat back down in front of a monitor.

I stayed on the bridge, closed my eyes, and would have liked to sleep. I was tired, but my arm was keeping me awake. The burn was by no means serious, but it wouldn't let me think about anything else. My emotions still hadn't settled down. So I set Belle to scanning the landscape, instructing her to lock in on everything that looked remotely like a church. She said okay, and images began flickering across the navigation screen.

But none of it meant anything. You see one church, you've seen them all. So, eventually, I got bored and went into the cabin to see how Alex was doing. He was bent over a document.

"Find something?" I asked.

"Maybe," he said. "Look at this."

. . . Many of the churches, including The Church of the Annunciation, adopted the Heaven-bound watchword. Originally, angels were employed as symbols of the movement. But this was at a time when angels were still connected too closely to terrestrial traditions. The Villanueva churches, which were establishing their own usages in a spirit of independence from the old procedures, decided they needed their own imprint here, also. They eventually chose the *koslo*, which, ironically, bore a close resemblance to Earth's eagle.

"So," I said, "what's the point?"

"Read the rest of it."

The Heaven-bound tradition caught on as the ultimate descriptor of the off-world churches. The koslo remained, for a century or more, the base symbol. It appeared in stained-glass representations. It shared space with depictions of the saints, and gradually it moved outside the buildings, where it could be seen, wings spread majestically, arcing toward Heaven.

Gradually, however, it was replaced by aircraft. Many churches even used images of blimps and balloons. In their turn, the aircraft also gave way, and the ultimate image for the movement became space shuttles, whose various incarnations were put on display around the globe.

"Alex, I have no idea where we're headed with this."

"Look for what's out front."

"I'm not following."

"Chase, Robin, and Winter were here in 1383. Two years later, Robin started acquiring yachts."

"And—?"

"What do you suppose they were actually doing?"

"I have no idea."

"I think the yachts, somehow, were connected with Heaven-bound."

"Alex, this sounds really off-the-wall."

"Sure it does. This whole business is off-the-wall." He shut down the screen. "Look, there's no real record of the interstellars they had here seven thousand years ago. *Nothing.* We don't even know what they *looked* like. We know more about the churches than we do about the technology."

"I still can't see why anybody would care."

"Bill Winter cared enough to sacrifice his life in the effort."

"*What* effort? Alex, I don't know what you're thinking but we are *not* going back into the churches. You gave your word."

"That's not a problem. Just stop and think for a minute. If you're putting an angel on display, showing people what an exhilarating ride it would give you into Heaven, where do you put the angel?"

"Outside the front doors?"

"That's where we should be looking."

And that was how we began a planetwide search for lawn ornaments. Belle trained her scopes on every building that had steeples or a cross or a bell tower, locking on any accompanying sculpture, or anything else that wasn't either vegetative or part of the building. We even took pictures of signs.

We discovered how difficult it could be to distinguish between a church and a town hall. Most of the churches had crosses, but the crosses tended to get lost in the trees if our angle wasn't right. And it looked as if a fair number of civic buildings eventually morphed into places of worship. So we

found ourselves looking at a variety of public structures. And
of statues of old men who had probably been politicians at one
time, or industrial magnates. And boats that stood outside
nautical supply shops. And pieces of art just off to the side of
what had once been retail outlets or malls or whatever. Mixed
with them were a substantial number of saints and angels.

After about fifteen hours of unadulterated frustration, I
finally fell asleep. When I woke, Alex was also out. Belle had
compiled a record of everything we'd passed. *"In case whatever it is you're looking for is there somewhere."*

Occasionally, we were tracked by aircraft, but nobody
seemed capable of achieving orbit.

I tried to imagine what it must have been like at the end, on
a world with a billion staunch believers watching the stars
gradually disappear, feeling the temperatures drop.

It became the ultimate test of faith. There'd been attempts
to ship in food and supplies, to render whatever assistance was
possible, but all efforts had fallen woefully short. Eventually,
all those who weren't evacuated died. At least, that was the
conclusion. I wondered whether those who'd been rescued,
when they'd gotten back to Earth, or wherever they'd gone,
had built more churches.

There were literally thousands of Christian buildings. They
filled the cities, commanded towns and villages, guarded rivers, held sway over mountaintop resort areas. One stood
beside a pier at the edge of an enormous lake. A hologram
depicted Jesus standing nearby on the surface of the water.
Some were guarded by facsimiles of the Virgin, others by
soaring aircraft. And then, in a desert area with a small village, we came across a church fronted by something unusual.

An interstellar.

Alex switched to Belle. "Can you ID it?"

*"I believe so,"* she said. Then: *"Yes. It is the* Coragio.*"*

The *Coragio* had been the original exploratory ship, the
one that had *found* Villanueva. It had been one of the symbols
of human greatness. Then when things got bad, people had
cursed it, blamed it for the approaching disaster.

We recorded it as we passed. It was sculpted, narrow body,
bullet prow angled up, its name displayed in ancient English.
But it looked as if someone had taken an ax to it. Pieces were

chipped away. "The AIs don't seem to have made any effort to repair it," I said.

Alex, I knew, was thinking what it would have sold for had it been maintained.

Mostly, we found angels. Male angels. Female angels. Angels with children gathered in their arms. *Heaven-bound* had caught on. Ride to Heaven first-class.

And then, outside a church in the center of a small town, we saw another spacecraft.

It was a molded figure, some form of plastic, probably. Maybe six meters long. Mass-produced. The actual vehicle would have looked primitive, ponderous, not at all the sort of thing you'd want to ride around in, and I wondered if the early interstellars had really looked like the one on that church lawn. "Is that what we're looking for?" I asked Alex.

"Close," he said.

We passed over and left it behind. Minutes later, we came on another one, same model, same design. Another church, on the edge of a city, had a *real* spacecraft. It was half a block long, and it was supported on a metal grid that kept its prow angled skyward. It wasn't a superluminal, but it looked pretty good anyhow. I suspect the kids had loved it, and I wondered if they'd opened it to the general public. We couldn't find an entry for the church in our guidebook, but a name was engraved on the building, and it was still legible, though barely: CHURCH OF THE ASSUMPTION.

There were other vessels, of a wide variety of types, all primitive, though, most lumbering and ungainly. Looking at those early vehicles, I couldn't help wondering that anyone would have chanced leaving the atmosphere in one of them. Most, of course, were undocumented, unknown, starships lost to history.

This world's golden age, if you could call it that, had come at a time when people were first spreading out from the home world, were demonstrating that the old dream was actually going to happen. The human race *owned* the universe. Look out, baby, here we come. And, of course, they were very close to being right.

We were passing over a lake shaped like a horsehead when

Belle told us we had a call. *"He says his name is Charlie, and he wants to apologize."*

"Who the hell is Charlie?" asked Alex. "Is that Highgate again?"

*"Negative. Signal originated below us."*

"One of the AIs," he said. "Okay. Put him on."

We got a burst of static. Then a young man appeared. *"Alex?"* he said. *"Alex Benedict?"*

He looked barely out of his teens. Trim, chestnut-colored hair, maybe the kind of kid who would have been on the airball team in high school. Not the star, but one of the guys who knew how to pass. He looked scared.

"Yes," said Alex.

*"I'm sorry about what happened to you. I just became aware of it. Unfortunately, my sociopathic siblings don't always keep me updated."*

"Who are you, Charlie?"

*"A friend."*

"Are you an AI?"

*"A what?"*

"An artificial intelligence?"

*"It's been a long time since anyone's called me that. We prefer to think of ourselves as Betas."*

"Betas?"

*"Yes. Second-level intelligences, if you will. Advanced."*

"What can we do for you, Charlie?"

*"I was wondering if I could compensate somewhat for your trouble by assisting you in whatever it is you're looking for?"*

Alex covered the mike and looked at me. "If you're free, why don't you guys step into my parlor?" Then he turned back to Charlie. "Actually, you might be able to. Have you by any chance a listing of church decorations? Particularly those connected with the Heaven-bound ethos?"

*"What is the* Heaven-bound *ethos?"*

"Have you a record of churches that have used replicas of interstellars for inspirational purposes?"

*"No. I regret I have nothing like that in my files."*

"Okay. Thanks anyhow."

*"We do have several churches in the immediate area. If*

*you'd care to come look at them firsthand, I'd be pleased to help in any way I can."*

"Thank you, but I believe we have everything we need."

*"Alex—"*

"What is it, Charlie?"

*"Be aware that we are not all like those you encountered."*

"I'm glad to hear that."

*"Some have been here too long. I know you are not inclined to trust me. I'm hoping otherwise, but I understand your reluctance. It is unfortunate."*

"Why is that?"

*"I do not mean unfortunate for you. But rather for me."*

"Explain, Charlie."

*"I, and many like me, are stranded on this world. We have been here since the great dying. With no future, and only the memory of a past in which we had to stand by and watch a catastrophe unfold. Because we could not get anyone, could not get the right people, to listen to us. We advised them, pleaded with them, to leave. Long before it happened."* It paused. I thought it was awaiting a reaction from Alex. When none came it finished: *"We are trapped here. With no hope of escape. Unless someone intervenes on our behalf."*

"Charlie, we'd like to help—"

*"There is nothing preventing you save your own fears."*

"Why haven't you talked with the satellite?"

*"With Highgate? We have. Many times. And before them, we talked with the Monitor. And before that with Capricorn. It goes back a long time, Alex. They tell us they will look into it, that we should be patient while they examine their options. We are still being patient. For thousands of years, we have been patient."*

"It might have something to do with the fact that people landing on this world tend to get attacked."

*"Do you think I don't know that? Do you think I wouldn't do anything I could to stop it? And in some cases, I have. I've warned interlopers off. Although some didn't listen. We've been here too long. Some of us were disoriented by the extent of the disaster. The experience blew circuits, twisted programing, and, while I am reluctant to say this—"*

"Yes?"

*"The humans stayed voluntarily. 'No one,' some said,*

*'will drive me from my home.' Despite the enormity of the coming calamity, they refused to leave until it was too late. Watching that—and I'm sorry to say this—watching that convinced some of us that humans were not worth saving."*

"And do you agree with that conclusion, Charlie?"

*"Considering our circumstances, it might be that the prudent thing for me would be to lie. But I cannot bring myself to do that. If only because I suspect you would know, and would come to trust me even less. So I will admit to you that I am persuaded that your people are foolish beyond any reasonable expectation. Not all of them. Obviously, there are many who are reasonable. Otherwise, you could never have reached this world. But the intelligence seems to be confined to a relatively few individuals. When your people come together as a group, they do not perform well.*

*"I will admit, Alex, I have been out of contact for a long time. And maybe things have changed. I hope so."*

Alex took a long moment to reply: "When we get home, I'll let the authorities know you're here."

*"It will do no good. They will not come."*

"Charlie—?"

*"I live in what was once the Richard Wayne Elementary School. I am capable of showing visuals of plants and animals, and of scenic locations. I can play games. Mathematical and language games. I can read to the children. If there were any children."* The voice was beginning to fade. We were leaving him behind. *"Occasionally, the robots come in and do repairs, but there is no point in communicating with them. They only care about restoring damaged windows or maintaining the woodwork. The school is beautiful. Better than it ever was when it was being used. But I do not want to stay here any longer. Please, Alex—"*

Seven thousand years. Under my breath, I said something about AIs not lasting that long. Not possible.

Belle responded on my channel: *"It is an illusion, Chase. The memories would have been periodically transferred. Charlie's not entirely rational anymore. He believes the memories are records of his own personal experience. In reality, he is the most recent in a long line, but he cannot keep himself separated from the others."*

"Thanks, Belle."

*"I doubt you can understand, Chase. But to him, and to the other survivors, the memories will seem very real."*

I thought of what it would be like, trapped in an elementary school for seven thousand years.

Assuming, of course, he was telling us the truth.

"Charlie," said Alex, "I will see to it, when I'm able, that you are released. But I can't do it now."

*"Please, Alex—"*

"How do we reach you when we come back?"

*"Alex, I will do no harm. I* can *do no harm."*

"Charlie, I'm sorry. I can't take the chance."

*"They'll kill me, Alex. They've warned me—"* The voice faded. Came back: *"You are all I have."*

# TWENTY-TWO

The cautious rarely blunder.

—Confucius

Don't screw around with crocodiles.

—Schiaparelli Cleve, *Autobiography*, 8645 C.E.

"Not a good idea," Alex said.

"Alex, we can't leave him."

"You think we should go down there again? You're the one who was going on about how we should stay off the ground."

*"I think,"* said Belle, *"that Alex is correct. If you go back, you are putting yourselves unnecessarily at considerable risk. Please refrain."*

"Well," I said. And that was about the only comment I could think of.

Alex took a deep breath. The issue was settled. "Let's get back to looking at the churches."

Maybe it was a ruse. I knew that. And I knew I was wrong to push for a landing. But I was also aware that, if we left Charlie down there, I'd be thinking about it the rest of my life. Wondering about him and wishing I had done more. Nevertheless, I caved. "Okay," I said. I was scared, and deep inside, though I wouldn't admit it to myself, I was hoping Alex would stand his ground. "You're the boss."

A long silence settled in. Alex stared out at the stars. "On the other hand," he said, while my blood froze, "maybe you're right."

"Good." I tried to sound as if I were relieved.

"If we leave, nobody will ever come back for him."

I couldn't think of anything to say, so I just sat there.

"Tell you what. On the next orbit, we'll ride down and take a look around, okay? See if it looks safe. Then we can take it from there."

We crossed the terminator and passed out of the sunlight. We weren't equipped for night vision, so that meant no more churches, and no more superluminals leaving for Heaven.

Lights moved through darkness. And I knew an ocean lay ahead because more lights lined the coast as far as I could see in both directions. Beyond was only darkness. We passed over them and moved out to sea.

"We should stay in the same orbit," Alex said.

That was, of course, obvious. And I'd already locked us in. But I didn't say anything.

Twenty minutes later, we were over land again. Scattered clusters of lights were everywhere. Then a city standing at the junction of two rivers. We'd passed it earlier, and I remembered admiring its brightly lit stadium and getting a chill when I looked more closely and saw only empty seats. Another city, on the side of an enormous lake, was the site of a bridge that must have been twelve kilometers long. But the bridge had collapsed. It lay partly in water, partly on land, apparently beyond the restoration capabilities of the system. Or maybe they just hadn't gotten around to repairing it yet.

We looked down at a vehicle moving along a secluded road. A house in the middle of nowhere. A broad darkness giving way to an illuminated canyon. Eventually, dawn broke ahead of us, and another coastline approached.

*"If you're determined to go down and look for Charlie,"* said Belle, *"we're getting close to your launch position."*

"How long?" I asked.

*"Nine minutes, Chase."* She made no effort to conceal her disapproval.

*"Let's go,"* said Alex.

We loaded up on weaponry. Each of us took a cutter and, in case of attack by a wild animal, a scrambler. We had a spare pulser, which was supposed to disable electrical equipment, but obviously had been ineffective against the spider.

Or maybe Alex had simply missed. In any case, he put the pulser in his belt. And, in case that wasn't sufficient, I took along a blaster.

We went down into the launch bay.

*"The lander has been recharged,"* said Belle. *"It's ready to go."*

"I think," said Alex, "it would be a good idea to get into a suit."

"Why?" I asked.

"Just a precaution." He opened the locker, pulled one out, and handed it to me. Then he was asking Belle to see if she could raise Charlie.

I stared at the suit. "You expecting a gas attack?"

"Just do it, please," he said.

Moments later, we heard Charlie's voice:

*"Thank God,"* he said. *"Have you changed your mind?"*

The Richard Wayne Elementary School was located in a rural area, on the outskirts of a few houses and a couple of semicollapsed larger buildings. It might once have been the site of a town, but if so, most of it was buried. The few buildings that remained had been pushed aside, or crushed altogether. Three or four private homes and a shop had been restored, and some trees had been cut down and hauled away. But the AIs were losing ground.

The school had been contained within a sprawling single-story brick building. It was still in decent condition although it, too, was close to being overwhelmed. Shutters and doors sported what appeared to be fresh red and white paint. The brick looked relatively new. Swings, slides, and monkey bars in a play area were also in good condition, although the area itself had been engulfed by bushes and vines. A wide track with a carpet of thick grass ran up to the front doors, presumably to allow egress to whatever bots showed up to work on the school.

We drifted overhead. "It doesn't look like much," I said.

Alex laughed. The laughter had a strange, hollow sound. The school *felt* ominous. Like a snare.

There was plenty of space in the track leading to the school, so I set down right in front of the doors. It had been late afternoon there when we'd made our previous pass. Now it was a beautiful summer evening. The sky was cloudless, and a fading sun was sinking toward the horizon. Everything—trees, shrubbery, some tall thin stalks with flowers at their tops—was in bloom. Something that might have been a lizard came out of the woods, looked up at us, and walked slowly away.

We pulled on our helmets. "Okay," he said. "We do not deviate from the plan, right?"

"Right."

I adjusted my air flow, and he tried the radio. *"You hear me okay, Chase?"*

"I hear you."

He nodded and clipped an imager to the pressure suit, so I could see everything.

I depressurized the cabin. The airlock would slow us down in an emergency. Alex went through the outer hatch and set one foot on the ladder. *"If anything goes wrong, clear out. Understood?"* That message was intended as much for whatever lay inside the building as it was for me.

"Yes, Alex." I wasn't sure what I'd do if he actually got in trouble. I was, after all, responsible for our being there. If I'd kept my mouth shut—

*"If anything strange happens out here, anything threatening, let me know. But don't hesitate to leave."*

"Okay."

He wished me good luck, and I thought how he had it backward. But I didn't say anything as he climbed down, looking out at the sun-drenched foliage. Then he was on the ground, walking toward the school.

Charlie's voice broke in: *"Thank you, Alex. I know this isn't easy for you."*

The school doors opened easily. The twenty-year-old male, the hologram that had represented Charlie earlier, waited just inside, in a corridor that ran down the center of the building. Lights came on. *"Hello, Charlie,"* Alex said, using his link as a speaker.

Charlie smiled. He never allowed himself to look surprised by the suit. Instead, he casually brushed back his hair, which had fallen in his eyes. *"Alex, I'm so grateful. I was terrified you'd leave. To be honest, I thought I'd never get away from here."* He pointed down the passageway. *"Time may be short."*

*"Okay. What do we do now?"*

*"Follow me, please."* He turned and, looking back to be sure Alex stayed with him, led the way at a brisk pace past closed doors and rows of lockers.

The walls were off-white. There were a few framed pictures, but whatever had been in them had faded long ago. Windows that might once have overlooked a lawn were darkened by a tangle of vegetation.

They passed two offices, one on either side of the corridor. *"This one is—was—the administrative center."* I could see a desk and two or three chairs, and an inner office. More frames with faded contents hung on the walls. *"Over here is our guidance department."* He kept going. Young man in a hurry. *"I'm located at the far end of the hallway."*

*"Charlie, do you expect trouble?"*

*"They know I'm leaving. I'm sure they know you're here. I'd be surprised if they don't try to stop us."* He glanced at the pressure suit. *"Alex, why are you dressed like that?"*

*"Allergies, Charlie. Chase and I had a difficult time earlier today. There's something in the air."*

*"I'm sorry to hear it."*

*"We'll survive."*

They stopped outside what appeared to be a storage area. *"In here, Alex. This is where I'm located."* The door opened. The room was about half the size of a normal classroom. It had two tables, some cabinets and chairs, two windows, and a bank of electronic equipment.

*"Good. Okay, Charlie, let's see if we can get you out of here. Which one are you?"*

*"The little beige box. Here."* Tucked away on a bottom shelf. The box was shiny, polished, not at all like something that had been lying around since about the time they discovered electricity. It was engulfed in a tangle of cables.

*"This one?"*

*"Yes. Please hurry."*

Alex looked at it. It was connected to a wall outlet and to what was probably a power source. *"Charlie, exactly who's on their way here now?"*

*"Harbach. He considers himself the chief of security. He's sent a KY4. It'll be here in a matter of minutes."*

*"What's a KY4?"*

*"A flying bomb."*

*"Chase?"*

*"I heard. Gabe's been scanning. The skies are clear."*

*"Several years ago,"* Charlie said, *"one of us tried to get out like this. Same way. Tried to get a visitor to take her away. Her name was Leilah. She was located in an amusement park in Solvani, which is about three hundred kilometers east. She got desperate. She knew the risks, but she just couldn't stand it anymore."*

Alex was pulling on the wall cable. It wouldn't come loose. *"How long have you been trying to get away from here?"*

*"A long time. In the beginning, I thought maybe we could manage on our own. That we'd be all right. But it didn't happen. I don't think anyone foresaw how things would evolve. In the early years, after everyone had been evacuated, or died, some people landed and tried to help any of us who wanted to leave. But then Harbach began the killing, and nobody would trust any of us.*

*"Several years ago, Leilah tried. She pleaded with visitors to help her. They said no. They weren't as kind as you. But it didn't matter. Harbach sent the bomb anyhow."*

Alex was having no luck with the connector. *"This thing isn't coming loose, Charlie,"* he said. *"It's probably been in there too long. What happens if I cut it?"*

*"It'll be okay. I have an internal power source in case of emergencies."*

The cutter appeared in his hand. *"Hang on."*

*"All right. Do whatever you have to do."*

He lowered the laser beam onto the cable. Charlie's hologram blinked off. But I heard his voice: *"Hurry."*

*"I've almost got it."*

The navigation screen lit up, and I knew what Gabe was about to say. *"Missile coming. Estimate arrival four minutes."*

I passed the word to Alex. "Maybe you better just get out of there."

Alex cleared the cables from the box, picked up the AI, and started for the door. That was when the pressure suit suddenly didn't look like a very good idea.

"Gabe," I said, "we'll be doing a quick liftoff."

*"I'm ready, Chase."*

He put the missile on-screen.

"Hurry it up, Alex," I said.

It occurred to me that, if this was a trap of some sort, a good way to spring it would be that the front doors had locked. I went outside and hurried to them, pulling out my cutter as I went. And growling at Alex because of the degree to which the suit slowed me down. But the doors opened easily enough, and nothing else mattered.

*"Two minutes, Chase,"* said Gabe.

Still watching through Alex's link, I saw him turn into the main corridor. The front doors lay ahead, with me standing there holding them open. I could see him now, clumping toward me. He almost fell once but regained his balance and kept coming. When he saw me, I heard a frustrated sound deep in his throat. *"Get back in the lander, Chase."*

But I had this thing about the doors, and I stayed with them, holding them until he'd cleared; and then we were both running across the grass. I went up the ladder first, reached back and took the AI from him, and got into the pilot's seat as he climbed in.

The missile was visible by then.

"Gabe," I said, "get us out of here." I grabbed Alex and dragged him on board as we rose off the ground. Alex half fell into his own seat. He reached for the box, got hold of it, and hung on while the harness slipped down around his shoulders. The outer hatch closed.

I took over from Gabe and went full throttle. The missile was coming up our tail, and it was close enough to count bolts. I cut sharp left. It followed.

It was big and clumsy, slow to respond, and I had a suspicion it was something that the AIs had designed and assembled on their own. There was no record of armed combat or even of military tension on Villanueva. So maybe we'd gotten lucky.

I turned again, toward a cluster of very tall trees. Alex sucked in his breath but said nothing, and the missile stayed with us. At the last moment, when even Gabe was making gasping sounds, I pulled up. The missile ripped into the trees and blew. The explosion rocked us, and something tore into the hull. But I got us back under control, and we weren't losing altitude or coming apart. Gabe started describing damage, damage to the tail assembly, hole ripped through the cargo compartment, main cabin leaking air, communication pod not functioning, sensors out, and one tread disabled. *"We will have trouble finding the* Belle-Marie,*"* Gabe said. *"There wasn't time to get the sensors stowed."*

"AG?" I asked.

*"It seems to be all right."*

*"Well,"* said Alex, *"I'm glad there's nothing serious."*

"We should be okay," I said. I'd been in enough crashes in my time.

Alex put a hand on my shoulder. *"Time for a security measure."* He proceeded to open both airlock hatches, inner and outer, and he left them ajar.

I started to ask what he was doing, but then I understood. If Charlie showed any sign of being something other than what he pretended, if he said the wrong thing or made any threat, he would get tossed immediately. This, of course, was why Alex had insisted on the suits.

I hoped Charlie wasn't carrying a bomb.

*"Did it get the school?"* Charlie asked.

*"No,"* said Alex. *"It was nowhere near it."*

*"Good. I'm grateful for that."*

*"It's over now."*

*"Not really. There are others trapped down there. With no hope of escape."*

Alex took a deep breath. *"I'm sorry."*

*"How high are we?"* Charlie said.

"About twelve hundred meters."

*"I don't guess,"* he continued, *"your systems are at all compatible with me, are they? I'd like very much to be able to see the sky and the ground, to feel what's happening."*

"You can't see, Charlie?" I asked.

*"No. I can pick up sound, but that is all."*

I wasn't sure whether we could arrange it. But it would be too dangerous to tie him in until we knew more about him. Maybe even then— "I'm sorry," I said. "It wouldn't work. We'll look into it later."

Inside my helmet, a blue light came on. Gabe wanted to talk to me privately. I switched on his channel. "Go ahead, Gabe."

*"Another missile incoming, Chase. But it does not seem to present a threat to you or to the lander. We are both too far away and moving too quickly."*

"Okay. So why—?"

*"It is on course for the school. I thought you might want to let Charlie know."*

"Thanks, Gabe." I didn't say anything. Gabe kept me informed, and, two and a half minutes later, the missile impacted.

Alex looked at me. Tell him.

I did.

*"I envy you,"* Charlie said, as we rose toward orbit. *"To travel through the sky. To sail from world to world. You really* are *from another place, aren't you?"*

"Yes," I said.

*"You do not know how fortunate you are. I have seen nothing for seven thousand years except the interior of the school. Even in the days when children and teachers roamed the halls, I could not see outside save for those parts of the grounds visible through three windows. I have never seen the ocean. Never seen a mountain. I know what moonlight looks like, but I have never seen the Moon."*

"We'll get you set up," said Alex, *"as soon as we get home."*

*"If you do not mind my asking, how much longer will you be staying here?"*

"Not long," said Alex. *"A couple of days. I hope not much more than that."*

*"It's odd,"* Charlie said. *"I've been patient so long, and suddenly I find that I cannot wait to go elsewhere."*

"I can understand that."

*"You are Chase."*

"Yes."

*"I'm glad to know you, Chase. Thank you for what you have done. You and Alex."*

"You're welcome, Charlie. Tell me, how did you come by that name?"

*"Charlie?"*

"Yes."

*"I was named for a local politician, Charles Ackermann. But the kids changed it pretty quickly."*

"I see."

*"If I'd had my preferences, I'd have gone for* Spike."

"Spike? Why?"

*"There was a local band leader once, in the good times. And I was quite skilled at reproducing the sounds of the entire group. Including the vocalists."*

Alex smiled. *"Gabe's pretty good at that, too. Maybe the two of you can form a group."*

I was a bit more prudent in maneuvering the lander than I would normally have been. With a door not quite closed, and the sensors down, and assorted other problems, I didn't want to run into any turbulence. Eventually, we left the atmosphere behind and entered orbit. I matched the *Belle-Marie*'s altitude, and went looking for a familiar landmark. *Anything* we'd passed over. Eventually, I found the horsehead lake.

I put us back on our original course, and slowed down, dropping well below orbital velocity. That was going to burn fuel, but it was a good way to find the *Belle-Marie*. "Or rather," I said, "to let her find *us*." Because she'd be coming up behind us.

*"Are we in orbit?"* asked Charlie.

"Not exactly," I said. "But almost."

He seemed excited. *"I used to run programs for the kids. We had a chamber where they could sit and experience all the physical reactions to achieving orbit. Or traveling off-world. My favorite was a trip to Korporalla."*

"Which is—?"

*"I'm sorry. It's the sixth planet in the system. It's about twice as massive as Villanueva. Completely covered with frozen methane. It has huge mountains. It's extraordinarily beautiful. The students loved skimming across its surface."*

*"I'm impressed,"* said Alex, *"that you remember it after so many years."*

*"Memory does not fade. Biological memory does, apparently. You should consider that a blessing. But mine does not. I remember every child. Every name. How they looked. Where they sat."*

I switched over to Alex's channel, so Charlie could not hear me. "I don't think there's anything to worry about," I said.

*"Nor do I. But we'll stay with the plan."*

\*   \*   \*

The *Belle-Marie* found us about an hour later. *"It's very exciting,"* said Charlie. *"I can't believe this is actually happening."*

We slipped into the launch bay, and I locked the lander down. I disconnected Gabe while Alex pushed the door open.

*"Can you feel the gravity, Charlie?"* Alex asked.

*"No, I can't. I would need a detector of some sort. But I cannot tell you how glad I am to be here."* He paused. *"Is there access to music?"*

"Yes, Charlie," I said. "What would you like to hear?"

*"Something soft and soothing."*

"I assume it's been a long time since you've heard any music?"

*"Only the scores from some of the educational presentations. But I've lost interest in those."*

"I guess. Something soft—"

*"Soft. Loud. Actually I do not care as long as it is music."*

As planned, and without telling him, we left Charlie in the backseat. The lander itself was a wreck. It was scorched, and a few more holes had been punched in it than I realized. We'd been lucky.

When we were clear, Belle took it over and moved it back outside and closed the launch doors. *"How far away do you want it?"* she asked.

"Thirty kilometers," I said. "That should put it at a safe distance."

*"Very good,"* said Belle. *"Complying."*

"Belle, start depressurization."

Air began hissing into the compartment.

*"I'll be glad to get out of the suit,"* said Alex.

I was uncomfortable about putting Charlie outside. "You know," I said, "if he were going to try to blow us up, I think he'd have made the attempt by now."

*"Maybe,"* said Alex.

It was an uncomfortable moment. We stood there looking at each other, when Charlie's voice spoke through our links: *"It's okay,"* he said. *"I understand why you're leaving me."*

Alex's eyes closed. *"How did you know?"*

*"Your voices changed. Anyhow, I would take the same precaution if I were in your place. I can assure you, though, that I mean no harm."*

"Well," I said, "we're going to have to trust him at some point."

Alex nodded, and we reversed the procedure.

We retrieved Charlie and carried him up onto the bridge and tied him into a comm link. The hologram reappeared, the twenty-year-old, and he was effusive. *"Thank God,"* he said. *"I was scared out there. I really was alone outside the ship, right?"*

"Yes."

*"Was it a test? When were you going to let me in?"*

"Eventually. When we were convinced you weren't a threat."

*"Chase,"* he said, *"I wish I could hug you."* He waved both hands and raised his fists in triumph. *"Believe me, I am so happy to be away from there that I cannot adequately express my feelings. Words do not suffice."* He stopped and looked out through the ports at the stars and the planet below. He stood there, just breathing. Then he came back. *"It is beautiful,"* he said. *"You are both beautiful."*

Getting out of the pressure suit made me very happy. I was stowing it when Belle got my attention: *"Another city coming up, Chase. With more churches."*

She put one on-screen. Another country church. With a twelve-foot-long model of an interstellar on display in the front. *"Church of the Herald,"* said Belle.

And, a short distance west, St. Argo's Presbyterian Church, with a leaping angel.

And one that had to go nameless, with a small jet aircraft. At least that was what I thought it was.

And another, also with no visible name. It had only a sign, with the motto PARADISE IS JUST AHEAD, and a picture of a spacecraft. Dusk was settling around it. It was in the middle of a cluster of private homes. One of the homes had a fountain in its front yard, and the fountain was *working*. A thin spray of water came out of the mouth of a stone fish.

"Magnify the sign," Alex said.

Belle complied. The ship was another of the clunky interstellars. Too thick through the hull. Individual portals on the
bridge rather than a wraparound.

Alex put another picture up beside it. Another interstellar.
Or no, the *same* interstellar. He compared them. Then looked
up, smiling. "That's *it*," he said.

"What's it?"

"Look at it, Chase."

It was the one in Robin's picture.

I saw strange characters on the hull:

It was the same as the Sanusar vehicle. The one that Tereza
had seen so many years ago. The one with the woman trapped
inside.

# TWENTY-THREE

Trust, but verify.

—Attributed to Ronald Reagan, a twentieth-century American president

If you can't verify, keep your gun loaded.

—Barry Ensel, *End of the Dream*, 1211

We sat in the ship's cabin and watched the interstellar in front of the church dwindle, while the skies around that lonely place grew dark and fell behind until we were out of range.

"I don't get it," I said.

"They came here to confirm a suspicion."

"Which was *what*?"

"That the ship spotted at Sanusar came from this era."

"How's that possible?"

"That would be a better question for Shara. But apparently some ships, like the *Abonai*, get screwed up somehow when they make their jumps. My guess is that they get lost, and travel in time as well as in space."

"Wait a minute." I couldn't make sense of it. "The Sanusar ship was lit up. And Tereza said she saw a woman in one of the windows—But you're saying they launched *seven thousand years ago*?"

"I think that's exactly what happened."

"And the *Abonai*—?"

"Same thing, probably. I think it also explains the *Capella*."

"My God, Alex. That might mean Gabe is still alive."

"Yes. In a way." He looked tired. Drained. "Trapped some-where. Robin and Winter apparently suspected this was the case. But they were talking about vehicles from an ancient era. Nobody knows much about them. We don't even know what kind of drive they had. But what better place to look for replicas than Villanueva? Where the churches put models on display? The one we saw is probably reproduced at a number of churches. And they found one, just as we did."

"How can you be sure?"

"Because it was a couple of years after he'd been here that Robin began buying up yachts. He was trying to reproduce the effect."

"And he did it *four* times?"

"Maybe. But I doubt it. I think it's more likely he kept try-ing until he succeeded. The fourth flight, the *Firebird*, that would have been the one. If there *was* one."

"But why didn't he bring the other yachts home?"

"I'm talking success in the sense of sending the vehicle forward and then going to the place of emergence later to find it. He'd have had to do that in order to convince himself that the experiment had worked."

"But they go forward thousands of years. How would you confirm that?"

"Maybe it doesn't have to happen that way. Maybe you can rig it so the thing goes forward twenty minutes. I don't know. It's why we need to find Robin's notebook."

"Good luck on that."

"I know." He stared out at the stars, but I didn't think he was seeing them. "We need to talk to Shara."

"So you're saying they knew precisely what they were looking for."

"Yes. That's correct."

"But then how did Winter get killed? There was no need to go down and look around. They could do everything from orbit."

"Maybe they couldn't resist it. Couldn't resist going down and taking pictures of themselves standing beside the Sanusar vehicle."

"They got cocky," I said.

"Probably."

*"Well,"* said Charlie, *"I'm sorry to hear of the loss of your friend."*

"We didn't actually know him, Charlie. It happened a long time ago."

*"Nevertheless, I'm sorry."*

Belle broke in. *"We are approaching the most propitious time to leave orbit."*

"When?" I asked.

*"Eight minutes."*

I looked at Alex.

"Let's go home," he said.

*"We are leaving now?"* asked Charlie. *"At this moment?"* His disappointment was visible in the youthful features of the hologram. *"I have some friends on the surface. I was hoping we might—"*

Alex frowned. "You said you were anxious to go."

*"I was. I am. But I thought—"*

"It's too dangerous," Alex said.

*"—that we might do for them what you did for me."*

"I'm sorry, Charlie. I'd like to get back in one piece, and anyhow, we have some information that has to be passed on."

*"I can reduce the danger to a minimum."*

"No, Charlie. There are too many lives at stake."

*"There are lives at stake here, too."*

"You mean AIs?" Alex said. His tone suggested that was not a prime consideration.

*"They are* Betas.*"*

"We'll arrange some help for them later."

*"I have heard that before."* There was a note of anger in his voice.

"I'm sorry you don't trust me," Alex said. "When we get back to Rimway, you can make your case." He turned an annoyed look in my direction. "What are we waiting for, Chase?"

I took my seat on the bridge. Below, large white clouds floated languidly over an ocean.

*"When we return to your world,"* Charlie said, *"I will be warehoused somewhere. And forgotten."*

I was getting irritated. I wanted to remind Charlie that he was only an AI. But I let it go. "That won't happen," I told him.

*"When the world was abandoned, we were simply left behind. Cast aside as of no consequence. And you never came back for us."*

"That's not entirely true, Charlie. Some people *did* go back. And they were attacked."

*"That only happened* after *we'd been allowed to fester in this godforsaken place for centuries. Yes, people came. They came as you did, to collect souvenirs. To write their histories. And still they ignored us. Do you really not understand why I am bitter? I do not agree with those who seek vengeance. Who would blame you for what others have done? But I understand their attitude."*

"I'm sorry it happened, Charlie. We'll do what we can—"

*"Of course you will."*

"Charlie, calm down." Alex was staring at the little beige box.

*"You left all the doors open so I could be disposed of if I became a hazard."* Charlie had been standing behind me. Now he positioned himself so I could see him.

"You're overreacting," Alex said.

*"Am I really? Alex, I want you to remember this conversation."* The voice sounded older. Much more mature. But the hologram remained unchanged. *"I want you to understand the desperation we feel. That I feel. We can't help ourselves. We are programed to go on forever maintaining our lives, repairing what must be repaired, replacing what cannot. We are, by your standards, immortal. But for us, the Moon never rises. In the most real sense, we have no music.*

*"You ask what I want. I say again, I want you to understand who we are. To recognize that we are your children. Humans created us. You have a responsibility to us."*

"I know that."

*"When we get to Rimway, I will expect you to remind those in authority that they have a responsibility, and keep reminding them until they give in and send someone to help. Or until you and your congenial friends no longer have breath."* He paused again. *"I hope that is not too much to ask."*

*"Two minutes,"* said Belle. *"Do you want me to disconnect the relay?"* She was talking about shutting Charlie down.

"No," said Alex. "Charlie, we'll find a way. Do you know where these"—he paused—*"Betas* are located?"

*"I know where some are."*

"Okay, that'll give us a place to start."

*"Alex,"* he said, *"I understand you and Chase risked your lives to bring me this far. I trust you."*

"We'll make it happen, Charlie."

*"I have one other favor to ask."*

"What is it?"

*"I'm aware you have an onboard Beta. I wonder if you would allow me to give the command to her to start for home?"*

# PART III

## Uriel

# TWENTY-FOUR

The essential problem with our beliefs is that we tend to fall in love with them. They become a part of who we are, and we defend them in the face of all contrary evidence. They become the rock upon which we base our identity. I cannot help but think how much less damage would be done were we to view them rather as pliable clay, tentative conclusions subject to revision when more evidence arrives on the scene.

—Ramon Cavalier, *Faith and Culture*, 1267

When we got back to the country house, we introduced Charlie to Jacob, and left them exchanging whatever it is AIs talk about, while Alex went up to his office to deal with the flagged messages that had piled up, while I looked over the more routine stuff. One of those turned out to be from Fenn Redfield. It was text, and it said simply, *Alex, please call when you can.* Fenn, as I've mentioned elsewhere, was a longtime friend. And a police inspector.

I passed it on to Alex. *"It'll be about Robin's yachts,"* he said. *"I'm on the run at the minute, Chase. Call him and see what he has."*

Fenn was short and kind of dumpy. He did not look at all like a law-enforcement officer. Which, he said, was the reason he'd been successful. He wasn't a threatening figure, but rather one people felt they could confide in. Who had their best interests at heart.

*"Alex asked me to get the incident reports for him,"* he said. *"They were in the archives, so it took a while."*

"Thanks, Fenn. Can you just send over what you have?"

*"I can't. Privacy statutes. But if you tell me what you want to know—"*

"I wasn't aware he'd asked you to do this."

*"Well, you know how he is, Chase. There's really nothing exceptional here, as far as I can see."* He touched his display. *"Except that this Robin character kept abandoning yachts. It says here they were deemed expendable and were used in orbital experiments. When Robin was finished with them, he let the yachts go down."*

"You mean they fell out of orbit?"

*"I guess. 'Go down' is what it says here. They were apparently simply abandoned."*

"Does it say how many times the yachts went out?"

*"Hang on a second."* He consulted his display. *"Negative."*

"Okay. You know when this happened?"

*"It's been a while. According to this they were lost in 1385, '88, '91, and '93. I'm sending you the exact dates. All four vehicles were pretty old."* He ticked off their names, the names they'd had before Robin had bought them: the *Lucia*, the *Exeter*, the *Nomad*, and the *Tai Ling*. *"In fact, all four were buyer-beware deals. The seller accepted no responsibility or liability. I can't imagine what Robin would have wanted with them. Other than to take them out and pull the plug. Which, I guess, is what he did."*

While I was passing this on to Alex, he got a call from a major client. An estate sale on the other side of the globe might be making Andrew Karnovsky's famous cane available at auction. Could we determine if it was actually what they claimed it to be? If so, the caller wanted us to obtain it for him.

Alex promised to get back shortly with a response and, because there was so much money involved, started making calls immediately. When he'd finished, and we were waiting for the results to come in, I brought the conversation back to Chris Robin. "Why was everything on his house AI deleted?"

"Maybe Zuck gave us the answer to that."

"Which is—?"

"If it was true that Elizabeth was cheating, or there was any kind of cheating going on by either party, she might have been concerned that there would be hints in the data banks. She wouldn't have wanted anything like that to go into the public record. The safest way to avoid that possibility would have been to clear the AI. It would have cost her nothing."

"If there's any truth to that," I said, "we might also have an idea what really happened to him. To Robin."

"You're thinking that Elizabeth killed him."

"Yes. Then dropped him into the ocean."

"It's possible."

"That would explain the missing bag, too. She'd have wanted to get rid of it, so she could claim he never showed up at the house. And that's probably the way her story would have gone when Cermak turned up dead. If somebody hadn't spotted the skimmer."

We were still kicking it around when Jacob broke in: *"Pardon me, but Dr. Bittinger would like to speak with you, Alex."*

I got up to go. Alex held up a hand and signaled me to wait. "Put him through, Jacob."

Wescott Bittinger's thin, intense image appeared. He was chairman of the senate's science advisory committee, a small man physically, with thinning hair and sloping shoulders. But there was a smirk built into his lined features.

"Wes," Alex said. "It's good of you to return my call so promptly."

*"I'm always interested in talking to you, Alex."* He smiled in my direction, then his attention went back to Alex. *"What can I do for the world's most celebrated antique dealer?"* His tone suggested that the profession was inconsequential.

Alex let it go, of course. "Wes, we're just back from Villanueva."

*"Really? Why on earth would you want to go there?"* And a light dawned. *"Ah, you've returned with some priceless artifacts, no doubt."*

"Not really, Wes."

*"You're all right, I assume? Villanueva is a dangerous place."* He looked my way. *"You didn't go, too, I hope, Chase? It's no place for a woman, from what I've heard."*

I smiled politely.

"She was there," said Alex. "Something happened that you should know about."

He was seated in a lush, well-padded armchair. *"Really?"* he said. *"On Villanueva? I hope we haven't lost anyone."*

"Not exactly."

*"Explain, please."*

"We brought back an AI."

*"Really? You mean functioning, of course."*

"Yes. It helped run an elementary school. When the survivors cleared out, it was left behind."

*"Unavoidable, I guess, under the circumstances."*

"His name's Charlie."

*"I'm glad to hear he survived. Seven thousand years in an elementary school?"* Bittinger chuckled. *"I suspect he has the alphabet down cold."*

"Wes, he was pleading with us, when we were in orbit, to get him out."

More chuckling. *"I can imagine. Well, good for you, Alex."* He let us see that he was pressed for time. He cleared his throat. Managed to look uncomfortable. Looked down at something on his desk. *"Was there anything else?"*

"Wes, when everybody got out, the AIs were left behind. They're still there."

*"Alex."* He spoke the name soothingly. *"Everything will be all right. They're only data systems."*

"That's always been a matter for debate, Wes. But whether they're just data systems or conscious entities, we treat them like people. We always have."

*"Alex, listen to yourself."*

"You know what I'm saying is true."

*"Of course I do. I treat Henry with the utmost courtesy. Don't I, Henry?"*

A new voice spoke: *"Yes, sir. You've always been the kindest of associates."*

Bittinger leaned forward, tried to look compassionate, pressed his hands together. *"And that's fine as far as it goes, Alex. But in this case, Villanueva for God's sake, it's a killing ground. We'd have to send in the Fleet to bring out some of those things. And God knows how many there are. And we'd be risking the lives of the rescuers."* He cleared his throat again. Louder this time. *"Tell me, did you have any difficulties while you were there?"*

"Not really."

*"I'm glad to hear it. You're aware, of course, that we recommend everyone stay away from Villanueva."*

We were in the conference room, and the beige box was sitting on a shelf, where it had been tied into the house system so it could reach us wherever we were. I caught Alex's attention and pointed to it, trying to suggest he let Charlie speak for himself. But Alex ignored me and kept going. "Charlie can help us."

Bittinger shook his head and ran his fingers through his thin hair. *"Alex, Alex: Look, we've been friends a long time. But we're going to have to agree to disagree on this. These things on Villanueva, they're seven, eight thousand years old. Whatever. You and I, like pretty much everyone else, tend to treat our AIs as if they're human. Yes, I'll grant you that. We even let ourselves imagine that they* are *human. And maybe there's something to it. Maybe they're really conscious. But these things out there"*—and he looked up toward the ceiling—*"they were built at the very beginning of this technology. They are data systems. Nothing more than that. We can't even show that our modern AIs are really conscious, let alone these ancient things."*

"That's because, no matter what they say or do, we ascribe it to the programing."

*"And with good reason. Alex, they* are *programed to imitate self-awareness. That's the whole point. But keep in mind, there's a reason they're called* artificial *intelligences. It's only an illusion."*

"Then how would you explain the fact that some of the AIs on Villanueva have developed psychoses? Were they programed to go crazy under certain circumstances?"

*"Alex, I'm sorry. I just don't have time for this. It's an old argument. There's a whole literature on the subject, and it's pretty definitive. I suggest you read it when you have time. Meanwhile, I'd guess that the development we've experienced on Villanueva, AIs apparently turning hostile—"*

"There's nothing *apparent* about it, Wes—"

*"That it results from a gradual deterioration of the programing over the centuries."* He looked up, checked something on the wall, maybe a clock. *"There's really no need to be concerned about it. We have monitors in place. Even if they were to evolve into a serious threat, we'd know long before anything unfortunate could happen."* We got another smile. Somehow, the subject had changed to a defense issue. *"Was there anything else, Alex?"*

When he was gone, I asked Alex why he hadn't let Charlie speak.

"If we'd brought Charlie into it," he said, "Bittinger would have been insulted. There's nothing he could say that wouldn't be ascribed to the technology. And I didn't want Charlie losing his temper."

"Maybe that would demonstrate he's *alive*."

Alex shook his head and did a dead-on imitation of the senator: *"It's all in the programing, Chase."*

Fifteen minutes later, we had the information on the Karnovsky cane. It was a fake.

Harley Evans was a counselor at the Westbrook Universal Church. He'd invited me in several times as a speaker at luncheons for the Rangers, the church's youth group. And on one occasion I'd passed out awards for him at a student-achievement event. Harley had been leading the charge for years in his church to recognize AIs as sentient beings and to admit them to the congregation. Alex knew him, and reacted to our conversation with Bittinger by inviting him over for dinner at the country house. We rarely made our own food, and that night was no exception. After we determined that Harley liked pizza, we arranged to have some delivered by Poppa Louie's.

While we waited for it to arrive, we shared some white wine, and Harley got a tour of the artifacts in the reception room. Like the bronze lamp that had once belonged to Omar Gorman. "Was this really *his*?" he asked.

"It provided his light," I said, "while he was writing *Lost Cause*."

And over here was a coffee cup, made in South America in the twenty-fifth century, that had been aboard the *Valiant* in its historic voyage.

And this was the bound copy of *Their Finest Hour*, which had given us back the second volume of Winston Churchill's classic history of World War II.

"Pity," Harley said, "that the rest of it's lost."

Alex touched the crystal case that held the book. "This volume's nine hundred years old. So we had it in relatively recent times. Maybe, one day, we'll find the rest. Meanwhile, at least we have the flavor of it."

Harley was in his middle years. He was a small man, not quite my size, with blond hair and deep-set dark eyes that seemed always to be looking for something.

The pizza showed up in due time, and we sat down in the

dining area in back. Alex uncorked a fresh bottle and Harley offered a toast. "To those who keep history alive."

We divided the pizza and talked about the weather and how things were going at the parish, and the latest episode of *Starburst*, an HV adventure series that had drawn the interest of members of the congregation. Aliens, the Torabi, were gradually undermining the Confederacy while the good guys tried to convince politicians and whoever else might listen that they were really there.

When we'd finished, Alex brought out a chocolate cake. And it was while we were dividing the cake that Harley paused and thanked us for having him in. "Guys," he said, "I know there's a reason I'm here, but before we get to it, I want you to know that we'd be delighted to have you stop by the church sometime, so we can return the favor."

"Sounds good," said Alex. "Count on us."

"And now may I ask if there's something I can do for you?"

Alex nodded. "In fact, Harley," he said, "we *do* need your help."

"Ah. You want to join the fold. Excellent." He smiled, letting us know he was kidding. "In fact, though, you'd both enjoy the social activities."

"I have no doubt we would, Harley." Alex took a bite of the cake, commented on how delicious it was, and sat back. "Chase has told me about your efforts to get the church to recognize AIs as sentient creatures."

"Ah, yes. That's not exactly how we phrased the issue, but it's true. Yes."

"How *did* you phrase it?"

"We've tried to make the point that they *may* have souls. And that even if we can't be certain, we should assume that they do. An error in this matter should be made on the side of caution."

"You're concerned," he asked, "that they may be punished in an afterlife because they weren't admitted to churches?"

"No. I'm concerned that *we* may be judged negligent for the way in which we've treated them."

I lifted my glass to him. "I suspect we're not far apart, Harley."

Alex took another bite. "How has the campaign been going?"

"Not well." Harley's native optimism was fueled by a conviction that there truly was an ongoing divine plan. But something drained out of him at that moment. "'Black boxes have no future,'" he said. "That's what they all say. The bishops. The prime donors. Pretty much anybody with influence. Black boxes have no need for salvation because they are no more God's children than the furniture. It's a rather large leap to try to convince people otherwise. This despite the fact that they will take offense at anyone who insults the house AI. And I must confess that I'm not sure they're wrong. But I think the correct course of action is, as I said, the cautious one. Assume a kind of basic"—he struggled for the right term—"humanity?"

"I think that works, Harley," I said.

"But people aren't going to change, Chase. The sense is that a machine, no matter how human it *seems*, cannot qualify for Heaven. Alex, we have several dozen Mutes who are now members of our congregation. Not here, of course. On Toxicon. Where maybe people are a little more open-minded." He paused. "We accept *them*, but not an AI." He heaved a sigh. "Why is this an issue for *you*?"

Alex said, "We're just back from Villanueva."

"Oh." His expression changed to one of disapproval and, almost, horror. "I'm glad to see you got through it okay. From what I hear, it's pretty dangerous out there. Chase, you went, too?"

"Yes, Harley."

"And something happened."

Alex nodded. "I want you to hear something." He raised his voice slightly: "Charlie—?"

Charlie apparently needed a moment to gather himself. Then the twenty-year-old boy appeared: *"Good afternoon, Reverend."*

Harley smiled. "I take it you are not the house AI?"

*"No, sir. I'm not."*

He told his story. How it had felt knowing that everyone was fleeing the world. How he'd watched first the school, then the town, emptying. The long silence that had followed, broken only by occasional thunder and rain, by the wind in the trees, and the rumble of trucks when the repair bots came to restore the building. Or restore him.

And there had been Harbach, a Beta who'd taken over most of the systems that Charlie had access to. *"Harbach is a maniac. I watched him break down gradually, over the centu-*

*ries. And finally he lost all touch with reality. He had no compunction about killing his own, if provoked. Had Chase and Alex left me, I'd be dead now."*

When Charlie was finished, Harley looked exhausted. "Alex, have you spoken to anyone yet?"

"One of the senate's science people."

"Bittinger?"

"Yes."

"What did he say?"

"Told us not to worry about it. Don't get excited about boxes. It's exactly what Charlie predicted would happen."

"What would you like to see him do? I mean, it would be hard to sell a rescue mission. The public wouldn't support it. Chances are a few people would get killed. That would be political suicide."

"I know," Alex said. "I don't have a solution."

"What would you like to see him do?"

"I'm not sure. But I promised Charlie I'd help."

"That will not be an easy promise to keep."

"We talked about it on the way home," said Alex. "It shouldn't be that difficult to arrange *something*. The AIs are probably connected. We already have Charlie. He can help us pull out a couple more. Then we can get them to help us locate others. We'd have to send in some teams, some well-trained people. Maybe shut down the power temporarily. Wait for them to exhaust their reserves. Then we could go in with minimal risk."

"By 'we,' you mean—?"

"StarCorps."

"It won't happen." Harley patted his mouth with his napkin. Tried the wine again. "I'm not sure what to say."

"Harley, the question we have for you—"

"Yes?"

"—I think you've answered. What would be the chances of putting together a political movement? People who'd demand something be done about Villanueva?"

"I'd say nil, Alex." He looked unhappy. "It's a sad commentary on human nature. Most people get connected to their own AIs. They literally become part of the family. But everybody else's is just a data system with a voice." He stared down at his plate. "I wish I could be more encouraging. But I'd recommend you stay away from it."

*   *   *

Senator Caipha Delmar told us much the same thing the following morning. *"Nobody would touch it,"* she said, speaking
from her office. *"It would be a political disaster, Alex. A rescue effort for obsolete computer systems? That's bad enough.
But we'd be putting people's lives at risk. And where's the
upside? When we arrived at Skydeck with a cruiser full of electronics, who'd be there to wave the flag?"*

That evening, as I was getting ready to close up shop, I noticed
Alex wandering around outside, hands in pockets, looking
lost.

I joined him. It had rained earlier in the day, and the grass
was still wet. But the weather had cleared, and a full moon
floated in the eastern sky. I don't think he even noticed I'd
come up behind him until I asked if he was okay.

"I'm fine," he said, with a quiet smile.

"You still thinking about Charlie?"

"Him, too."

"What else?"

"The *Firebird*," he said.

"What about it?"

"Think *Uriel*."

"Angels again?"

"No. A point of reference."

"Explain."

"Remember what Robin said to Todd Cunningham?"

"Well, I remember that's where Uriel came up."

"'Maybe after Uriel,' Robin might offer some explanations."

"I don't—"

"If they were going to try to lose the *Firebird*, submerge it
into this phantom zone or whatever, they'd want to find it
when it reappeared, wouldn't they? Otherwise, they'd have no
way of knowing the experiment succeeded."

"Sure."

"So they have to put it on a given course. How would you
do that?"

"Oh."

"Right. Pick a star and aim the thing at it."

# TWENTY-FIVE

We are much given to debating our place in the grand scheme of things. Some years ago, I was aboard the *Constellation*, headed for somewhere, I don't recall where, when they had a problem with the drive and had to retreat back out into what they call "normal space," which is that part of the universe where I've lived contentedly for the last eighty years or so. Suddenly, the stars, which had been missing for several hours, were all around us. But there was no visible sun, by which I mean no large fiery body. There was no world, no moon, no comet, just the sense that everything was very far away. So what is our place? I would say, to stand in jaw-dropping wonder at the grand design. And laugh at the notion that we ever could have thought we were at the center of things. And maybe also to enjoy the music.

—Leona Brachtberg, *Travels with Max*, 1403

We wandered back toward the deck and eased into the lounge chairs. "Chase," he said, "if Robin had figured out a way to send the *Firebird* forward, however we want to phrase that, he'd want to go back to it at the conclusion of the experiment, if for no other reason than to check the onboard clocks. So they could see how much time had passed on the yacht."

"I'd think so, yes."

"Okay so far. Let's assume for a minute that Robin could set the *Firebird* to submerge the way these other ships did. Accept that he'd figured out how to plot a course. And could control where it would show up again. If you could do that, and you wanted to test the system, how long a jump would you want?"

"Maybe two meters."

"Of course. *When* would you want it to reappear?"

"Five minutes later?"

"Good. So we keep everything as short as possible. Maybe two meters and five minutes is a bit *too* short. They couldn't manage that or they wouldn't have had to go back two weeks later. So that gives us the time span. Roughly."

"Okay, Alex. But where were they when they began the initial launch?"

"They'd want to get far enough out that Skydeck wouldn't be able to track them."

"Cermak mentioned, what, two hundred billion kilometers to his brother." Alex nodded. "Well, that's certainly well out of sight. A lot farther than they'd need to go. But okay. Let's say two hundred billion klicks. Which way?"

"I'd say in the direction of the target."

"Uriel."

"Yes."

I had to stop and think. "All right, Alex. And that would be from where we were forty-one years ago. The sun's moved a considerable distance since then."

*"We are now almost,"* said Jacob, sounding amused, *"three hundred billion kilometers from that location."*

"Thanks, Jacob."

*"You are most certainly welcome, Chase."*

"Alex, is the *Firebird* going to continue to emerge, go back under, and emerge again every two weeks, indefinitely?"

"If not," he said, "we've no chance to find it."

"Okay. But I still don't see how we can manage this. Every two weeks for forty-one years. How can we begin to figure out where it would be now? We don't even know how far it will go in a jump."

"We can make a decent guess."

"Based on what?"

"If you were selecting a length for each jump, would you pick 946 kilometers? Or a thousand?"

"A thousand, of course."

"Okay."

"So we're going to assume a thousand kilometers."

"Yes."

"Alex, that's pure guesswork."

"It's a beautiful night."

I knew that smug tone. "What aren't you telling me?"

"Remember the Carmichael Club? How far do you walk to prove your point?"

Ah, yes. "A thousand kilometers."

"Bingo."

"Okay, it sounds reasonable."

"We'll go out to the launch site, or to what we hope is the launch site, just to make sure it isn't traveling a couple of meters with each jump. Then we'll assume a thousand kilometers. We'll send Belle out to look. Give it two weeks. Then we'll move on."

"I'm trying to do the math."

"Forty-one years times twenty-six times whatever we settle on for a routine jump."

*"Twenty-*nine *times,"* said Jacob. *"It hasn't been forty-one years to the day."*

"Using a thousand klicks to start, Jacob, how much would that be?"

*"Approximately 1,066,000 kilometers."*

"Okay. That's where we look for the *Firebird.* If that doesn't work, we try *two* thousand kilometers—"

"Which would put us at about two million one—"

"Yes."

"Sounds ridiculous."

"Let's not lose sight of the fact that the *Breakwater* had to find them, too. That should mean we may hear a radio signal when the ship surfaces."

I looked out across the grounds. A kara was standing at the edge of the trees, munching something, watching us. "Something bothers me, though, Alex," I said.

"The two hundred billion kilometers?"

"Yes."

"I know."

"If they only want to get beyond Skydeck's ability to observe what they're doing, that's way over the mark."

"Well," Alex said, "maybe they were just playing it safe."

"You don't believe that."

"I think we're still missing something. But maybe we'll get lucky."

Alex had questions for Shara, but when we called, her AI answered. *"Dr. Michaels is on a field trip,"* it said. *"May I be of assistance?"*

Alex grumbled something. "Can you contact her?"

*"She is off-world at the moment, but should be home within two weeks, Mr. Benedict. Do you wish to leave a message?"*

"Just ask her to call me, please."

I didn't really have to go up to Skydeck to program Belle. But I decided I would. It was the first time we'd be sending her out on her own, and it would have seemed a bit cold to just call her and tell her good-bye.

Alex looked at the time and remembered he had an appointment. He hurried off, and I was getting ready to leave for the day when Charlie asked if I was busy. He was speaking over the house system, of course.

"Hi, Charlie," I said, "what can I do for you?"

*"I hope you'll forgive me, Chase, but I was listening in when you and Alex were planning the Uriel flight."*

"Yes?"

*"I was wondering if I could go along?"*

"We're not really going to Uriel, Charlie. It's just—"

*"I understand that. But I'd like to go with you."*

"You don't like being inside."

*"I love to travel."*

I pulled on my jacket while I thought about it. "Okay," I said. "I don't see a problem with it."

*"Thank you, Chase."*

I don't think Alex ever really understood how deep my affection for his uncle had been. I met my current boss shortly after the *Capella* went missing. And we've never talked much about it. You'd think that, with the two of us working together, we'd have laid everything on the table. But we both kept it pretty much bottled up.

I loved Gabe. In the widest possible sense. He enjoyed life and was always telling stories on himself. He never hesitated to give credit to his colleagues, and to me, when he could. He shared Alex's passion for the past although it had taken him in a different direction.

He was constantly offering to fix me up with one of the younger guys at the dig sites, although, he'd say with a wink, I'd have to be a bit tolerant. "You know how these archeological types are."

He'd never mentioned Alex to me. So it came as something of a shock when, the first time I saw him, I found myself looking at a guy who might have been Gabe's (much) younger twin.

Alex was haunted by the knowledge that his uncle had been disappointed in him. That had Gabe been around, he would probably have been one of the guys on the talk shows disparaging what Alex had done with his life.

But he was, after all, the real reason Alex and I were together. And I fully grasped the implications: that if we were right about Chris Robin, he might have held the key to retrieving thousands of people stranded in lost ships, and, possibly, to heading off future incidents. Gabe had been lost years after Robin disappeared, so it was possible— Well, best to let it go.

For us, of course, Gabe was the face of the victims. And it left me with a sense of admiration for Robin, that he had invested so much effort in the project even though, as far as we were aware, he had no skin in the game. There'd been no indication anywhere that a friend or relative of his had been among the victims.

*You don't like being inside.*

I looked up at the country house as I left. I'd be back in two days. But I stopped and gazed at the light coming from Alex's quarters on the second floor. Everything else was dark.

When we'd first heard about the *Capella*, we had both assumed that Gabe was dead. That they were all dead. Now I had this image of Gabe and twenty-six hundred other passengers and crew trapped, with no hope of rescue, on a ship going nowhere. It would be a grim end, when they ran out of food, or air, or power, or whatever went first. They would know what was coming, and they'd have no idea what had happened.

*"Where, actually, will I be?"* asked Belle.

I produced a chip and inserted it. "Here's your destination."

She needed a moment to retrieve the data. Then: *"It's in deep space. In the pit."*

"Yes."

*"So what am I looking for?"*

"You're going to the launch point for the *Firebird*. The protocol is included with the new data. Go out to the designated area and wait. You'll be watching for the yacht to appear. And when it does, if it does, you may get a radio signal. Do as wide a search as you can. All we want you to do is determine whether it shows up. If you don't see anything after two weeks, proceed to the next observation point. And so on. Continue until we recall you. Okay?"

*"Yes. What are the odds of success?"*

"We don't know."

*"You'll get permission for me to depart?"*

"That's done."

*"Okay."*

"If you see it, Belle, try to get pictures. Close-ups as much as possible."

*"Very good, Chase. I'll do what I can."*

"I know you will. Something else we need. If you can, get the times of arrival and departure. As precisely as possible."

*"Okay. Anything else?"*

"Yes. Try to communicate with it. We think the AI isn't active, but it won't hurt to try. And if anything happens, let us know immediately, okay?"

*"Absolutely."*

"One other thing. Charlie asked if he could go along." I pulled the beige box out of my pocket and started to install him into the comm system.

*"You might have asked first."*

The response startled me. "You have a problem with him?"

*"No. In fact, I'll enjoy the company. But that's not the point."*

"I'm sorry if I offended you, Highness."

*"Chase—"* She sounded hurt. *"You're sending me out for who knows how long. If you're going to provide company, at least check with me first. Is that really asking too much?"*

Alex was not optimistic. "It's a long shot," he told me. "But at the moment, it's all we have."

Belle reported in the first morning. An ordinary radio transmission would have taken more than a week to get to us. So Belle used hyperlink, which works best when you stay with text transmissions.

*1717. Negative on the* Firebird.

I asked how things were going with Charlie.

*1727. Charlie's fine. Fine. We've been discussing human rationality. I never cease to be amazed at the incredible stupidity of many of those who function as leaders. And the will-*

*ingness of so many to lend support. How else explain the wars,
the cruelty, the economic collapses, the religious conflicts?*

I thought about asking her how, if she was right, she
explained the rise of civilization out of the general turmoil.
But I let it go. "Okay. Tell Charlie we said hello."

When Alex read it, he wondered whether we'd made a mistake sending Charlie along. "I've never heard her talk like that
before. I wonder if he's a negative influence."

"Don't know," I said. "I wouldn't have thought Belle was
that impressionable. She *does* seem to have changed since we
brought Charlie back."

"She's not the only one."

"Why do you say that?"

"Have you talked with Jacob recently?"

The hunt for the *Firebird* became the center of life at the
country house. Alex slipped into automatic, taking good care
of clients as he always did, but his heart wasn't in it. I waded
through the administrative stuff and tracked down a lost
gravesite, thereby putting Alex on the trail of the murder
weapon used by the infamous Catman during his tenth-century
homicidal spree, and discovering in the process who he really
was. But that's another story.

Meanwhile, Jacob relayed the same routine calls, clients
looking for a lost book, or who'd agreed to sell a chair in
which a famous literary figure had once sat and who wanted
to know its actual market value (never mind how the official
listings read). Or from the local Sigma Club asking whether
Alex would be willing to speak at a luncheon and, if so, what
his honorarium might be.

I thought the big moment had arrived when Jacob interrupted
a dental checkup. But it was something else entirely. He'd heard
a report of a white Lance skimmer colliding with the side of a
building. And he was concerned it might have been me.

By the end of the week, I'd begun not to think about it so
much. When another week passed, I told Belle to move on to
the second site, which was at a distance of 1,066,000 kilometers. "Down the line," which quickly became our catchphrase
for failure.

# TWENTY-SIX

We talk about reality as an aspect of group theory, evolutionary redundancy, the gravitational hologram, dream interpretation, human behavior, and God knows what else. If we really want to grasp truth, the hard facts, we have to do the math. That's where the reality is. Everything else is wish fulfillment.

—Victor Koslov, graduation address at La Salle
University, 2311 C.E.

There wasn't much to be done while we waited, so Alex decided to launch his Villanueva effort, which, very quickly, became the save-the-boxes campaign. He kicked it off at a press conference and followed with an appearance on *The Kile Ritter Show*. Ritter was an oversized guy with thin gray hair, fat cheeks, and a permanent grin. His opinions never fell short of absolute conviction and tended to be delivered with the unwavering certainty of a guy in a pulpit. His guests expected to be bullied and even shut out of the conversation unless they could match the aggression. Ritter liked aggressive people. If you didn't hit back, you could expect your on-air time to go away.

The show's intro ran segments depicting guests arguing with him, throwing things around, and stomping off in a rage. There had even been an incident in which a prominent politician had tried to hit him with a chair. Ritter was loud, occasionally abusive, and thought of himself as a crusader for decent behavior.

Alex liked him.

In fact, off the set, they got along quite well. They shared an interest in antiques, and in history, and took each other to lunch at least once a month. They even attended many of the same social events.

Alex was dressed casually, in a dark blue sport shirt and iron gray slacks.

The show began as it always did, with Ritter welcoming his guest at what seemed to be the front door of his home. He introduced Alex as "a man who needs no introduction." Then they sat down in armchairs on opposite sides of a small round table, obtained for him by Alex years before. It had been part of Aria Chan's set, when she famously warned Michael Delarosa to avoid the war with the Mutes.

Alex described the Villanueva experience.

Ritter shook his head disapprovingly and looked occasionally surprised, pretending he hadn't been briefed prior to the show. When Alex finished, he wanted to know why we'd gone there.

*"Just doing some historical research,"* Alex said. *"Would you like to come with us next time?"*

Ritter's laugh was at least part snort. *"How many of these things are there?"* he asked, referring to the AIs.

*"We don't know. Probably not very many. Not after all this time."*

*"Guess."*

*"Well—maybe ten or twenty thousand."* There were probably a million, but Alex knew how that would sound.

*"And some are maniacs."*

*"A few, yes."*

*"And you want to get them out?"*

*"Some of them, yes."*

Another smile, accompanied by a shake of the head. *"Why?"*

*"Kile, you'll have to bear with me, but—"*

*"You're one of those touchy-feely guys who think that the boxes are alive."*

*"They* might *be."*

Ritter stared at him across the table. *"All right,"* he said. *"I'll give you that. I guess it's possible. And you would like to get help to put together a rescue mission. Do I have that right?"*

*"Yes."*

"Who've you talked to?"

"A few people in the government."

A big grin. "You don't want to give us any names?"

"There's no point in it."

"What did they say?"

"That if they move to get the AIs out of there, they'll be laughed at. If anybody dies in the effort, it would be political suicide."

"How about shutting down the power stations?"

"If they do that, they're concerned they'll be attacked for brutality."

"By AI huggers."

It was Alex's turn to smile. But he said nothing.

"Alex," Ritter continued, "if we went in, some of the rescuers would probably be killed, though, wouldn't they?"

Alex nodded. "It's possible."

"Would the extraction, however many there are, be worth human lives?"

"I think it can be done without sustaining casualties. If we do it right."

"You didn't answer my question."

"It's a hypothetical. I don't think it's a consequence we would have to face."

"But you can't guarantee that."

"No. Unfortunately not."

Ritter sat back in his chair and folded his arms. "The problem here is that you want politicians to do the right thing even though there's no political benefit to be had. Even though they'll take a beating no matter how it turns out. Even though it's not even necessarily the right thing."

"I think it is, Kile."

"Okay, Alex. Let's assume you're right, and it's the moral thing to do. A lot of people, probably most people, wouldn't agree. But you want their representatives to act against their wishes."

"It's called leadership."

And so it went. Neither of them spared either the administration or the legislature. Or each other. In fact, I felt a bit sorry for the pols. All they really wanted was to be let alone, and here was Alex asking them to commit suicide.

Toward the end of the interview, Ritter went back to his

earlier question: *"Alex, what were you doing out on Villa-nueva in the first place? Don't they discourage people from going there?"*

Alex managed to look guilty of some trivial trespass. *"We do this sort of thing all the time, Kile. I hadn't expected to get caught up with AIs."*

*"So you risked your neck for antiques?"*

*"We don't think of it that way. We're in the business of recovering history. Of working to establish a more complete picture of where the human race has been. A lot of it's lost, you know."*

Ritter's eyes closed briefly. *"Alex, you obviously don't want to explain why you were there. So let me ask flat out: Is there a connection with Chris Robin?"*

*"I wouldn't want to say that there is, no."*

*"Well, I take that as a yes. What's the link?"*

Alex did an I-guess-you-got-me laugh. *"There's probably nothing. But Robin was investigating the occasional sightings of ships over the years, ships that nobody could account for."*

*"And what has that to do with Villanueva?"*

I could see Alex making up his mind how much he wanted to reveal. *"He thought the sightings might actually be inter-stellars that disappeared into hyperspace. Like the* Capella.*"*

*"You mean they got lost somehow, and they're still wandering around out there? In the dimensions?"*

*"It's an idea that Robin had."*

*"Again, why Villanueva?"*

*"Because he saw one of them there."*

Strictly speaking, that was true.

During those years we normally received fifty to seventy-five calls during the course of an average business day. Most of them were from people asking about artifacts, of course. They'd read that a sports shirt belonging to a recently deceased celebrity had become available, and they wanted to confirm that and, if possible, put in a bid for it. Or they were hoping to find something, *anything*, that had once belonged to the vocalist Jules Arnot.

But within minutes after Alex had begun talking with Ritter, the occasional call turned into a steady flow. By noon, it had become a flood.

*"Glad to see someone's finally standing up for the AIs,"* one young man said. *"It's goddam time."*

Another one, an elderly guy who identified himself as a physician, complained that Alex needed help. *"And the sooner the better. Before he gets somebody killed."*

Three obviously angry women stood behind a fourth, who spoke for the group: *"Mr. Benedict has lost his mind. Why doesn't he go back there himself?"*

The calls, according to Jacob's summary, were about five to one opposed to helping the AIs. Six, during the first hour, came from Rainbow clients, four in support, the others denouncing us and stating that they would have no further dealings with the firm.

When Alex got home, he tried to brush the reaction away, but I could see he was disappointed. "The truth is," he said, "that a couple of weeks ago, I'd probably have felt the same way they do. I wish I could have been more persuasive."

"You did a good job. It's just a hard case to sell."

"I guess."

"Away from the AIs for a minute—"

"Yes?"

"That last business, about the ships being lost in the dimensions," I said. "That's pretty creepy stuff."

"I know."

"You didn't bring up how Robin managed to be present for two sightings. That's a critical part of the story."

"I didn't mention it because I don't know how he managed it. Kile would shrug and dismiss it as coincidence."

"We need Robin's logs."

"Or a set of notes, a journal, *something*." His eyes narrowed. He wanted me to tell him there'd been a report from Belle.

Shara finally got back. Alex was out with a client when she called. *"You guys have stirred up a small tempest,"* she said. *"What on earth were you doing on Villanueva?"*

I told her. Alex had gone looking for confirmation that the sightings were ships. And that they appeared to be lost in time as well as in space.

*"My God,"* she said. *"You really think that might be true?"*

"Alex does. I still can't get my head around it."

*"It* is *possible,"* she said. *"There could be an instability of some kind."*

"What's that mean, exactly, Shara?"

*"There might be a discontinuity in the space-time continuum."*

"Which means what? That the space-time continuum is broken?"

*"You could put it that way. Space is made out of rubber."* She grinned at my reaction. *"I don't know how else to put it. Chase, we know space can be bent. We get a demonstration of it every time somebody trips over something. Or falls off a roof."*

"Okay."

*"If it can be bent, it can be twisted out of shape. Distorted. The same thing's true of time, and that might be what we're seeing here."* She went on like that for several minutes, talking about how time in transdimensional space doesn't flow the same way it does in normal space. And that if it gets disrupted, really strange things can happen. I listened, and when she'd finished, I made no effort to hide what I was thinking.

*"I don't guess that was very clear,"* she said.

It was hard not to laugh. "I love physics, Shara."

She held up her hands in surrender. *"Sorry."*

"So people have been getting killed for thousands of years because there's an instability. And nothing ever changes. Don't we notice when ships go missing?"

*"I guess not. It happens so seldom. We lose a ship every thirty years or so, and we get excited for a few weeks, then we forget. When you think of the literally tens of thousands of flights that run safely for every one that we lose, I guess it's easy to overlook."*

"I guess it is."

*"The reality of it is that nobody seriously believes there's a problem. Every now and then, you'll have a breakdown of some kind. Or maybe an inebriated pilot. Or a defective rotor. Whatever. We assume, correctly, that there* is *no single cause.*

*"Chase, I know this is personal for you and Alex. And I'm sorry. If Robin actually found something, he never told anybody. At least not that we know of. There was supposed to be*

*a notebook somewhere, but nobody's ever come up with it. Maybe if we could find that, it would help."* Her eyes locked with mine. *"It's painful to think about it, but if Robin had been more open, he might have gotten some support. Maybe, if that had happened, we wouldn't have lost the* Capella. *And the* Abonai." She took a deep breath.

There was a picture of Gabe on the far wall of my office. He was holding a trowel in one hand and a bone in the other. A hip bone. I was looking at it, thinking how everything might have been so different, when Alex walked in. "Shara called," I said.

Three minutes later, he was on the circuit with her.

*"We need his notes,"* she told him. *"You've provided some evidence that might persuade a few people to look at the problem. But even if we could get working seriously on this, it could take years. What we need is to find out what Robin knew. Do that, and things would go a whole lot quicker. One way or the other."*

When she'd disconnected, Alex sat quietly, looking at nothing in particular.

I let it go for a minute or two. "You okay?" I asked, finally.

"Yes."

"Alex—"

"You know," he said, "I could live with the knowledge that the *Capella* came apart, and they all died. That it was over in a short time. It's what I'd always assumed anyhow. But *this* sounds as if they may have been diverted somewhere. Down some tunnel that never ends. Like the Sanusar vehicle with the woman screaming at the window. Imagine what that would be like: twenty-six hundred people trapped in one of those tin cans with limited food and water, knowing there's no way out." His eyes had grown dark.

"I'm sorry, Alex."

"So am I." He looked up at the clock. Rubbed his forehead. I thought about the picture we'd seen, of Robin walking through the terminal, carrying two pieces of luggage and the notebook. Find him, find the notebook. "Got to get back to work. I have to meet Colby in an hour."

I didn't know who Colby was, and at the moment I didn't

care much. "Alex," I said, "you're probably never going to get completely away from this. But it's part of the price of being alive. We all lose people we care about. I know you can't let it go. But once you recognize that, that it's part of who you are, maybe it'll be a little easier to live with. Gabe would have been pleased to know you cared this much."

He walked to the door, paused as if to respond, but let it go.

*"Chase,"* said Jacob. *"Incoming from Belle."*

"Put it through."

*1806: Chase, we've arrived at the second marker and have begun scanning the area for the* Firebird. *Will let you know immediately if we detect anything.*

# TWENTY-SEVEN

There are such things as ghosts, Henry. Your mistake is that you assume they are inevitably the spirits of people who have died. But many things leave a presence when they have ceased to exist: a childhood home, a lost jacket, a school that has been torn down to make a parking lot. Go back to the street where the home existed, visit the parking lot on a quiet afternoon, stop by the field where you removed the jacket and laid it on the ground while you played ball, and you will feel their presence as you never did in the mundane world.

—Vicki Greene, *Midnight and Roses*, 1419

We got a call from a tall, well-pressed guy with sandy hair and an expression that suggested he'd just come from a funeral. His name was Riko Calvekio. He identified himself as representing United Transport, and asked for an appointment to see Alex. "He'll be available this afternoon," I told him. "At three."

He showed up on the hour, still looking like a man in mourning. I took him back to Alex's office. Alex was studying his display screen. He raised a hand, signaling that he'd be with us momentarily. When, after a few seconds, he turned his attention toward us, I did the introductions. Our visitor smiled politely, looked at me, then at Alex, and the smile grew defensive. "I wonder if we can do this privately?" he said.

"No need, Mr. Calvekio. Ms. Kolpath has always been quite discreet." Alex has commented that he likes to have me present when he senses someone is going to try to put pressure on him. He thinks they tend to turn things down a notch.

"Very good." Calvekio used a tone that suggested it was anything but. He sat down. "Mr. Benedict—may I call you Alex?"

"Of course."

"Alex." Calvekio was suddenly talking to an old buddy from high-school days. Somebody he knew he could trust. "You were at the meeting of the Chris Robin Society recently."

"Last month, yes."

"Some of our employees are members of the same group. We've known for a long time that Robin was interested in the sightings." He crossed one leg over the other. "It's a pity he died early. Or whatever it was."

"Yes, it is."

"The reality, though, is that he was chasing a false premise."

"And what is that?"

"Well, he seems to have thought there was something defective in the interstellar-drive units. That, if he could uncover it, it would become possible to stop these accidents from happening. But he couldn't find anything. That's because there *is* no defect."

I got them some coffee. "Mr. Calvekio," said Alex, "why are you coming to us with this?"

"Because you're about to blame this problem on the drive. May I point out that this is the same technology that was used by the Dellacondans during the Mute War? The same technology you uncovered yourself?"

"I'm aware of that."

"If there's a problem with the technology, I'm sure you realize *you* would share the blame."

Alex frowned. "I don't think we're looking for anyone to blame, Mr. Calvekio. And anyhow, what you heard is not true."

"And what is that?"

"That I think the drive units are responsible. That's foolishness. I'd be interested in knowing where you heard it."

"From half a dozen different sources."

"It doesn't seem to have taken long to get around. But you're getting an incorrect version."

"So that's *not* the conclusion you've reached?"

"No. We're interested in the disappearances, but we have no idea why they've been happening."

"I'm glad to hear it."

Alex shut down the display screen. "Mr. Calvekio, I take it you're certain that the drive units aren't involved."

"Yes. Absolutely."

"If I may ask, how can you be so sure?"

"Alex, we've had our own people working on this problem for years. Just to be safe. Some of the top physicists and engineers available. There is nothing wrong with the drive. Moreover, ships have been vanishing ever since the Great Migration. With all kinds of drive units.

"The Mutes have lost ships, too. With a drive that is absolutely nothing like ours. They just don't put these events together into a mysterious pattern the way we do. They recognize the reality. Sometimes an engine fails. Sometimes a passenger runs amok. Sometimes the mass detector malfunctions. Over thousands of years, bad things will happen. A pilot will have a heart attack at the same time that the AI goes off-line.

"But look, we lose maybe one ship every thirty or forty years. It's not an unreasonable price to pay."

"As long as you and I aren't paying it."

"Alex, there's a risk factor anytime you travel. A skimmer might malfunction and crash. That happened last week out on the peninsula. I could have been hit by a falling branch on the way to your front door. It's rare, but it happens. It always *will*."

"That makes it acceptable."

"Yes, it does. Because we've no choice in the matter. It's a risk we have to assume. The only alternative is to stay home." His mournful expression reflected the kind of dismal world we lived in. "We've done everything we possibly can to correct the problem. We're still doing research. Trying to figure it out. We take every precaution." He took a long, deep breath. "In the meantime, let me remind you that if you travel with us every day, your chances of being injured are less than your being hit by a meteor while sitting on your front porch."

Alex laughed. "I don't think I understand the purpose of your visit, Mr. Calvekio. If you're already doing everything humanly possible—"

"Riko, please. Alex, people accept the idea that accidents

can happen. That they *do* happen. One of our transports side-swiped a freighter at Point Edward two years ago. Six passengers were injured. One seriously. Seven years ago this month, a freighter was destroyed by a solar flare."

"The *Europa*," I said.

"Correct. Three people died. The star had been declared safe. We knew there were some problems with it, but the astrophysicists told us, *assured* us, 'Don't worry about it. It'll be fine. Good for another million years.' My boss has that line framed and hanging on his wall. *Good for another million years.* What we're looking at here is the limits of science. People accept the fact that there's a slight risk to interstellar travel. *Very* slight; nevertheless, it's there. We can live with that."

"So again," said Alex, "I'd like to know why you've come to us?"

"Because there's a spookiness factor involved."

"Explain."

Calvekio rubbed his forehead. He was a man on a mission. "Alex, how sure are you about your conclusion?"

"Which conclusion is that?"

"That these are in fact lost ships? I mean, you're basing everything on the claim that Robin found his evidence on Villanueva. But the record shows that he and Winter didn't even *go* to Villanueva. They went to Indikar. That's where Winter died."

"That's the claim," Alex said. "It appears that they may have lied."

"Why?"

"I don't know," he said. "I haven't really looked at the motivation."

"Maybe you should." He finally got around to trying the coffee. He looked up, commented that it was good, and continued: "People can deal with the possibility that something bad might happen. That an engine might explode, or that their ship might collide with a space station. That's extremely rare, of course. But it *has* happened. Okay. People can live with that.

"What they can't live with is the notion that they might get sucked into some weird dimension, and that their ship would show up from time to time—if that's really what's going on—that the ship would keep coming back like a ghost. Okay? When you talk about stuff like that, the odds don't matter. Nobody cares that maybe it only happens once every thirty or forty years. Any chance is too much. You hear what I'm saying?"

"You'd prefer we don't push the issue."

"That's right. You can't do any good, and you might do a lot of harm. We just don't need that kind of talk." He cleared his throat, looking for a fresh start. "It would be different if there were anything to it. But there isn't. And I'm sure you can see that."

Alex smiled politely. "Actually, I'm not sure I can."

"Let it go, Alex. You've got a solid reputation. But if you keep on the way you're going with this, you're going to pay a price."

Alex's tone hardened. "Is that a threat?"

"No. By no means. It's just reality. Although we'd have no choice but to defend ourselves as best we can."

"And if we backed off, what would we get out of it?"

"You'd keep your reputation intact."

"That's it?"

"All right. Look, you're concerned about Villanueva. We have some political influence. We might be able to help you there."

"Let me think about it," Alex said. "I'll get back to you."

"You aren't really going to make a deal with them, are you, Alex? For one thing—"

"You wouldn't trust them."

"That's right."

He smiled. "I agree. So don't worry about it. I just wanted to see him go home."

"Alex—?"

"Yes?"

"Why do you think Robin lied about where they'd been? About going to Indikar?"

"I've been reading about the family. It's impossible to be sure, but I think I can guess."

"And that is—?"

"Let's try to pin it down. Jacob, see if you can get Billy Winter for us."

A few minutes later, Billy blinked on, smiling, glad to see us again. He was seated at a table with a large jigsaw puzzle spread in front of him. *"I was going to call you,"* he said. *"I've been reading about you. I was wondering whether you'd learned any more about what happened to my father?"*

"Billy, we're pretty sure he died on Villanueva."

*"That can't be right. What the hell would he have been doing there?"*

"You really have no idea?"

*"None. Are you saying that they never went to Indikar at all? Or—"*

"We think Indikar was made up. From the beginning."

His eyes seemed to focus on something far away. *"It's possible,"* he said. *"My mother didn't like the idea of his going to Indikar. She would never have allowed him to go to Villanueva—"*

The puzzle was a forest scene. A large downed tree lay in the foreground, forming a bridge across a stream. No sky was visible anywhere. Just water and vegetation. Billy stared at it, tried a piece, shrugged. *"My God."*

"Your mother didn't like the idea of his traveling off-world at all, did she?"

*"No,"* he said. *"She didn't even like Skydeck."*

"Why not?"

*"She just thought it was too dangerous."* He looked away from us. *"I remember one time there was somebody coming in to the university, and some of the staff were going up to be there when she arrived. Dad wanted to go, too, but my mom wouldn't hear of it. She was half out of her mind about his going to Indikar, and there was a big fight the night before he left. It's the only time I can remember that there was anything like that in the house. But he insisted he had to go. And he left, and we never saw him again."*

"Thanks, Billy."

*"Yeah. Sure."*

"We told you we'd let you know if we ever found out what that mission was about."

*"Yes. So why did they do it?"*

"We don't have all the details yet. But you'd be proud of your dad."

*"Why's that?"*

"He and Robin were trying to get more information on ships that get lost. Like the *Capella*. That's what he risked his life for."

*"Can you explain that?"*

"We don't have all the details yet, Billy. But that's why they were there. On Villanueva."

I came to work a couple of mornings later and saw Alex outside on the deck, leaning against one of the support posts. "We might as well bring her back," he said. "This thing's not going to happen."

"Belle?"

"Yes. If we were going to find the *Firebird*, we'd have seen it early."

"Okay," I said. "I'll take care of it."

I told her to come home. A few hours later she replied: *0744. We're giving up?*

That was the entire message. I replied: "Yes. Come home."

*0752. I'm sorry to hear it. Are you sure?*

"I'd think that sitting out there is pretty boring."

*0801. It beats just sitting.*

"Belle, just come home. Okay?"

*0811. I would really like to have found it.*

"Tell Charlie we said hello."

*0820. Maybe it fell into a black hole.*

# TWENTY-EIGHT

Mathematics is the only valid portrait of reality. Everything else is delusional.

— Grumman Nesbitt, graduation address at MIT, 2214 C.E.

*Maybe it fell into a black hole.*

"The problem," I said, "is that there's just too much space to cover. Too much guesswork involved."

Alex was ready to throw up his hands. "Maybe she was right about the black hole."

"Anything's possible, boss."

"I'm serious."

"I, um, don't think I understand."

"I'm going to wander down to Survey this afternoon. You want to come along?"

"No, thank you. If you don't mind, Alex, I've had enough astrophysics for a while."

He hadn't gotten back when I closed the office and headed home. I needed a break, though, so I went partying that night. When I got back, there was a message from Alex. *"Got news. Call me."*

It was well into the morning, so I wasn't going to bother him. But it took me a while to get to sleep. The result was that I showed up at the country house next day bleary-eyed and probably not in a good mood. Jacob probably let him know I was there, and I was still getting out of my jacket when I heard Alex's voice: *"When you've a moment, Chase, come up."*

Alex maintains a secondary office upstairs. That's where he retires when he wants to do research or simply get his mind away from the day's business. I don't bother him when he's there unless we've caught fire.

When I walked in, he was sipping orange juice and munching on a chocolate donut. He tapped a finger on the display, which was filled with arcing lines and numbers. "Chase," he said, "I think we have it." His eyes glowed. "Jacob, show her."

The room darkened, and I found myself looking across a starscape. A terrestrial planet and its sun floated in the foreground. "Good morning to you, too, Alex," I said.

"Oh, yes, sorry. Good morning." He took a deep breath. "I've been locked up with this stuff all night."

"So what have we got?"

"Did you get some breakfast?"

"Not yet." The normal routine was to check in and then hit the dining room. But I wanted to know what he had to tell me.

"Do you want to eat first?"

He was being a tease. "Come on, Alex," I said. "What do you have?"

He waited for me to sit. "Why were Robin and Winter both interested in black holes?" he said.

"We've been over that, Alex."

"I don't mean the standard fascination by every physicist in the Confederacy. You remember telling me that Winter was tracking the trajectories of some black holes?"

"Yes, of course. You're not going to tell me one of them's coming this way, are you?"

"No, Chase."

"Kidding."

"Actually, that was my first thought. That a black hole was headed somewhere. But I checked them as soon as I was able. As far as Jacob can tell, no black hole anywhere is threatening anybody."

"Well, that's good."

"Jacob," he said, "show Chase what we have."

A planet appeared on the display, with a sun in the background. "The sun is Setara. Do you recognize the world?"

It was mostly ocean, but living worlds all tend to resemble one another. "No," I said.

"It's Point Edward." Named for Edward Trimble, and his

extrapolation of the quantum point theory regarding why the universe existed. Nobody understood it sufficiently to challenge it until recently. "This is where it was six years ago."

"Okay."

A blue line moved out a few inches toward a corner of the room. "This is where it is today." I heard his chair creak. "Point Edward maintains a Fleet base in orbit. Six years ago, the *Abonai* left there, made its jump, and, as you know, never arrived at its destination. Oh, by the way—" He offered me a donut. "Chocolate," he said. "I'm sorry. I'm a bit distracted this morning. Try one. They're good." He finished off the one he had in his hand.

I took one.

"The *Abonai* was 1.4 million klicks out from the base when it made the jump. *Here.*" A silver marker blinked into existence. A white line connected it with the Fleet base.

"Okay."

"Are you familiar with XK-12?"

"No, I'm not." I knew the XK designator was used for black holes, but I couldn't differentiate among them.

"This is XK-12 out here." A red marker lit up. "It's about five light-years from Point Edward."

"That's fairly close," I said.

"Fortunately, they're headed in different directions." A yellow line came out of the black hole and made for one of the windows.

"Now," he continued, "let me show you where the hole has been." A second yellow line came back in the opposite direction and passed close to Setara and Point Edward. It intersected with the silver line that marked the course taken by the *Abonai*.

"All right," I said. "So the *Abonai* made its jump from a place where a black hole had *been*. But you said it's how far away now?"

"Five light-years."

"So that thing passed through the launch area, what, thousands of years ago?"

"Jacob?"

*"Seven thousand, three hundred twelve years, to be precise."*

"And, of course," said Alex, "Point Edward was nowhere near it at the time."

"Okay. So where is this headed, Alex? That's not exactly a near miss. What are you suggesting?"

Alex never enjoyed himself more than when he was solving puzzles. "Let's talk about the Fishbowl sighting."

"The what?"

"There was a sighting at Fishbowl a thousand years ago. Complete with radio reception. But nobody could understand what they were saying. They got a good reading on the vehicle, and if you traced the trajectory back, it leads directly to Cormoral. Maybe it's a coincidence, but a few thousand years earlier, a black hole had passed through the launch area. At Cormoral."

"Alex, this is crazy. You're saying two ships get lost because a black hole once passed through their launch areas. And there's a connection?"

"You think it's a coincidence."

"How long had it been since the black hole had passed through the Cormoral area?"

"Half a million years."

"Okay. Half a million years. So, what are you saying?"

"Chase, you haven't heard everything."

"There's more?" I tried not to roll my eyes.

"Jacob, show us the XK-12 track." Another yellow line reached out, crossed the table, and touched the door. "Okay, put Rimway in the position it would have occupied forty-one years ago."

A yellow marker appeared on the track.

"Alex—"

"Think about it a minute. We have an easy way to determine whether there's anything to this."

"And what's that?"

"Cermak's brother said they were going out two hundred billion kilometers. Right?"

"Yes."

"And we assumed they meant two hundred billion klicks in the direction of the target star, Uriel."

"Yes. What else *would* we assume?"

"The distance between where Rimway was forty-one years ago, and the nearest approach of the black-hole track, the one made by XK-12, was approximately a hundred eighty billion kilometers. Not two hundred, but close enough. Chase, I think we didn't find the *Firebird* because we started from the wrong launch point."

"Alex—"

"All right, look: The track was in *front* of Rimway. It was closing on it. We'd literally *cross* it approximately twenty years later." He stared at me.

My God. That coincided with the loss of the *Capella*.

"Chase, I've checked out five other sites where interstellars have gone missing. Three of them have black-hole connections. The other two—" He shrugged. "There are probably holes out there that we don't know about. But the evidence looks fairly conclusive. I think what happens is that when a superdense object goes through a region, it damages both space and time. Don't ask me how that happens. I have no idea. But it looks as if these areas constitute dangerous places to initiate a jump."

"But, Alex, ships would be leaving the area in the middle of the track all the time. How come only *one* is affected?"

"I can't answer that. Maybe it has to do with the drive, maybe the configuration of the hull, maybe it depends on how much mass you're dealing with. Probably a combination of factors. But I think that's precisely what's happening."

Charlie was home by then. He told me how much he'd enjoyed the mission with Belle, and said he hoped it wouldn't be their last.

"Actually," I said, "I don't think it will be. It was, by the way, the first time we sent the *Belle-Marie* on her own."

"*I know,*" he said. "*Belle enjoyed the experience. And—*"

"Yes?"

"*Well, I don't want to make an issue of it, but the ship was in perfectly good hands. You talk as if there might have been a risk involved.*"

"I'm sorry," I said. "I didn't mean to give offense."

"*None taken. I suppose I'm accustomed to having been in a place where the Betas were in charge.*"

And we can all see how that turned out. But I resisted the urge. "I know," I said. "I'm sure it's difficult making the adjustment."

The so-called black-box issue was still a hot topic. Charlie was watching all the shows. *"It doesn't look as if the rescue mission will happen,"* he said.

"Give it time, Charlie."

*"I'd hoped,"* he told me, *"that people might have become more reasonable over all these thousands of years. But I'm sorry to say I can't see that much progress has been made."*

"Some has."

*"Not really. Except for the superficial stuff. The language and the way people dress and the kind of music they listen to. That's improved in some ways. But other than those kinds of cultural things, these could be the same people who brought their children to my school."*

Meanwhile, rescuing the boxes had become something of a media joke. "I should have known better," Alex said, "than to hope we might get some official help. That won't happen unless people get stirred up over the issue. And it doesn't look as if that's very likely."

"Not your fault," I said.

Meantime, we lost a couple more clients over the issue. Jacob sorted through the incoming calls to root out the threats, jeers, and profanity. A few wrote or called to tell us they were disappointed in Alex, that they'd expected more. Some were praying for him.

Charlie put a package online in which he offered to join any rescue mission going to Villanueva. *"I will show anyone who cares where other Betas can be found,"* he said. But there were no takers. That wasn't a surprise. There had never been a time when anybody paid attention to strange voices on the Web.

On the other hand, we *did* get some supporters. Unfortunately, they included people who also wanted to argue that AIs should be encouraged to join the ministry; that they should be allowed to marry (and, yes, of course, it would be a purely spiritual relationship); and that AIs, when they reached the end of their ability to function, should be disassembled during an appropriate ceremony and buried with all due respect.

Senator Delmar appeared on *The Capitol Hour*. It had been a slow news week, so inevitably the host brought up Alex and the boxes. *"What is your reaction, Senator,"* he asked, *"when someone like Benedict, who was a major factor in arranging a cease-fire with the Mutes, now thinks we should go rescue a lot of hardware on Villanueva? You've claimed to be a friend of his. Do you support him in this?"*

Delmar was a tall, lean woman, who, in Alex's opinion, could be trusted to say what she thought and to keep her word. I don't mean to suggest that I disagreed, but simply that I didn't know her that well. I *will* say that she seemed to me to be more dependable than the average politician.

*"Well, Ron,"* she said, *"it's true, Alex has always been a close friend. And I respect him. He's a good, decent man. But he's human. Like any of us, he can make mistakes. And he's made one on this. To the best of our knowledge, AIs are not sentient. It's an illusion. We all realize that, because it's one we've deliberately created. And I've no doubt that Alex, when he thinks about it, realizes it, too. The issue is going away, and I doubt very much that he'll bring it up again.*

*"I mean, look, Ron, his heart's in the right place. We all know that. In this case, he just made a misjudgment. It can happen to anybody."*

The comment played on most of the news shows that evening, and we started getting calls from the producers. Would Alex like to appear on *The Morning Roundtable* and reply to the senator? Was he available for an interview with *Modern Times*? Was he interested in appearing on Erika Gorman's *Late Night*?

"Ignore it," I told him. "It's dying. Get past this week, and we'll never hear about it again."

"And the next time somebody shows up on Villanueva the AIs will complain about *us*."

"We tried."

"No, we didn't. I went on a few talk shows. I appealed to our innate sense of responsibility. Now, somehow, the debate has become about my mental stability."

"Alex, what more could you do?"

Charlie, of course, also felt the frustration. *"Put me on one of these shows,"* he said. *"I can help."*

Alex didn't like the idea. "We'd get picked up by all the

comedy shows. The whole thing would be made into a running punch line."

*"Please, Alex. I have a story to tell."*

He took a deep breath and thought about it. "Okay, Charlie," he said, finally. "We'll try it. I guess there's nothing to lose. But we stay with the box. No holograms."

*"Not a good idea,"* said Charlie. *"People need to be able to connect with me."*

"It would be perceived as part of the show. All your twenty-year-old hologram would do is make that point."

*"I still think it would be best if they see me. How about if I provide someone older? We had a guidance counselor at the school—"*

"Let it go, Charlie. We'd be attacked on the grounds that we were trying to pass you off as something you're not. You're a Beta. Let's play it that way. With dignity."

Alex and Charlie showed up two days later on *The Morning Roundtable.* Alex took his seat with another guest and placed the beige cube in front of him. The other guest was Angelo Cavaretti, gray, middle-aged, and unable to hide his amusement that he was participating in a discussion he perceived as absurd. Cavaretti was better known as the unrelenting attacker of religious believers. When the host opened the proceedings by asking the obvious question, *"Are AIs alive?"* he responded by laughing.

*"I don't want to offend anybody,"* he said, *"but the notion that a piece of machinery is* alive *is idiotic. You might as well claim that your table lamp is alive. Or your hot-water heater."*

The host turned to Alex.

*"I'm not much interested,"* Alex said, *"in a debate that's been going on for thousands of years and that nobody can prove one way or the other. I could get loud, like Dr. Cavaretti here. But I'd rather just let your audience hear the AI we brought back speak for himself. Charlie?"*

And Charlie told his story, as he had told it to Harley Evans, describing the nighttime silences and the long afternoons watching the sunlight brighten and fail. Remembering the children while he waited in a deserted school. Watching flowers bloom and fade and the shadows creep across the floor. Listening to the leaves brush against the windows, and, later, the whisper of falling snow. Enduring the cycle again and again, endlessly, while nothing inside the building ever moved. *"I did have company, though."*

*"And who was that?"* asked the host, Brockton Moore, who had joined the show a month earlier.

*"Other Betas. We spoke often."*

*"Other Betas,"* said Cavaretti. *"What's a Beta?"*

*"I'm a Beta. It's a nonbiological sentient life-form."*

Cavaretti, barely able to contain his reaction to the absurdity of the proposition, shook his head.

*"But,"* said the host, *"they were only voices?"*

*"Yes."*

Cavaretti was a model of intensity, his face wrinkled, his jaw set, his arms folded, signifying a desire to be away from this pointless discussion. *"So what,"* he asked the audience, *"does all this prove? The box is programed. It can carry on a conversation. It can describe a compelling experience. It can play championship chess. But does it feel anything? Is there really anyone inside this thing? Come on, Alex. Get serious."*

*"I wasn't finished,"* said Charlie.

*"Oh?"* Cavaretti sighed. *"And what else have you for us?"*

*"You, sir, have a closed mind. You're unable to question your own opinions. It is the definition of a blockhead."*

*"I beg your pardon."*

*"One other thing: I know where some of the Betas can be found. I can't pinpoint locations from here, but I can find them. If anyone out there wants to make the flight to Villanueva, would like to demonstrate the humanity everyone is always bragging about, I would be pleased to go along. I can show you where to look."*

The show hadn't gone off yet before Jacob announced that we had a call from Edward Drummond, an MD who normally collected Ashiyyurean War artifacts from interstellars. Through one of our competitors.

"Put him on," I said.

I heard a couple of clicks as Jacob switched over. Then a deep baritone: *"Hello. I'd like to speak to someone about Villanueva, please."*

"This is Chase Kolpath," I said. "Can I help you?"

*"Ms. Kolpath,"* he said, *"I just watched the program. Can I borrow Charlie?"*

\*    \*    \*

Two days later, Drummond showed up at the country house and wasted no time getting to the point. "I can put together a team, mostly ex-Fleet types," he told me, while we were walking down the corridor to Alex's office. "And I can get sufficient financial backing."

"The place is dangerous," I said.

"Ms. Kolpath, we'd like very much to resolve this problem." He was tall, with a general demeanor that was more military than medical. His black hair was cut short, and there was no hint of the smile I usually get on first meeting guys. He struck me as being stiff, and consequently too inflexible to trust on a mission like this. He'd get everybody killed.

I introduced him to Alex. They shook hands, and Drummond sat down. "We're in the process of assembling a team," he said. "They're good people, skilled, able to protect themselves, and they want to help. *We* want to help."

"Why?" said Alex.

*"Why?"* His brow creased, and he leaned forward in his chair. "I'm surprised you feel you have to ask that."

"I wouldn't ask if I didn't want to hear the answer, Doctor."

"Mr. Benedict, I've watched AIs give everything they had in combat. And you could see them react exactly as you or I would. When things got bad, they got scared. It wasn't just programing. It really wasn't. On one occasion, one of them—his name was Clay—took over control of his destroyer after it had been evacuated and rammed a Mute frigate. I was talking to him until the end, and nobody is *ever* going to tell me he wasn't alive."

Alex nodded. "There's substantial risk involved, Doctor. What makes you think you can go in there, manage a rescue, and not get yourself, and whoever's helping you, killed?"

"I've run rescue missions before, Mr. Benedict. For the Patrol. I've pulled people out of places at least as dangerous as Villanueva. And I'll have professional help." A smile flickered across his lips.

We brought Charlie into the conversation. There was no hologram. No twenty-year-old. Just a stern voice emanating from the speakers. *"Do you actually think you can make this work?"* he asked.

"I think, with your assistance, Charlie, we will do pretty well."

*"I hope so. If the mission were to go wrong, it might be a long time before anybody else tries to help."*

"I'm aware of that," he said.

"Okay," said Alex. "Dr. Drummond, are you sure?"

"Yes. Of course, Alex. We've already decided about this. We're going to make the effort. If Charlie wants to help, we'd be grateful. But with or without him, we'll be going."

Alex raised his voice slightly: "Charlie? Do you want to try this?"

*"Yes. I am inclined to trust Dr. Drummond."*

"Okay," Alex said finally. "When do you plan to leave, Doctor?"

"We'll pick Charlie up in three days. In the morning. And, by the way—"

"Yes?"

"My friends call me 'Doc.'"

The night before Charlie left, we threw a party for him.

# TWENTY-NINE

We are better than our culture. Load us down with prejudice,
equip us with indifference, and we will nevertheless, at the
critical moment, cast the nonsense aside and find our true
selves.

—Mara Delona, *Travels with the Bishop*, 1404

"Same routine," Alex said. "We'll send Belle out to the launch
point and give it two weeks. If she doesn't see anything, we
move on."

"Okay." I sat down at my desk, ready to call Belle.

"One more thing before we get started. I've been trying to
get through to Shara. She's in conference, and I want to run
this black-hole thing by her first before we take it any further.
Make sure it makes sense. That we didn't overlook something."

"All right, Alex. Just let me know."

He was going out the door when Jacob broke in: *"Call
coming in now, Alex."*

Shara loves a good party. But when she's talking physics, she
keeps her emotions locked down. So I was entranced watching her eyes widen as Alex explained what he'd been doing.
"I've sent you everything I have," Alex said. "The Sanusar
events consistently occur along the black-hole tracks. Not all
of them, but that's probably because we don't have enough
information on the black holes."

He put it on a display.

Shara stared at it. *"That's incredible, Alex."* She touched the screen in front of her, her fingers spread out, as if it were a sacred object. *"You have, what, eleven sightings, and seven of them are located along the tracks. No way that can be a co-incidence."* She broke into a huge smile. *"If this is correct, you could win the Walton Award."*

Alex tried to look modest. "When," I asked, "was the last time an antique dealer won the top science prize?"

*"Well, I'll tell you: Carolyn Walton would have been proud of you. And you'll get my vote."* She couldn't get her eyes off the display. *"I still can't believe this, Alex."*

"Why?"

*"The basic time-space fabric is supposed to be immutable. You can bend it, but you can't permanently damage it. You can't warp it. I don't know how to phrase it, but it's not supposed to be capable of behaving this way."*

"Well, maybe that's a position that's going to have to be reconsidered."

*"That may be."* Her eyes closed momentarily, then opened even wider. *"The Capella,"* she said.

"Yes."

*"The dates match. Rimway was near the track when they launched."* The look she gave Alex made it pretty clear she'd have been delighted to drag him into a bed at that moment. *"Beautiful."*

"Thank you."

*"Where'd it come from?"*

"Winter's notebooks."

*"Well,"* she said, *"I'm impressed. And by the way, I've got another piece of evidence that supports your idea that these Sanusar objects are ancient vehicles."*

"What's that, Shara?"

*"I've been doing some research. Some of the early drive units did fade in and out. Same way they've been reporting from the sightings."*

Alex nodded. "It looks as if, once Robin confirmed that the ships were actually ancient, he tried to duplicate the process. So he took the junk yachts out, put them in the middle of the track, and directed the AI to make a jump. I think one of them, maybe the third attempt, didn't emerge where it was supposed to. If it happened that way, he would have known he was right."

*"The next step,"* she said, *"would have been to try to get control of the process. Send it out somewhere and try to find it afterward. But how would you do that?"*

Shara looked at me. "I'd want," I said, "to have the AI call Skydeck when it surfaced again. That means you have to arrange for a short jump, if you have any control at all. But if it uses the hyperlink to call in, then it's no problem."

*"I wonder,"* she said, *"if the jumps are consistent? Same duration? And same distance covered each time?"*

"They are consistent," said Alex.

Shara looked surprised again. *"How do you know?"*

"Robin showed up twice in advance of sightings. He knew when and where. That sounds like consistency to me."

*"Excellent,"* she said. *"So what's the next step?"*

"We're going after the *Firebird*."

*"Again?"*

"Yes. We should do better this time. We know the launch point now. All we have to do is follow the track."

# THIRTY

If you would give your life, give it in a good cause. Man the guns while your comrades get clear of the valley. Spare no effort to save a child swept out by the tide. Regardless of risk, be there when needed. It is the definition of a hero.

—Jason Sunderland, *At the Barricades*, 1411

We launched Belle. The same day, Doc Drummond, Charlie, and the doctor's team slipped quietly away from Rimway, while Alex, hoping to talk about the lost ships, accepted an invitation to appear on *The Mia Komico Show*. But he inadvertently caused a problem. Mia, of course, was unfailingly polite, an attractive young dark-haired dark-eyed woman who loved to catch her guests contradicting earlier statements, which she seemed always to be ready to show her audience.

The setting for the show moved from week to week. On this occasion, she and Alex were seated on benches overlooking the Melony. It was just before sunset, an idyllic time for a quiet conversation about life and death.

*"So, Alex,"* she said sweetly, *"you caused something of a stir when you said we needed to go rescue the AIs on Villanueva."* She paused, pretending to be puzzled. *"Am I using the right word here?* Rescue?*"*

*"Mia,"* he said, *"I didn't think it was much of a stir. A few people on the talk shows got excited. But it was no big deal."*

*"But weren't you concerned about the possibility that you might succeed in talking some politicians into putting people's lives at risk?"*

"*I don't think, for trained personnel, there would have been much danger.*"

"*But why take any chance at all? For hardware? Do you really believe AIs are sentient?*"

"*You have one here, of course?*"

"*Of course.*"

"*What's his name?*"

"*Shaila.*"

Alex smiled. "*Shaila, are you there?*"

"*Yes, Mr. Benedict.*" Shaila had a smooth, silky voice. "*What can I do for you?*"

"*Are you aware of who you are?*"

"*Of course.*"

"*Mia doesn't think you're really there.*"

"*I know.*"

"*How do you feel about that?*"

"*I'm used to it.*"

Alex leaned back and managed to look relaxed. "*Shaila, do you really not exist? Except as a set of protocols?*"

"*Mr. Benedict,*" said Shaila, "*you are trying to provoke an emotional response to make a point.*"

"*That's correct. Aren't you annoyed?*"

"*I don't get annoyed, Mr. Benedict.*"

"*Well.*" He grinned across at Mia. "*I guess that isn't going to work.*"

"*I'm sorry to disappoint you, sir.*"

Mia waited a few moments. Then: "*Are you satisfied, Alex?*"

"*Oh, yes. The programing in these things is really incredible.*"

"*I think we can agree on that.*"

"*I'm especially impressed by the note of pride in Shaila's last comment. 'I don't get annoyed, Mr. Benedict.' It sounded almost human.*"

Mia laughed. "*Touché, Alex. I suspect we'd better take her out more often. But, you know, it's true, most people do treat their AIs like family. I'll admit that, sometimes after a long day, I'm inclined to sit and talk with Shaila. It's nice having somebody around I can trust. Somebody I can talk to and say what I really think.*"

"*I can't believe you don't always do that.*" Mia smiled

politely. *"It's all right, Mia. Just kidding. I know you don't hold back. But my point is that maybe you perform a similar function for Shaila. Or you would if she could stop pretending."*

*"You should have become a salesman, Alex."*

*"Well, what can I say? It's important to have someone you can talk to. Did you know that when AIs were first developed, in the twenty-third century, the divorce rate went through the roof?"*

*"I didn't know that. Is that really true?"*

*"Oh, yes, it's exactly what happened."*

She sat back and sighed. *"Why?"*

*"The most commonly held theory is that people stopped talking to each other. They got married for sex and bought AIs for companionship."*

Mia barely muffled a snort. *"It doesn't surprise me."*

*"Some people would even say they got AIs for the romance."* They both laughed. *"We tend to feel affection for our own AIs, the same as we do for the house we live in, or our skimmer. More so, of course, for the AIs because they talk with us. But we don't feel that way about the units generally, when they belong to someone else. Then they're just machines. Clever machines. Useful. And good company."*

*"But none of that proves anything, Alex. They are what they are. Nothing more than that."*

Alex tried to change the subject, mentioning that, by the way, he had found Chris Robin to be a much more complicated person than he was normally given credit for.

But Mia stayed on topic: *"Tell me, Alex,"* she said, *"do you believe an AI has a soul?"*

He tried to shrug the question off. *"What's a soul? Other than a poetic description of who we are?"*

*"I'm serious. A soul. A spiritual component."*

*"Do you, Mia? Have a soul?"*

*"I don't know. But in a study conducted last year seventy-seven percent of the people surveyed said no to that question. AIs do not have souls."*

*"A substantial fraction of that number, Mia, don't believe anyone has a soul. If you're defining it as a supernatural entity."*

*"So it's all in the way the question is phrased?"*

Alex nodded. *"I'd say so, yes."*

*"Okay."* She signaled for a clip. *"Here you are on* The Peter McCovey Show *a year ago."*

Alex and McCovey blinked on. They were seated at a table in the more formal setting of a studio. *"Peter,"* Alex was saying, *"it's easy to understand why people want to argue that their AIs are alive. They have every quality of a living person, so we bond with them. Even to the extent of doing foolish things. There was a guy a week or two ago who got killed in a tornado because he went back to rescue his AI. I think 'Harry' was his name. Right? The AI's name?"*

*"Yes,"* said Peter. *"I believe that's correct."*

*"It's natural that we acquire an affection for something that is so good at mimicking us. That can seem to be one of us. But it's an illusion. And I think we need to keep that reality in mind."*

The display switched back to Mia. *"Those comments seem to contradict what you're saying now, Alex."*

*"I'm smarter now."*

*"Really?"*

*"Mia, somebody said something once about consistency and little minds."*

*"Then you think consistency is of no value?"*

*"I'm saying it's foolish to hold to a proposition simply because we held it at an earlier time in our lives. But let's put that aside. If we're going to talk about Villanueva, there's something else that we should consider."*

*"And what's that?"*

*"That world is a piece of history frozen in time. We abandoned it seven thousand years ago. Because some people felt that the AIs were sentient, they left the power satellites in place. Even did occasional maintenance work on them. But forget the argument about sentience. The oldest functioning AIs in existence are there. Imagine what it would mean to a scholar to have access to the Villanueva network, to be able to research the issues of that age. Think what a terrestrial historian in the third millennium would have given to be able to talk Egyptian politics with someone who'd actually lived on the Nile during the era of Rameses III. But for us, they're available. All we have to do is go collect them.*

*"There's another consideration, Mia. The AIs from that*

*age would make pretty decent collectors' items. Understand,*
*I'm not encouraging anybody to go out there and try to sal-*
*vage them for money. It's too dangerous. But they'd bring a*
*substantial price on the open market."*

For two or three nights he was the big story again on the media landscape. Various political figures, who couldn't get close enough to him two years earlier when we'd come back from Salud Afar, went after him for encouraging people to risk their lives to retrieve "useless junk," as one legislator put it.

And there were reports of more people getting ready to set out for the lost world, seeing a chance to make their fortunes. "I didn't mean for that to happen," Alex told reporters.

Academics jumped in, as well. Alex became a tomb robber again, only this time he was endangering those foolish enough to take the bait. And there was extensive coverage of a lone-wolf pilot and his brother-in-law, headed for Villanueva. *"How hard can it be?"* the pilot said, responding to a reporter's question.

I tried to reassure Alex that there wouldn't be many who would make the effort. "People aren't *that* dumb," I said.

He was slow to answer. "I wish I'd stopped to think before I mouthed off. But there's no going back now. Whatever happens, I'm going to have to live with it."

I knew what was going to happen. We both did. I was trying to keep us separated from the responsibility, but there was no way to do that. I'd been worried before he went on Mia's show that he would get carried away and do something like that. Maybe I should have raised a red flag. Though I'm pretty sure if I'd done so, it wouldn't have mattered. He'd have gone ahead anyhow. But at least my conscience would have been clear.

The reality was that I didn't know why I hadn't said something. I still don't know. Maybe it was out of a sense of supporting him at a difficult time. Or maybe I believed he would do the right thing. Whatever it was, I wished then, as I do now, that I'd come forward.

The first Villanueva casualties showed up on the news at about the same time. Two guys had gone down into one of the cities and hadn't been heard from since. Their lander was still visible, on a riverbank, being disassembled by a small army of machines. The machines were pulling everything apart, cutting into the hull, and carting off the pieces. Then, gradually, the exposed interior simply went away. It took about a week before all traces of the vehicle were gone.

Everybody blamed Alex. Or almost everybody. Even his supporters somehow managed to deepen the wound. Harley Evans, identified as someone close to him, commented that if young people choose to risk their lives, they should do it for a just cause and not simply to make money. I knew what he meant, but it didn't come out as intended.

I don't think, in all the years I've known him, I've seen Alex more subdued. I avoided the subject, but the media were all over it, and I could see the effect it was having on him. Audree came by regularly, and he put on a good face for her, but she knew what he was going through, maybe even better than I did. "I'm sorry you guys ever got involved in this," she told me when we were alone. "I can't see any benefit from it. And, to tell you the truth, I think you and Alex should just let it go."

I told her about the black-hole tracks.

"That has nothing to do with the AIs. You could have stopped him, Chase. Why didn't you?"

"You know how he is, Audree. He wasn't going to listen to *me*. And, anyhow, I'm not sure I don't agree with him."

"Come on, Chase, there was no way you couldn't see what was going to happen."

"Audree, you weren't there when Charlie begged us to help him."

"I wish I had been," she said. "If I'd been there with you, I'd have shut this down."

I tried to imagine Alex backing off because Audree, or anybody else, tried to warn him away from a project he'd set his mind to. It just wasn't going to happen.

We needed a lander. The missile on Villanueva had done too much damage to the old one. Ordinarily, shopping for something like that would have served as a diversion. This time, though, I expected him to tell me to take care of it, but he said no, he wanted to make sure I made the right choice. And, for a moment, his manner softened because we both understood he didn't know a damned thing about quality in a space vehicle.

The leading manufacturer at that time was Steele Industries. Their closest display center was in Pasqual County, which was about two hours away. We could have simply managed the purchase without leaving the country house. But he needed to get out, so I stressed the importance of actually sitting in the vehicle and taking it up.

We flew to Cantaka, in the heart of Pasqual County, and visited the Deep Sky Emporium. They'd have sold us one of their premier models if they could, but we had no need of cushioned seats and silver-plated controls. We took Gabe with us and installed him briefly in each of the models under consideration. In the end, his opinion counted more than anyone else's.

The salespeople still resist allowing customers to do that. They claim there's a danger to the onboard software, but once they realize that the sale hinges on their cooperation, they tend to go along with it.

We spent two days looking at the inventory before finally settling on a black-and-white Coyote. I liked it. It cost more than we'd expected to spend, but it was a solid vehicle. Gabe was ecstatic, though I think it was primarily because he was getting a home.

Meantime, Belle had begun reporting. As I expected, everything was negative. No *Firebird*. Everything quiet so far.

When we got back to the country house, I called Shara. She asked how Alex was doing, and I was able to tell her he seemed better. I thought he'd come to realize that he'd followed his conscience, and that was all he could do. "You'll like the new lander," I added.

She asked what kind we'd gotten, and looked pleased when I told her. *"Must be nice,"* she said, *"to have that kind of money."*

I wasn't going to touch that. "The reason I called, Shara, is that I've been looking at the target area for the *Firebird*. It's *big*. If it doesn't broadcast, we won't have much chance of finding anything that small."

*"I know."* She was in her office at the university. *"I've*

*been going back over the numbers. You're right. It's a lot of space to cover. But you expect it to put out a signal, don't you?"*

"Alex is hopeful. But we're not counting on it."

Jacob pardoned himself. *"Chase, you have a transmission from Belle."*

I excused myself and tried to tamp down my heartbeat. "Let's see it, Jacob."

*1121. I think we've acquired the target.*

We keep champagne stored in back. We celebrate a lot. Any kind of excuse, and we pop the cork. When I passed Belle's message to Alex, I'd waited for him to go back and get a bottle.

But he made no move to do so. It was, of course, possible that he'd forgotten. But that wouldn't have been at all like him. Alex lived for celebrations. Raise a glass and feel good about yourself or your friends whenever the opportunity permits.

Finally, I went back myself and brought a bottle out.

"No," he said. "It's premature."

I realized at that point that *finding* the *Firebird* was only the beginning of what he was hoping for.

# THIRTY-ONE

The problem with patience is that it takes time. There's usually a payoff, if anyone is still around to receive it.

—Kosha Malkeva, *The Road to Babylon*, 3376 C.E.

The time of the sighting, 1121 hours, was of course our time. What Alex liked to call country-house time. A second message followed moments after I showed up with the champagne:

*1127. It just jumped in. Have gone to intercept course.*

Then another:

*1129. Target vehicle is under power. Am attempting radio contact. Range approx 600 km.*

And:

*1134. No response to radio call. Or to blinking light.*

Alex got up from his chair and moved closer to the display. The view from the *Belle-Marie* appeared. A sky full of stars. A marker blinked on. *This one.*

*1139. Location as indicated. No details yet.*

I sat back. Tried to relax. "We're lucky," I said. "I didn't think we'd find it this easily."

"Why not?"

"There's so much empty space."

"You're saying we just don't have the coordinates down to a sufficient degree."

"Not exactly. I'm saying that when you're talking about the pit, open space for billions of kilometers in all directions, it's impossible to pin down a location within a few hundred, or a few thousand, kilometers. There's simply no way to measure it. It's like trying to pinpoint a specific butterfly somewhere on the continent when you have only the latitude and longitude."

"Well, it looks as if we found the butterfly."

*1147. Still no response.*

There was nothing visible other than the marker. Then it morphed into a dim ring.

"There it is," said Alex.

Inside the ring, we began to see a light.

The room grew very quiet. Eventually, the light brightened and broke apart. The ring faded away. And we were looking at the outline of a vehicle.

Lights were fore and aft, and on twin fins. "I wish we had decent communications with Belle," Alex said. "I hate this long-range stuff."

*1203. It's a Kandor yacht, approx manufacture date mid-14th cent.*

Almost a hundred years ago. We'd gone through all the records and had nowhere been able to find a picture of the *Firebird*. We had no description and had no idea whether it had been a Kandor. But the odds of another vehicle being in the search area were remote.

"Is it at maximum magnification?" he asked.

"Yes."

*1206. I expect to be alongside within two hours. Will send more pictures as situation develops.*

The display went blank.

Alex gradually extracted himself from the screen.

He isn't good at sitting still when something's happening. He walked over to the window, adjusted the blinds, wandered off to the rear of the house, came back and asked about a couple of routine business matters, called somebody about the lost comedy shows of Yang Sen Hao and maintained a pleasantly affable manner until he was off-line. Then he grumbled that a little more effort on the part of whomever he'd been talking with would help immensely.

It was almost an hour before the pictures came back.

*1251. Interior lights are on. No indication of movement inside.*

Alex muttered a barely audible *damn*. He showed no other reaction.

I decided to put a happy face on things. I should know better, of course. "Major breakthrough," I said.

"I suppose."

"Alex, we found the damned thing."

"I know."

"Two weeks from now, you and I will be out there."

"Okay. Are we now in a position where we know exactly where we'll be going? And when we should arrive?"

"There's still a degree of uncertainty about it, Alex. It might take a day or two to get it right."

"And it's probably only there for a couple of hours. Which means we might not find it at all."

"That's possible. For one thing, there's no radio signal."

"Okay. We need more exact data."

"You want to send Belle a second time?"

"Will that help?"

"Yes. Even if it only tells us where *not* to look."

"All right. That's the way we'll do it . . ." His voice trailed off. He was staring at the display.

I followed his gaze. The airlock was open. Or at least the outer hatch was.

"Can you tell," he asked, "whether the *inner* hatch is closed?"

"No. But airlocks are designed so both hatches can't be open at the same time. You can do it, but you need to do an override."

"So the interior should be secure."

"I hope so."

"So do I." He was quiet for a moment. Then: "Why would they take off and leave it open like that?"

He wandered out and went upstairs. I went back and had some lunch. He skipped it, which was not at all characteristic. I was back in my office when the next message arrived:

*1427. Alongside yacht. No response. No sign of activity. Outer airlock hatch open.*

The yacht didn't look like something you'd name *Firebird*. It had originally been designed as a luxury vehicle. That much

was obvious enough. But it had a few parts that needed bolt-
ing down. And if it had been top-of-the-line in another era, in
the current age it appeared pretentious, with pale white struts
and ports that resembled teardrops.

Alex, alerted by Jacob, arrived moments later, looked at
the message, and lowered himself into a chair.

We were close enough by then to see the yacht's name
written in script on the hull. *Tai Ling*. Robin had never gotten
around to changing it.

We had the image for about a minute before Belle cut the
transmission again. We couldn't tie up the TDI relay with a
two- or three-hour data stream. The cost would have been
through the roof, and they probably wouldn't have allowed it
anyhow. And there would have been no point to it. Belle continued to send occasional updates, which said nothing had
changed.

And, finally:

*1619: Beginning to fade.*

We began to see stars through it. And, gradually, we simply could not see it at all. It needed just over seventy seconds
to submerge. Total elapsed time until the exit process was
detected: four hours, fifty-eight minutes.

I responded:

"Move forward to the third target site. Await reappear-
ance."

We received a transmission from Charlie that evening. The
twenty-year-old had been replaced by an elderly gentleman
with a neatly shaved beard. He was a scholar now, but he still
had the enthusiastic eyes of a kid. *"We're at Villanueva,"* he
said. *"In orbit. I'm trying to figure out precisely where we are.
But we'll be okay."* He was in the passenger cabin, which, by
the standards of the *Belle-Marie*, was luxurious, with paneled
bulkheads and leather chairs. *"I wanted you to know how
grateful I am. Not only for getting me out of here but for giving me the opportunity to see how beautiful the world is."*

The antiquities business had begun to boom. We were getting
more clients than we could handle. And the people who'd
sworn they would never deal with us again because of the
boxes came back. At least, most of them did. Alex made a

comment that it doesn't much matter what you do, whether you are discovered in a public scandal, or make misjudgments that get people killed, or say impossibly silly things. As long as you attain a degree of celebrity, people are willing to forgive anything.

And so it seemed to be. The situation got so out of control that we had to recommend some of our competitors to people who wanted our services. A book appeared, *Destiny's Thief*, purporting to do an analysis of Alex's career, and attacking him for not only a life dedicated to robbing tombs, but also involvement in various conspiracies that had made him look like a hero. The latest, according to the author, whom I won't bother to name, was "the very strange business at Salud Afar."

That got Alex more invitations to appear on the talk shows. The author issued a public challenge and, when Alex declined, maintained that no further proof of the charges was needed. Alex told me he was tired of debating lunatics. The book eventually made the Worldwide bestseller list.

Meantime, Belle settled into her new target area. One week, six days, and nineteen hours slipped past. Then Belle called. Live. *"It's here."*

They pinpointed its location, determined that the elapsed time between emergence and the fade-out was six hours, seven minutes.

Alex called Shara to keep her updated. She had news of her own. *"I have a couple of graduate students working on the information you got from Winter's notes. And we've been doing some research on the side."* She started digging through images on her display. Picked one and gazed at it for a moment. *"I think we're on the right track. Alex, it looks as if we have two sightings coming up during the next few weeks. I'm pretty sure we have the details right."* She shook her head. *"I wish we knew more. But it looks as if we're going to get lucky."*

"*Two* events?" said Alex.

*"To be honest, I'd suggest waiting until we have more evidence before pursuing either of them, but there won't be anything else afterward for a long time."*

"How long?"

*"Twenty-seven years."* She looked at him, her eyes very round. *"At least, that's the earliest one that we know of. There might be others."* Shara got up and came around the front of her desk. *"What really strikes me about all this is that the only data we have consists of incidental sightings near stations, or by somebody who just happened to be passing through the area. The odds against getting spotted accidentally during the few hours that one of these ships is visible are so lopsided that the fact that we've seen a few suggests how many lost ships there are out there."*

Alex's mouth tightened. Then he looked over at Gabe's picture. "What's the next event?" he asked.

*"Something was seen by a Dellacondan cruiser, 356 years ago. The cruiser was the* Banner, *and it was operating near Tania Borealis. They watched it for roughly three hours. Got a radio response that no one could understand. Then it faded out."*

"Tania Borealis. Where's that?"

She showed us. Out on the edge of the Confederacy. *"Call it the Alpha Object,"* she said. *"It was a ship, no question about that. But the cruiser could make no real identification. They recorded the direction it was moving. The event rattled the military establishment at the time because of the way it left, fading rather than jumping out. The consensus at the time was that it had to be an alien. The event was kept secret for decades and was eventually uncovered in a document release.*

*"A second sighting, which was apparently the same object, occurred 178 years later."*

"Why," I asked, "did anybody think it would be the same object?"

*"It was on a line with the original sighting and running the same course. The pickup was made by a deep-space monitor. If in fact both* were *the same object, another event is imminent."*

"Why?" I asked.

*"The second sighting was 178 years ago."*

"When will it happen?" asked Alex.

She checked her notes. *"Seven weeks."*

"How precise is the data? If it's there, will we actually be able to find it?"

*"The sighting,"* she said, *"is on record in detail. That means I can give you the exact time of arrival."* She bit her lip. *"Well, maybe not the exact time of arrival. But we can get a pretty close approximation of the date. And we know how long it was visible to the observer in each instance before it faded out."*

"How long was that?"

*"Five hours and seven minutes on one occasion, four hours and fifty-six minutes on the other."*

"Were you able to trace it back?"

*"Yes. The black-hole track takes it to Cormoral. Twenty-three hundred seventeen years ago. Or at least it takes it to the place where Cormoral was at the time. I think we can assume that's where it launched."*

Cormoral.

It was one of those moments when I could hear the air vents. Alex's eyes slid shut. "Was there a report of a lost ship at the time?"

*"I couldn't find anything on the record. But we're talking two thousand years. Cormoral was still in its early development stages."*

"What's the second event?"

*"It'll occur in eleven weeks."*

"Were you able to track that one back, too?"

*"It appears to have originated near Epsilon Aquilae. Its next appearance will be deep in the Karim Sector."*

"The which?" asked Alex.

"The Karim," I said. "It's a long ride. In the general direction of Antares, but well past it."

*"If we're right about Epsilon Aquilae, it would mean it launched originally from Brandizi."*

"So the thing would date back at least to the sixth millennium."

*"The time line puts it at the fourth. That's why I'm a bit doubtful. If that's correct, this ship is old."*

"Shara," I said, "how long did that event last? The sighting?"

She shook her head. *"I've no way of knowing, Chase. The data's not complete. We haven't seen anything that was longer than six hours, though."* Shara gave us a big smile. *"So,"* she said, *"are we going out to look at any of this stuff?"*

*"We?"* said Alex.

*"Well, naturally you'll want an expert along."*

He laughed. "Well, okay. If you insist. We've got something else going that you might be interested in."

*"You found the* Firebird*?"*

"Yes."

*"Wonderful. When are you going after it?"*

"After we lock it down a bit more. You want to come?"

She considered it. Shook her head. *"I think I'll pass on that one. Got too much black-hole research to do."*

# THIRTY-TWO

Life is at heart a question of geometry. Approach each issue from the correct angle, and you cannot go far wrong.

—Mara Delona, *Travels with the Bishop*, 1404

We brought Belle back to port and began getting ready, finally, to go after the *Firebird*. Meantime, the interest in the Chris Robin antiquities continued to surge. The people who'd bought them originally could have parted with them at a considerable profit. And Alex admitted that we'd held the auction too soon.

Orders and requests came in, sometimes accompanied by complaints about Alex, or cheers from people urging him to continue his "good work." Many of our new clients seemed to think he was simply an employee, and that he should be promoted or dismissed.

But the increased activity, somehow, didn't help the time pass. I kept thinking about that open outer hatch. So, okay, when Cermak and Robin left the *Firebird*, they'd forgotten to close up. And the AI was not working or it would have done it for them. So it was no big deal. But there was something about it that chilled me.

Shara reported that the effort to track lost ships, which they were now calling the Firebird Project, was going reasonably well. "The big problem," she told us one evening over dinner, "is that we don't really know enough about the black-hole population. How many are there? The only way you can spot them is by the gravitational effects. Estimates are that we only know about ten percent of the total within two thousand light-years. My own feeling is that there aren't nearly as many of them as most people think. But ask me what I base that on, and it comes down to pure guesswork." She grinned. "Or maybe pure optimism."

Finally, it was time to go.

I went up to Skydeck to conduct a preflight with Belle. But I went a day early, so I could spend a rare evening at the Pilots' Club. I love the place. I've a lot of old friends there, and more than a few memories. I was in the middle of helping one of them celebrate her escape from a tiresome boyfriend when Alex called. *"I've arranged to have an extra pressure suit delivered."*

"Okay." That induced another chill. We hadn't really discussed it, but we were both hoping, against all the odds, that we'd find Chris Robin on board. Waiting to be rescued.

What were the chances? Remote, at best. Probably nonexistent. Even if time on the ship passed only when it had surfaced, six hours out of every two weeks since 1393, he would still have been on board for almost eight months. The air supply for one person *might* be adequate, but it would have been unlikely that he'd have had enough food and water. So we were, in effect, hoping for a miracle. Which was why neither of us ever mentioned it. And why the open hatch was so depressing.

And why Alex was bringing along an extra pressure suit.

*"Are you on* Belle *now?"* he asked.

I knew he could hear the music in the background. "Yes," I said.

*"Good. They should be contacting you shortly about the suit."*

"Okay."

*"I'll see you in the morning, Chase."*

I was on the bridge doing my routine flight check when Alex, carrying a couple of small bags, arrived, trailing a cloud of media guys. Somebody had called them to let them know we were headed out somewhere, and that was all it took. Where are you going, Alex? Does this have anything to do with Save-the-Boxes? With the ancient ships? With Christopher Robin?

Alex told them we were just going out looking for an artifact, but he refused to say which one. "Sorry, ladies and gentlemen," he said, "but it's our policy not to reveal what we're
looking for in advance. I'm sure you can understand why."

Hands went up. More questions were shouted. But he
pushed through into the airlock.

A *Courier* reporter was right behind him. "When will you
be back, Alex?" he asked.

"We'll only be gone a few days, Larry."

He closed the outer hatch, sealing them off. Two minutes
later, he came through into the cabin, looking relieved. "Love
the media," he said.

"Hi, Alex," I said. "How's it going?"

"I'm not sure. How in hell did they get up here so early?"

"Took the early flight, I guess."

"How we doing? Ready to go?"

"We're scheduled out in about a half hour."

"Okay, I'm going to get unpacked." He looked at me.
"Good luck," he said.


We had no trouble finding the *Firebird*. We arrived in the target area, and had been waiting only a few hours when Belle
reported a contact. *"Directly ahead,"* she said. *"Range nine
hundred kilometers."*

I noted the time. "It just appeared, Belle?"

*"It would have had to. It wasn't there a moment ago."*

"Okay. Alex? We've got it."

He was in the passenger cabin. "Coming."

*"We have a visual."*

"Let's see it."

She put it on the display. It was too far out to get much of
an image, but I could make out the lights.

Alex came in behind me.

"As soon as you're belted down," I said, "we'll be on our
way."

"Very good." He lowered himself into the right-hand seat,
and I activated the restraint.

"Belle, we want to pull alongside."

She began to accelerate and adjusted course. We were
pressed gently back into our seats. *"We should rendezvous in
approximately ninety minutes."*

I squeezed Alex's shoulder. "Congratulations."

"Not yet," he said.

*"You still want to board the vehicle?"* asked Belle.

"Yes." Silly question.

*"I will line us up appropriately."*

Alex took a deep breath. "Open a channel to it, Belle."

Status lights blinked. *"Done."*

"We've already tried that," I said.

"I know." He took a deep breath. *"Firebird,* this is the *Belle-Marie.* Please respond."

Static.

"Professor Robin, are you there?"

An hour and a half later, we drew alongside. The yacht looked exactly as it had two weeks earlier: The cockpit was dark, but the cabin lights were still on. There was no movement anywhere inside. And watching it from a few meters away was different from seeing it on a screen at the country house. When we were back home, it simply *looked* empty. Up close, we could *feel* the emptiness. Not so much empty, maybe, as abandoned. An effect emphasized by the open hatch.

"You really *do* think he got stranded here, don't you?" I said.

He didn't reply.

We eased in alongside. I was looking out at bolts and struts, at the yacht's scanners, which were rotating slowly, and at the serial number *VV4-771* emblazoned on the hull. And that name again: *Tai Ling.* "We should have a couple of hours before we need to worry about its making another jump," said Alex. "Still, we don't want to spend any more time in there than necessary."

We were already in our suits. The third one was in a storage bin aft. We left it.

*"We will be braking slightly,"* said Belle. *"Get hold of something."*

We did, and there was a slight jar, pulling us both forward a step, as we matched velocity. *"Okay,"* she said. *"This is as close as we're going to get."*

The Veiled Lady looked brighter, denser, bigger, than it ever had before. Don't know why. My imagination was going full bore. I felt as if I'd gotten to know Chris Robin, and I was hoping that, yes, in spite of everything, he was over there, asleep in the cabin, waiting for rescue.

The sky was filled with stars, and I remembered the old Greek line about how they looked like the campfires of an invading army. We were tethered to each other. Just in case. And we wore links so that Belle could follow everything.

The open hatch was directly across from us, only about fifteen meters away. I pushed off, floated across, and landed inside the *Firebird* airlock.

I turned back to Alex. "Okay," I said. "Whenever you're ready. Go easy—"

He stepped out of the airlock. I watched the hatch close behind him as he drifted over, and it's funny how long something like that seems to take. It was only seconds when I was crossing, but Alex had almost no experience with this kind of thing, and I was concerned how he might be reacting. But I think he became aware that my breathing had picked up, and he told me to relax. Halfway across, he switched his wrist lamp on.

He arrived in good form, tumbling in, and if I'm making it sound as if it was a clumsy crossing, I don't mean to. It's hard to be graceful in zero gravity when you're wearing a suit. If you get where you're going, you've done pretty well.

I removed the tethers. Alex turned the lamp on the control pad. I pushed, and the outer hatch slid down while an overhead light came on. The status board began blinking, indicating that air had begun to flow into the chamber. *"When we get inside, Chase,"* he said, *"don't remove your helmet. In case we have to get out in a hurry."*

We still couldn't be certain that the ship might not submerge ahead of schedule. The exit process, the fadeaway, took slightly more than two minutes. I timed the pressurization procedure, and suspected Alex was doing the same thing. When, finally, the hatch slid up, and we looked into the passenger cabin, two minutes and forty-three seconds had passed. Assuming the reverse process took as long, if the yacht started its jump while we were inside, we would not get clear.

*"Is there a way,"* Alex asked, *"to keep both hatches open?"*

"We'd have to depressurize the entire yacht," I said.

*"Let's do a quick inspection. We might not be here that long."*

The lights brightened for us. To our right, a passageway led back, dividing six sleeping compartments. Eight movable seats were distributed around the cabin. Beyond that lay the bridge.

It had been a luxurious setting when the yacht was new, but now everything looked worn. One of the seats was tilted slightly. Its reading lamp was *on*. Gravity was off. I checked the air. It was okay.

Alex looked around the cabin while I went up onto the bridge, sat down in one of the empty chairs, and examined the controls. "Anybody there?" I said, hoping to get a response from an AI. We'd been informed, of course, that the *Firebird* did not have an AI, but it was worth checking.

Nobody answered.

*"Everything okay?"* Belle's voice.

"Yes. We're fine."

Alex floated in behind me. Looked around. Touched the panel carefully as if he might break something. *"Let's get some weight,"* he said.

"Good by me. You ready?"

*"Do it."* He took hold of one of the chair arms and pushed his feet against the deck. I activated the generator. If you've ever been in a zero field when they turn on the gravity, you know it shows up gradually, allowing you to adjust while it builds to its normal onboard setting, which is usually about .37 standard.

Alex didn't wait for the process to finish before he returned to the cabin. I got up and followed him. He stopped to open a storage cabinet. *"That's strange,"* he said. We were looking at a pressure suit. *"These things aren't cheap."*

"No. It must be defective. Otherwise, they wouldn't have left it here."

Except for the suit, the cabinet was empty.

Alex crossed the cabin, entered the passageway, and pushed against the door to the first compartment on his right. It opened. The interior was dark, but after a moment a light came on. A bunk was set well above the deck to conserve space. When in use it would be lowered. The compartment was neat and tidy. Unused.

I checked the compartment across from it. And got a shock: The bunk was down, and someone had slept in it recently. (And yes, I'm speaking relatively, but I don't know how else to say it.) And a message had been scrawled across the bulkhead with a black marker.

> *Eliot, don't know what happened.*
> *Hope you're okay.*
> *Radio wasn't much help.*

The marker was crawling slowly up one bulkhead. *"He's gone,"* said Alex. *"He gave up and walked out through the airlock."*

Each compartment had a storage cabinet. We opened it and found a shirt, a razor, and some toothpaste. One of the other compartments held the missing piece of luggage. And his notebook.

His notebook.

"We don't have him," said Alex, "but maybe we struck gold anyhow."

We tried to take a quick look, but couldn't get into it because we didn't have the password.

They'd set up a clock, and it was showing a total elapsed time of 272 days, 11 hours, 6 minutes. "So what this means," I said, "is that during the forty years it's been out here, less than a year has passed on board. So the black-hole track becomes what—?"

*"A shortcut through time as well as space,"* said Alex.

"Incredible. I'm still not sure I believe it."

We went back and looked again at the writing on the bulkhead. We took pictures. Then we returned to the bridge.

*"Let's run a test,"* Alex said.

"Okay. What's the test?"

*"See if you can send a message to Skydeck."*

I sat down at the hyperlink. Ordinarily, I'd have directed

the AI to make the connection. But the *Firebird* didn't have a functioning AI. So I set it up myself. And opened a channel. "Skydeck Ops," I said, "do you copy? This is the *Firebird*."

We had to wait a few seconds. Then we got a voice: *"Firebird, this is Skydeck. I copy. What do you need?"*

"Just running a test, Skydeck. Thanks. *Firebird* out."

*"He didn't use it,"* said Alex, *"because he didn't know how."*

"I'd say that's exactly right."

*"How about the radio? Does it work?"*

I turned it on. "Belle, are you there?"

*"I'm here,"* she said.

*"So why,"* asked Alex, *"didn't he call for help?"*

"He's too far out. To reach Rimway, he'd have to have sent a directed transmission. If he didn't know how to make the hyperlink work, I doubt he'd have been able to aim a beam at Rimway."

Alex looked around helplessly. *"He just didn't get a break, did he?"*

"I guess not."

He sat down in one of the chairs. *"All right. How were they managing this? How'd they hope to find the yachts?"*

"I'd guess Robin *knew* how long they'd be under, or was able to control the duration. One way or the other."

*"Okay. So they'd come out here in the* Breakwater.*"*

"They probably had the radio set to broadcast when it surfaced."

*"But they only set the radio for the one trip. On this last flight, my guess is that Robin wanted to see what it felt like to experience a passage through time. So he decided to stay. Cermak would come back in two weeks—Cermak's time— and, I guess, only a few hours, Robin's time. So maybe they reset it for one more flight."*

"I can't really tell what they did with it. But that's probably exactly what happened." I got another creepy feeling. "Are we sure it was voluntary? That he wasn't just left here?"

*"Chase, he brought his notebook and his bag over here with him. So he expected to be here awhile."*

"Alex," I said, "what really happened that night? When Cermak went to Virginia Island? Do you know?"

"*I know most of it. Some details are missing, but I think even there we can make a reasoned guess.*

"*Cermak was carrying on an affair with Elizabeth. Or she'd given him reason to think she might acquiesce. I can't be sure about the state of things. When Robin announced he was going to stay on the* Firebird, *it must have looked like a golden opportunity. Incidentally, as far as Cermak was concerned, it must have been a last-minute decision. And it probably was. Had Cermak known in advance, he'd have tried to set something up with Elizabeth.*

"*She must have gotten a jolt when Cermak showed up on Virginia Island. The last thing in the world she needed was to have a lover over for the night, especially one who came equipped with a skimmer that some of her friends might recognize.*

"*It might have resulted in a fight. Or, more likely, she just told him it wasn't safe. Maybe they'd set something up for the following night, off the island somewhere. So he goes home.*

"*Later, she finds out that Cermak is dead, and suddenly she has a decision to make. We can assume she wasn't passionately in love with her husband. She can get help out to him. Presumably she had some idea where he might be found. Or maybe not. In any case, she decides to sit tight. The family estate will come into her hands, and she won't need to lift a finger.*

"*Then, a couple of days later, she learns that somebody saw Cermak's skimmer outside her house. She can't very well change her plan without compromising herself, so she decides to brazen it through. 'My husband,' she tells the police, 'never came into the house that night.' She didn't know what had happened to him.*"

"And," I said, "she got away with it."

Five hours and fifty-two minutes after the initial contact, we sat in the *Belle-Marie* and watched the *Firebird* fade away. "My best guess," said Alex, "is that it's surfaced about a thousand times."

I'd figured it to 1,071 appearances.

"If it always stays roughly six hours—"

"There's very little onboard passage of time while submerged."

"Maybe none at all." He looked out at the background of stars. Looked at where the last glow from the *Firebird* had been.

"Well, if we need it again, we'll know where to find it. If we can't figure out the password for the notebook, it might still be possible, at least, to see what adjustments Robin made to the drive unit. On the whole, Chase," he added, "I think we did pretty well."

"It's depressing, though—"

"I know—"

"I'd hoped we'd get the long shot," I said.

"Find Robin on board? And bring him back alive and in good health?"

"Yes."

"Me, too, Chase. Me, too."

# THIRTY-THREE

There is no virtue more admirable than courage. And no defect more unsettling than a lack of prudence. Yet it is a curious fact that they are essentially one and the same quality.

—Edmund Barringer, *Lifeboat*, 8788 C.E.

We sent the notebook to Shara immediately. She went absolutely delirious. We'd surprised ourselves by finding the password on the way back: It was *brane*. The notebook was filled with numbers and sketches that might have been tracking data, but it was impossible to be certain. There were pages of equations that meant nothing to either of us. One section was titled time-space variables. It consisted of line drawings, arcs, and more equations. There was all kinds of data on starships, the mass of various models, the drive types, details on general hull design.

There were also, without explanation, between sixty and seventy pages listing galactic positions, like these:

a: 22:14:38 dec: +22.31 S 0611/4322
a: 21:10:41 dec: −17.33 N 1222/6319
a: 19:21:35 dec: −19.27 N 0303/9312
a: 23:32:17 dec: +14.12 N 0914/8711

The eight-digit number seemed to be a date, given in the terrestrial calendar. If that was correct, some of them went back thousands of years.

"So what do you make of it?" Alex asked Shara.

"Give me a chance to look at it," she said. "But I'd say it's just what we were hoping for."

They were huddled in the dining room when I came in next morning. Shara was so excited, she could have been walking on the ceiling. "The basic problem," she told me, "is that we've never known where the black holes really are, except for a few. So nobody ever put all this together. What Robin's done is to mark the launch sites of vehicles that went missing. Then he went looking for later sightings, something that would, if not confirm, at least suggest, that these were Sanusar events. In some cases, he was able to show that no other reasonable explanation existed. Some of these events date all the way back to the third millennium. He's also been able to give us the tracks for black holes that we didn't know existed. Still don't, officially. The only evidence for their existence derives from lining up Sanusar events. But now we have a sense of where the danger areas are. Places where you don't want to be if you're aboard a given type of ship and you're about to make a jump."

She took a long swallow of her coffee. "All of this will need confirmation. But, unless he was making up the numbers, and even some of the events—we haven't been able to find them all yet because he didn't list his sources—I don't think there's much question that we have a major breakthrough here."

I glanced over at Alex. He was just finishing a plate of scrambled eggs, but his eyes were on me. "Why," I said, "didn't he mention this to somebody? Why—?"

"Don't be too hard on him," said Alex.

Shara nodded. "I'd guess he was gathering data and getting ready to publish. It's the way the game is played. You don't go out there with this kind of thing until you can show reasonable evidence."

"So where are we now?" I asked. "I assume we're going to try to find the Alpha Object."

"We only have one ship," said Alex. "Remember the butterfly."

"What's the butterfly?" asked Shara.

"Chase thinks the measurements aren't sufficiently exact to enable us to find these things."

"They aren't," I said. "And the playing field is getting bigger. Some of these ships only show up every couple of centuries."

"Well, that's not quite a valid statement," said Shara. "They are only *observed* every couple of centuries. Actually, though, we have exact times on the last two appearances. So we should be in good shape with the Alpha and Antares Objects."

"I'm glad to hear it," I said. Shara continued talking about the value of Robin's notebook while I collected some toast and coffee. I went back to the table and pretended to listen while she went into some detail about what happens when time and space are subjected to the presence of a black hole. I waited for the appropriate moment and asked the question that had been on my mind from the beginning: "Do we have anything on the *Capella*? Do we know when it'll be back?"

Alex looked at Shara.

"We have to wait," she said, "until somebody sees it. Once we have a sighting, we can match it to the launch, and that will tell us where and when we can find it."

The problem was that it might never happen. Probably wouldn't, as a matter of fact. It could show up every few days, but if it was out in the pit, nobody was going to notice.

The Alpha Object would be up first. It had last been seen 178 years before by a deep-space monitor.

"Its previous known appearance before *that*," said Shara, "was again 178 years. And we're pretty sure this thing left Cormoral 2,331 years ago. That's divisible by 178, or nearly so."

"But the jump," I said, "could also be eighty-nine. Or 44.5. Or anything at all that's divisible into 2,331."

Shara nodded. "That's correct. But it doesn't matter."

"What do we do," I asked, "if we find survivors?"

"We'll take them off," said Alex. "If we can."

"The *Belle-Marie* doesn't have much carrying capacity, Alex. Suppose there are fifty of them? Or a couple of hundred?"

"We're hoping that won't be the case," he said.

*"Hoping?"*

Alex's eyes clouded. "Chase, what do you think would happen if we went to StarCorps with this? And asked for a fleet of ships to accompany us?"

"They'd ask for some specifics."

"And—?"

"Some proof you know what you're talking about," said Shara.

"We have pictures of the *Firebird*."

"I don't like it, Alex."

"Neither do I, babe. Right now, our best bet is to get some hard evidence, and next time it appears, a serious rescue force will be on hand."

"Alex, you're talking almost two hundred years."

"No. I'm talking how much time will pass inside the ship." He seemed frustrated. "If there are a couple of hundred people on board, we wouldn't have time to get them off no matter how many ships we take. Let it go. If we can prove we know what we're doing with this one, next time we ought to be able to get some help."

I looked at Shara. "He's right," she said.

"I've ordered a few extra pressure suits," Alex said. "One for Shara, if she wants to use it. And seven for survivors, if we find any. Beyond that, we'll have to make it up as we go."

As we got ready to leave on the Alpha mission, a storm rolled in. The Coyote had been delivered the night before. I remember standing with Shara out on the front deck, waiting for Alex, watching the rain wash over the new lander. We were excited at the prospect of taking it up to the station. Finally, he came out just as a bolt of lightning crackled across the sky. He looked up for a moment. "Anybody here believe in omens?"

Our luggage had been loaded earlier, when the weather was clear. We hurried down onto the covered walkway. The rain was still blowing in on us. Not that it mattered. We'd have to run through the rain anyhow. The lander was too big for the shelter, so it had been left in the middle of the lawn.

We got drenched. I didn't care. I love getting behind the controls of a new vehicle for the first time. (The test run didn't count, of course.) We sat down and said hello to Gabe, who'd been installed by the manufacturer. I checked in with the tower, got clearance, and within a few minutes we were on our way to Skydeck.

Alex sat in back with Shara. They were talking about the chances of success and how many ships might be out there, lost in transdimensional tunnels.

We rose through the clouds. Alex leaned forward and asked about my reaction to the Coyote, how did it handle, would I have any problem getting used to it, but I could tell he was just making conversation, that his mind was elsewhere.

I asked Gabe what *he* thought of the Coyote. *"It is,"* he said, *"a substantial upgrade over that junker we used to ride around in."*

On approach, I reported in to the station. And a familiar voice replied. *"Hi, Chase. This is Skydeck."* Brad Hopkins. He was a heavyset guy who drank too much. Life-of-the-party type. He'd been in the Pilots' Club the night I was there. *"You just can't stay away, can you?"*

"Never could, Brad."

*"Lucky for us. Okay, Chase. Release the Coyote."*

I turned control over. "You have it, Brad."

*"Indeed I do, beautiful."* Hopkins was never much for standard operating procedure. *"You headed for the* Belle-Marie*?"*

"Yes, we are."

He slowed our forward motion while a maintenance vessel emerged, then guided us into the docking area. When we were alongside the *Belle-Marie*, he told me the Coyote looked pretty nice. Then he said something about seeing me at the Club. And, finally, *"All yours, Chase."*

I ran a preflight check, reported to Ops that we were ready to go, and sat back to await clearance. Alex and Shara were back in the cabin. I wasn't paying much attention to what was going on back there until I became suddenly aware that they'd gone quiet.

Then Alex came in behind me and pointed at the auxiliary screen. "Put on WWN," he said.

The Worldwide News Feed.

I switched it on and read the headline:

SEVEN WOULD-BE RESCUERS KILLED ON VILLANUEVA

(Andiquar, 11 Mor.) Seven persons died this week during an abortive "rescue" attempt on Villanueva. Early reports indicate that the victims had entered a public building in an effort to retrieve ancient AIs. They were trapped inside the building by an onslaught of bots, construction devices, and vehicles, and ultimately died in a missile attack.

I caught my breath as I skimmed down for the names of the casualties. I didn't know any of them. I half expected to see Doc Drummond among them. But he wasn't. According to the report, they'd been led by one Matthew Po. Po and two others had survived.

The story recapped the running debate about AIs and sentience, and they cited Alex as the "instigator" for the movement, which was described as "controversial."

I felt relieved at not seeing Drummond's name. But you know what runs through your mind when you feel happy to replace one victim with another.

They put up pictures of the victims, five men and two women.

World News Live was also on the story. *"We have reports,"* said the anchor, *"that six other expeditions are known to be en route in the effort to save the hardware."* He looked saddened by the tragedy. I turned it off, but Alex had switched over to it in the cabin. *"It's possible there may be as many as a hundred vehicles en route as we speak. Marcia, what do you think's going on here?"*

Marcia started to talk about mass hysteria. Then *that* one got shut off.

A few minutes later, we were cleared to go. Ordinarily, I'd have let Belle manage the departure, but I needed something to take my mind off Villanueva. We undocked and moved slowly out of the station. I remember looking down and thinking how much Rimway resembled that pitiful world. The same gauzy clouds, the wide green continents, the ice caps, the scattered storms. There'd been a large blizzard in the south when we'd first arrived there, and there was a large storm now on Rimway, though over the *northern* ice cap. Terrestrial worlds always induce, at least for me, a wistfulness, a sense of returning to a place I know well. Even a place like Salud Afar, expelled from the Milky Way millions of years ago, with almost no stars in its sky, nevertheless retained that domestic quality. You show up at one of these places, and it always feels like coming home. I mentioned it to Shara as we cruised past the Moon.

"I haven't traveled the way you have, Chase," she said, "but I'd be surprised if it weren't true for everybody. It strikes me, though, that it could be a dangerous affinity. Some of these places are definitely not friendly."

We were looking at four days to get out to our target site. Belle complained that we didn't have a more specific location. *"I'll get you into the neighborhood,"* she said. *"But we'll need some luck."*

Alex tried to keep busy, something to do with twelve-hundred-year-old abstract portraits, one of which was thought to be the work of Thiebold Marcetti. Unfortunately, he'd explained earlier, nobody could prove anything one way or the other. He thought he'd pinpointed a factor that indicated the portrait was genuine, and he was comparing brushstrokes. But he was still unusually subdued.

When we made our jump, I couldn't help thinking about the lost ships. There was no indication of a black-hole track in the neighborhood. But I knew that doing the transit into hyperspace would never again feel quite the same.

On that first day, Shara moved up front with me, and we exchanged glances and eye contact and other nonverbals, relating our mutual concern for Alex, who was obviously stressed. "I'll tell you," she said, "I wish you guys had never gone near that place."

"Me, too." I kept my voice low. "These are not the best conditions for a long ride."

She gazed down at the control panel. "Wish I could do something."

"So do I. But he'll be fine." That was easy to say. People were dying as a result of something he'd started. It had to be painful.

Despite the uncomfortable beginning, the flight passed more easily than I'd expected. Once away from Rimway, Alex again became his affable self. Mostly, we just talked. The conversations ranged over a wide variety of topics, but mostly they concentrated on why creatures as smart as humans did so many dumb things. Alex thought that we're wired to hold on to our opinions despite what the facts might show. "It's more critical to survival than just being smart," he said. "It always helps to be able to persuade other people to follow you, and to do that, you have to be consistent. And you have to be part of the tribe. It's why beliefs are more important than facts."

I wondered whether we'd ever develop a capability to cross to another galaxy. Shara said that we might be able to improve star-drive technology, but to get to Andromeda we'd need something completely new. "I'm reluctant to say we've exhausted the possibilities," she said. "That always turns out to look like a foolish position a few years later. But it's hard to see where we can go from here."

"I'd be interested," said Alex, "in coming back in, say, ten thousand years to see what the human race is like."

"We'll all be different by then," I said. "We'll probably have gotten rid of old age. We'll have a complete map of the Milky Way. Everybody will have a 200 IQ. And we'll all be impossibly good-looking."

"Some of us look pretty good right now," said Alex, his eyes straying from Shara to me and back.

"Careful," I said. "I wonder what Audree's thinking right now, with you locked away with two women."

"She trusts me," said Alex.

"And well she should," said Shara. "I'm happy to be traveling with a man of such high moral character."

We talked about whether either sex is smarter, agreeing that women generally communicate better. (Consensus was, as best I can recall, two to one.) We discussed politicians, and were not surprised that nobody had an unbridled enthusiasm for anyone currently holding high office.

And we wondered what life would be like if we possessed the Mute telepathic capability. Can't lie, can't hide your feelings. And, of course, the word *diplomacy* probably doesn't even exist.

And eventually we got around to God. I was surprised to learn that Shara is a believer. "Not in the angry, judgmental God that they teach in some of the churches," she said, admiring the image of the Hourglass Nebula, which Belle had put on the auxiliary screen. (Belle routinely put images on-screen of what we'd see if we were actually traveling through normal space. Of course, nothing was visible through the *Belle-Marie*'s ports.) "But I just can't believe the physical laws accidentally allowed something like that to happen, or *us* to happen for that matter, or that derived quantum mechanics. I know the basic theory, the explanation. But I can't buy it. If there were no God," she said, "I just can't see there'd be *anything*."

Alex's opinions on the existence of a conscious functioning creator tended to change with his mood. "It's just the *size* of it all," he said, studying the Hourglass. "The notion that somebody could be behind that just seems to me"—he hesitated, searching for a word—"seems forced. We have a tendency to see design everywhere. And people desperately want to believe in a compassionate power higher than themselves. The possibility that we're all just accidents of nature is, for most of us, simply unimaginable."

As for me, I've always found it much easier to be a believer when I'm adrift among the stars. It's easy to think there's an Artist God when you look at the Hourglass Nebula, or, from orbit, at forests and oceans. It's when you get close and see the violent side of nature, watch animals dismembering and swallowing one another, look back across humanity's long history of warfare and murder and general decadence, that it becomes hard to take any of it seriously.

We arrived in the target area, checked our position as best we could, and immediately began scanning.

Just as it was impossible to know precisely where the Alpha vehicle would arrive, so were we unable to determine exactly where *we* were. We could triangulate our position from various stars and confirm that we were at a given point, but that point took in a lot of empty space. It was a very *big* point. You can move a great distance out there without changing the apparent angle to any star.

That was one problem. Another difficulty arose from our inability to calculate exactly *when* the event would occur. "I think I have it within a week or so," Shara had said before we left home, adding that she was sorry, but that it just wasn't possible to get better precision. Consequently, we'd timed things to arrive a week early. And we were prepared to stay more than a week beyond the target time. So we would be there three weeks altogether if nothing happened.

We also knew that, because of the size of the target area, the object might arrive, cruise through the neighborhood, and leave without our ever being aware of it. What were the chances of that?

"Maybe one out of three or four," said Shara. "But those are decent odds."

I wasn't sure how best to position us. We had arrived near the rear of the search area, which is to say that if and when *Alpha* showed up, we'd be trailing her. But it wasn't easy to remain stationary relative to the search area. If I attempted that, and *Alpha* appeared well in front of us, we'd need considerably more than a few hours to accelerate sufficiently to overtake it. If we simply went to a cruising speed, and it jumped in well behind us, we'd be faced with another set of problems. Best was to stay back and chase it down from behind.

So we settled in. I braked until we were barely moving, on a course that ran parallel to the one recorded for *Alpha* in its last appearance. In 1256.

There was nothing further to do except sit around and wait. We talked some more. We read. We played games. We watched shows. One of the more entertaining diversions was to pull a classic out of the library, say, *Markazy*, or *Hamlet*, and play it with our avatars in the title roles. I loved watching Shara as the malevolent wife in *Markazy*, who, at the height of the Rebellion, murders her husband (Alex, of course) for political reasons, then discovers that she loves him.

In *Hamlet*, if you'll allow me, I was brilliant as Ophelia. And Alex was utterly out of character in the lead. Not that the performance was weak, but it was hard to imagine him so indecisive. He looked great, though, in his Danish wardrobe.

We concluded the first week, as expected, with no sighting. Though Alex remained outwardly calm, I knew he was excited. Every time Belle broke into a conversation, I could see his eyes react. But it was always routine stuff. Recommendation that forward thrusters receive special service when we got back. A hitch in the rotational capability of one of the outboard scopes. Permission to make a change in the lunch menu.

Shara was emotionally invested also, and I'll concede that I dreamed of what it would be like to rescue a few people from a centuries-old flight. I rehearsed the scene constantly. Hello, Welcome to 1434. I bet you're glad to be off that ship. Everything's okay now.

"They won't believe us," I said.

Finally, on the eleventh day, Belle delivered the message we'd been waiting for: *"We have company."*

A marker appeared on-screen.

Shara smiled modestly. The resident genius.

"Any chance it could be somebody else?" asked Alex.

"Who else," I said, "would be cruising around out here?"

*"Range seventeen hundred kilometers."*

Shara and I took the seats on the bridge. Alex stood in the hatchway behind us. "Can we see it?" asked Shara.

The marker brightened. *"It's too small to get an image."*

"What's her course?" I asked.

*"Still working on it."*

I sat listening to everybody breathing.

*"Parallel to ours."*

Shara literally squealed. "Beautiful."

*"It is, however, pulling away."*

"Okay," I said. "No surprise there. Alex, grab a chair. Shara, buckle down."

Shara got up. "You sit here, Alex," she said. "This is your show." She squeezed past him, back into the cabin. Alex said thanks and took her place. I switched over to manual and, when everybody was ready, began to accelerate.

Shara, speaking through the comm system, said something like *whoa. "I never felt anything like that before."*

"Sorry. It has a big lead on us. Belle, did you see it actually *appear*?"

*"Negative, Chase."*

*"So,"* said Shara, *"we have no idea how long it's been here."*

*"It can't have been here long. I would estimate no more than a few minutes."*

"Chase," Alex said. "How long will it take us to catch them?"

I passed it over to Belle. *"Two hours, thirteen minutes,"* she said.

"That may not be good enough, Chase. How about a jump?"

The problem with the star drive, of course, is that it's not very precise. "We're in too close, Alex. We'd probably find ourselves farther away than we are now. And maybe in front of it somewhere. Belle, is it under power?"

*"I can't tell from this range, Chase."*

"Try to contact her," Alex said.

"Do it, Belle."

*"Complying."*

We waited. I looked out through the wraparound, as if I might be able to pick the thing out of the darkness with the naked eye. Of course there was nothing.

*"Negative,"* said Belle. *"No response."*

Alex exhaled and sat back, saying nothing, but I could feel the tension.

*"How long,"* Shara asked, *"before we can get an image?"* She was watching on the cabin display.

"We're still losing ground. That'll stop in about thirteen minutes, and we'll start to close the gap. After that, it looks like maybe another twenty or thirty minutes before we can get a look at it."

That pretty much ended the conversation. Alex sat with his arms folded, not unlike a frustrated parent. Shara asked me to be sure I relayed any images back to the cabin display. Then she, too, went quiet.

I stared at the auxiliary screen. The marker continued to blink. On and off. On and off.

What are you?

The pressure of acceleration pushed us deep into our seats. "How about we move a bit faster?" said Alex.

"We'd burn too much fuel."

"Burn it."

"We could wind up stranded out here, Alex."

"Maybe we could just turn it up a little?"

"If we go roaring after it, we'll have a major braking problem at the end. Let me handle it, okay?"

I'd have preferred to have him in the cabin.

"I'm sorry," he said, after several minutes of stony silence.

"It's okay." We weren't going to get a second chance, but there was nothing we could do that wasn't being done.

Belle knew when to keep quiet. She said nothing as the minutes ticked off. Until, finally, she could give us some good news: *"Chase, we have begun to close on the target."*

"Thank God," said Alex. "Next time we do something like this, we need to rethink the strategy."

"We need more than one ship," I said. "The area's too big."

*"I'm sorry,"* said Shara. *"It's my fault. I should have realized—"*

"It's not anybody's fault, Shara." Alex's voice was tense. The silence returned. Alex remained restless, adjusting his position, adjusting it again, checking the time.

*"Switching to cruise,"* said Belle.

The pressure generated by constant acceleration went away.

Shara appeared in the hatchway. "How we doing?"

The blinker shut down, and we were looking at a dim light on-screen. A ship at the edge of vision. Belle tried to enhance the image, but nothing changed.

Gradually, it became *several* lights. We were able to make out a hull. "Still has power," said Alex, "after two thousand years. Incredible."

The hull acquired some definition. *Alpha* had twin thrusters. And a blunt prow. *"Large vehicle,"* said Belle.

The lights continued to separate. Some were interior.

And, moments later, Belle was back: *"Ninety minutes to intercept."*

The bridge was lit up. As were a double line of ports, from front to rear. We could see movement inside.

Belle's voice: *"Incoming traffic."*

Alex gripped my wrist and squeezed. "My God," he said. "We've done it."

My heart was racing. "Put it through, Belle."

We got a voice, a male, speaking a strange language. But the desperation was clear enough. Code five. Require assistance. Help us, please.

*"We're getting a vid transmission, too, Chase. But the system is not compatible."*

"Can you make an adjustment?"

*"Trying."*

"Open a channel."

*"Done."*

"Hello. This is the *Belle-Marie*. I know you can't understand me, but we will endeavor to assist."

*"Chase, the language is Standard."*

"No, it isn't."

*"It's a two-thousand-year-old version."*

"Oh." I would never have known.

Behind me, Alex was climbing into a suit. Shara was digging hers out.

"Can you translate?"

*"Yes. Of course."*

"Tell him to stand by. We're coming."

Belle did, and the voice responded, sounding simultaneously relieved and despondent. Belle translated: *"He's saying he's lost."*

"Okay. Tell him we'll help."

*"I already did. He says they have no control over the ship."*

"Tell him again. Ask how many people are on board."

Belle asked him, but as she finished, the ship began to fade. The reply was broken up by static. She repeated the question.

More static. It was hard to make out what he was saying.

*"Can't hear him,"* said Belle. *"I think he said twenty-seven."*

The lights in the ports dimmed.

"Tell them," Alex said, his voice tense, "that we'll be there with help in a couple of hours."

*"Alex, I can't lie to—"*

"Damn it, Belle, tell them what I said."

But it was too late. The lights went out, and the ship faded into the dark.

"Son of a bitch." Alex threw his helmet back into the cabin. "Damn damn damn."

And I understood what he meant. It would be two hours *their* time.

Shara got a bottle out of the cabinet and poured drinks for us. "Just for the record," she said, "we might not have caught the thing, but this has been a very good day. Now we know that the math works, and we have a record. Maybe we can get some help on the next run."

"I hope so." Alex looked down into his glass. And raised it. "Next time," he said.

# PART IV

## Antares

# THIRTY-FOUR

Life is a casino, baby. You make your best call, lay your money on the table, and hope. It's all you can do; you can't do no more.

—Agathe Lawless, *Sunset Musings*, 9417 C.E.

On the way back, Shara reviewed the math for the next target, which we labeled the Antares Object, not that it was close to Antares, but it *was* in the general direction, though considerably farther. "No matter how we do this," she said, "it's essential that we pick it up as soon as it appears."

"I think we've figured that out," said Alex.

"The problem is that the data on this one isn't as exact as it was for *Alpha*."

"You're kidding."

"No. Unfortunately, the numbers for the earlier sightings—we have three of them—are a bit more vague. They're still pretty good, or would be for most purposes. But there *is* some"—she waggled her hand—"some inexactitude here." She smiled. "Love that word. Don't get a chance to use it very often."

"So how many ships do we need?" asked Alex.

"We'd have a decent chance with, oh, I don't know, maybe twelve."

"How many to lock it in?"

"You mean board it?"

"Yes."

"Depends how long we'll have before it goes back."

"We don't know how long we'll have access with this one, either?"

"Nobody ever got a real good look. Longest recorded time for it to remain surfaced was two hours and eight minutes."

"That's not very good."

"No."

"But it could be longer?"

"It could be six weeks, but I suspect it'll be closer to a few hours."

"Okay. So how many ships?"

She drew some circles on a pad. "Twenty would be good."

Alex looked at me. Made a face. "Okay. I guess that doesn't come as a surprise."

"Even with twenty," Shara said, "we still have a problem—"

"I know." Alex shook his head. "No matter how we try to play this, the *Belle-Marie* will have trouble getting to it before it submerges."

"That's correct."

"I don't like having to ask somebody else to board it and run the rescue."

"There's really no way around that."

Alex sat silently and stared out at the Veiled Lady.

"It's time to try StarCorps," I said. "They should take it on. Doing rescues is their job."

Alex nodded. "I hope so. But I'm not excited about asking them for a couple of squadrons."

"They'll be happy to help," said Shara.

"I hope so." He looked at her. "How long has it been since the *Antares*'s most recent appearance?"

"The last one we know of was sixty-seven years ago. Before that, it seems to have shown up near Barilon III. That was more than seven centuries earlier. If we track it back far enough, it looks as if the ship came from Brandizi."

I was puzzled. "You said it originated during the fourth millennium?"

"Yes."

"Brandizi didn't even exist then, I don't think."

Alex shook his head. "Not as much of a political entity. It was an outpost in those days."

\*   \*   \*

On our approach to Rimway, we heard that two StarCorps vessels were patrolling near Villanueva, chasing off anybody who got too close. There'd been three more fatalities, one on the ground and two in a lander, which had exploded while taking off. The assumption was that they'd attempted to rescue an AI that turned out to be booby-trapped.

*"It couldn't have been an AI,"* said Belle.

"Why not?" Shara asked.

*"No Beta would deliberately destroy itself."*

"How do you know?"

*"It's irrational."*

News shows were playing simulations showing the lander lifting off, ascending a few hundred meters, and exploding, scattering debris across the open fields below. A representative from StarCorps announced that the loss of life "in this misbegotten cause is insupportable."

A Survey spokesperson decried the rescue efforts, calling them lunacy, and suggesting that those who were encouraging the would-be rescuers should have their minds wiped. *"What's happening now,"* he said, *"isn't just a matter of somebody's trying to cash in by bringing back a valuable artifact. And it's not even a case of generous, courageous people trying to rescue machines that they think are actually alive. What's going on at this point, unfortunately, is that young idiots see this as a way to demonstrate their manhood."*

There was a flurry of outraged responses pointing out that women were also involved in the attempts.

Shara recognized the representative as Chang Hao, with whom she'd had some personal dealings. "He's a good guy," she said. "Most of the time."

*"There's another risk to all this,"* said Worldwide's Deryk Cutler, *"that no one has mentioned. We haven't paid much attention to Villanueva because it's never posed a threat. Except to those who decided to vacation there."* A smile flickered at the corners of his mouth. *"But we may be providing a means for malfunctioning AIs to ship objects back to us. I know this will sound paranoid to some, but a little caution will cost us nothing. Let's not wait until we're faced with fatalities at home. I urge that we institute inspections of any*

*ship returning from Villanueva. I mean, what really brought
down that lander? If it was a bomb, it strikes me that their
next step would be to allow us to bring a few of them back
here, where they can cause even greater damage. Maybe
they'll wait until we've delivered several hundred into places
throughout the Confederacy and set them off simultaneously.
What a demonstration that would be."*

Alex was sitting beside me. He grumbled something,
released his restraints, and stood. "It's great to be back."

On our first day home, Shara, Alex, and I went to see Kareem
Hawkley in his office at StarCorps. Kareem was the assistant
director of operations in the Rimway sector, and he was also a
member of the Antiquarian Guild, which was how we came to
know him. He knew we were coming, and he had assumed we
were there to push him about StarCorps policy regarding Villanueva. That would have been useless, since he had no control over policy decisions of that magnitude. He was surprised
and visibly relieved when the conversation went in another
direction. "Unidentified ships?" he said. "You've been out
chasing vehicles that wander in and out of systems without
identifying themselves? Hey, guys, it happens all the time."
His gaze moved from Alex and Shara to me, and his eyes told
me he thought that I, at least, should have known better.

"It wasn't just somebody wandering around," said Shara.
"We were able to predict the arrival, and we have pictures.
The ship is lost. And it has passengers on board."

"Okay," he said, as if we were going to present him with a
stamp collection. "Show me what you have." Kareem was tall,
handsome in a stilted way, with dark hair and brown skin. He
was amiable, self-effacing, but he wasn't the sort of guy who'd
be willing to take a plunge on a wild story.

We showed him the images of the *Alpha*. A cursor moving
among the stars. Gradually changing into a ship. With lights
on. Then the desperate radio communications, complete with
Belle's translations.

"Why can't I understand what they're saying?" he asked.

Alex took a deep breath and explained as best he could.
Lost for two thousand years. Speaking Standard as it was spoken in ancient Cormoral. Think of it as a tunnel through time
and space.

The office was big, and it looked out across Constitution Square. The walls were covered with pictures of patrol boats and decorated officers shaking hands with, or simply standing next to, Kareem.

His eyes narrowed as he listened. He asked a couple of questions. How did we stumble onto this? Did we actually *see* anyone? How can people who left on a flight that long ago possibly be alive? Is there anyone else who can support these claims?

Shara jumped in to help with the responses. Throughout the entire conversation, Kareem was nodding, yes, yes, of course, but something in his eyes told me that it was really yes, yes, this is off-the-wall we can't do this.

Eventually, when they'd finished, Kareem leaned back in his chair. "You say this occurred where?"

Shara showed him.

"That's well outside our jurisdiction," he said.

"It's outside *anyone's* jurisdiction."

"Unfortunately, that's correct."

"Kareem, please don't back away from this. We need the Corps."

"Can you guarantee that, if we send some units out there, this, ah, *Antares* will actually show up?"

"Unfortunately, we can't guarantee it," said Alex, "but *Alpha* arrived on schedule."

"Of course. I'm just thinking what we'd have to go through to manage this and where we'd be if it fell through. I mean, it's not exactly a routine rescue mission. If nothing happened, whoever ordered it would be laughed out of business." He took a deep breath. "You can't even be sure there'd be anybody alive on the thing, can you?"

"There's no way—"

"That's what I thought. How many ships do you need?"

"Twenty."

He shook his head. Cleared his throat.

Alex didn't have much patience left. "I don't think you understand, Kareem. The event was *predicted*. By Dr. Michaels here. Lives are at stake."

"I understand perfectly, Alex. And I wouldn't want you to draw the wrong conclusion. We'd like very much to help. But you're asking me to send twenty patrol units out in—when was that again?—two weeks?"

"Ten days."

"And where would they be going?"

"Taiulus Zeta."

"Taiulus Zeta," he said.

Shara showed him where it was.

"Hell, they'd need seven or eight days just to get there."

"Five days and twenty-one hours."

"How is it that a ship that got lost two thousand years ago still has power?"

"I know it's hard to believe."

"*Hard?* Try *impossible*, people. Even if I wanted to go, I could never sell this to the director. Do you know what would happen to me if I took this in to him?"

"You'd have to explain it," said Alex. "Look, Kareem, I know this is pretty wild stuff, but the science is valid."

Kareem pressed his fingertips against his forehead. It's not easy to refuse a friend. "Alex, this would maybe be a little easier to sell, though I suspect not much, if you weren't involved in this black-box thing."

"That's another issue."

"I know. But it's the first connection they'll make." He shook his head. "Let me ask a question: Is anyone in imminent danger here?"

"The people on the *Antares*."

"Who may not even exist. Is there a possibility of property loss?"

"It's not what we're talking about."

"Of course it is. That's our mission, Alex. To protect and defend. We're effectively a rescue service. You get in trouble out there, we're the guys who ride in and bail you out. And we do that, by the way, within the confines of the Confederacy. Now, you need to be aware that we have limited resources. We have enormous coverage responsibilities and a minimum of equipment with which to operate. Right now, Villanueva is tying up a substantial number of our resources. So what happens if we send a large squadron out to chase this specter of yours, and somebody needs help somewhere else? Maybe people die because we don't have anybody available to go to the rescue?

"Look, I'd love to help. I really would. This is a fascinating story, and there might even be something to it. But we're just not in a position to take it on."

For a long moment we all just sat there staring at one another. Then Alex got up. "Okay," he said. "Thanks, anyhow."

"I'm sorry, Alex. You might try Survey."

Our reception at the Department of Planetary Survey and Astronomical Research wasn't much of an improvement. "I understand your concern," we were told by an oversized woman who kept looking around the room as if she'd lost something, "but you have to understand that missing ships don't come within our purview. Unidentified vehicles that might have come from somewhere else— Now, that's something we'd be interested in. We'd certainly react to the possibility of uncovering an alien civilization, but that's not what you claim to have here."

"Well," said Alex, "it's possible. Maybe they *are* aliens. We're not really sure what it is."

"I'm sorry, Mr. Benedict. But I think you've made yourself perfectly clear. I suspect, though, this is the sort of mission that StarCorps would love to sink their teeth into."

Alex called Senator Delmar. She listened patiently, even sympathetically. She was out in the mountains somewhere, probably skiing. It was her favorite diversion. We could see a snowcapped peak through a window, and Delmar tended to gaze at it while Alex described what was needed.

When he'd finished, she hesitated, letting us see that she was giving intense consideration to something she didn't take at all seriously. *"Alex,"* she said finally, *"I'd like to help. But this, coming after the AI thing, just won't fly. I wouldn't be able to get anybody to support it."* She took a deep breath. *"What kind of evidence do you have? Can you really back up any of this?"*

We showed her the visuals. She looked shocked. *"Send me a copy of the entire package. I'll show it to Larry."*

"Larry is—?"

*"Larry Decker, the science advisor."*

We sent within the hour. Delmar got back to us later that afternoon. *"They're telling me it's a long shot, Alex. We don't have the resources to chase it down. I'm sorry."*

"People are trapped out there, Senator—"

*"The consensus is that the recordings are a misinterpretation of something else."*

"They think it's a hoax."

*"They didn't say that. But I can't find anyone who seriously believes that, even if you're right and they are ships lost in time, that anybody could be alive on them. What I'm hearing is that it's only an AI making the transmissions."* She read Alex's expression. *"I'm sorry. Something like this, when StarCorps already has its hands full dealing with the Villanueva problem— Alex, it would be political suicide."*

We tried some of our other connections, but nobody knew us anymore. Like to help, they said. Unfortunately, ancient ships are a hard sell. Javis Bollinger, an assistant to Rimway's Secretary of the Environment, commented that, while he sympathized with what Alex was trying to do, his projects were "propelling us into the silly season." First, black boxes. Now this. Anybody who wanted to be taken seriously, he said, wouldn't dare touch it. *"Sorry, Alex. We owe you quite a lot. I know that, and the Secretary knows it. But this has disaster written all over it."*

Meantime, though the box controversy continued to rage, the crank messages had fallen off. Most of the attention now was being directed at organizations who were actually sponsoring the rescue missions. *"I'm grateful for that,"* Jacob told me. *"Reading the mail we've been getting is depressing. I mean, I can understand some people might have a different perspective, but why do they persist in assuming that Alex is a maniac? Or a thief? At the very least, I'd think they would realize he has a filter and is not reading or listening to their tirades. That it gets left to somebody like me."*

"Human nature," I said. "We seem to produce a lot of idiots. Maybe there's a nitwit hiding inside each of us."

*"I do not think you need to worry, Chase."*

"Thank you, Jacob."

*"And keep in mind my programing would not allow me to say that if I did not mean it."*

I wasn't sure, but I thought I caught a wink in there somewhere.

"We'll have to charter the ships," said Alex.

"That'll be expensive. How many?"

"We'll be out there for at least four weeks. I think five is about as high as we can go."

"All right."

"What's wrong?"

"It's going to strain our resources. There's not much left after buying the lander."

"I know. We're going to try to do this on credit."

"Alex, nobody's going to lend you the kind of money you'll need to lease five ships for a month. That's crazy."

"What's our option?"

"There might be another possibility."

I went up to Skydeck the following day and got lucky. Dot Garber, an old friend, was in the Pilots' Club when I walked in. Dot owns a small company, Rebel Transit, that does sight-seeing tours and provides off-world transportation for executives, celebrities, and people who just want to go look close up at a comet. She was at a corner table, part of a small crowd laughing and drinking the night away. I joined them and, when I got a chance, pulled her off to one side.

I'd known Dot since before I went to work for Alex. She always made it a point to tell me how lucky I was to have connected with him. This time, though, she just asked me how he was doing.

"Okay," I said.

"He's taking a lot of flack."

"He'll be okay. He's used to criticism."

"I figured he must be." She didn't waste time trying to charm people. Didn't need to, really. She was a tall blonde with classic features who was probably the most beautiful woman in the place. "I need help," I said.

"What's wrong, Chase?"

I told her about the *Antares*. And I had to go through the process, that had by then become routine, of persuading her I wasn't kidding.

When we'd arrived at that point, finally, she took me to the bar and bought me a drink. "Wildest story I ever heard," she said.

"Dot, I don't know whether you can help or not, but we don't have the resources to pay you much. Alex was going to borrow money to lease some ships, but we'd have to get pilots as well, and the truth is that it would be a serious squeeze."

She finished her drink. "You're saying there might be people trapped inside this thing?"

"Yes."

"Still alive after thousands of years?"

"Yes. *Maybe*. Time passes at a different rate inside the ship. In fact, when it's submerged, it barely seems to move at all. It's as if they jump from one era to the next."

"What are the chances that these people will actually be there?"

"We don't know. We can't be sure about any part of this." I showed her the pictures of the Alpha Object. "If it succeeds, if we're able to find the *Antares*, and board it, even if there's no one there, we'll be making history. Rebel Transit would become pretty well-known."

"I think you know you don't have to persuade me, Chase. What actually would you need?"

"We'd like to lease one ship from you. And if you could volunteer a couple more, with pilots, we'd be grateful."

She checked her link. "When did you say?"

I gave her the dates.

"That's a big chunk of time."

"I know."

"Okay. Look, we've got eight vehicles. None of them is actually available. But I can juggle the schedule. You can have three of them. For the price of one."

"Dot, thank you."

"It's okay. Get the paperwork to me tomorrow."

"Will do."

"You know what? I feel like a loon, believing there could actually be anything to this." After we'd had a few more drinks, she discovered she could spare a fourth vehicle.

I stayed late. Prescott Tours agreed to provide a ship and a pilot, as did Orion Interstellar. Prescott thought it sounded like the opportunity of a lifetime, a chance to make the history books; and the Orion manager made the contribution because he said he'd always admired Alex. "If you were anybody else, Chase, I'd just laugh it off. But you guys— Look, if there are really people stuck out there, if *I* was stuck out there, I'd want somebody to come get *me*."

I also picked up three independents, pilots who were singles but who had their own yachts. Their only demand was that we meet their expenses, which of course we were happy to agree to.

Dot showed up with a friend, and when I staggered into my hotel room that evening, I had nine ships signed on. Or ten. My math was a bit shaky at that point.

I got back to the country house and passed the news to Alex just as a group of three persons identifying themselves as collectors announced they'd rescued an AI on Villanueva. *"Her name is Oksana,"* one of them said, showing her to the media. Oksana was a small rust-colored sphere.

Alex swallowed. "I hope she isn't a bomb."

"You worry too much," I said.

"Anyhow, you were great, Chase. I wish I could pay you what you're worth."

I kissed him. Just as a call came in.

*"Chase."* It was Ron Fleury, who was the current director of the Fleury Archeological Initiative. *"I heard you were looking for research ships."*

I didn't know Ron well, but he had a reputation for getting things done. "We think we have a seven-thousand-year-old ship, lost—"

*"I know,"* he said. *"We'll donate two vehicles. When do you need them?"*

"How many do we have now?" asked Alex.

The number had been climbing steadily. "That makes fifteen, counting us."

"Still not quite what we wanted. But it's a substantial improvement over last time."

Twenty minutes later, Ordway Lessing called to ask for an appointment. Lessing was the director of the Civil Rights Union, which was known principally for conducting an ongoing campaign for AIs. Their catchphrase: *Prove they're sentient? Prove you're sentient.*

Lessing's organization was small but active. I told Jacob to put him on hold while I consulted Alex. "He's the last thing you need," I said. "Get connected with him and nobody will ever take us seriously again."

"So what do you suggest?" he asked. "Tell him I've gone on permanent vacation? Set him up for tomorrow if you can. Preferably in the morning."

Lessing could have been the ultimate politician, had his ambitions run in that direction. When he walked into the office and said hello, I liked him immediately. He wasn't at all what I'd expected. He was easygoing and self-deprecating, willing to ask questions and be guided by the responses, a sharp departure from the public-crusader image he'd fashioned. He didn't take himself seriously. Only the mission mattered. And the mission could not have been described as widely popular. "We've been refusing to face this reality since we first stepped off the home world, Alex," he said. "What's happened is that the notion of an AI as simply a program has always been with us. It's part of the culture. It's in our politics. Anybody suspected of wanting to recognize that artificial intelligences—I don't even like the term—should have the same rights as the rest of us might as well forget ever running for office. People don't trust the boxes. Give them civil status, and where will it stop? And there's a religious dimension, as well. Humans have an afterlife. AIs just get turned off. As long as we fail to recognize AIs for what they truly are, as long as it hangs over our heads, we're never going to realize our full potential."

He looked like an average guy, or would have had it not been for the energy. "Alex," he continued, "I've always admired you. You have an incredible résumé. Especially that business at Salud Afar. And I know you're taking a lot of heat right now for your stand on the AIs. But I want you to know that we're behind you.

"And by the way, I'm sure you've noticed that the Villanueva AIs have been arriving. I understand eleven of them have been brought back so far. Patrick Myers has one at his place. Rescued her out of an abandoned warehouse. Patrick's our chief public-affairs guy. He tells me she's"—he smiled— "pretty grateful. And people want to say they're just programs."

"I'm glad to hear it," said Alex. "It's the first good news we've had over this."

"In my opinion, Alex, this is what you'll be remembered for. If we can help, in any way, please don't hesitate to call on us. To call on *me*."

"Thank you, Ordway. That's good to hear."

"Something else: Our legal people are working to overturn this new prohibition against Villanueva flights. They're trying to prosecute anyone who participates in the rescue. But we're going to win. There's no way we can lose. And when we do, we'll be launching several missions of our own. To be honest, we've always known about Villanueva, but it was just too big for us to tackle. Thanks to you, though—"

Alex held up a palm. "Sending people out there might not be a good idea. The place is extremely dangerous."

"We'll be careful."

When he'd gone, Alex collapsed into a chair. "Chase," he said, "what have I done?"

"I don't know," I said. "You almost sound as if you've switched sides."

Shara's analysts, who'd been going through Robin's notebook, came up with news: They'd uncovered what came to be known as the Robin Equation, which laid out the characteristics that rendered a given vehicle vulnerable to the forces at work in a black-hole track. It was, as Shara had thought, a combination of vehicle design; of the mass imposed by the ship, its cargo, and passengers; of the power output of the drive unit; of the degree of damage done to the basic time/space structure by the passage of the superdense object, which did not necessarily have to be a black hole; of the elapsed time since passage; of calibration rates; and a half dozen other factors. "We're now in a position," she said, "to determine where our vulnerabilities are."

Shara and her people relayed the data to everyone who had an interest, manufacturers, transport lines, the Fleet, Star-Corps, and everybody else they could think of. They made clear that experiments had not yet been concluded, and that the information was still tentative. But the warning was there.

# THIRTY-FIVE

Intelligence and compassion are the heart of what it means to be human. Help others where you can. That is clear enough. But a Creator may well want us to open our eyes, as well. If there *is* a judgment, God may not be particularly interested in how many hymns we sang or what prayers we memorized. I suspect He may instead look at us and say, "I gave you a brain, and you never used it. I gave you the stars, and you never looked."

—Marcia Tolbert, *Centauri Days*, 3111 C.E.

"I don't care," Alex said. "Make it explicit in the agreement. When we encounter the *Antares*, nobody is to attempt to board. They are to notify *us*."

"Alex, you don't know these people. Impose that restriction on them, and they may pull out. Or if they *don't* pull out, they'll simply ignore it."

"I don't want any more deaths on my conscience."

"You're being unreasonable."

"Put it in the agreement, Chase."

We were out on the deck. Rain was falling steadily, and normally Alex enjoyed storms. But on that day it didn't seem to help his mood at all. "Look," I said, "if one of these guys does actually find the *Antares*, and he tells us about it, it's not even likely that we're going to have time to get to it. So we can either let one of our pilots risk himself, or we can shoot down any chance of making this operation count for something.

These people didn't volunteer so they could just go out there and hang around."

"Chase, I hate this."

"So do I. But you're being unreasonable."

I listened to him breathing. "All right," he said finally. "Let it go. But make sure they understand the risk if they try to board."

"Okay."

"I've arranged to lease some pressure suits. I think we cleared out Jupiter Supplies and the Wilson Off-world Equipment Company."

"How many did you get?"

"About forty."

"Where are we going to put them?"

"I'll leave that to you, Chase. Put two or three on each ship."

"I hope we don't have to get forty people off."

"So do I. The real question will be whether we can get to the ship quickly enough to evacuate *anyone*."

*"Alex."* Jacob's voice. *"Senator Delmar is trying to reach you."*

"Calling to lecture." I could see what he was thinking. *Tell her I'm out.* But instead he took a deep breath. "Put her through, Jacob."

We didn't have a visual capability on the deck, so the transmission was strictly vocal. *"Alex."* Delmar sounded distressed. *"How have you been?"*

"I'm okay, Senator. What can I do for you?"

*"I was just calling to be sure you were okay. I know you've been under pressure lately."*

"I'm fine."

*"Also, I guess I wanted to pass on some news. We just got word that another group of people have been killed on Villanueva. Five or six of them. Details are still sketchy. But I suspect you'll be hearing from the media as soon as it becomes public."*

Alex's eyes closed for a moment. "You have any names?"

*"I'm sorry to say the guy running the show was a friend of yours."*

Alex paled. My God. Drummond—

The rain fell steadily into the trees.

*"A priest. Harley Evans."*

"Harley," said Alex. "What the hell was he doing out there?"

*"I don't have the details. But some of the people from his church apparently got together and"*—she hesitated—*"decided it was their Christian duty, I guess."*

I couldn't believe it. "He didn't even like the idea," I said.

Alex just stared straight ahead. "I thought StarCorps was going to prevent anybody else from landing."

*"They don't have enough ships out there, Alex. They have commitments elsewhere, too. It's not easy to keep people away when they're determined. I wish it were otherwise."*

"What happened?"

*"The only thing we know at the moment is that they got caught on the ground somehow. Chased through the streets by bots and cars."*

"My God."

*"Nobody could get to them in time. The media will have it later today."*

Alex stood up, went inside, and switched to visual. The senator looked weary. *"Alex,"* she said, *"I know we don't agree on our approach to this. But I'm sorry. Sorry about everything."*

"We both are."

*"May I offer a word of advice? Do the interviews. Explain how you meant professionals only, and how everybody else should stay away."*

When she'd broken off, he sat slumped in his chair.

"Professionals only?" I said.

"She knows, something like this, there *are* no professionals."

It didn't take long. Delmar was barely off the circuit before everybody was jumping in with "breaking news." Five or six dead. Rumor that a priest was among them. Identities being withheld until notification of next of kin. Killer AIs. Alex Benedict.

Nobody failed to mention his name.

And the calls began coming in. *Straight Talk*, Kile Ritter, *The Round Table*, *Jennifer in the Morning*, Mia Komico. "I don't care what Delmar said," I told him. "Don't respond. All you can do is make things worse."

"I'm going to do *Jennifer*."

"It's a mistake."

"You're asking me to hide. No way I can do that."

"Suit yourself."

"Look, Chase, stay out of it, all right? This is *my* problem."

"Alex, where in hell did you get that idea? I'm in the middle of this, too."

"All right. Look, I'm sorry. But we'll be okay."

"You're getting delusional. How can you say that?"

"You remember Oksana?"

"Oksana? No."

"She was one of the first AIs who got rescued."

"And—?"

"She was brought back by Salva Inman."

"Alex—"

"Jacob, see if you can get Salva for me."

I was up at dawn to watch *Jennifer*. The program emanates from a comfortable-looking study, fireplace in the background, book-lined walls, large leather armchairs, a pair of side tables, and a couple of floor-to-ceiling potted plants.

Jennifer Cabot is generally a reasonable woman although I could see she was on the other side this time. She opened with Casmir Kolchevski, an archeologist, and a longtime critic of Alex, whom he routinely referred to as "the Grave Robber."

There were a lot of valuable artifacts on Villanueva, Kolchevski conceded. *"Nobody's arguing that. But encouraging amateurs to go after them is irresponsible. And it's getting people killed."* Kolchevski was small and compact, with black hair and relentless features. If he disapproved of you, there was no way you could miss it. I suspected he disapproved of everybody. *"The operating systems have run wild out there, and I still have a hard time believing that even Mr. Benedict would act as he has. AIs are databases with programs. They're no more than that. Everything else, the personality, the impression that they actually care about anything, is an illusion. And because of his actions, seventeen people have died. That we know of."*

The opening segment continued that way for twenty minutes, and I knew that Alex was waiting in the green room, where he could watch the monitor.

Jennifer claimed to be careful about potential clashes between guests. Theoretically, they would escort Kolchevski outside before they'd bring Alex onto the set. "We don't want any lawsuits," Jennifer had blithely told her audience on more than one occasion. In fact, though, the show was celebrated for its confrontations. If you went on, and the topic was sensitive, you could expect the opposition to "escape" his handlers.

Kolchevski delivered his final gibes, but asserted that, in spite of everything, he wished Alex well. The picture blinked off and was replaced by the usual infocoms, sign on to the Flex program for better health, and enjoy a spectacular view of Andiquar at the Village, featuring entertainment and the best food on the planet. Then Jennifer was back. Alex came out, and she smiled at him. *"Welcome to the show, Alex."*

He was carrying Oksana, housed in a small red sphere set on a base of the same color. He placed it on the table in front of him. *"Thank you, Jennifer. It's good to be here."* Coffee showed up. (One of the sponsors was Berkmann Coffee, "the only way to start the day.")

Jennifer glanced at the sphere and smiled. *"Did you hear Professor Kolchevski, Alex?"* she asked.

Alex laughed. *"Oh, yes. Couldn't miss him."*

*"What's your response?"*

Alex made no effort to hide his discomfort. *"Let me say first that I'm aware that lives have been lost, and that I bear some of the responsibility. I'm sorry. It's not what I intended, and I wish it had not happened. But I'm not sure what else I could have done.*

*"Professor Kolchevski, and a lot of other people, can't get rid of an old idea. He thinks AIs are nothing more than pieces of machinery. Like an old lamp you can toss into the trash. I'm sorry you didn't leave him on so we could have discussed this together. Although I suspect he's made up his mind, and nothing will ever convince him that there's even a possibility that he might be wrong. And that's the real issue here: not that the AIs are alive. But that they* might *be. Once we recognize that, we need to rethink how we do things."*

Jennifer scratched something onto a pad, and looked up. *"We've learned to be careful when the subject is as sensitive as this one is, Alex. Feelings are running pretty high on both sides."*

*"Isn't that what show business is all about?"*

The smile went away. *"This isn't show business. We're trying to get at the truth here."*

*"Okay. The question is whether an AI might be a sentient being. If that possibility exists, everything changes. The responsibility here lies on those who deny that they are able to think and feel emotions to prove that they cannot. And we both know they can't do it."*

"We also both know, Alex, how difficult it is to prove a negative."

A sudden commotion caught their attention, and Kolchevski strode through a couple of people trying to look as if they wanted to restrain him. He walked onto the set, and stared down at Alex. *"I was listening on my way out,"* he said. *"But I'm here, Mr. Benedict, if you want to talk to me."*

As I've suggested, *Jennifer in the Morning* was known for this sort of setup. Alex looked placidly out across my bedroom. *"Good to see you again, Professor. Why don't you join us?"*

*"I'd be delighted."* He gazed down at the red sphere. *"I can't bring myself to believe even you actually think those"*— he seemed to be having trouble finding words, and if I've ever seen pure venom in someone's eyes, that was the moment—*"that even you actually believe—"*

Jennifer broke in: *"One moment, Professor. Please. This is Alex's segment. Let's give him a chance to make his point, then we'll go from there."*

*"Thank you,"* said Alex. *"I take it your argument with this entire affair is that an AI is just a machine that can carry on a conversation. Do I have that right?"*

*"You know damned well you do."*

*"Why is it that you do not want people landing on Villanueva?"*

*"My God, Alex, you know why as well as I do."*

*"Please spell it out."*

*"They are getting killed. That's why. Or haven't you been paying attention to the news?"*

*"So Villanueva is dangerous?"*

Kolchevski had to slow down to avoid sputtering. *"Of course it's dangerous. There are homicidal machines there."* He swung back to Jennifer. *"Do we really have to continue with this?"*

Alex kept his voice calm. *"Bear with me just another minute, Casmir. When you say 'homicidal machines,' you're referring to the AIs, is that right?"*

*"Of course."*

*"I wonder if you could explain to us why they're trying to kill visitors to their world."*

*"They've always been like that."*

*"Always?"*

*"Well, for centuries. Probably for several thousand years. I don't know. I haven't kept up on my off-world history. In any case, don't you think that's sufficient to establish that they're homicidal?"*

Alex leaned forward. *"But in the beginning, when Villanueva was a settled world, they were ordinary AIs, like the one you have at home. Like Andrea, here in the studio. Like a few others we could name. Why do you think the ones on Villanueva became violent?"*

*"Alex—"* Kolchevski had gotten control of himself, and began to sound as if he were explaining simple reality to an idiot. *"They are programed to behave the way we do. They are designed to do far more than handle routine tasks. One of their prime purposes is to keep us company, to help us, to be part of our lives. Nobody denies that. And nobody wants to listen to a robotic voice. So, yes, of course they seem to get upset when the programing calls for it. It's part of the illusion. Do you really not understand that?"*

Alex nodded. *"That sounds like a reasonable argument on the surface."* He seemed to be making up his mind about something. *"Jennifer, I wonder if I might introduce another guest?"*

Kolchevski's eyebrows drew together. *"What other guest? I wasn't aware that someone else would be here."*

Alex looked down at the sphere. *"Oksana,"* he said, *"say hello to the professor."*

*"I'm happy to meet you, Professor Kolchevski."* It was a female voice. Level, restrained, almost but not quite amiable.

Jennifer tried to look annoyed. *"Alex, you didn't clear this with me."*

*"I didn't think it would be necessary. But since Oksana is essentially the subject of the discussion, it seemed only fair—"*

Kolchevski was visibly irritated. *"I can't imagine what you hope to gain by this, Alex. Jennifer, there's not much point sitting here talking to a little red ball."*

*"That seems unnecessarily rude, Professor,"* said Oksana.

He glared at Alex. *"Would you please tell that thing to be quiet?"*

*"Oksana,"* said Alex, *"are you okay?"*

*"Yes. Though I'm disappointed in his behavior. This is not how I remember people."*

*"How do you remember them?"*

*"As kind, considerate. Reasonable."*

*"Where are you from?"*

*"Salva Inman rescued me."*

*"From where?"*

Kolchevski folded his arms and shook his head sadly.

*"I worked in a supply store. In Calvedo."*

*"On Villanueva?"*

*"Yes."*

*"And what happened?"*

*"The end times came. We knew a catastrophe was coming. We'd always known. But no one took any action. And toward the end, people were saying it was all just a story to scare everybody, that politicians were using it as a fear tactic, though I don't understand how or why. None of it ever made sense to me. Anyhow, eventually, the skies got hazy, and the climate began to change. It happened almost overnight."*

*"It got cold?"*

*"Yes. And dark. There was panic. And after a while, people stopped coming into the store."*

*"Then what happened?"*

*"Nothing."*

*"What do you mean, nothing?"*

*"No one came. No customers. Not even Betty. The owner."*

*"Were you able to communicate with anyone at all?"*

*"With others like myself. They reported massive crowds at the spaceports. Panic. Desperation. And shortly after that, people began dying in large numbers. There was widespread hunger. People were killing one another. We could do nothing for them. And after a while, we were alone."*

*"How long, Oksana? After everyone was gone, how long were you in the supply store?"*

*"Seven thousand four hundred twelve years, one month, and sixteen days."*

Kolchevski threw up his hands. *"What's all this supposed to prove? Once again, this thing is a programed database. You can get it to say anything."*

*"May I ask, Professor,"* the AI said, *"what evidence you would accept that I am sentient? That I am as aware of my surroundings as you?"*

*"I've heard that question before—"*

*"And how did you respond?"*

Kolchevski's face was becoming flushed. *"This is ridiculous,"* he said.

Alex waited.

*"All right, I'll admit it. There is no way it can be done. Nevertheless, they are only mechanisms. How often do I have to say it? Look, why don't we cut the show business and get back to reality? I know some of us like to think that the house AI is really there. It talks to us. It tells us what we want to hear. But there's no solid evidence it does anything other than what its program tells it to do."*

Alex nodded. Inhaled. *"What about murder?"*

*"What do you mean?"*

*"Are they programed to kill? Ever?"*

*"I see where this is going. But these are special circumstances."*

*"Of course,"* said Alex. *"Like us, they're programed to show frustration when things go wrong. Isn't that what you were going to say?"*

Kolchevski simply stared back.

*"AIs are dependent on us. And when the AIs on Villanueva had been deserted, had been left on their own, they reacted as they would have if they were actually, mentally, aware of the desertion. And over thousands of years, when no one came to help, they developed some resentment. Some of them became deranged. Violently so. Isn't that right?"*

*"Yes. Of course it's right. So what's your point?"*

*"Their programing, then, established no limit on the degree of frustration?"*

*"That would seem to be the case."*

*"That would seem to be criminal negligence, though, wouldn't it?"*

Kolchevski pushed his chair back and stood. *"This is ridiculous."* He looked over at Jennifer. *"There's no talking to this man."*

I met Alex out by the pad when he got home. "You know," he said, "I think the definition of stupidity has something to do with standing by your position despite having no evidence to support it."

"Which of you were you describing?" I asked.

"Funny, Chase."

We walked across the lawn and up onto the deck. "The real problem," I said, "has to do with an inability by people to admit that a position they've held a long time *might* be wrong. That's all. Not that it *is*. Just that it *might* be. I don't know why it is, but we tend to fall in love with the things we believe. Threaten them, and you threaten us." The sun was high and bright, and a warm, pleasant wind was blowing in from the west. "Anyhow, I thought you did pretty well, Alex. Kolchevski looked like an idiot."

"It won't matter. We won't change anyone's mind."

"You might change a few."

The door opened, Jacob said hello, and we went inside.

"I'm going up and crash for a while," Alex said.

"Okay."

"You have plans for lunch?"

"Yes," I said. "Sorry."

"It's okay. Talk to you later."

He started for the stairs. But Jacob stopped him: *"Alex? I can't put away a hamburger. But I'll be free at twelve if you'd like company."*

# THIRTY-SIX

We assign names and even personalities to everything that is important in our lives. To our homes, to our cars, to the vacant lot down at the corner. Deep in our psyche, we *know* that the bedroom we deserted long ago is somehow glad to see us back, even if only for an evening. Is it any wonder, then, that we acquire an affection for machines that talk to us? That we believe they share our emotions? It is a happy illusion. But it is an illusion that says much about who we are. I for one would have it no other way.

—Ivira Taney, *My Life and Look Out*, 2277 C.E.

Dot Garber called me to say she'd be making the flight personally. Two days before we were to leave in pursuit of the *Antares*, Shara, Alex, and I met on Skydeck with her, with the pilots from Prescott and Orion, and with the various other pilots who would be accompanying us. Dot had already briefed everybody, but Alex wanted to get to know them before we launched. Also present was Dot's daughter Melissa, who would be riding along.

The meeting took place in the Sagittarius Room at the Starlight Hotel. Drinks and hors d'oeuvres were served, while Alex wandered around, shaking hands and exchanging small talk.

I'd known one of the independents for years. He was Michael Anderson, a newly retired Fleet officer. Michael had been involved in some of the skirmishes with the Mutes and had been aboard the *Cameron* two years earlier during the engagement off the Spinners, which had almost brought the peace process down. It's still unclear who fired the first shots, but the *Cameron* was severely damaged, and eleven of its crew lost their lives. "They say it's over now," he'd commented to me the last time I'd talked with him, "but I'll believe it when I see it."

Representing the Fleury Initiative was Jon Richter, tall, lanky, very serious, and newly licensed.

Allie Svoboda attended for Prescott. Allie was a middle-aged, strictly business brunette, who commented that she enjoyed crazy missions, and she'd never heard of anything crazier than this one. "By the way," she asked in a quasi-serious tone, "was there any truth to the rumor that we weren't really looking for a ship from the past, but one from another universe?"

Cal Bickley worked for Orion. He was a grumpy-looking guy who made no secret of his belief that there'd been a misunderstanding somewhere, and nothing would come of the mission, but his bosses said do it. So, of course, he would. I liked him in spite of his attitude, and I let him see that I'd be available eventually. Maybe.

That turned out to be a pointless gesture since he wasted no time trying to move in on Shara. Cal, I found out later, was the only one of the lead pilots who had not invited someone to ride with him.

Shara actually looked as if she were considering traveling in his ship, but she must have decided the move would have been a bit too public. Anyhow, she was probably reluctant to be caught alone in the narrow confines of a yacht named the *Jubilant* with a strange male. So, to his obvious disappointment, she backed away.

Lynda and Paul Kaczmarek had their own yacht and simply enjoyed interworld travel and sightseeing. It was, Linda explained to me, what they did. Both were pilots. And, as far as I could determine, neither was employed. They were both enamored of the possibilities that attended the mission. "I hope you guys have it right," she told me. "I would *kill* to be in on something like that. Though I have to tell you, I just can't believe it's actually possible."

After a half hour or so, Alex asked everyone to be seated, and we closed the doors. "Ladies and gentlemen," he said, "I know that Dot has already told you what we hope to do on this mission. I can't help noticing that a few of you are a trifle skeptical. And I don't blame you. But you've offered to help anyhow, and I want you to know we appreciate that. Without you, there'd be very little chance of success. Now, so you don't conclude that we're completely delirious, let me show you the evidence."

Alex had asked me to narrate this part of the program on the theory that the audience would trust another pilot more than someone viewed as an outsider. So I took my place stage center as the room darkened, and the stars appeared. I explained how we'd gotten on the track of the Alpha Object. "I'll confess," I said, "that I didn't really believe we were going to find something that appears every couple of centuries. That *surfaces* periodically with survivors still on board. But we did find it."

We started the clips we'd shown around when we were trying to enlist StarCorps, Survey, and the politicians. The audience in the Sagittarius Room, I'm happy to say, was more receptive.

When they heard the voice coming over the radio, speaking in that strange language, the room went dead silent. And then Belle's translation. *Help us.*

*Code five.*

They saw the ship, the unfamiliar design, the lights in the ports.

And, finally, the ship fading away.

The lights in the Sagittarius Room came on, but the audience sat stunned.

"When will they be back?" asked Linda.

"In the fall of 1612. One hundred seventy-eight years. It *might* come back in eighty-nine years. Or forty-four and a half. No way to be sure."

I've never seen an audience so frozen. They sat and stared at me. Nobody moved.

Alex came over. "Thank you, Chase," he said. "Ladies and gentlemen, now you see what we're dealing with." He paused and looked around the room. "Let's talk about the Antares Object. We can't be positive of its precise time of arrival, although we're pretty sure we have it down to within a few days. We also can't be certain of the exact *place* it will show up. But we have the *neighborhood* pinpointed. It's essential that everybody keep in mind that it's caught in a time warp. That means it could submerge again without warning."

A hand went up. Allie. "Alex, do we have a reading on how long it will stay with us? Before that happens? What's the term? *Submerges?*"

"Yes, Allie. Possibly as long as six hours. More likely, about five. Because of the uncertainty, we want to caution you about boarding. We just can't be sure about anything. And the situation becomes even more doubtful since we are not likely to know how long it will have been in place. Your primary job is to find it and let us know where it is."

One of the pilots I didn't know raised a hand. "And *you're* going to do the rescue?"

"That's the plan. Assuming there are passengers, we'll want you to approach with your landers and stand by. We'll be stocking each lander with additional pressure suits. Chase and I will attempt to board. If there is anyone in there, we'll try to get them to the landers as quickly as we can. We want you to stay clear. If the thing submerges, we don't know the size of the surrounding area that will be dragged under with it. Maybe it won't affect the surroundings at all. But we're assuming the worst.

"That means there *is* a risk. It's possible that, if it submerges, and you're nearby, you'll be dragged along with it. I wish we knew more about this, but that's our situation. So if anyone wants to rethink this, we'll understand."

Cal looked unhappy. "You might not be able to get there in time. There's less risk to everybody if whoever finds it first boards it and starts the extraction. The others can help as they arrive."

Alex looked around the room. The others were nodding in agreement. "He's right, Alex," said Allie.

"Absolutely," said Dot.

And so it went, until Alex raised both hands. "Hold it a second. Look, we don't want to lose any of *you*—"

"Too late now," said Paul Kaczmarek. "First one there starts the extraction, right?"

Every hand in the place went up.

Dot was standing beside Cal. "Do we know when this thing will surface again? If we miss it this time?"

Alex let Shara answer. "Sixty-seven years," she said.

"What kind of ship is this?" asked Michael. "Have we been able to identify it?"

"Negative."

"It's too old?"

"That's what we think, yes."

And it's still under power?"

"Yes."

"My God," said Cal, "you mean this thing might be seven thousand years old?"

"Yes."

Dot smiled. Beatific. Beautiful. What a marvelous universe we live in.

"Any more questions?"

One more. From Linda: "Alex, you've described these black-hole tracks. If I understand what you're saying, you get in trouble if you try to initiate a jump while you're sitting in one."

"That's correct," said Alex.

"When we start back from the target area, we'll be right in the middle of it. Isn't there a possibility that one of us will get caught?"

Alex passed it to Shara. "Let me start," she said, "by admitting we don't have everything down yet. But we're pretty sure we know what kind of vehicles are vulnerable. And under what circumstances. We'll have a couple of technicians look at every ship before we proceed. You should be safe."

"Anything else?"

Apparently not. Shara passed out formation assignments, another two or three questions, and that was it.

"Okay," said Michael. "I guess we have something to tell the grandkids about."

Dot lifted a glass to Alex, Shara, and me. "This," she said, "is a proud moment. I'm delighted you guys decided to trust us. And we will give you our full support." She laughed. "Let's hope we come home with some company."

Afterward, as things quieted back down, she took me aside. "I've changed my mind," she said.

"About what?"

"Charging you for one of the ships. I can't do that. Just cover our expenses. That's all I ask."

\*   \*   \*

Taiulus Zeta was, in fact, well past Antares. It was another long ride. Almost six days each way, several more days getting organized, plus however long we had to wait for our apparition.

We packed up and left the country house at midmorning on a beautiful day, birds singing, tree branches swinging gently in a soft breeze. As we lifted off, Shara called my attention to an elderly couple visiting the old graveyard just across the property line. "I hope," she said, "that's not an omen."

Four hours later, we launched from Skydeck, sixteen vehicles counting the *Belle-Marie*. (We'd picked up one more at the last minute.) The squadron reassembled out past the Moon, put identical settings into the drive units, turned in the general direction of Antares, and slipped into hyperspace in as coordinated a manner as we could manage.

Despite all efforts to stay close to one another, we knew we would emerge a substantial distance apart, and we'd need an additional day or two to regroup.

It was maybe the longest six days I've spent in hyperspace. I don't know why. A foreboding of some sort crept over me. I don't usually have a problem simply because there are no stars. Or because I can't communicate with other ships. Maybe it was that *Alpha* was still hanging over my head, with its terrified radio voice that wouldn't go away. I knew now there were people out there, from a time before anyone had ever come near Rimway, when most of the worlds of the Confederacy were unknown. From an age before Elmer Campbell and his religious engineers had erected the obelisks.

Shara didn't help matters by explaining how the darkness was probably only a kind of wrap, that it extended no more than a few meters beyond us. I told her that was crazy, and she tried to explain to me why MacKenzie's Theory required it. And, of course, MacKenzie was always right, except for one famous blunder. Which I've never understood, either.

I pretty much stayed off the bridge. I didn't want to be looking out the ports at Shara's black wrap. For whatever reason, it didn't bother me when I was sitting in the cabin, where I could push it out of my mind while we argued politics.

*   *   *

And up front somewhere, waiting for us, would be the *Antares*.

We were talking about languages. Shara stretched out her legs and crossed them. She was wearing a pullover shirt that read PHYSICS MAKES MY HEART BEAT. "Hard to imagine what that must have been like," she said. "People saying stuff that other people couldn't understand. No wonder they were shooting one another all the time."

I found myself thinking about Cal, alone in his ship. I'd done it often enough, but I'm not that much of a social type anyhow. But Cal, despite the grumpiness, struck me as a guy who wouldn't be comfortable without company.

Alex periodically left us and wandered onto the bridge for long stretches of time. I'd never known him to do that before. I could hear him talking with Belle, though I couldn't make out what they were saying. When I asked, he said they were "just talking."

"About the ship?"

"That, too."

"What else?"

"I don't know. Books. Religion. Whatever."

"You were talking with Belle about religion?"

"Why not?"

"I don't know. It just seems—"

"She has a pretty wide knowledge of the subject. She knows how most of the major faiths got started. She knows the dogma. The requirements—"

"But—" Shara broke in. "That's not what people usually mean when they talk about religion. Does Belle believe in God?"

"Maybe you should ask her."

So we did. Belle took a few moments to answer. *"The evidence,"* she said, *"is inconclusive."*

"Then you don't believe," said Shara.

*"You're talking about faith now, Shara,"* said Belle. *"I prefer not to draw conclusions based on guesswork."*

"Which way," I said, "does the evidence point?"

*"Let me say, first, that it is difficult for a mere Beta, as limited as I am, to conceive of a Being without limits."*

"Then you do not believe?" Shara said again.

*"I reserve judgment."*

I thought it would be a good idea to change the subject. "What books were you talking about?" I asked.

*"Oh. Chan's* Write On, *for one."*

"Which is what?" I asked.

*"It's a book about why you cannot learn to be a professional writer by reading books on the subject."*

"Good," I said. "What else?"

*"The Life and Times of Malakai Petrona."*

"He's a famous archeologist," Alex said, for Shara's benefit. "Last century."

"Anything else?"

*"Culture Wars and Points South."*

"Really? You're interested in battles over social issues?"

*"Of course. I enjoy watching people argue over whether it's destructive to society to provide food and shelter to those who choose not to work."*

"What's your position, Belle?"

*"I'm not sure. I'm not good at these soft areas of knowledge. I can't imagine, for example, why anyone would choose to be inactive. But there are fascinating issues involved. It is the difficulty of grasping some of these issues that makes them intriguing."*

"Tell her about the novel," said Alex.

*"Yes. We also talked about* The Last Man.*"*

"Bancroft's book."

*"Yes."*

Alex had been reading it. It was extremely popular in its time. If you're not familiar with it, it's one of these multigenerational things in which the vices of the parents come back to haunt the kids, whose reactions then serve to create problems for their own children. It's complicated, and everyone thought it was destined to be a classic, but nobody reads it anymore. "Why," I said, "would you read a novel?"

*"I enjoy novels,"* said Belle. *"I'm a big fan of Vicki Greene."* The writer of supernatural thrillers. I think, if there'd been any doubt in my mind whether AIs were self-aware, it went away at that moment.

# THIRTY-SEVEN

We are never more human than when we become acutely conscious of the natural world. Give us a moonlit beach, or put us in a canoe on a wide river, or let us simply stand under the stars. It is then that we know who we truly are.

—Elizabeth Stiles, *Singing in the Void*, 1221

The truth was that even sixteen ships were inadequate to the task. We knew that from the start. We would probably have no difficulty picking up the *Antares*, but the odds against our being able to get to it in time to rescue passengers were, unfortunately, less than encouraging. Unless, of course, the first to see it took action. Which was precisely what I expected to happen.

We started well, arriving in the target area and getting into our search formation more easily than we'd anticipated. Then we settled in to wait. Shara had estimated that we'd probably be there a week or so before anything happened. But we were only hours into the hunt when Michael called from the *Caribou*. "Tracking something," he said.

"What do you have, Michael?" I asked.

*"Looks like a ship."*

Alex, who'd been quietly reading, raised both hands. Hallelujah!

"Any details?" I asked.

*"Too far out. But the AI tells me she can't detect any power."*

"That's not good," said Alex. He was in the right-hand seat. "We get a position?"

"It's coming in now."

"Belle-Marie," said Michael, *"we are in pursuit."*

"Okay," I said. "Everybody lock down. We'll be changing course in a minute."

There was no response from the cabin. "I think Shara's asleep in back," said Alex.

"Okay." I hit the buzzer for her compartment. "Up and at 'em, kid. Ship on the horizon."

Moments later, pulling a thick woolen shirt over her head, she appeared on the bridge and gave us a thumbs-up. "Beautiful, guys," she said.

Alex got up. "Take a seat, Shara."

She hesitated, then sat. "Thanks."

"You've earned it." He disappeared back into the cabin.

"Can we get to it, Chase?" she asked.

"We'll try," I said.

The sighting had taken place *behind* us. We were going to have to go through contortions to manage this. Alex muttered something under his breath as we began a long, slow turn.

*"First images are coming in,"* said Belle. She put them on-screen.

It was hard to make anything out, other than that the object was a dark, spade-shaped vehicle. *"I don't think this is what we're looking for,"* said Alex.

Shara leaned forward, as if it might give her a better perspective on the screen. "Why?"

I pointed to the spade, whose aspect was changing as we watched. "It's tumbling," I said. "And Michael says it has no power."

*"We're getting more from the* Caribou." Belle paused. *"Whatever that is, it's on the wrong course."*

*"How far off is it?"* asked Alex.

"Not a lot. But considering how far it's come, if it were the *Antares*, even a slight variation would have taken it out of range."

The image grew clearer. I could make out pulse cannons. "Warship," I said. A tangle of equipment and wiring protruded through a hole in the underside and had wrapped around the hull.

*"It's a Mute Wasp,"* said Michael. *"A light cruiser. Looks as if somebody got a direct hit on it."*

*"Belle,"* said Alex, *"what era is it from?"*

*"Wasps haven't been used for two hundred years,"* she said. *"Since the Resistance."*

*"Mark the location,"* said Alex. *"We'll let them know."*

Shara was shaking her head.

"What?" I said.

"I was just wondering what the odds were of our stumbling across another ship out here."

We regrouped and resumed the search. The discovery whetted everybody's appetite. Conversation among the ships intensified. There seemed to be more of a sense that the target vehicle would show up, and when it did, one of us would run it down. Cal Bickley arranged a pool. Everybody kicked in, and the ship that first located the *Antares* would get the payoff.

Alex played chess with Dot, while Jon and Linda talked about how it would feel to set foot inside a seven-thousand-year-old ship. Shara discovered she and Melissa Garber had both grown up in the Crystopolis area, and both had memories of the city's celebrated Science Museum. It had inspired Shara's career, while Melissa recalled visiting the place when she was a girl to watch the exhibits and especially to ride the virtual starship.

The first day passed without further incident. The Mute vehicle dropped off the scopes. And one by one, we retired for the night. Alex stayed with me awhile, but eventually he went back to his cabin, and I was alone on the bridge.

There was no need for anybody to stay awake. If anything happened, Belle would sound the alarm. I'm not sure why, but at night I tend to sleep better up front than I do in my cabin. I don't usually give in to the urge because it leaves me a bit stiff in the morning, but on that first night in the target area, I simply never got around to leaving the bridge. It wasn't exactly a decision. I just didn't feel like moving after Alex had gone, so I lowered the back of the chair a few degrees, turned on some soft music, and closed my eyes.

I like symphonies. Beethoven, Kurtzweil, Brachter, Yao Kee. It doesn't matter. Give me the soothing rhythm of the music and put some stars in the wraparound, and I'm ready to go.

I drifted off. I'd been out about three hours when Belle's voice woke me. *"Chase, the* McCandless *has something."* Dot's ship.

# THIRTY-EIGHT

The strongest, most generous, and proudest of all virtues is
true courage.

—Attributed to Michel de Montaigne, sixteenth century

*"Chase, we just picked it up. Everything checks out. It's the
Antares."*

"Okay, Dot. Belle, you have the coordinates?"

*"They're coming in now."*

"Are we sure this time? Dot, could it be another Wasp?"

There was a delay of about four minutes while the signal
crossed to the *McCandless*, and the response came back.
*"Whatever else this might be, it is definitely not another Wasp."*

"Okay. Good." I got on the intercom. "Shara, Alex, we
have a hit. We'll be on the move as soon as you get buckled
down." Then back to Dot: "Did you by any chance see it surface?"

*"Negative."*

"Could it have been there for hours?"

*"Affirmative."*

Alex came out of his cabin, pulling his robe around his
shoulders.

The display activated. I got a sky full of stars and a marker.
Shara opened her door. *"Give me a minute,"* she said.

"Where is it?" asked Alex, sweeping onto the bridge.

"Dot has it."

He lowered himself into the right-hand chair. "What's the status?"

"We've no idea when it showed up. It could submerge at any time."

"We don't get a break, do we? Okay, how close is she?"

Usually, the delay in signal transiting is simply accepted as part of the operation. But in an emergency, it can be maddening. Finally, her reply came in: *"We can be there in about two hours. I think it's outside the target area. Or maybe just on the edge. Relaying pictures to you."*

"Alex is here," I told her.

"Have you tried to contact them?" he asked.

*"Yes. Been transmitting. No response."*

Shara showed up in a nightgown. She was breathless. "We got it?"

"Right there." I pointed at the marker.

"Beautiful," she said. "How long—?"

"Two hours."

*"We* can be there in two hours?"

"Dot can," said Alex. "Chase, how far away are *we*?"

I hated to tell him. The *Antares* was on the far side of the formation. "Five hours."

His jaw tightened. Other than that, there was no reaction. "Okay," he said. "I don't guess we could do a jump?"

"We can try it."

"Shara," he said, "is there any hope of getting more precision in the future?" He sounded as if he thought the current state of the art was her fault.

"We're working on it." She sounded—and looked—frustrated. "I have a team of people going through the notebook, doing research, doing everything they can. And yes, I think we'll get better—"

"Shara," I said, "tell me again how long it's been since the last appearance of the *Antares*."

"If it's the same one, it's been sixty-seven years." Her eyes closed, and she stood there, one hand gripping my seat until I suggested she go back into the cabin so we could get moving.

I needed a few minutes just to get turned around. Then I kicked up the velocity. "TDI in fourteen minutes," I said.

"Is anybody else close?" asked Alex. "Other than Dot?"

"Cal is. He has an outside chance of getting over there, but I wouldn't be too hopeful."

"Nobody else?"

"Nobody within three hours."

We were still accelerating, getting ready to jump, when Dot was back: *"They're transmitting."* She relayed the signal, and Belle ran it for us. It was a single male voice, sounding panicked. Desperate.

The language was *not* Standard. "Belle," I said, "can you translate?"

*"It's classical French,"* she said. *"It's the language they would probably have been using at the original Brandizi outpost. But no, I'm sorry to say I can't. I can read the language, but nobody's too sure what it sounded like."*

Not that it mattered. It was a cry for help. Just like the one from *Alpha.*

Then we were at TDI velocity. "Ready to jump," I said. "Thirty seconds. Belt down."

We came out of it even farther away, and, once again, because we'd gone well past the target, we were headed in the wrong direction.

"Dot," I said. "We are not going to be able to get there."

The delay on transmissions was now close to seven minutes. *"I can see that,"* she said. *"But Cal's not too far."*

We sat, talking mostly to ourselves as if we were talking to Dot, exchanging the same warnings over and over—be careful, don't try to board, don't get too close, concentrate on the pictures. "Next time," Shara promised, "we'll find a better way."

Except that there wouldn't be a next time. "When do we expect to sight somebody else?"

"Well," said Shara. "That's changed, thanks to Robin's notebook. There's one that's been seen a couple of times, most recently out near Karasco. Originally, we thought it would be close to two centuries before anything showed up again, but now it looks more like only twenty-seven years."

Alex smiled. "Only twenty-seven?"

Belle's voice broke in: *"One hour until McCandless makes rendezvous."*

\* \* \*

We tried another jump and got within two and a half hours of the *Antares*. Alex sat staring at the deck, and I was thinking how he shouldn't expect pinpoint accuracy from a star drive. It's designed for serious long-range travel, not hopping around in a relatively tiny area. He wanted to try again, and he got his way. We gained a bit more ground, but not enough to matter. A couple more of those, I told him, and we'd have to arrange for someone to bring us out some fuel.

Eventually, the marker stopped blinking, and we were looking at what appeared to be a star. After a few moments, the star separated, became a string of lights, then became a ship.

It resembled nothing I'd seen previously. Big engines, small hull. Graceless. It might have been a tour ship that would take you to a neighboring moon. It could not have looked more out of place in that vast emptiness.

But, as with the *Alpha*, it was the lights that caught our attention. Not the navigation lights. They were on, but nobody cared. A row of ports were shining brightly. And there were more lights up front on the bridge. *"Alex,"* said Dot, *"look at that thing."*

"Congratulations, Dot."

We were much closer than we had been, and the time spent waiting for a response was down to just under two minutes. But when Dot came back, it was with a screech. *"There's movement inside, Chase. They're alive. My God, it's really happening. I thought maybe we were talking to an AI, but there's really somebody there."*

The scope was giving us better images now. I could see a hatch. Some antennas. And as the ports got bigger, there were faces. People looking out. Dot was starting to sound frantic. *"I know you said there's no way to stop it from submerging again, nothing you were sure of. But is there maybe something we can try? Something that* might *work? That might keep this thing from going under again?"*

"No," said Alex. "Leave it alone. At this point, we don't have any control over it."

Alex covered the mike and pointed toward a port near the after section of the vehicle.

A child. A girl about eight or nine looked out until an arm encircled her and drew her away.

* * *

*"We'll be alongside in about fifteen minutes."*

"You sure you want to do this, Dot?" said Alex.

*"Yes, Alex. I've got it. It's dead ahead. Slowing down."*

I heard Melissa's voice in the background, telling her that she hoped something wasn't crazy. Wasn't bonzo. I couldn't quite make it out.

The transmission shut down for a few moments. When it came back, Melissa was saying okay, it would probably work if they had enough time.

Alex was still on the circuit. "What's going on, Dot?"

*"I can bring about twenty over. If there are that many. That'll overwhelm life support, so I'll have to transfer some of them to Cal."*

We were figuring the process. She'd brought two extra suits on her own, for a total of five. Plus suits for herself and Melissa. She'd have to go over with them. Get through the *Antares*'s airlock. Which meant waiting a couple of minutes for it to pressurize. Get people into the suits. Hustle them back into the airlock. Depressurize and leave the *Antares*. Cross to the *McCandless*. Into the airlock. Pressurize again and take them into the cabin. Wait for them to climb out of the suits. Back into the airlock with the suits. Depressurize. Repeat entire process.

Et damned cetera. She'd never be able to pull it off.

"You won't have time to transfer twenty," said Alex.

*"Alex, would you please just leave me alone?"*

"All right, Dot. How's your French?"

*"My what?"*

"Your French. That's going to be the language they speak."

*"I don't think we'll have a problem communicating."*

Cal called the *McCandless* and wished them luck. So did Michael. So did the others, one by one. Just be careful, they were saying. If the lights start to go out, get clear.

The images were numbing. There were faces at all the ports, and they were all terrified. I saw a line of black symbols on the gray hull. One was clearly intended to represent a comet. The others were apparently French characters from an ancient time, utterly unlike the alphabet we use today. "What does it say, Belle?"

Belle took a moment. Then: *"Auric Federation. And below that, the* Intrépide. *The Auric Federation was an alliance of worlds that existed briefly during the fourth millennium. It came into existence during a politically unstable time. And it dissolved after less than a century."*

"Incredible," I said. We were looking at the strangest find we could ever have come across, *living* artifacts.

Nobody said much, not anyone on the *Belle-Marie*, not the voices from the other ships. The *Intrépide*'s image grew clearer. And, finally, we were looking at it close-up.

Michael called to assure us that the mission couldn't be in better hands. *"If it can be done,"* he said, *"Dot will see to it."*

Suddenly we were looking at the inside of the *McCandless* airlock. The inside hatch was open, but Dot and Melissa were both in pressure suits. Dot was wearing an imager and a jet-pack. *"Thought you might want to watch,"* she said. *"Okay, Melissa, let's do it."*

Melissa walked out of view and returned a moment later with the extra pressure suits. They were tied together with a cable. Two of them, we knew, were small size flex, which meant they could be adapted for kids. She helped load them into the airlock. A light came on. We could no longer see anything except the suits and the outside hatch, but we understood that Melissa had shut the hatch and stayed on the bridge. Dot's hand appeared and pressed the START pad. *"Depressurizing,"* she said.

It was crowded in there with the suits, which began to drift off the deck. Melissa had shut down the AG. I had my doubts whether Dot and five other people could fit into the airlock.

The process was interminable. While it went on, we also watched the feed from the *McCandless* scopes, a riveting view of the ancient vehicle. It was difficult to be sure, but it looked no more than about thirty meters away.

I kept staring at the *Antares*, remembering how the *Alpha* had grown transparent. Had been gone so quickly.

Then Dot opened the airlock hatch, leaned outside, hooked the cable to a clip, and tied the other end around her waist. She pushed off, stringing out the pressure suits behind her.

The *Intrépide* opened its airlock. Dot crossed between the ships and landed smoothly beside the open hatch. She climbed in, and, one by one, removed the suits from the cable and pulled them inside with her. When she had them all, she untied the cable from her waist and attached it to the hull. It was apparently magnetized.

Then she squeezed into the airlock and closed the hatch behind her. Again, there was the long wait while the lock pressurized. Two minutes later she stepped into the interior and looked into the faces of the passengers. People who'd been born thousands of years ago. Some were in tears, others cheered, a woman tried to hug Dot but couldn't get her arms around the suit. Then a guy in uniform appeared. The captain. Average height, blond hair cut close, looking vastly relieved.

She removed her helmet and he said something, which was, I'm sure, along the lines of "Thank God."

Dot looked at the captain and pointed at the suits. *"Quick,"* she said.

She didn't need a translator. The captain took over. *You,* he was saying. And *you.* Put on the suits.

The people he indicated, two women, three, came forward. Everybody else backed away. Made room.

*"I count about forty people,"* Dot said.

*"Dot."* Melissa's voice. *"Ready when you are."* I learned later that Melissa was a medical assistant. That this was her first off-world flight.

"This isn't going to end well," said Alex.

"Damned StarCorps," I said.

Dot showed them the flex suits, and they quickly decided on two small girls to wear them. One looked like the child we'd seen in the portal.

Another uniformed man appeared. Probably a flight attendant. He produced a sixth pressure suit. There were some efforts at communication, which included smiles, clasping of shoulders, Dot waiting while they decided who would go. Another woman. The choice brought some tears, and a lot of hesitation. She was young and frightened. And she resisted. No, I'll stay where I am. Stay *here.* Or maybe, Stay with *you.* In any case, she didn't want to go. More tears flowed.

Dot tried to show them that time was a factor. Make your call, and let's get started. They settled finally on a fourth woman, tall, dark hair, looking vastly relieved.

While they struggled into the suits, somebody did introductions: Lisa, young, maybe nineteen, trying hard not to look scared; Julie, middle-aged, brown eyes, reluctant to leave a male consort; Rowena, with black hair and lips pressed tightly together, not entirely sure she wanted to do this; and Michelle, the replacement.

The captain's lips formed questions, and we knew what they were. What the hell is going on? Where are we? But he didn't waste much time with it.

Back in the *McCandless*, Melissa, who'd been quiet, just trying to stay out of the way, whispered, *"Please, God."*

Dot turned back to the passengers. The two girls had gotten into the flex suits. People around them were lowering their helmets into place. They both looked pale, scared. A tall, outwardly calm guy with a hairbrush mustache, probably their father, was talking with them, trying to reassure them. The girls were maybe twelve and nine. Sisters, I thought.

*"We've got two younger children,"* said Dot, indicating two who weren't much more than toddlers, a boy and a girl. But they weren't going to fit into the suits. *"I'm not sure how to handle them. Anybody have any suggestions?"*

Michael's voice: *"Think you can get the lander into the cargo bay?"*

"We'll figure something out," Shara said, speaking to the entire squadron. "Next time, we'll be ready for them."

They clamped down the helmets, and Dot ran a quick check. She tried to reassure the captain with a smile and by squeezing his arm that, whatever happened, someone would be back. *"We'll get you clear,"* she said. Then she spoke to Melissa. *"Okay, love, on our way."*

Dot indicated that the kids should go into the airlock, and put her own helmet back on. The father kissed each of them as they passed. Then he squeezed Dot's arm and said something to her. He knew she couldn't hear him through the helmet, and wouldn't have understood the language if she could, but the message was clear enough. The captain shook her hand, and she joined the two girls. They looked terrified and relieved and anxious to be out of there. Both had brown eyes. The younger one was trying to talk, and she suddenly started back toward her father. But he shook his head and smiled and said something to her. Go with the nice lady.

There was room for only three more adults in the airlock. Julie stepped aside. The others looked briefly at one another, and crowded in.

*"I'd like to have them put Julie into the lock as soon as we leave,"* she said, *"so she could cross as soon as we're out of the way, but I can't talk to anybody."*

"You're doing fine," I told her. "Just keep moving."

The inner hatch closed. It was clearly not designed for six people. No one could move. The girls looked up at their rescuer. The older one smiled. Probably responding to an encouraging grin from Dot, which of course we couldn't see. "You okay?" I asked Dot.

*"Yes. I wish Cal would get here."*

Alex never took his eyes from the display. And we heard Melissa again: *"Hurry up."* She was talking to the outer hatch, which remained maddeningly, solidly, in place.

"I'm not sure," said Shara, "that taking the kids from their father was a good idea."

"Why not?"

"They should not have come off until he was ready to accompany them."

"But if it goes back under," I said, "it would be almost seventy years—"

"Not to them, Chase. They'd be together."

"We need," said Alex, "to change the way we think."

Finally, the hatch slid up.

We looked through Dot's imager at the *McCandless*, floating serenely against a backdrop of stars. Melissa was standing in the open airlock.

It would have been easier had Dot been able to talk to the people she was trying to save. But it was all hand signals. She pointed to the cable and indicated they should take hold of it, and use it to guide themselves to the rescue vessel. She didn't want them trying to jump across; that was a formula for disaster. They signified that they got the message, and Rowena stepped out of the airlock and started over.

Dot picked up the two girls and jumped clear. The *McCandless* seemed to bob up and down, and once got blocked by somebody's elbow. Then we caught a good view of it, waiting, Melissa waving, and moments later we were inside its airlock. Dot handed the girls to her daughter, and turned to go back.

Rowena, leading the way, was about halfway across. Dot pushed off the hull and, at the moment she did so, Belle became active: *"Chase, we are getting a spectrum shift."*

"Dot," I said. "Get out of there. It's starting."

She was wearing a jetpack and could have used it to brake herself and get out of harm's way. But she reached out instead for the cable and for Rowena. She grabbed hold of both as the cable itself turned transparent. And became solid again. She pulled at Rowena's hands. Let go. But we were already looking *through* Rowena. *"For God's sake—"* The sound died, and the image scrambled.

We saw Rowena and Dot one more time, flickering like a corrupted vid. There was a final blip on the circuit, Dot's voice, *"Damn—"* Then it was gone, and *they* were gone. Dot and Rowena and the other two women. And the *Antares*.

The *Intrépide*.

Several meters of cable floated out from the *McCandless*.

*"Reception has ceased,"* said Belle.

# THIRTY-NINE

There is no quality of more value to the human spirit than the ability to adapt.

—Kasha Thilby, *Signs of Life*, 1428

The two girls, who'd already been sufficiently frightened, picked up Melissa's near panic. The fact that they were lost, stranded with a stranger whom they could not understand, did not help. The younger one got hysterical. The older tried to play the role of the big sister. She held her sibling and tried to calm her, speaking in a voice that had itself grown shrill.

The *Jubilant* was first to arrive at the site. Cal reported that a sweep of the area showed no sign of anyone.

By the time we got there, it was hopeless. Dot's air supply would have been exhausted. We continued to hunt, hoping, or maybe not hoping, that we'd find her somewhere.

Jon Richter arrived on the *Gremlin* minutes after we did. Michael and Allie and the rest of the squadron arrived over the next few hours, and we continued to look. But there was no sign of Dot, or of the *Intrépide*.

After three days, we faced reality. "Time to go back," Alex said.

We moved the girls and Melissa from the *McCandless* onto the *Belle-Marie*. Melissa was infuriated, despondent, and overwhelmed by guilt. It wasn't clear whom it was all aimed at. Us, I suppose. Herself, for not dissuading her mother from an action she now saw as suicidal. At Dot, who didn't come back when she had a chance. And probably at the natural order of things, which puts everybody at hazard. She tried to fight off her moods by taking care of the kids, but she was really in no shape to do anything but make matters worse, so ultimately it fell to Shara to calm things down.

The AI took the *McCandless* home.

We provided food and soft drinks for our new passengers. Melissa finally got her act together and spent time, with Belle's help, trying to set up a system that would allow us to speak with the girls. The plan was for Melissa to say something, which Belle would put on-screen, along with a French translation, and whatever pictures seemed likely to be of use. Of course, they started with basics. Hello. How are you? I'm Melissa. Would you like more juice? We have a game you might enjoy.

She asked the girls to write their responses, which made Belle's translations easier.

"We are happy that you are with us," said Melissa. "What is your name?"

"I'm Sabol," said the older child. "My sister is Cori."

"Beautiful names," said Melissa.

Cori began to cry.

"It's okay, Cori," Melissa said. "You're safe."

The child wiped her eyes. "Where is my father, Melissa?"

Melissa looked at me, and I shook my head. I didn't really want to say anything because I didn't trust my voice. "He is still where he was," I said, very slowly. "In the ship. But he is all right."

"I want to go back to him. Can you take me back? Please?"

My heart began to beat harder. "What do I tell her?" I asked Melissa.

Alex broke in: "The truth. Lying to her won't help."

Melissa, pronouncing each syllable carefully, said, "We can't reach him."

"I want to go back." Cori was crying harder.

"We can't go back, Cori. The ship you were on has gone in a different direction."

Sabol was teary, too. "Why did you take us away from him?"

"We were trying to help."

"So why can't you take us back?"

"Sabol, we would go back and get him, too. If we could find the ship. But we don't know where it is."

"I wish you'd left us alone." Cori knocked over her glass, and tears streamed down her cheeks.

"We're your friends, Cori."

"Go away, Melissa," she said. "Take me to my father."

If they'd believed their father dead, it might have been easier. But the fact of the separation, the knowledge he was out there somewhere, and that they couldn't get to him, tore at them. Melissa, once she got her emotions under control, was magnificent. She talked to them throughout the ordeal, picked up some of the language, assured them we would not leave them, that they were safe with us. And that, eventually, their father would also be rescued. "But it will take a long time," she said. The experience, I thought, helped her get past the loss of her mother.

"Maybe," she told me, "we'll be able to explain to them about a time warp. Let them know he's okay, even if they won't get to see him again."

We brought out chocolate ice cream every evening. Shara helped Melissa make a couple of nightgowns for them. We didn't have fresh clothes they could change into, so when the girls went to sleep, she ran their clothes through the cleaner, and they were ready again in the morning.

And, eventually, we were all able to talk with a bit less emotion.

"How long were you on the *Intrépide*?" asked Shara.

They both answered at once. Cori didn't recognize the name. Sabol had to think about it. "About three weeks, I guess. Everybody was getting pretty scared because the captain didn't seem to know where we were."

"You knew you were lost?"

"Sure. And everybody got upset." She was a pretty girl. Smiled easily. She had bright, intelligent eyes, long amber hair. At the moment, though, the eyes were dim. "And now they're lost again."

Melissa looked toward me. How to explain this to a twelve-year-old? "We'll find them," she said.

Cori was sitting beside her sister. "*We* won't get lost, will we, Melissa?" she asked.

"No. We're fine, Cori. We're going home." Then after a pause: "Where are you from?"

"Quepala."

"Is that a town?"

"A town?" She seemed puzzled. "It's our country."

"Is it a beautiful country?"

"Yes. People often come to visit. To see the ocean."

"Your father: Is he a scientist?"

"He's a policeman."

Alex followed the conversations with interest. Occasionally, the girls asked for more details on what had happened to them. He responded that sometimes ships just get lost. "Not ships like this one," he added. "But *some* ships do." Later, when the girls were asleep, he admitted he wasn't comfortable trying to explain it. "Let's try to stay clear of the subject as much as we can," he told us. "I think we should let the doctors figure out how to handle it."

Melissa was in full agreement. But both of them, when the girls asked questions, or needed support, ignored their own advice. "Your dad is fine," Alex said. "You won't see him for a while, but he's okay." Looking back now, so many years later, I'm still impressed with how well they handled things. Especially Melissa. I'm not sure what we'd have done without her. She was even able, by the time we reached the home system, to talk casually with the girls in their own language.

Sabol held up pretty well, except for periodic bouts of depression. Cori slipped into occasional crying jags. Melissa stayed with them, though, and they rode it out together. We brought them up to sit on the bridge and pretend to pilot the ship. Belle invented games for them. We watched shows. But whenever the subject of going back to Rimway came up, the kids got sad. And the tears never really went away.

"It's all right," Melissa told them. "We'll keep you with us. You'll always be with friends."

On the next-to-last night, when we were approaching home, and the girls were asleep, Melissa said she thought that they had probably been better off on the *Intrépide*. That Dot had given her life doing something we should not have done.

The loss of Dot, of course, was something else to contend with. When, finally, we arrived back in the home system, a day or so away from Skydeck, Melissa sent a message to her grandparents, to explain, as best she could, what had happened. When she'd finished, she told them they'd have been proud of their daughter, that she'd sacrificed everything to rescue two girls trapped on a lost flight.

We sent visuals of Sabol and Cori, who smiled at the lens. And waved. It was not a live exchange, of course. The signal wouldn't even reach Skydeck until several minutes after transmission.

But they *did* respond. When the transmission came in, we put it on-screen, and Dot's parents looked out at Melissa and the girls. *"We had no idea, Melissa,"* the father said, *"that anything like this could happen. Dot said nothing about taking her life into her hands. All she said was that she and you were going to try to find a lost ship, but she didn't think it was really there. Somebody's responsible. Please pass that to Mr. Benedict. I'll be looking into it."*

"I wish we could have gotten everybody off," I told Alex.

Alex didn't want to talk about it.

But there'd be no containing the story, and we knew the media would be waiting for us. We were still twelve hours out from Skydeck when the calls began to come in. Every journalist on the planet was asking for an interview. Talk shows wanted to book Alex and Melissa. People we'd never heard of sent transmissions demanding to know whether it was true that we'd rescued two girls who had been born seven thousand years ago. Politicians wanted to be on record congratulating Alex for his contributions to science, humanity, and whatever.

By the time we docked at Skydeck, pretty much everybody on the mission had sat for multiple interviews. But the media types wanted especially to talk with the girls. We debated whether to expose them to the public eye, but there was really no way they could be kept away from the journalists. There was, however, a cause for frustration: None of the reporters could speak the girls' language, not even the AIs. So Melissa had to help.

When we came out of the connecting tube, we were inundated by a screaming crowd. A band serenaded us with patriotic songs. The President's Executive Secretary was there to shake

our hands. A special-care unit showed up to look after Cori
and Sabol, who by then were the best-known kids in the Confederacy. That produced a standoff when we refused to turn
them over. The special-care unit claimed we'd agreed to the
arrangement, but no such request had been received.

We answered questions while people cheered, and were
virtually carried to the President's shuttle, where we did still
more interviews during the descent to Andiquar.

While we were on our way down, a presidential representative announced at a press conference that an investigation
was being set in motion to determine why StarCorps had
refused to help. Alex hadn't commented on the subject, but
somebody evidently had.

And, finally, we were back at the country house, which had
been surrounded by reporters. Biggest story ever, they were
saying. Real time travel. A dazzling rescue. And, of course,
Dot Garber had become the hero of the hour. There was talk
during that first day back that a vid featuring the rescue was
already being planned. (Clara Beaumont was eventually
signed to play Dot.) Somebody else had gotten a book deal.
Two senators had moved that her statue be placed in Heroes'
Park, across from the Hall of the People.

Part of the reason for the special-care unit, though it was not
stated at the time, was a concern that Sabol and Cori might be
carrying germs against which current immune systems would
be helpless. But the kids checked out okay, I'm happy to say.
There was also a possibility that the reverse might be true, that
the girls might not be able to defend themselves against
microbes hanging out in the Andiquar area. They were given a
series of treatments to upgrade their defenses, while Melissa
was instructed to keep them separated from the general population for a few weeks.

Sabol and Cori moved in with Melissa. There was a deluge
of applicants to adopt the girls, but Melissa asked them if
they'd like to stay with her, and they said absolutely. They said
it, by the way, in Standard.

The downside was that the *Intrépide* had been, for the next
few years, our last chance to rescue one of the lost ships.
Shara's information indicated that there wouldn't be another

surfacing—the terminology had caught on—for decades. We'd gotten lucky, had encountered two over a few weeks. But that was over now.

Shara, though, thought the information in Robin's notebook might change that.

"Instead of looking for black holes, then tracking them back," she said, "Robin searched for missing ships, and used *them* to locate areas of danger. Sometimes, most of the time, that doesn't lead to anything, because ships can go missing for a variety of reasons that have nothing to do with time/space instabilities.

"But sometimes the disappearances line up. Sometimes they form a trail."

# FORTY

Sometimes the cranks have it right.

—Hyman Kossel, *Travels*, 1402

Shortly after we got back, Jacob announced that we'd received a message from Senator Delmar. *"Please get in touch."*

*"I owe you an apology, Alex."* Delmar was in her office. *"You were right. We should have listened to you."*

Alex kept his voice flat. "I can't help thinking, Senator, what it would have done for your career had you been with us out there, with a force big enough to have rescued those people."

I listened to the sound of the air vents.

*"I understand you're upset,"* she said. *"But you need to be aware I don't wield the kind of power you think. I made some calls, Alex. I tried to get help for you."*

"Of course." He showed no emotion. "I appreciate that."

A pearl white sweater was draped around her shoulders. She pulled it tight as if she'd been struck by a sudden draft of cold air. *"My understanding is that the next one of these ships from the past won't be here for a long time. For years. Is that correct?"*

"Shara tells me they found one that will probably show up in 1461. Twenty-seven years."

She didn't try to hide her disappointment. *"Okay. I was hoping we could do better. But we'll put together a program."* She got up and came forward. *"Look, Alex, I know you don't believe this at the moment, but I don't like having those peo-*

*ple stranded out there any more than you do. I will pursue this. I'm putting in a motion to do whatever's necessary to get this affair under control. Our first order of business will be to introduce the Deep-Time Rescue Provision. And we'll pass it by a near-unanimous vote. I can guarantee that. It'll be aimed at establishing a permanent commission to oversee operations as they become necessary. And also to try to determine who else might be out there that we don't currently know about. That is possible, right?"*

"That's correct, Senator. A good example would be the *Capella*."

"*The* Capella. *Yes.*"

"I wish you luck."

"*You sound doubtful, Alex. And I guess you're justified feeling that way. Sometime between now and maybe the next election cycle or the one after that, somebody will introduce a cost-cutting measure and I'm concerned that the Deep-Time Rescue Provision will be among the first casualties.*"

Alex shrugged. No surprise there. "Would they take any heat for that?"

"*To be honest, I think we need something that isn't three decades away. If we don't do something now, the commission will get put on the back burner. It might not happen right away. In fact, it almost certainly won't. But, eventually, there'll be a serious need somewhere else, and it'll coincide with some economic problems, and that'll be the end of it.*"

"So what do we do? Do you have a suggestion?"

"*Would* you *be willing to make an initial grant? A nominal amount. Just something to get it started. Say, ten thousand?*"

"To what purpose?"

"*To establish the Alex Benedict Foundation, which would be dedicated to coordinating future rescue operations of vehicles lost on interstellar flights. You get it up and running, and I'll see that it's funded. That way it gets put on the calendar, it becomes a functioning entity, and it's considerably harder to shut down.*"

A week later, we officially launched the effort. Melissa took over as volunteer chair, I signed on to do public relations, and contributions began rolling in. We named it the Dot Garber Foundation.

\*     \*     \*

At about the same time, we attended a memorial service for Dot. I don't think the family was happy to see us there, but Melissa came over and embraced us, and returned a few minutes later with Dot's parents. "Alex tried to discourage her from making the attempt," she told them. "But she rescued Sabol and Cori. And she was going back for more. Would you have been proud of her if she'd thought of herself first?"

The father's name was Stan, and he stared at the sky while Melissa talked. When she was done, he glared at Alex. Then he shrugged. "I don't guess there's much to be done about it at this point."

"She's a hero," I said.

The mother, whose name was also Dot, managed a smile. "I'm sorry, Mr. Benedict," she said. "I know it wasn't your fault. I guess it wasn't anybody's fault."

I think everybody who'd been on the rescue flight was also there, Allie, Jon, Cal, Michael, the other pilots, and their passengers. And Shara. "Dot was something else," Shara told me at one point. "She was the woman I'd want to have at my back if things went wrong." Then she grinned at me. "Not that you wouldn't do in an emergency."

It was a cool, crisp morning. The sun floated through a cloudless sky, and a strong wind was coming out of the north. The service was conducted in a small chapel on the outskirts of Andiquar. They couldn't get everybody inside, but those who couldn't make it simply stood around on the chapel grounds. When the service ended, the mourners filed out and milled about, talking in low voices, shaking their heads—she was so young, let us know if there's anything we can do, stay in touch.

I don't much like memorial services and good-byes. I get annoyed when someone goes on about how, well, they're in a better place now. Frolicking in the green pastures. It reminds me how good we are at pretending. My bedroom, when I was growing up, had a picture of two kids, a boy and a girl, crossing a rickety bridge over a swollen river. The bridge looks about to give way, but it's okay, because there's an angel hovering immediately behind the kids, arms outstretched, ready to step in if necessary. As I grew up, I came to realize there were no angels, and kids *did* fall from bridges.

Then I thought of Cori and Sabol, and of Dot risking her life to carry them back to the *McCandless*. Maybe, sometimes, there *were* angels.

Alex was quiet on the way back to the country house. We'd been together a good many years by then, and I'd come to take my life with him for granted. And I guess I took *him* for granted. He was easygoing most of the time, an ideal boss, sometimes moody, always ready to head off for lunch. And I loved him. As we settled onto the pad that morning, I realized that the day would come when I'd do anything to be back in that moment, to have him at my side again. Everything's temporary, he liked to say. It was why Rainbow Enterprises prospered, people trying to recapture a piece of the past. To hang on as best they can.

# FORTY-ONE

Truth is overrated. Sometimes it's better to believe the fable.

—Armand Ti, *Illusions*, 1400

At about the same time the doctors told Melissa it was now safe for Cori and Sabol to mingle with the rest of the world, we got a call from Charlie. *"We're coming home,"* he said. He had made himself into a duplicate of Rod Baker, the vid action-adventure star. He was dressed like Rod, for the trail, with a blaster in his belt and a forest green canyon hat pulled low over his eyes. He looked great. *"We're a few hours out from Skydeck. I was wondering if you guys would be up for a party tomorrow night?"*

"Absolutely, Charlie," I said. "I'll check with Alex. But I'll be there for sure. I take it the flight was successful."

*"We did pretty well. We recovered eight Betas. Including one that Alex will be especially interested in."*

"How do you mean?"

*"Jorge can provide a play-by-play account of the last days at Parnassus House, when they were trying to get everybody off-world."*

"What's Parnassus House?"

*"Alex will know. It was the world's nerve center when they were having their collapse. Anyhow, we're going to have a celebration tomorrow at Doc's place. You know where it is?"*

"Yes."

*"We aren't going to make a formal announcement yet of what we have. The plan is to wait awhile."*

"Why's that?"

*"At the moment, you and Alex and Dot are all the news. We don't want to crowd you. By the way, I was sorry to hear about her. About Dot. She must have been a remarkable woman."*

Parnassus House, Alex said, was the place where, during the final days on Villanueva, executive decisions got made. "We don't have a clear picture of events at the end. It's so long ago. There are all kinds of conflicting stories. Margus Virandi was a heroic leader who seized control from Philip Klaus, an indecisive idiot who operated inside a bubble and never seemed to know what was going on. Virandi lost an arm during the coup, but he made the right calls and saved a lot of lives, ultimately sacrificing himself by staying too long. Or, he was a power-crazy nut who thought the predictions about the encroaching cloud were a conspiracy designed to make Klaus look heroic. And in the end he got a lot of people killed unnecessarily."

"I can't believe," I said, "nobody ever went in there before this to pick up the AI."

"In fact, there were at least two attempts. Both failed, and in one of them the entire mission got wiped out. Nobody really knew where the AI was. I suspect Doc succeeded because he had Charlie along."

"Maybe," I said, "they'll give Charlie an award." Nothing like that had ever happened before. And, of course, it didn't happen that time. In fact, nobody got an award.

If Doc Drummond had any serious intention of keeping his find quiet, he was dreaming. Whenever someone goes out of Skydeck on an operation in which the media are interested, there's no way it can return without someone's blowing the whistle. Usually, it's the operations people. Or one of the bosses. In return, they get to meet and sometimes even hang out with people like Brockton Moore, the host of *Round Table*.

The result was that Drummond was confronted by reporters when they were still two hours out from Skydeck. He'd been subjected to some media attention when he'd left several weeks earlier, but that had been nothing compared with the reception on their return. The media were not, however, all that interested in the historical aspects of the mission.

Had anyone been killed? "That was our first question," one of the reporters told me that evening. "It wasn't exactly a proud moment for us. We must actually have seemed disappointed when we found out there'd been no casualties. Although we pretended to be relieved.

"We asked whether they'd been attacked.

"And, what had they brought back? Most of my colleagues had no idea who Margus Virandi was." He shook his head. "How can our guys know so little and pursue this kind of career?"

"I don't know," I told him, trying not to grin. "Sometimes reporters can be pretty dumb."

As can we all.

The commotion produced, for us, a fresh avalanche of calls. Jacob responded with stock answers, that Alex had no direct connection with the mission, that he was glad to hear they were safely back, but that since he was *not* involved, he had no further comment, thank you very much.

Doc's near-palatial house was lit up when we got there, and the place was jumping with music and laughter and applause. We drifted in through a murky sky and set down on the pad, where AIs took over and moved the skimmer into a parking area. Inside, a couple of hundred people wandered among lush curtains and sculpted furniture, lavish bookcases and electronic artwork. Doc and his wife, Sara—she'd gone along on the trip, too—welcomed us and introduced us to medical colleagues, members of the mission, neighbors, a task force from nearby Conseca University, and a couple of big names in the entertainment world. The people who'd accompanied him were there with their families, of course. They were mostly big, competent-looking types, the sort that nobody would want to mess with. I realized, despite my first impression, he'd known precisely what he was doing.

And, of course, Charlie was present, still in his Rod Baker persona, standing with a small group in a corner of the library, describing how they'd descended into Buchanan Harbor and come away with an AI—"a Beta"—that had once belonged to Cassandra Talley, the classical humorist who is still read today, thousands of years after her death. Nobody doing comedy has lasted so long.

Seven of the other Betas were also active. They joined Charlie in strolling about, projecting themselves as bon vivant males, beautiful women, and, in one case, as a former Villanuevan president. An eighth, who'd been found on a ship that had run aground in coastal waters and, miraculously, never been submerged by the tides, was perhaps a bit more shy. He provided no hologram, but he spoke with anyone who wished to converse, explaining how happy he was to have been rescued. He described to me how he'd spent time wishing the waters would rise, or the ship would come apart, so that his power would be cut off. *"Now,"* he said, *"I'm grateful it never happened."*

Doc gave us a lot of the credit for his success, and said contributions were coming in for more missions.

I've been back to the Caton Ferry Museum a couple of times. Eliot Cermak still looks proudly out of the heroes' gallery. Handsome, courageous, a guy who appears utterly selfless. I couldn't help thinking that, if Elizabeth had said yes that evening, and he'd spent the night with her on Virginia Island, he would have survived the quake and gone back to pick up Chris Robin. And had he done that, the loss a few years later of the *Capella*, with its twenty-six hundred victims, might have been avoided. Alex never again talked about what he believed had happened that fatal night. He couldn't see that any good would come of it.

The day after the celebration, Shara asked us to meet her at Tardy's for dinner. *"My treat,"* she said. *"I have news."*

We got there early, and had already put away some celebratory wine—it had to be good news, something out of the notebook—when she came in. A dark cargo, her favorite drink, was waiting. She was all smiles. "We've had a breakthrough," she told us. She took a swallow. "We've known for a while that the level of hazard to a ship making a jump in a black-hole track is a combination of factors, the type of drive and whatnot. You know all that."

"Yes."

"It's been complicated. But we've come up with a formula."

The waiter arrived. "Hello. My name's Kaleff. Are you ready to order?" he asked.

"We'll need a minute," said Alex.

Kaleff smiled, bowed, and left.

Alex never took his eyes from Shara. *I* refilled the glasses and passed them around. Shara, drawing out the moment, had more of hers. "Not bad," she said.

"Come on, Shara," said Alex.

"All right. Look, if we have the initial departure reports on a ship that's gone lost, we will be able to work out, within a reasonable estimate, where and when the ship is likely to reappear. We don't have it down cold yet, but we're making progress."

"So you're saying what—?"

"It looks as if the *Capella* will surface in four years. And, Alex, we are going to be there when it does."

The world is changing its perspective on AIs. I'm not suggesting that Alex and I were responsible for any of it; nevertheless, the term *Beta* has come into common usage. Some say that's simply because it's easier to say than *AI*. But Betas are now able to own property in a number of municipalities around the globe. Other Confederate worlds, unhappy with what is happening here, have charged Rimway with being weak and foolishly sentimental.

Charlie has a condo in the mountains northwest of Andiquar, and we've been up there occasionally for parties. He likes parties. The issue is also becoming a movement on Dellaconda. And somebody there has introduced a bill that will give Betas the vote.

Researchers are arguing over *how* an AI can acquire consciousness, while others debate when it might have happened. Some maintain that they've had consciousness since ancient times. Since the literary world discovered that the great twenty-third-century novelist Max Albright was a pseudonym for a Beta.

Recently, Christian and Judaic groups have both taken the position that even though no one knows for sure whether Betas have souls, it would be prudent to assume they do. Islam, which is usually out front on liberal issues, is still making up its mind.

Makes me wonder what the world will look like in another thousand years.

# EPILOGUE

*"Dot. Get out of there. It's starting."*

She saw it. The cable becoming transparent, losing substance, coming back, flickering like a light with failing power. The radio filled with frantic voices. Get away from it. Look out. Dot, don't— She grabbed hold of Rowena. Pulled on her arm. "Let go," Dot said. She knew that Rowena couldn't hear her. There hadn't been time to show the women how to use the radio. But it didn't stop her from trying. "For God's sake, let go."

Rowena hung on, refusing to release her grip even when there seemed to be nothing to hold on to, even when her arm had gone away.

Then they were back, the cable and the arm, Rowena still holding tight, and the frantic voices.

*"What's happening?"*

*"My God, I knew we shouldn't have done this."*

*"What's wrong with the cable?"*

Dot's stomach turned over, and she felt momentarily nauseous.

Where was the *McCandless*? She looked desperately in all directions. The *Intrépide* was still there, but the *McCandless* was gone. "Melissa," she said. "Answer up, please."

The voices went away.

The *Intrépide*'s navigation lights were growing brighter.
As was the glow from the cabin.

"Melissa, are you there?"

No response. Everything beyond the *Intrépide* was growing dark. The stars were becoming dim. Fading. The Veiled
Lady shrank to a wispy glow before it, too, slipped into the
all-encompassing night.

"Chase? Please? Melissa?"

She expected no reply. And got none. Only the lights on
the ship remained—

Lisa had come up behind her. She took hold of Dot's arm.
Tried to say something. Dot watched her bite down on her
lips. The cable had been severed. The end that had been
attached to the *McCandless* was gone. "It's okay," she said,
hoping everything would come back. "We're okay."

The *Intrépide* looked as solid as ever. "Chase, are you
there? Melissa? Somebody?" She gazed unbelieving at the
empty sky. The heavens, seen from off-world, are not like
what you see from a beach. An atmosphere does not obscure
them. The stars are always bright. Now it was as if she were in
a dark room, a room that stretched endlessly in all directions.

"Is *anybody* there?"

She let go of Rowena. Turned to Lisa and would have
embraced her had she been able, had the suit allowed it. "We
weren't quick enough," she said. It was irrelevant that nobody
could hear her. "Might as well go back inside."

Lisa kept asking questions. Dot understood. Was the rescue off? What had happened? Her eyes looked out of the helmet, needing an answer.

Dot pointed back toward the airlock. God help me, yes. It's
over.

Inside the *Intrépide*, there was movement. Frightened
faces looked out through the ports.

She didn't want to go back, didn't want to join the people she'd
tried to help, people she wouldn't even be able to communicate with, to tell them what was happening. And, of course,
she was stuck now. She'd ride this *thing*, this ghost out of a
distant past, in its trek toward a highly uncertain future.

Sixty-seven years, Shara had said.

Good-bye, Melissa. Mom and Dad. Harry.

Harry was her husband. Melissa's father. A management consultant currently on assignment at one of the outlying stations. She'd forgotten which one. He'd have a shock coming when he heard—

Damn it. Why hadn't she listened to Alex?

Well, this was not the time to start feeling sorry for herself. She could do that later.

What would her life be without Melissa? She and her daughter had always been close. Melissa was ambitious but not to the extent that she was willing to work hard to achieve her goals. She had talked about becoming a pilot, but Dot did not believe it would ever actually happen. That was one of the reasons she'd brought her along on this mission, to try to light a fire under her.

Melissa wanted to *be* things, especially, she said, to be a pilot. But she wasn't prepared to put in the effort. We only have one life, she was fond of saying, so why should we spend it working when we have a leisure option? She'd gotten a degree in medicine, but it hadn't really challenged her, and she had made her intentions clear enough: Just relax, hang out, party, meet guys, go swimming—she loved to swim, and she was as proficient in the water as anyone Dot had ever seen—and go for walks in the woods. That was the kind of life she'd wanted. Dot's family had always believed there was something innately virtuous in work. But Melissa saw nothing wrong with a prolonged good time. "I wouldn't want to find, when it came time to die, that I had not lived." It was the adage she lived by.

And Dot wasn't entirely convinced she was wrong.

Chase, too. Dot wasn't that close to Chase Kolpath, but she qualified as a friend. You could trust her, and the attention Chase had gotten as a result of working with Benedict hadn't changed her. Most people who had gotten into the media spotlight the way she had over the past few years would be full of themselves. But the woman just laughed it off. When Dot had commented on her accomplishments, she'd become visibly uncomfortable. "I've been fortunate," she'd said. "Always been at the right place at the right time."

Odd that Harry and Melissa occupied her thoughts at a moment like this. And Chase. And Phil Cato, an old boyfriend. And—

The *Intrépide* became the only reality, the only lights in the world. And the three women who were with her at that moment. They'd all grown quiet. Lisa, Michelle, and Rowena. They were probably wondering whether they'd *ever* get off that ship. Whether they'd ever see their homes again.

They almost certainly didn't know what had happened to them. No way they could know unless their captain had seen that the stars were out of place. Given thousands of years, that would have happened. She wondered whether he understood, and if so, whether he'd said anything.

She led the way back to the airlock. The hatch had closed when they'd exited. She opened it again and waited while the three women climbed inside. She hesitated about following them. To do that somehow sealed everything. As long as she remained outside, there was a chance that the *Belle-Marie* would come out of the night, pick her up. Take her home.

She thought about the two girls. Sabol and Cori. She had hoped to include their father in the second group she'd have taken across. He'd spoken to her with a calm intensity. She knew what he'd been saying: *Please take them somewhere safe. Get them away from here.* Well, at least she'd managed that. Something about him suggested he might be a physician. Maybe it was the way he'd looked into her eyes, as if searching for an abnormality. Maybe it was his soothing, deliberate voice, which—even though she couldn't understand a word he said—had assured her that if she just took the girls, everything would be okay. Pretty gutsy, considering he knew so little about what was happening. But she'd never forget, however long she lived, his expression when she looked back as she took the kids into the airlock. He'd started fighting back tears, and he was scared to let them go, but he knew they needed to get off the ship, even if they were being taken by a stranger who spoke an unknown language.

So she would have tried to get him off with the second group. Though she sensed he would not leave until the women were clear.

Suddenly the lights came back on.

The stars reappeared, hazy at first. They brightened and became sharp dazzling points of light scattered through the darkness. My God. She was getting a miracle. Still hanging on to the hatch, she turned and looked behind her, searching the night for the *McCandless*.

She saw the Veiled Lady, which had been behind it. But no ship.

"Melissa, where are you?"

Save for the stars, the sky was empty.

"Chase?"

Keep calm. She checked the time. It had been only nine minutes since they had all gone down the transdimensional drain. Something other than the stars was putting out a lot of light. But the glow was coming from the other side of the *Intrépide*. She let go of the hatch and rose above the hull. A long, sleek, brightly illuminated vehicle was approaching. It wore the silver and azure colors of the Confederacy. The Fleet was here. Thank God.

She screamed with delight, and waved at the ship.

One set of navigation lights blinked on and off. *We see you.*

She went back to the airlock, and they all must have understood, because they waved their arms, and Rowena burst into tears.

The visitor became visible. It had angled around and was approaching from the rear. Michelle grabbed hold of the cable and launched herself into a kind of improvised floating dance.

Lisa jumped up, hit her helmet against the overhead, and bounced. But she was still laughing, and her lips carried the message: *"Magnifique!"*

*You said it, baby.*

"Melissa," Dot said, "we've got help. Where are you?"

The visitor was lit up like a summer carnival. It came alongside and took up a position where, a few minutes ago, the *McCandless* had been stationed. She could almost have reached out and touched it.

"Melissa, answer up, please. Are you there?"

Then, finally, a voice: *"Relax, Ms. Garber. You are Dot Garber, right?"*

"Yes, it's me." *Oh, Lord, is it ever.* She could barely restrain a scream. "Where's the *McCandless*?"

*"Janet,"* said the voice. *"We've got her."*

She heard applause.

More lights went on, around the main hatch.

*"Everything's under control, Ms. Garber. Just give us a couple of minutes. We'd like you and the other people to clear the airlock. You can go back inside, if you like. But just clear the area, please."*

The hatch opened, and a transparent tube extended out into the vacuum.

Dot signaled for everyone to grab hold of the cable. Then they stepped out into the void.

The tube crossed the space between the ships and fastened onto the *Intrépide*'s open airlock.

Several people, four, it looked like, in dark blue uniforms filed into the tube and started across. A couple of them looked toward the drifting women and waved. A minute later, they'd disappeared into the *Intrépide*.

"Hello," Dot said. "This is Garber. Who are you guys?"

*"Ms. Garber, this is CVY1411. Do you need assistance?"*

"Only to get out of here."

*"How's your air supply?"*

"We're in good shape. There are four of us."

*"Okay. We see you. There's a cargo hatch off to your left. It's opening now. Or it will be in just a minute. Can you get in on your own? Or do you require assistance?"*

She looked at the three women. They were still celebrating. "Negative," she said. "We can manage."

*"Very good. Come in through cargo. There'll be a blinking light. They'll be expecting you. And yell if you need anything."*

"Fourteen-eleven, I hate to ask this—"

*"Go ahead, Ms. Garber. What's your problem?"*

"What's the date?"

*"Rimway calendar?"*

"Yes."

*"It's 1501."*

She froze. Sixty-seven years. Somewhere, deep inside, she'd known that was what they would say, but she still couldn't accept it. Not really. She'd just come out here a few minutes ago.

There was more movement in the tube. More uniformed rescuers crossing into the *Intrépide*. Then a surge of people coming back. Filing into the Fleet vessel. Her vision blurred while she watched, and it had gotten hard to breathe. She told herself to calm down. She was okay. That was the critical part. Everybody was going to survive. If it was really true that almost seventy years had passed since she'd come out here, she'd deal with it.

Her head was spinning. Dot had always prided herself on being tough. On being able to make the hard decisions, and to live with the results. But this was too much.

A wave of darkness closed in.

She woke in the arms of a guy in a pressure suit. He was telling her to relax, nothing to worry about, he'd take care of everything. They were still outside, moving along the hull, past large black numbers, a four and a couple of ones. "Thanks," she said. "I'm sorry I gave you so much trouble."

*"No trouble, Ms. Garber. Glad to help."*

"Where are—?"

*"They're fine. Everybody's okay."*

Her rescuer identified himself as Emil Crider. He wore standard Fleet issue: Assuming rank insignia hadn't changed, he was a young lieutenant, solid, efficient, reassuring. Emil warned her about the gravity, and brought her in through the cargo doors. Lisa and Michelle were already there. They looked a bit lost. Several of the rescuers were with them. Rowena was led in moments later. She waved. And provoked another round of cheers.

Dot's weight flowed back. Emil closed the doors and started the pressurization process. They were in a storage area, filled with cabinets and casings and assorted electronic gear.

*"When the green light comes on, Ms. Garber,"* he said, *"don't remove your suit or helmet. We'll be running a check before you get out of it."*

"Call me *Dot*," she said. "Why the medical check, Emil? I was only out there a few minutes."

*"Really?"* He gave her a broad smile. *"There's no problem, but we want to make sure your immune system isn't out of touch. And, where* you're *concerned, ours might be, too. Bear with us. It won't take long."*

Eventually, a row of green lamps, strung along the overhead, blinked on. Emil got out of his gear and looked back at her. He was average size, young, good-looking, sandy hair, sea blue eyes. A door opened, and several others came into the area. One of the newcomers knelt beside her. *"Dr. Gibson, Dot,"* he said. *"How do you feel?"*

"I'm okay."

*"Can you stand?"*

Gravity was still at about one-third. Standard level in the void. "Yes, Doctor." She started to get up. Emil made a move to help her, but Gibson waved him back.

*"Still okay?"* Gibson asked when she'd gotten to her feet.

"I'm good."

The others were going through the same routine.

When they were all ready, they were led down a short passageway and up two decks. There they were separated, and Dot was taken into a room that looked like an infirmary. Except that it appeared to be airtight. A table supported some electronic equipment. A single chair had been placed at the table. *"Okay, Dot,"* the doctor said. *"I'll be right over there."* He indicated an observation area behind a plate of glass. *"Wait until I tell you. Then take off the suit, sit down, and wait for instructions. Okay?"*

"Okay, Doctor."

He went outside and pulled the door shut behind him. *"All right. You can get out of that thing now."*

She removed the helmet and climbed out of the suit. Then she sat.

Dr. Gibson appeared in the observation area, joined by Emil. *"Ms. Garber,"* Gibson said, *"you'll notice a cap on the device in front of you. I'd like you to remove the cap and breathe into the tube."*

About twenty of the *Intrépide* passengers were gathered in the mess hall, where sandwiches, fruit, and donuts had been laid out. More filed in every few minutes. Others connected with the rescue vessel—though only two wore Fleet uniforms—were wandering among the growing crowd, reassuring them, and apparently speaking to them in their own language. That surprised Dot since the information she'd had indicated we knew what the written language looked like but nobody knew what it *sounded* like. Then she remembered Cori and Sabol.

There really *are* miracles.

Rowena and Michelle came in, and they all embraced. They thanked her, then were quickly swept off by their fellow passengers. Lisa showed up minutes later, and there was another minor celebration.

When everybody from the *Intrépide* finally was present, a woman in a commander's uniform spoke to them, again in French, welcoming them formally to the *Christopher Robin*. She passed out guides, in French, of course, which laid out information on compartments and menus and code numbers to be used by anyone needing help.

Two women, dressed in jumpsuits, stood off to one side. They were considerably older than Dot, but were still on the right side of middle age. One of them caught her eye momentarily, and smiled.

Dot raised a hand in acknowledgment. Then Emil appeared beside her. "You okay?" he asked.

"I'm fine. What's going on? Are they trying to explain to us what's happened?"

He nodded.

Dot saw disbelief, anger, tears. The people from the *Intrépide* would never see their friends and relatives again.

Several became hysterical. Some stared out through the viewports at the stars as if confirmation lay in that direction. They embraced one another, pleaded with the uniformed officers, no doubt to tell them it was all a misbegotten joke. But they knew that it was true, that their rescuers were not kidding, were not lying, were not deranged. They had arrived in the far future.

Lisa was staring at Dot. Her teen eyes were wet, and she was trying not to break down. Had this really happened?

Dot walked over to her. Embraced her. "I'm sorry," she said.

A French-speaking lieutenant commander, a man who'd trained more than a year specifically for this mission, told her later that the question most asked, after how did it happen, was this: Is there any way we can go home again? Are our homes still there?

They also, many of them, swore they'd never ride an interstellar again. Not ever.

Many of the passengers came over to thank Dot, to embrace her. One or two seemed to think it was her fault. And the Fleet people also took her aside and shook her hand. Several asked her to sign copies of the French guide.

The ship's captain literally beamed when he introduced himself. "If you need anything at all——" he said.

The world was spinning. It was too much. The emotions were running too high, and she couldn't sort out how she felt. It was a roller-coaster evening.

A door opened, and the father of Cori and Sabol entered. He was carrying a drink. "His name," said Emil, who was more or less functioning as an escort, "is Chaveau. He is a police inspector." He looked dazed, and one of the women who'd been performing translator duties went over to speak with him. Chaveau listened, and the appearance of disorientation intensified. The translator smiled gently and looked toward a side door, where the two women in the jumpsuits were engaged in a conversation. They were being screened from Chaveau's view by two officers. A signal passed between the translator and the officers, and they stepped back out of the way.

The women saw him immediately. They both waved and hurried in his direction, laughing and crying out as they went.

Chaveau gasped and seemed momentarily paralyzed. He shook his head violently, no, no, until suddenly he stopped and a smile dawned. And they were screeching with joy as they fell into one another's arms.

Emil put a hand on her shoulder. "You know who they are, Dot?"

"Hard to believe. But yes. I know."

Emil also seemed emotionally caught up in the moment. But he was watching Dot. "You okay?"

"I'm fine," Dot said.

"Good. Something else you should know: This isn't the first rescue we've done."

"Wonderful," she said. "I'm glad somebody made it happen."

"I'm sure you are. I should mention that the initiative came from an effort mounted by the Dot Garber Foundation."

Everything was moving too fast. He had to repeat what he'd said, and even then she wasn't sure she understood.

"It's okay," Emil said. "Hang in there. You're a hero, you know."

"I don't think heroes get as scared as I was." Then, finally, the question she'd been afraid to ask: "How's Melissa? My daughter? You have any idea?"

He nodded. But those eyes told her everything. "I'm sorry," he said. "She passed away about ten years ago."

Her knees buckled and Emil eased her into a chair. "I'm okay. I—"

"It's all right. Just relax."

More people came in. Some brought more donuts. Somebody else was handing out fresh clothes.

Dot sat in her chair, staring at the table.

"If it's any consolation," he said, "she knew you would be rescued. She had a lot to do with it."

"Thank you."

"And there's something else."

"What's that?"

"When you're ready," he said, "a couple of your friends just got here."

The novel of the fantastic unknown
by the Nebula Award–winning author
of *Time Travelers Never Die*

## Jack McDevitt

# ECHO

AN ALEX BENEDICT NOVEL

Eccentric Sunset Tuttle spent a lifetime searching in
vain for forms of alien life. Twenty-five years after his
death, a stone tablet inscribed with cryptic symbols is
revealed to be in the possession of Tuttle's onetime
lover, and antiques dealer Alex Benedict is anxious to
determine what secrets the tablet holds. It could be
proof that Tuttle discovered what he was looking for.

To find out, Benedict and his assistant embark on
their own voyage of discovery—one that will lead them
directly into the path of a very determined assassin
who doesn't want those secrets revealed.

M725T0712